BLOOD AND ICE

ALSO BY ROBERT MASELLO

FICTION

Vigil

Bestiary

Black Horizon

Private Demons

The Spirit Wood

NONFICTION

Robert's Rules of Writing

Writer Tells All

A Friend in the Business

Raising Hell: A Concise History of the Black Arts

Fallen Angels . . . and Spirits of the Dark

ROBERT MASELLO

BLOOD and ICE

BANTAM BOOKS

BLOOD AND ICE
A Bantam Book / March 2009

Published by
Bantam Dell
A Division of Random House, Inc.
New York, New York

Book design by Catherine Leonardo

Library of Congress Cataloging-in-Publication Data
Masello, Robert.
Blood and ice / Robert Masello.
p. cm.
ISBN 978-0-553-80728-8 (hardcover)
1. Journalists—Fiction. 2. Crimean War, 1853–1856—Veterans—Fiction.
3. Antarctica—Discovery and exploration—Fiction. I. Title.
PS3613.A81925B56 2009
813'.6—dc22   2008032682

Printed in the United States of America
Published simultaneously in Canada

www.bantamdell.com

BVG 10 9 8 7 6 5 4 3 2 1

For Laurie

ACKNOWLEDGMENTS

In writing any book, especially one of this scope, you often have to call upon the wisdom of friends and experts. I would like to thank François Sauzey, Carol Weston, Professor Roberto Véguez, Susan Williams, and James Donlan. I would also like to thank Brooks Peel of the State Climate Office of North Carolina, and Captain George Galdorisi, U.S. Navy (Ret.). I am in debt, too, to the noted historians Cecil Woodham-Smith, whose landmark book, *The Reason Why*, was such a help to me in writing about the Crimean War, and Gillian Gill, whose *Nightingales* provided invaluable research on Florence Nightingale and her nurses. The nurse's quotation about her cap, which appears on page 271, was drawn from Gill's book, which cites *Letters from the Crimea* as its original source.

Any mistakes are, of course, my responsibility alone.

I also happened to be blessed on this book with a great editor, Anne Groell, and an agent who, as always, kept encouraging me whenever my confidence flagged. Thank you, Cynthia Manson.

BLOOD AND ICE

PROLOGUE

Aboard HM Brig *Coventry,* in the Southern Ocean.
Lat. 65 degrees 28 minutes S.,
Long. 120 degrees 13 minutes W.

December 28, 1856

Sinclair bent low over the wooden bunk where Eleanor lay. Though she was snugly wrapped in his greatcoat and buried under every blanket and sheet he could lay his hands on, her teeth still chattered and her breath fogged in the dank, freezing air. By the flickering light of the oil lamp, he could see that her eyes were rolling up under her lids, and her face was as white and cold as the ice that had surrounded the ship for weeks.

With his own numb hand, he stroked her brow, brushing a wisp of her dark brown hair away from her eyes. The skin felt as lifeless and implacable as the blade of a sword, but underneath it he could still detect the slow coursing of her blood. She would live, somehow, but he would have to see to her needs, and soon. There was no way around it, anymore; he would have to leave the cabin and go below to the stores.

"Rest," he said, gently, "and I will be back before you know I've gone."

She sighed in protest, her pale lips barely moving.

"Try to sleep." He pulled the woolen cap more tightly around her head, kissed her cheek, and stood up, as much as the low ceiling of the stifling cabin would allow. Holding the lamp in one hand—its glass was smudged, and only an inch or so of whale oil remained at its bottom—he listened at the door for a moment before easing it open to the black passageway outside. He could hear the muttering of the crewmen somewhere in the hold. He didn't need to hear their words to know what they were saying. Ever since the ship had been blown off course, driven farther and farther toward the southern pole by unrelenting storms and wind, he had overheard their curses and seen the growing enmity in their eyes. Sailors were a superstitious lot, even at the best of times, and he knew it was their mysterious passengers—Eleanor and himself—that they had come to see as the source of their present calamity. But what, he wondered, would they choose to do about it? He did not like to leave Eleanor alone for even a few minutes.

He had long since removed the spurs from his boots, but it was impossible to move down the corridor without the creak of the timbers underfoot. Sinclair tried to take a step only when the ice battering the hull was especially loud, or the sails up above flapped in the night wind; but as he passed the galley the light from his lamp fell on Burton and Farrow huddled over a bottle of rum. The ship pitched to starboard, and Sinclair had to reach out and steady himself against the wall.

"Where you off to?" Burton growled. There were ice particles in his gray beard, glinting like diamonds, and a large gold hoop through one ear.

"The stores."

"What for?"

"That's none of your affair."

"We could make it that," he heard Farrow mutter, as the ship righted itself with a thundering groan.

Sinclair stepped to the ladder leading to the storerooms below. The rungs were coated with frost, and as he descended them the oil in the lamp sloshed from one side to the other; wild shadows flickered across the vats of salted pork, dried cod, and hard tack—all nearly empty—and the Chilean rum that the crew had broken into. His own cargo lay just beyond, in a large chest secured with heavy padlocks and chains. At first glance, it looked unsullied.

But when Sinclair bent lower and the feeble glow from the lamp fanned across the top of the trunk, he could see scratch marks and subtle indentations, as if someone had tried to pick the lock or even pry it loose. It came as no surprise. In fact, he could think of only one reason his belongings had not been rifled: The crew not only hated, but feared, him. He knew that they looked on him—a hardened cavalry veteran of the Crimean campaign, and an ac-knowledged master with pistol, lance, and saber—as someone to be reckoned with. He pulled the collar of his army tunic higher around his neck, then drew from its vest pocket the keys to the chest.

After glancing behind him to make quite sure he was alone and unobserved, he opened the padlock, slipped the wet chain loose, and lifted the lid. Inside, beneath a layer of riding tackle, uniforms, and several books—the works of Coleridge, Chatterton, and George Gordon, Lord Byron—he found what he had come for. Two dozen bottles, bearing the label MADEIRA—CASA DEL SOL, SAN CRISTOBAL, carefully wrapped and packed. He wiped one clean with a pair of riding breeches, tucked it under his arm, and secured the chest again.

Climbing back up the ladder, while juggling the lantern and the bottle, was a tricky proposition, made worse by the sight of Burton lurking at the top.

"Find what you were looking for, Lieutenant?"

Sinclair made no reply.

"Give you a hand there?" Burton went on, extending one mit-tened hand.

"No need."

But Burton had seen the bottle by now. "Spirits, is it? Well, couldn't we all use a warming cup."

"You've been warmed enough already."

Sinclair stepped away from the ladder and brushed past Bur-ton, then Farrow—who was beating himself with both arms to stim-ulate the circulation—and once out of their sight, ducked into the galley. He held the bottle near the stove, where a low coal fire still smoldered, to thaw its contents, then returned to his cabin, praying that he would find Eleanor no worse.

As it happened, she was not alone. A guttering light shone from beneath the door, and within Sinclair discovered the ship's physician, Dr. Ludlow, hovering over her. Ludlow was a revolting specimen of a man, baggy and hunched, with a manner at once obsequious and arrogant; Sinclair wouldn't have trusted him to cut his hair (another of the good doctor's shipboard duties), and he especially mistrusted him around Eleanor, in whom he had shown an unseemly interest ever since they had come aboard. At the moment, he was holding her limp wrist in one hand and shaking his head. "The pulse is very low, Lieutenant, very low indeed. I fear for the poor girl's life."

"And I do not," Sinclair declared, as much for Eleanor's benefit as the wretched doctor's. He removed her hand from Ludlow's damp grasp and slipped it under the blankets. Eleanor did not stir.

"Even my leeches are frozen, I'm afraid."

That at least was good news. The one thing Sinclair knew Eleanor did not need was any further loss of blood. "A pity," Sinclair said, knowing full well that it was the application of the creatures to Eleanor's bosom and legs that the doctor most enjoyed. "If you will leave us alone, I can manage quite well on my own."

Dr. Ludlow gave a cursory bow, then said, "I came with word from the captain. He wishes to speak with you on deck."

"I'll be there when I can."

"I'm so sorry, Lieutenant, but he was rather insistent."

"The sooner you leave, the sooner I shall speak to the captain."

Ludlow paused, as if to prove that he had not been dismissed, then left the cabin. The moment he was gone, Sinclair braced a stool against the door and used the dirk sheathed beneath his tunic to open the bottle. "Wait," he said to Eleanor, though he was not sure if she was beyond hearing, "wait for me."

With one arm, he raised her head from the makeshift pillow— a bundle of rags stuffed into a burlap sack—and put the bottle to her mouth. "Drink," he said, but she still didn't respond. He tilted the bottle until the liquid met her lips, turning them pink, giving them a semblance of life again. "Drink."

He felt her breath on the back of his hand. He tilted the bottle more, until a rosy trickle ran down her chin and spotted the ivory brooch she wore at her collar. The tip of her tongue appeared, as if chasing the errant drops, and Sinclair smiled. "Yes, that's it," he encouraged her. "Take more. More."

And she did. After a minute or two, her eyes opened. She looked up at Sinclair with a confused expression, one that mingled deep regret with an even deeper thirst. He held the bottle steady as she suckled at its tip. Her eyes became more focused, and her breathing more regular. When he felt she had had enough—too much and she might regurgitate the lot—he laid her head back on the pillow, wedged the cork back in place, then hid the bottle beneath the pile of bedclothes.

"I have to see the captain," he said. "I won't be gone long."

"No," she said, barely audibly. "Stay."

He squeezed her hand. Was it already warmer to his touch?

"Talk to me," she said.

"And so I shall, so I shall...About coconut palms as tall as St. Paul's..."

The tiniest hint of a smile creased her lips.

"And sand as white as Dover." It was one of their private catchphrases, drawn from a popular ditty, and they had often murmured it to each other in moments far less trying than this.

Sinclair took the stool away from the door, extinguished the lamp—what oil remained had to be conserved—and left it in the cabin. Only a pale shaft of light penetrated from the upper deck to the passageway, but it was enough to guide his way to the steps.

Cold as it was below, it was far worse above, where the wind, like a bellows, sucked the very breath from the lungs and filled them instead with a chilling blast. The captain, Addison, stood at the wheel, wrapped in several layers of clothing, the last of which was a torn sail; in Sinclair's eyes, he was nothing but a privateer, who had extorted three times what the fare should have been for his and Eleanor's passages. The man could sense desperation and had no scruples about exploiting it.

"Ah, Lieutenant Copley," he declared. "I was hoping you might pass the time with me."

Sinclair knew it was more than that. He looked around him, at the rolling, gray sea, strewn with great slabs of ice, and the night sky that, at such a southern latitude, gave off a kind of unchanging pewter gleam. Two crewmen stood watch, one on either side of the deck, looking for especially jagged or insurmountable bergs; another clung to his perch, high above, in the crow's nest. The ship's progress was slow and precarious, and the mutable winds made the frosted sails—those that could still be unfurled—flap and luff with the rumble of thunder.

"How is your wife faring?"

Sinclair came closer, his boots sliding on the slippery deck.

"The good doctor," Addison continued, "tells me she remains unwell." His tricorner hat was tied to his head with a frayed crimson sash running under the chin.

Sinclair knew that if there was one thing on which he and the captain could agree, it was on the utter unreliability of the ship's physician. Every man aboard, in fact, was of a suspect nature, but it was only on just such a boat that Sinclair could have booked immediate and unquestioned passage.

"She is better," Sinclair replied, "and resting."

Captain Addison nodded thoughtfully, as if he cared, and gazed at the overcast, starless sky. "The winds remain against us," he said. "If we don't change course soon, we shall find ourselves at the pole itself. Never seen such winds, in all my time."

Sinclair read into the remark precisely what the captain doubtlessly intended—a reminder that the foul weather was attributed to the presence of these mysterious passengers on board. Women were considered bad luck to begin with, but the fact that Eleanor was ailing—that she appeared as white as a ghost—only made matters worse. Initially, Sinclair had done all that he could to enter into the life of the ship, to make himself a steady and agreeable guest, but between his duties to Eleanor and the conditions imposed by his own secret infirmity, there was simply no way that he could carry it off. Even the two crewmen on deck—their names, if he was not mistaken, were Jones and Jeffries—glanced at him from under their woolen caps and the rags knotted around their faces with unconcealed malevolence.

"Tell me again, Lieutenant," Captain Addison said, "what was your business in Lisbon?"

It was in Portugal that Sinclair had booked passage.

"Diplomatic matters," Sinclair replied, "of a sensitive nature. Nothing that I may disclose even now."

The wind picked up, whipping the ragged sail around the captain's legs as he stood with both hands gripping the wheel. In the strange penumbral glow of the night sky, he looked to Sinclair like an image from some daguerreotype, washed of all color, reduced to shadows and shades of gray.

"And was it there your wife fell ill?"

The plague, Sinclair was aware, had visited the city only a few years before.

"My wife is ill with no contagion, I can assure you of that. It is an internal disorder, which we will see to when we reach Christchurch."

Sinclair noticed one of the sailors—Jones—throw a glance at Jeffries, a glance that clearly said, "*If* we reach Christchurch..." It was a question that haunted Sinclair, too. Would they have come so far, in such haste, only to perish in a frozen sea?

The next words from Addison's mouth were swallowed in a sudden gust of wind that set the sails billowing and the masts creaking, but which carried with it a strange sight indeed—a giant, soaring bird. An albatross. Sinclair had not yet seen one, though he knew from the lines of Coleridge's marvelous poem that this must be one now. It hovered overhead, its underbelly white, its outspread wings—no less than ten or twelve feet wide in Sinclair's estimation—tipped with black, its long beak a ruddy pink. Even in the tumultuous air, the bird maintained an attitude of utter serenity, dipping and turning around the masts, tacking on the invisible currents with no greater movement than a slight adjustment of its feet.

"A gony," Jones said, using the seaman's term, and Jeffries nodded appreciatively; the albatross was a bird of good omen and brought misfortune down only on those who tried to do it harm.

The ship hit a rising wave, its hull grating on chunks of broken ice, and Sinclair had to grab hold of a rope with both hands to keep his footing. The albatross swooped low, across the brig's prow, then up again and onto a shuddering yardarm. There, it perched, its wings now furled, its claws clutching the slick wood. Sinclair marveled at the sight; how, he wondered, could the great bird survive, flying for countless miles over nothing but rolling seas and slabs of ice, under such a desolate sky?

"Captain, sir! Captain Addison!"

Sinclair turned his head, and saw Burton clambering up onto the deck from below, his frozen beard as stiff as a plank; right behind him came Farrow, cradling something beneath his black seal-skin jacket.

His legs spread wide for balance, Burton marched toward the wheel, without so much as a glance in Sinclair's direction. "Something to report, sir!" he bellowed. "Of great concern!"

Sinclair had to crane his neck to see, as Burton and Farrow seemed intent on blocking his view. He saw the flash of something—glass?—and heard the men jabbering away, in low tones, over one another. Addison held up his hand, as if to calm them, then looked down at the prize they carried. Sinclair could see it, too, now, and to his dismay, saw that it was a wine bottle, marked MADEIRA.

The captain looked puzzled, then indignant, as if he were not a man to be trifled with. "See for yourself, Captain!" Burton urged, but Addison was still resistant. Farrow pulled a glove off with his teeth and used his bare fingers to pull the cork from the bottle. He held the open bottle under the captain's nose. Spitting his glove onto the deck, he said, "Smell it! Better yet, Cap'n, touch it to your lips!"

Addison reluctantly lowered his face to the bottle, then recoiled, as if affronted by an especially foul odor. But it was only when Dr. Ludlow crawled up on deck, too, and silently nodded his agreement, that the captain, an expression of horror on his face, peered at Sinclair.

"Is it true?" he said, taking the dark bottle from Farrow's hand.

"It's true," Sinclair said, "that you hold my wife's medicine. Stolen, no doubt, from our cabin."

"Medicine?" Burton blurted.

"Bloody hell it is!" Farrow threw in.

"Didn't I tell you they was trouble?" Burton shouted to Jones and Jeffries, who understood nothing but looked ready to welcome any mayhem about to ensue.

"Found it under the bedclothes, I did!" Farrow cried, in an apparent bid to claim the lion's share of the credit. "That's no denying!"

"And ask 'im what happened to Bromley!" Burton went on, his beard shaking with fury. "Ask 'im how a man like that, an able-bodied seaman who twice rounded the Horn, fell overboard while keeping watch!"

Suddenly, everyone's voices were raised and a half dozen other crewmen spilled from the hold, four of them carrying the trunk that Sinclair had just secured. They dropped it upside down on the ice-rimmed deck, with the sound of spurs jangling against the bottles still inside. Before Sinclair could even reach for his sword, he felt his arms pinioned and a coil of rope slipped over his wrists, then knotted tight. His shoulders were pressed against the main mast, and while he shouted his protests, he saw Burton and Farrow charge back below.

"No!" he cried out. "Leave her be!"

But there was nothing he could do now; he couldn't even move. Captain Addison shouted at one of the seamen to take the helm, then strode across the deck. Staring directly into Sinclair's eyes, he said, "I'm not one to believe in curses, Lieutenant." He kept his voice low, as if confiding a secret. "But with this," he went on, brandishing the bottle, "you have pressed my hand beyond endurance."

The sailors holding his arms tightened their grip.

"The men already hold you responsible for the death of Bromley, and I no longer doubt it myself." Weighing the black bottle in his hand, he whispered, "I'll have a mutiny on my hands if I don't do it."

"If you don't do what?"

But Addison didn't answer. Instead, he looked over at the hatchway, where Burton and Farrow were maneuvering themselves back onto the deck, holding Eleanor in a blanket like a sling. Her eyes were open, and one arm was held out toward Sinclair; her makeshift bonnet had fallen off, and her brown hair, once so thick and glossy, blew in loose tendrils about her head.

Farrow brandished a rusted chain in the air and Captain Addison, neither nodding assent nor demanding a halt, turned away. As he went back to the wheel, he hurled the black bottle, without so much as following its course, over the side.

"Sinclair!" Eleanor cried out, her terrified voice nearly lost in the tumult. "What's going on?"

But it was all too clear to Sinclair; he struggled at the rope and tried to kick his way free of the mast, but his riding boots scrabbled on the icy deck, and Jeffries suddenly landed a roundhouse punch to his gut. Sinclair doubled over, trying to catch his breath again, and saw only boots and ropes and chains as he was dragged toward her. She was standing now, though barely, held up by Burton, as Sinclair was forcibly pressed against her, back to back. How he wished he could embrace her, one more time. But all he could do was whisper, "Don't be afraid. We'll be together."

"Where? What are you saying?"

She was not only frightened beyond words but delirious, too.

Farrow, cackling like a hen, kept circling them, using his gloved hands to wrap the chain around their knees, their waists, their shoulders. Their necks. Wherever the freezing metal touched their bare skin, it seared, like a plaster. Though he was facing in the other direction, Sinclair could hear her ragged breath and feel her mounting panic.

"Sinclair," she gasped. "Why?"

Jones and Jeffries, having abandoned their watch, hauled them, bound together like two fireplace logs, over to the gunwale. Sinclair instinctively dug his boots into the wood, but someone kicked them loose, he lost his footing altogether, and in a matter of seconds, he found himself staring down into the churning water below. Oddly, he was glad that Eleanor's gaze would be fixed on the sky, on the white albatross he hoped still clung to the yardarm.

"Shouldn't we say some words?" Dr. Ludlow said, a tremor in his voice. "It all seems so . . . barbaric."

"I'll say the words," Burton shouted, leaning low to glare into Sinclair's face. "May God have mercy on your souls!"

Sinclair felt many hands lifting the two of them off the deck.

"And the Devil take the hindmost!"

Someone laughed, and then he was plunging, headfirst, with Eleanor screaming in terror, down, down, down, toward the water. It seemed to take longer than he expected before they crashed through a thin scrim of ice. Her scream stopped dead, everything went silent, and with the chain weighting them down, they sank swiftly, spinning in circles, into the frigid, black water. He held his breath for many seconds, but then, even though he might have sustained it for several more, let it out in one great rush . . . embracing Death, and whatever else might await them both, at the bottom of the sea.

PART I

THE VOYAGE OUT

"And now the STORM-BLAST came, and he
Was tyrannous and strong;
He struck with his o'ertaking wings,
And chased us south along.

With sloping mast and dipping prow,
As who pursued with yell and blow
Still treads the shadow of his foe,
And forward bends his head,
The ship drove fast, loud roared the blast,
And southward aye we fled."

The Rime of the Ancient Mariner,
Samuel Taylor Coleridge, 1798

CHAPTER ONE

PRESENT DAY

November 19, noon

THE DOORBELL WAS RINGING, and even though Michael heard it, he did not want to wake up; the dream he was in was too comforting. Kristin was with him, and they were driving in his Jeep on a mountain road. She had her bare feet up on the dashboard, the radio was blasting, and she was laughing, her head held back, her blond hair blowing in the wind from the open window.

The doorbell rang again, a series of short bursts. Whoever it was wasn't going away.

Michael lifted his head from the pillow—why was there an empty bag of Doritos next to his face?—and glanced at the lighted numerals on the clock—11:59. And then, even as he rubbed his eyes, it flicked over to noon.

The doorbell, again.

Michael threw the blanket back, dropped his feet onto the floor. "Yeah, yeah, hold your horses," he mumbled. He grabbed a bathrobe off the back of the door and shuffled out of the bedroom. Through the opaque glass in the front door, he could see a shape—

somebody in a hooded parka—standing on the stoop. Michael moved closer.

"I can see you, too, Michael. Now open the door—it's freezing out here."

It was Joe Gillespie, his editor at *Eco-Travel Magazine*.

Michael turned the bolt and opened the door. A cold rain spattered against his bare legs as his visitor hustled in. "Remind me to get a job on the *Miami Herald* next time," Gillespie said, stamping his feet.

Michael picked a sodden copy of the *Tacoma News Tribune* from the stoop, then gazed off at the shrouded peaks of the Cascade range in the distance. That was why he'd originally bought the house—for the view. Now it was just an awful reminder. He gave the paper a shake and closed the door.

Gillespie was standing on the threadbare hook rug—the one Kristin had made—with water dripping from his parka. He brushed the hood back, and what was left of his hair fuzzed out around his head.

"You ever check your e-mails anymore?" Gillespie asked. "Or maybe your answering machine?"

"Not if I can help it."

Gillespie blew out a frustrated sigh and looked around the messy living room. "Jesus, Michael, do you own stock in Domino's? You ought to."

Michael did note a couple of pizza boxes, and some empty beer bottles, scattered around the coffee table and stone hearth.

"Get dressed," Gillespie said. "We're going to lunch."

Michael, still barely conscious, just stood there with the wet paper in his hand.

"Come on, I'm paying."

Michael said, "Give me five," tossed the paper to Gillespie, and went to get started.

"Take ten," Gillespie shouted after him. "Throw in a shave and shower."

Michael took him at his word. In the bathroom, he switched on the space heater—the house was always cold and drafty, and though he often swore to himself that one day he'd do some insulating and basic maintenance, that day never came—and turned on the hot water. It would take a minute or two to get warm. The medicine chest above the sink was open, and half a dozen orange prescription bottles sat on the shelves. He grabbed the one on the bottom shelf—the latest antidepressant the therapist had prescribed—and downed a tablet with a handful of the now-tepid water.

Then, much as he dreaded the prospect, he closed the cabinet and looked at himself in the mirror. His shaggy black hair was even more unruly than ever this morning, curling off his head on one side and mashed down flat on the other. His dark eyes were red-rimmed and cloudy. He hadn't shaved in a couple of days and he could swear—was this possible?—that even though he had just turned thirty, a couple of the chin whiskers were coming in gray. Time's winged chariot...damn. He slapped a fresh blade into the razor and made a few hasty swipes at his stubble.

After a lukewarm shower, he put on some jeans, a denim work shirt, and the cleanest, driest pair of boots he could find by the front door. Gillespie was sprawled in his worn leather armchair, carefully peeling the pages of the newspaper away from each other. "I took the liberty of raising your blinds and letting in some light. You might try it sometime."

They drove in Gillespie's car—a Prius, of course—and went to the same diner they always did. Though there wasn't much to recommend the place in the way of décor—vinyl booths, linoleum floor, and a pastry carousel with garish white lighting—Michael liked it at the Olympic. It was about as far from a chain restaurant, or God forbid, a Starbucks, as you could get, and it had the added virtue of serving breakfast all day. Michael ordered the lumberjack special, and Gillespie had a Greek salad with a side order of cottage cheese and a cup of herbal tea.

"Whoa, there," Michael said. "Sure you're not overdoing it?"

Gillespie smiled while pouring half a packet of Equal into his tea. "What the hell—it's on the expense account."

"In that case, I'm having dessert."

"Good idea," Gillespie said. "I dare you to order a slice of the lemon meringue."

It was a running joke between them, that the lemon meringue pie on the top shelf of the carousel had not budged, much less been replaced, in the five years they'd been coming here.

While they ate, Michael couldn't help but notice that Gillespie had placed a FedEx envelope on the seat next to his thigh. Occasionally,

Gillespie would reach down and touch it, just to make sure it was still there. Must be something important, Michael thought, and since it hadn't been left in the locked car, it was probably something that was going to involve Michael somehow.

They talked about the magazine—a new photo editor had been hired, ad sales were up, the good-looking receptionist had quit—and the Seattle Mariners. Sometimes, Gillespie and Michael went to the games together at the Safeco Stadium. What they didn't talk about was Kristin—Michael knew that Gillespie was steering clear—and they didn't talk about the envelope either, until Michael, mopping up his egg yolks with the English muffin, finally broached the subject.

"Okay, I'll bite," he said, gesturing with the crust of the muffin. "The suspense is killing me."

For a second, Gillespie pretended to be uncertain of what he was referring to.

"Is that the layout for my Yellowstone story?"

Gillespie looked down at the envelope, pursing his lips, as if still trying to come to some decision. "No, the Yellowstone story ran last month. Looks like you're not even *reading* the magazine anymore."

Michael felt caught out—especially because it was true. For the past few months, he'd hardly ever read his mail, checked his AOL account, called people back. Everybody understood why, but more and more he felt the world was losing patience.

"This is something I think you should see," Gillespie said, sliding the envelope across the table.

Michael wiped his fingers on his napkin, then opened the packet and took out the papers inside. There were photos—some of them, in black and white, looked like satellite reconnaissance shots—and a sheaf of papers with the National Science Foundation name and logo on top. Many of them were datelined "Point Adélie."

"What's Point Adélie?"

"It's a research station, and pretty minimal at that. They study everything from climate change to the local biosphere."

"Where is it?" Michael asked, reaching for his coffee cup.

"The South Pole. Or at least as close to it as you can get. The Adélie penguins migrate there."

Michael's coffee cup stopped in the air, and despite himself, he felt a quickening in his blood.

"It took me months to set this up," Gillespie went on, "and get the necessary clearance. You have no idea the kind of paperwork and red tape you have to go through to get somebody onto the base down there. The NSF makes the CIA look friendly. But now we've got it—permission to send one reporter to Point Adélie, for a month. I'm planning on getting an eight-to-ten-page spread out of it—four-color photos, maybe three or four thousand words of text, the whole enchilada."

Michael sipped the coffee, just to give himself a second to think.

"I'll save you the trouble of asking," Gillespie said. "We're paying the usual rate per word, but I'll bump you up on the photos. Plus, we'll cover your expenses, within reason of course."

Michael still didn't know what to say, or think. Too many things were tumbling around in his head. He hadn't worked—he hadn't even thought about working—since the Cascades disaster, and he wasn't sure he was ready to take up his old life again. But another part of him was vaguely insulted. The project had been in the works for months, and Gillespie was only now mentioning it to him?

"When do you need it by?" he asked, just to buy some time again.

Gillespie sat back, looking just the littlest bit pleased, like a fisherman who's felt a tug on the line.

"Well, there's the catch. We'd need you to leave on Friday."

"This Friday?"

"Yes. It's not easy getting down there. You'll have to fly to Chile—Santiago—then on to Puerto Williams. From there you'll take a Coast Guard cutter as far as the ice allows, then they'll chopper you in the rest of the way from there. It's a very narrow window of opportunity, and the weather can close it at any time. Right now, it's summer down south, so there should be days when it's actually well above zero."

Michael finally had to ask. "Why didn't you tell me sooner?"

"I knew you weren't interested in working just now."

"Who was?"

"Who was what?"

"Come on, Joe. If you've been setting this up for months, you must have had somebody else lined up to do it."

"Crabtree. He was going to do it."

Crabtree again—the guy was always breathing down Michael's neck, trying to snag his assignments. "So why isn't he going?"

Gillespie shrugged. "Root canal."

"What?"

"He's got to have a root canal, and no one's permitted to go down there unless they've got a complete bill of health. Most of all, since there isn't any dentist on call, you've got to have a note from your dentist saying everything's in perfect working order."

Michael couldn't believe his ears. Crabtree had lost the assignment because he had a gum problem?

"So, please," Gillespie said, leaning forward, "tell me you don't have any cavities and your fillings are all intact?"

Michael instinctively ran his tongue around the interior of his mouth. "As far as I know."

"Good. So, that just leaves the main question. What do you think, Michael? Are you ready to get back in harness?"

That was indeed the million-dollar question. If he'd been asked last night, the answer would have been no and don't call again. But there was something stirring in him, something he could not deny—a flicker of that old excitement. All his life he'd been the first one to accept any challenge, to climb the sheer cliff, to bungee jump from the top of the bridge, to dive for the bottom of the coral reef. And though he'd tamped it down for months, that feeling was welling up in him again. He glanced at the satellite photo on top of the pile—from above, the base looked like a bunch of boxcars, scattered on an icy plain close to a rocky, barren shoreline. It was about as bleak a picture as could be, but it called to him as if it were a beach in Brazil.

Gillespie watched him closely, waiting. A wintry gust blew raindrops against the diner window.

Something started to turn in Michael's mind. His fingers rested on the grainy photo. He could always say no. He could go back to his place and...what? Have another beer? Beat up on himself some more? Throw away some more of his own life, to make up for what had happened to Kristin? (Though how that would make up for anything, even he could not say.)

Or, he could accept. He glanced at the next photo in the pile. This one, taken at ground level, showed a hut, raised on cinder blocks a few feet above the ice. A half dozen seals were lying around it like sunbathers.

"Do we have time for some pie first?" Michael asked, and Gillespie, after smacking the table in triumph with the palm of his hand, signaled for the waitress.

"Lemon meringue," he called, "all around!"

CHAPTER TWO

November 20 to November 23

THE NEXT FEW DAYS were a total blur as Michael struggled to get everything in order for a trip to the Antarctic. Most of the cold-weather gear he already had on hand, procured for previous assignments in Siberia and Alaska, but getting all the rest done wasn't easy. His first stop was the dentist, where Michael feared, for a few minutes, that everything might stop dead.

"You know you've still got that wisdom tooth on the upper right side," Dr. Edwards said. "That could give you a lot of trouble down the line."

"But it's not giving me any trouble now."

"Still, if I were you..."

"I can't get it taken out now. There isn't time for it to heal up."

"Well, don't say I didn't warn you," Dr. Edwards said.

"I won't, I swear. I just need you to sign that NSF release form."

Dr. Edwards pushed his trifocals back up his nose and studied the form while Michael lay flat in the chair. "Twenty years in practice, and you know, I've never seen one of these."

"Me neither." Michael waited to see him sign.

"Antarctica, huh?" The dentist still studied the release.

"Yep."

"I envy you. Wish I had the time to fit in a jaunt like that."

He made it sound like a quickie trip to Acapulco. Michael kept thinking of the unfortunate Crabtree and his imminent root canal.

The dentist glanced one last time at the X-rays he'd just taken, still mounted on the light board. "But I don't see anything else amiss, aside from that darn wisdom tooth . . ." Finally, he pulled a pen from his shirt pocket and scrawled his signature on the dotted line. Michael was up and out of the chair before the hygienist had even had time to remove his paper bib.

Next stop was his internist, where another battery of tests had to be performed and another raft of papers filled out. Michael had had more than his share of physical mishaps over the years—a dislocated shoulder, some torn tendons, several broken bones—but considering his line of work, which often entailed going places no human being was supposed to go, he'd escaped relatively intact. And the internist couldn't find anything new to worry about. He had only one question, he said, before signing the release forms.

"How are you doing, psychologically? Are you seeing the therapist I referred you to?"

Michael was afraid that would come up.

"That's all okay now," he said. "She's got me on Lexapro, and it's working great." In actuality, he couldn't tell if it was having any effect at all; he just didn't want to risk anything interfering with his clean bill of health. "The best thing for me," he added, with as bright an expression as he could muster, "is to get out of town and get back to work."

The internist bought it. "I agree," he said, scribbling his name on the bottom line of the form. "I wish I were going myself."

Michael never would have guessed so many people harbored Antarctic dreams.

But there was one last stop, and that was going to be the hardest by far.

Ever since he'd had that lunch with Gillespie, he'd known it was coming, and he'd done everything he could think of to put it off. He'd kept going full speed ahead, getting everything organized for the trip. He'd stopped his mail delivery and his newspapers; he'd enlisted the neighbor to keep an eye on his place and run the pipes if a freeze set in. He'd spent several hours at Tacoma Camera Supply, buying every battery, lens, tripod, and flash card he might need. Sure, he had plenty of that stuff already, but on an expedition like this, in a place where there wouldn't be any way to replace a faulty light meter or get hold of additional supplies, he wanted to be positive that he had everything he'd need. In a way, he'd welcomed all these distractions; for once, he wasn't absorbed in his thoughts, in an endless cycle of guilt and self-recrimination. He could focus on something else, something in the future, and coming at him fast.

But in the back of his mind, that last stop had always been there, and he couldn't delay it any longer. He was due at the Tacoma Regional Hospital.

In the coma ward.

Where he knew he was not welcome.

On the way over, he steeled himself for any possible confrontation. Kristin's parents were almost always there, or at least one of them. But he thought if he went around dinnertime, he might not run into them. When he got to the ward, he signed in—the nurse said, "Good to see you again, Mr. Wilde. I know Kristin will be glad you're here"—but as he walked down the hall, he wondered what that could possibly mean.

Kristin had not come out of her coma for months. Kristin, from everything the doctors had told him (even though he wasn't a family member, and technically should not have been told) was never *going* to come out of her coma. The fall had been too great, the delay in treatment too long, the insult to the brain too devastating. For all intents and purposes, Kristin was already gone.

All that remained of her was what he could see—a still form, so slim it hardly raised the pale blue blanket, nestled amidst a tangle of tubes and blinking, beeping monitors. He waited outside the glass, just looking between the slats in the venetian blind. And if he allowed himself to, he could almost slip into believing she was okay. Her blond hair (which her mom washed regularly) was spread out around the pillow, her face was calm, her eyes closed. Only her complexion—once burnished by the sun—was now pale and spotty, especially around her mouth and nose. Too many tubes and instruments had been put in and taken out.

But, to his relief, there was no sign of her folks. Michael

unzipped his parka and went inside, stopping only at the sound of a voice.

"Hello, stranger."

For one shocking second, it was as if Kristin had spoken to him again, but then he turned around and saw her sister Karen, curled up in a chair in the corner.

"Didn't mean to scare you," she said. She had a ponderous book in her lap, probably one of her law-school texts, and to his sorrow she reminded him, as she always did, of her big sister. They looked a lot alike—same penetrating blue eyes, same straight white teeth and tousled blond hair. They even sounded similar. Everything they uttered had a wry, knowing tone to it.

"Hey, Karen." He never knew what to say to her; he never really had. While Kristin had always been the boisterous one, the one who was constantly on the go and out of the house, Karen was the quiet, diligent student, the one who was hunkered down over the dining-room table with a scattering of textbooks and papers around her. Michael used to exchange a few words with her when he came by to get Kristin, but he always felt like he was interrupting something more important.

"So, how's she doing?" A stupid question, he knew, but all he could think of.

Karen smiled—Kristin's smile, the right side slightly up-turned—and said, ruefully, "The same." There was a note of resignation in her voice. "My parents just like one of us to be here nearly all the time, so I said I'd sit in while they caught the Early Bird Special at Applebee's."

Michael nodded, looking down at Kristin's hand, which was lying atop the blanket. The fingers were thinner and more fragile than he recalled, and a little black thimble, a monitor of some kind, had been attached to her ring finger.

"She hasn't had any seizures, or anything like that, all week," Karen said. "I don't know if that's a good sign or not."

What *would* a good sign be? Michael wondered. He knew that Kristin—the real Kristin, the alive Kristin, the Kristin who wanted to scale every peak with him and explore every forest—was never coming back. So what were they hoping for? Signs that she was finally failing? Signs that even the machines would not be able to keep her going, in a limbo state, forever?

"Okay if I sit on the bed?" he asked.

"Be my guest."

Michael sat gently on the edge of the bed, resting his own hand atop Kristin's. Hers felt like it contained the brittle bones of a bird.

"Law-school stuff?" Michael asked, nodding at the heavy book that was still spread across Karen's lap.

"Federal Tort Legislation and Reform." She closed the book with a whomp. "They'll be making a movie of it soon."

"Tom Cruise?"

"I'm thinking Wilford Brimley."

An orderly bustled in, lifted the plastic bag out of the wastebasket, and tossed it into the barrel on wheels outside. When he left, Karen said, "It's good to see you again. What have you been up to?"

"Not much." Truer words, he knew, had not been spoken. Karen knew—who didn't?—that he'd been adrift since the accident.

"But I wanted to come by," he added, "before I left town, on Friday."

"Oh. Where to?"

"Antarctica." Even Michael wasn't used to saying it yet.

"Wow. It's on assignment, I assume?"

"*Eco-Travel.* They just got clearance for me to go; I'll be staying for a month at a small base close to the Pole."

Karen put the book down on the floor beside the chair. "Kristin would be so jealous."

Michael couldn't help but glance over at Kristin. But her face, of course, betrayed no expression, no life, at all. Whenever he was in this room, he found himself torn—did he speak as if Kristin were somehow present, as if she could hear him and follow what was going on around her (even though he knew she could not), or did he just carry on as if she wasn't there? The first option felt fraudulent, and the second one cruel.

"You know, Krissy had a couple of books on Antarctica," Karen said. "They're still on the shelves in her room. Ernest Shackleton's expedition, things like that. If you want them, I'm sure she'd like you to have them."

And now they were distributing her belongings. With her right there. Or not. Where was she? Michael wondered. Was it possible that there was something, some vestige of consciousness, that they weren't aware of, still floating around out there, somewhere in the cosmic void?

"Thanks. I'll think about it."

"Just don't mention it in front of my folks. They still think Kristin's coming home and everything's going to be fine again."

Michael nodded. He and Karen had an understanding on this, unspoken though it generally was. They both knew, and had accepted, the medical diagnosis. Karen had even seen the brain scan that showed—in black, appropriately enough—the vast section of her sister's brain that had already atrophied. She had described it to Michael as "a dark village, with only two or three tiny lights glimmering through the windows." And even those were dimming. Sooner or later, the darkness would swallow those up, too.

Michael heard her dad's booming voice in the hallway—he was the most successful car dealer in Tacoma, and he treated everyone like a potential customer—greeting the nurses at the reception desk. Michael stood up, exchanging a glance with Karen; they both knew what was coming and saw no way to avoid it.

When he came through the door and saw Michael by the bed, he stopped so abruptly his wife bumped into him from behind. Karen also stood up, ready if necessary to come to Michael's defense.

"I thought I told you not to come here anymore," he said.

"Michael just came to say good-bye," Karen interjected, moving into the gap between them. "He's going away."

Mrs. Nelson maneuvered around her husband, a doggie bag from Applebee's in one hand. Michael was never quite sure where she stood. Mr. Nelson, he knew perfectly well, blamed him for the accident; he'd never liked Michael—but then he'd never have liked any man who stole his daughter's affections from him. But when it came to Mrs. Nelson, she seldom got three words out before her husband started talking over her, so it was tough to know what she really thought about anything.

His only ally, Michael knew, was Karen. "He just got here a few minutes ago," she was saying now, "and Kristin would have wanted him to come."

"Nobody knows what Krissy wants—"

Michael noticed how her dad had instinctively returned the conversation about her to the present tense.

"—but I know what I want," her dad continued. "And what her mother wants. We want her to rest, and recuperate, and not think about what happened. That kind of thinking can only set her back."

"I'm sorry you feel that way," Michael did venture, "but I'm not here to upset you. I've said good-bye to Kristin, and I'll just go now."

Michael turned back to take one last look at Kristin, as still and silent as a statue, then brushed past the burly shoulder of her dad, who refused to budge even an inch to get out of his way. For a split second, he thought he detected a sympathetic glance from the cowed Mrs. Nelson.

He was halfway down the hall when he heard quick footsteps approaching from behind. It was Karen—why did she have to remind him so much of her sister?—and she clutched his sleeve as she spoke. "I know Kristin's not there, you know Kristin's not there, but my parents still think..."

"I know they do."

"But if you did want to see those books..."

"Thanks, I'll think about it," he said, knowing he wouldn't. And knowing that it wasn't the books she was talking about, anyway.

The orderly rumbled by with the trash barrel.

"But just in case there is, I don't know, some part of Krissy that's still hanging around," Karen said, "I know she'd be glad you came."

There were tears, he could see, starting to well up in her eyes.

"I know you really loved her, and I really loved her, too," she said, fumbling for the rest, "except maybe once, that time she stole my skates and broke the blade"—she laughed and let go of his coat—"and all I know is she'd want me to tell you to be careful on your trip."

Michael smiled. "I will."

"No, really," she said, with greater urgency. "I mean it. Be careful there."

Michael put an arm around her shoulders to comfort her. "I solemnly swear to keep my mittens on and my ears warm at all times."

She gently pushed him away. "If you don't, Krissy will be really mad at you... and so will I."

Michael said, "I wouldn't want that."

"No, you wouldn't."

"Karen!" Mr. Nelson shouted, his face poking out of the door of the room. "Your mother wants to talk to you."

Karen bit her lip.

"*Now*, Karen!"

Michael rubbed her shoulder, turned, and headed back past the nurses' station. This time, nobody said a word to him as he went by.

CHAPTER THREE

1889

GREEN . . . DEEP, *gleaming emerald green.*

That was what she dreamt of.

The green of the grass in the Yorkshire pastures.

The green of the leaves on a sunny day in Regent's Park.

The green baize of the billiards table at the club in Pall Mall. (Women were prohibited from going upstairs, but Sinclair had found a way to sneak her past the porter and up the back service stairs.)

The green waters of the Bosporus . . .

So long as she could immerse herself in the green, she was content. She could remember the scent of the fields where she grew up . . . the damp grass, as it lay flat in the summer breeze, the cows standing white and black against it . . . the rolling green hills at dusk, the sun gleaming like her father's gold pocket watch . . .

She could feel the texture of the leaves, smooth and even and waxy, as she passed through the city park on her midday break from the hospital. It was only for half an hour, but in that time—and if the wind was blowing back toward the Thames—she could take a breath of fresh air, air that had no trace of blood or morphine or ether in it. Sometimes she would tuck leaves and sweet-smelling flowers in the pockets of her uniform before going back into the wards . . .

The green of the sea . . . she had never been at sea until leaving for Turkey. She had always imagined it to be blue, or perhaps gray—it had appeared so in every picture she had ever seen—but staring down from the deck, into the churning wake, she had been surprised by its greenish cast, like the dull patina on the statues at the Royal Museum (Sinclair had taken her there, shortly before his regiment departed) . . .

But there the reverie ended . . . as they all did, eventually . . . and a cold hand settled upon her heart. She had to struggle, once again, to fold herself into the green, to wrap herself in a bower of her own imagining . . . to warm the icy hand that had stolen beneath her clothes and frozen the very marrow in her bones. A thousand times she had come this way, and a thousand times more, she feared, she would have to come again, before she could awaken . . . before she could be released from whatever strange dream this was that still ensnared her . . .

CHAPTER FOUR

November 24, 10:25 a.m.

MICHAEL HAD SPOTTED the little red-haired guy getting off the plane at Santiago and knew he was a scientist right off the bat. There was something about scientists that gave them away, though he'd have been hard put to say exactly what. It wasn't something easy, like the smell of formaldehyde or protractors sticking out of their pockets. No, it was more a matter of their mien; with scientists—and Michael had been around plenty of them while photographing and writing about the natural world—there was something both detached and highly observant. They could be part of a group, and not part of a group, at the same time. And hard as some of them might try to fit in, they never really did. It was like that massive school of sunfish that Michael had photographed underwater in the Bahamas; all of the fish, for safety's sake alone, tried to move toward the center of the swarm, but some of them, for whatever reason, were kept to the margins and never made it.

And of course they were the easiest for predators to pick off.

During the layover before he could catch the prop plane to Puerto Williams, Michael dragged his duffel bag into the crowded café area of the airport. The red-haired guy was sitting alone at a table in the corner, his head lowered toward his laptop. Michael got close enough to see that he was studying a complex chart littered with numbers and arrows and intersecting lines. To Michael, it looked vaguely topographic. He stood for only a second or two before the guy in the chair whipped around; he had a small, narrow face, and pale red eyebrows, too. The guy sized Michael up, then said, "This can't possibly be interesting to you."

"You'd be surprised," Michael said, approaching him. "I didn't mean to disturb you. I'm just waiting for my connection to Puerto Williams."

He was waiting to see if that worked, and it did. "Me, too," the guy said.

"Mind if I sit down?" Michael said, taking the empty chair at the table—the last empty chair in the whole place.

Dumping the duffel on the floor, with one foot through the strap (a habit he'd gotten into on lots of late-night travels in foreign locales), Michael extended his hand and introduced himself. "Michael Wilde."

"Darryl Hirsch."

"Puerto Williams, huh? Is that your last stop?"

Hirsch clicked the keyboard a few times, then folded up the laptop. He looked at Michael as if unsure what to make of him yet.

"You're not some kind of government intelligence agent or anything, are you? Because if you are, you're doing a terrible job."

Michael laughed. "Why would you think that?"

"Because I'm a scientist, and we live in an age of idiots. For all I know, you're tracking me to make sure that I don't prove the earth is getting warmer—even though it plainly *is*. The ice caps *are* melting, the polar bears *are* disappearing, and Intelligent Design is perfectly designed for dolts. So go ahead—you can arrest me now."

"Relax. You're sounding a little paranoid, if you don't mind my saying so."

"Just because you're paranoid," Darryl observed, "doesn't mean you're not being followed."

"True enough," Michael replied. "But I like to think I'm one of the good guys. I work for *Eco-Travel Magazine,* doing photos and text. I'm going down to the Antarctic to do a story on life at a research station there."

"Which research station? A dozen countries have planted stations there, just to stake their claim."

"Point Adélie. About as close to the Pole as you can get."

"Oh," Hirsch said, digesting the news. "Me, too. Huh." He sounded like he still hadn't given up on his conspiracy theory. "That's really something." His fingers tapped on the closed lid of his laptop. "So, you're a journalist."

Michael detected that first glimmer he had seen before, a million times. When people found out he was a writer, there was that first mild surprise, then acceptance, and then—a nanosecond later—the dawning realization that he could make them famous. Or at least write about them. It was like watching little lights go on in their heads.

"That's great," Hirsch said. "What a coincidence." With studied nonchalance, he opened his laptop again and started tapping at the keyboard. "Let me just show you something." He turned the screen so that Michael could see it. The same elaborate chart appeared. "This is the seafloor of the continental shelf, under the ice around Point Adélie. You can see here where the shelf extends, and here"—he put a nail-bitten finger to the screen—"where it drops off precipitously, into what we call the abyssal range. I'm planning to go down maybe a couple of hundred meters on this trip. I'm a marine biologist, by the way. Woods Hole Oceanographic. I'm particularly interested in the *notothenioidei*—Antarctic icefish—as well as sea snails, eel pouts, rat tails. You know what those are, right?"

Michael said yes, though, privately, he'd have to concede his knowledge was extremely sketchy.

"—and how their metabolisms function in this incredibly hostile environment. A lot of what I do, now that I think about it, would offer some great photo opportunities. These creatures are fantastically adapted to their ecological niches, and to me at least, they're phenomenally beautiful, though some people, I gather, have trouble seeing it. But that, I think, is just because they seem so foreign at first..."

There was no stopping him. He didn't even need to take a

breath. Michael glanced at the espresso cup next to the computer and wondered just how many of those his new travel pal had imbibed.

"... and many of these animals, no matter how small or simple, carry a veritable world of parasites, in everything from their anal glands to their eye ducts."

He said it as if he was describing the array of wonderful rides at an amusement park.

"And as I'm sure you know, the parasite's best bet, in order to ensure its own survival, is to make sure that the host it's devouring is in turn devoured by something else."

Michael wondered if this was the guy's usual small talk.

"Did you know, for instance, that the larval *acanthocephalan* deliberately drives its amphipod host crazy?"

"No," Michael admitted. "Why would it do that?"

"So that the host will leave its hiding place, usually under a rock, and wildly gyrate through open water where it will surely be eaten by a fish."

"You don't say."

"Don't worry, I'll show you a lot of this when we get there," Darryl said, consolingly. "It's thrilling to see."

Michael could see that he was just about to launch into another paean on the glories waiting to be discovered on the ocean floor when a tinny loudspeaker announced—first in Spanish, then in English—that those passengers going on to Puerto Williams could board their plane.

Hirsch kept up his chatter all the way across the cold, wind-blown tarmac, and up the short flight of steps into the prop plane. He didn't even have to duck to enter, while Michael had to bend far forward to keep from getting bonked. The plane had just ten seats, five on each side, and with everyone wearing heavy coats and parkas, boots and gloves and hats, it was a very tight squeeze. All the others seemed to be rattling away in Spanish or Portuguese. Darryl Hirsch took the seat right across from Michael, but once the plane taxied down the windy runway, its props whirring and its engines growling, all attempts at conversation came to a halt. They'd have had to shout at the top of their lungs just to be heard across the narrow aisle.

Michael buckled in and stared out the small round window.

The plane had some trouble lifting off, buffeted by strong head-winds, but once it did, it quickly veered away from the land, soared over a ridge of jagged cliffs, and turned south along the Pacific coastline. It was a minute or two before Michael's stomach caught up with the rest of him. Far below, he could see the white-topped waves rolling and cresting, chopped by fierce and incessant winds. He was heading, he knew, for the windiest—in addition to the dri-est, coldest, and most barren—place on Earth. It was early after-noon, but the light would last around the clock. It was the austral summer, and the sun would never go down. It appeared on the northern horizon like a sliver of dull coin, bathing everything in a muted luminescence, punctuated by passages of either glaring brightness, or storm-covered shadow. Over the coming weeks and months, the sun would travel slowly across the sky, reaching its zenith on the solstice of December 21, before departing altogether in late March. Then, the moon would rule just as unequivocally as the sun did now.

Although Michael wanted to stay awake, to remember every moment of the journey, it became harder and harder to do so. He had been traveling for what felt like days, from Tacoma to Los An-geles, from Los Angeles to Santiago, and now from Santiago to Puerto Williams, the southernmost town in the world. He lowered the plastic shade on the window and closed his eyes. The plane was warm, too warm really, and his feet were sweltering in their hiking boots. But he was too tired even to reach down and try to unlace them. He settled back in his uncomfortable seat—he could feel the knees of the guy behind him prodding through the thin fabric cush-ion and into the small of his back—but dropped off into sleep any-way. The constant thrumming of the engines, the closeness of the cabin, the never-changing light . . .

He started out dreaming, as he usually did, of Kristin—of some occasion when they were happy together, when they were kayaking in Oregon, or parasailing off the Yucatán—but the deeper he went, the darker and more troubling the dreams became. Too often, he found himself in this same weird state—asleep, but simul-taneously, it seemed, aware of that fact—trying hard to marshal his thoughts and move them in another direction, but stuck all the same. Before he knew it, he was back on the barren ledge in the Cascades, huddling against the cold, with Kristin cradled in his arms. He was holding her so tight his arms ached, and pressing his feet against the rocky wall so hard that he lost all feeling below the ankles. He was talking to her, telling her how mad her dad would be, how her sister would claim she was being such a drama queen. But when he awoke, with the flight attendant shaking him to say he had to sit up for landing, he found that he was clutching his own back-pack, and his long legs were entangled in the metal runners of the seat in front of him.

Darryl was wide awake—that's what a few espressos will do for you—and grinning. "Look out your window!" he shouted over the engines. "It's on your side!"

Michael sat up, rubbing the rough whiskers on his chin, and lifted the shade. Again, he was struck by that eerie light that made him want to close his eyes or look away. But far ahead and far below, he could see the very tip of the South American continent, tapering like the sharp tip of a shoe, winnowing itself down to almost noth-ing where the Pacific and Atlantic Oceans merged. And on the very tip of the shoe, he saw a tiny, black smudge.

"Puerto Williams!" Darryl cried, exultantly. "Can you see it?"

Michael had to smile—he kind of liked this guy, but he was defi-nitely going to take some getting used to. He gave him a thumbs-up.

The pilot issued some instructions in Spanish, which Michael as-sumed meant something like return your seats to their upright posi-tion, and the plane banked steeply toward a long, spiky line of brown mountains. When it was parallel to them, and presumably protected from the easterly winds, it swiftly dropped altitude—Michael's ears popped like corks—and the pilot cut back on the engines. For a mo-ment, it felt like the plane was in a free fall, before Michael heard the rumbling of the landing gear coming down and felt the nose of the plane coming up a bit. The engine noise subsided considerably, and the plane seemed to glide, like a seabird, onto the gravel runway, touch down with a bump, then roll, unimpeded, toward a couple of rusted hangars, a ramshackle terminal, and a control tower that Michael could swear was tilting ten degrees.

Several of the passengers applauded, and the pilot came on to say, *"Muchas gracias, señoras y señores, y bienvenidos al fin de la tierra."*

That much Michael didn't need a translator for. Welcome to the ends of the earth.

CHAPTER FIVE

November 24, 4:15 p.m.

CAPTAIN BENJAMIN PURCELL, the Commanding Officer of the icebreaker *Constellation*, was getting impatient. From his cabin, he'd heard the arrival of the prop plane carrying his last two passengers, but that had been well over an hour ago. Where the hell were they? How long could it take to get from the airstrip to the port? It wasn't like Puerto Williams (pop. 2512 at last count) offered much in the way of sightseeing. Once you'd stopped to pay homage to the *Proa del Escampavia Yelcho*—the preserved prow of the cutter that had been used to rescue Ernest Shackleton's starving crew from Elephant Island in 1916—there wasn't a lot else to capture your interest. And Purcell should know—he'd been running his ship among the southernmost Chilean and Argentine ports for nearly ten years—and he still hadn't seen any more cooperation or amity between those two countries than when he'd started. To this day, there wasn't a reliable boat connection between Puerto Williams, on the northern shore of the Isla Navarino, and Ushuaia on the Argentine side of the channel.

He went up to the bridge, where Ensign Gallo had been placed on duty while they remained at dockside. Short of the aloft con tower, which rose another forty-five feet above the bridge and was used as a lookout post for oncoming bergs, the bridge afforded the best available view of the port and what passed for the town just up the hill. A few hundred yards away, at the *Muelle Guardian Brito,* or main pier, a Norwegian cruise ship had berthed, and he could hear one of the old Abba hits—was it "Dancing Queen"?—blaring from its party room.

"Give me those," he said to the ensign, gesturing at the binoculars that were lodged beside the wheel. He trained them uphill, toward the Centro Comercial—not much more than a few crafts shops, a general store, and a post office—looking for anyone who might look like a photojournalist or a marine biologist. The few people he could see were elderly tourists, carefully framing pictures of each other with the towering granite needles, known as the Teeth of Navarino, in the distance behind them. But then, if you were going to take the trouble to travel to one of the most remote spots on the planet, you probably did want to have incontrovertible proof of that fact when you got back home.

"How's the doc settling in?" Purcell asked Ensign Gallo.

"Fine, sir. No complaints."

"Where'd you put her?"

"Petty Officer Klauber volunteered, sir, to give up her cabin to Dr. Barnes."

That was a lucky break, Purcell thought. Berths were hard to come by. The doc—one of the three NSF passengers he was to transport to Point Adélie—was an African-American woman of considerable bulk (good padding, he thought, for the Antarctic) and strong demeanor. When she arrived the day before and shook his hand, he could feel his fingers crunch in her grip. She'd do well out there. It was no country for weaklings.

Purcell swept the town again, and this time, finally, saw two men looking down at the docks, and one of them—a little guy with red hair—asking a Chilean fisherman something. The fisherman nodded, then swung one arm, still holding a chum bucket, down toward the *Constellation.* The other guy was tall, with black hair that was whipping around his head (this was hat country, as he would soon learn) and carried a massively overstuffed duffel bag. He also had on a blue nylon backpack that betrayed the outlines of a laptop computer case.

As the two men came down toward the harbor, Purcell saw that the little guy had also hired a local teenager to push a wheelbarrow loaded with his own gear.

"There they are," Purcell said. "Give 'em a kick in the ass." The ensign obliged with a couple of short blasts on the ship's whistle.

"Single up all lines," the captain continued, "and prepare to get under way."

———————

As Michael dragged his bag down the metal-and-concrete pier, he saw a crewman in navy whites descending the gangway. The boat was bigger than he'd expected—he'd have guessed maybe four hundred feet long—with what looked like a helicopter secured under an enormous tarp on the aft deck. The sides of the ship were painted red, except for a wide white diagonal stripe across the bow. At the stern, there were gigantic propeller-like screws. Break the ice with the hull, Michael figured, then chop it up with the screws. The boat, in short, was like a huge, floating ice-cube maker.

"Dr. Hirsch?" the sailor called out, "Mr. Wilde?"

"Yo," Darryl replied, and Michael lifted his chin in acknowledgment.

"Petty Officer Kazinski. Welcome aboard the *Constellation*."

Kazinski grabbed the bags out of the wheelbarrow and, while Hirsch dug out a few bills for the teenage porter, turned around on his heel and marched briskly up the ramp. "The CO—Commanding Officer," he said over his shoulder, "is Captain Purcell. He has requested your company at dinner tonight, in the Officers' Mess. Seven o'clock. Please dress appropriately."

What, Michael wondered, did *that* mean? He'd forgotten to pack a tux. (Not that he owned one, anyway.)

Once up on deck, Michael looked around. The bridge, rising at least fifty feet above him, struck him as unusually high and wide, running virtually the entire width of the ship, and perched above that was a kind of crow's nest, mounted on what looked like a chimney stack. That must be some view. He should try to get some wide-angle shots from up there on the voyage to Point Adélie.

"You'll be sharing a cabin aft," Kazinski said. "Follow me, and I'll show you to your quarters."

As they headed for a narrow stairway, several sailors hustled past them, and Michael heard a few others clattering down the stairs above their heads. He heard some shorthand comments about mooring lines, switching fuel tanks, and some crack about a sonar tech that made no sense to him but made the sailors laugh uproariously. The ship was clearly being readied for immediate departure.

"How many men do you have on board?" Michael asked.

"The crew consists of one hundred and two men and women, sir."

Michael stood corrected. He hadn't seen any females yet, but apparently some were around. As if to prove the point, a tall, thin woman with a clipboard tucked under one arm of her uniform suddenly emerged from a hatchway; Kazinski immediately stood at attention and saluted.

She acknowledged the salute, then extended her hand to Hirsch. "You must be Dr. Hirsch. I'm Lieutenant Commander Healey—Kathleen—the Operations officer on board." She had a crisp, no-nonsense attitude about her; even the short brown hair peeking out from under her cap seemed cut for maximum efficiency. "And you're the journalist?" she said to Michael. "I'm sorry, I saw your name in the morning report, but I've forgotten it."

Michael introduced himself and said, "Glad to be aboard."

"Yes, we were waiting."

Michael began to get the impression that he and Hirsch had been holding up the works.

"You're the last of the NSF contingent," Healey said.

"There are others?" Hirsch asked.

"Only one. Dr. Charlotte Barnes. She arrived two days ago."

There was another long, blaring whistle from overhead. Three more sailors went flying by. The deck rumbled with the sound of the starboard engine coming online.

"If you'll excuse me . . ."

Michael nodded, and as she strode off, he could hear her calling out orders right and left.

"This way," Kazinski said, disappearing into the hatchway. Michael waited for Hirsch to go through, then followed. The passageway was so narrow it was tough to maneuver with the huge duffel—especially as it contained his camera equipment, painstakingly packed to protect against breakage; the camera and gear were in metal cases at the core, further insulated by all his clothing wrapped around them. But the bag was damn heavy, as a result.

"The *Constellation*," Kazinski was saying, "is among the largest icebreakers in the Coast Guard fleet. She weighs just over thirteen thousand tons, and she runs on half a dozen diesel engines and three gas turbines. We're carrying over one million gallons of fuel. At full throttle, she can muster seventy-five thousand horsepower and travel through open water at seventeen knots. In high seas, she has a maximum roll of ninety degrees."

What, Michael wondered, would that feel like? He'd seen some heavy weather off Nova Scotia, and been caught in a squall in the Bahamas, but he'd never been on an icebreaker in an Antarctic storm.

"Any chance of that?" Hirsch asked. "Rolling ninety degrees, I mean?" He didn't sound like he'd be looking forward to it.

"You never can tell," Kazinski said, stepping over the threshold of another hatchway, then warning, "Watch your step there. Summer seas are not as bad as winter down here, but it's still Cape Horn. Anything can happen, at any time. Watch your step again."

He took them down another short flight of metal steps, and the portholes suddenly vanished: Michael figured that they had just descended to below water level. Even the air became closer and danker. Fluorescent tubes in the ceiling flickered, and as they continued to make their way toward the stern, the vibrations in the floor got stronger. So did the noise.

"And here we are," Kazinski said, ducking into a cabin door. "Home sweet home."

When Michael and Darryl followed him in, there was barely room for the three of them to stand. There were two narrow bunks attached to opposite walls, with striped woolen blankets pulled military tight; a flat metal tray was folded down from the wall between them. There was one overhead light fixture, burning brightly in a frosted globe, and a plywood door that led to the head; Michael could smell the mildew.

"Is this the deluxe cabin?" Michael joked, and Kazinski laughed.

"Yes, sir. We save this one for visiting dignitaries only."

"We'll take it."

"Good decision there. Last two berths on board, sir."

Darryl, fortunately, didn't seem to mind, either. As soon as Kazinski left, he unzipped one of his bags and started tossing some things onto the bunk on the right. "Say," he said to Michael, stopping for a second, "did you want that one?"

Michael shook his head. "It's all yours." He slung his backpack off his shoulder and onto the cot. "But if they leave us chocolates on our pillows at night, I want mine."

While Darryl unpacked, Michael dug out one of his digital cameras—the Canon S80, good for down-and-dirty wide-angle shots—and went up on deck. The *Constellation* had left the dock, and was passing slowly southeast down the Beagle Channel, named after HMS *Beagle,* the very ship that had carried Charles Darwin into those waters in 1834. The air temperature wasn't bad, maybe thirty-six or thirty-seven degrees, and since the ship was still in a relatively protected waterway, the wind was mild. Michael was able to get off a few shots without worrying about gloves and without his fingers going numb. He probably wouldn't be using these for the piece anyway, but he always liked to have a few photos recording every important phase of his trip. He used them as memory aids when it came to the writing part, and it never failed to surprise him that something he remembered one way would show up quite differently when he looked at the photos. The mind could play a lot of tricks on you, he had learned.

The port had slipped into the distance, and the coastline was dusted with a pale green cover of moss and lichen. Patagonian Indians had once populated the wind-ravaged country, and when Ferdinand Magellan, searching for a sheltered westward route in 1520, had seen their burning campfires dotting the barren hills and shore, he had dubbed it Tierra del Fuego, or "The Land of Fire." There was nothing fiery, or warm, about it now, and certainly no sign of the original Patagonians; they had been decimated by disease and the usurpation of their home by the European explorers. The only signs of life that Michael could see onshore were flocks of snowy petrels, darting among the scoured cliffsides, tending their nests and feeding their young. When his fingers got too cold to handle the camera anymore, he tucked it back in his parka, zipped the pocket closed, and simply leaned over the rail.

The water below was a hard, dark blue, and broke from the sides of the ship in a constant curling motion. Michael had been reading up on the Antarctic ever since getting the assignment from Gillespie, and he knew that this ice-free water wouldn't last long. As soon as they left the channel and entered the Drake Passage—and Cape Horn—the sea would become the roughest on earth. Even now, in the southern hemisphere's summer, icebergs would pose a constant threat. He was actually looking forward to their appearance. Photographing bergs and glaciers, bringing out the delicate hues that ranged from a blinding white to a deep lavender, was an artistic and technical challenge of the first order. And Michael liked a challenge.

He'd been standing there for some time before he became aware of a fellow passenger also at the rail—a black woman with braided hair, bundled up in a long, green down coat. He wondered how long she'd been there. She was maybe twenty feet away, and fumbling with her own camera. From where he stood, Michael thought it looked like a Nikon 35 mm. She was aiming at the water—a couple of sea lions had just popped up, their sleek black heads glistening like bowling balls—and Michael called out, "Not easy from a moving boat, is it?"

She looked over. She had a broad face with high cheekbones and arched brows. "It's never easy," she said. "I don't even know why I try."

With one hand on the rail for balance—the sea was fairly calm, but the boat still rolled on the swells—Michael strolled over.

"You must be the photographer we've been waiting for," she said.

"I am." He was starting to feel like the class problem. "And you must be the doctor who got here ahead of time."

"Yeah, well, when you're coming from the Midwest, you make the connections you can."

They introduced themselves, and Michael glanced at her camera. "You're using film," he said.

"I've had this camera for ten years, and I've used it maybe twice. What's wrong with film?"

"Right now, it'll be okay. But when the polar weather really hits, you can run into some problems. Film cracks pretty easily in extreme cold."

She looked at the camera in her hand as if it had betrayed her. "I only brought it 'cause my mom and my sister said I had to bring back pictures." Then she brightened. "Maybe I can just borrow some of yours. They'll never know."

"Help yourself."

The sea lions bleated, then ducked their heads back under the waves.

"You work for the National Science Foundation?" Michael asked.

"I do now," she said. "I've got a ton of medical-school loans to pay off."

Michael guessed that she couldn't have been out of med school more than five or six years.

"Plus, the hospital I work for in Chicago is under active investigation by about six different agencies. I thought it might be a good time to get away."

"To the Antarctic?" Michael was already making mental notes, thinking she'd be a great character in the *Eco-Travel* piece.

"You know what they pay for anybody crazy enough to sign up for a six-month stint?" A gust of wind suddenly kicked up, blowing the braids of her hair, some of them streaked with a hint of blond, back over her shoulders. "I can tell you this—it sure beats working in the ER. In fact, I heard about this gig from a friend there, who did it himself about a year ago."

"And he lived to tell the tale?"

"He said it changed his life."

"Is that what you're looking to do?" Michael said. "Change your life?"

She pulled back a bit, and paused. "No, I'm pretty happy with my life so far." But she looked at him a bit warily. "You sure seem curious."

"Sorry," he said, "bad habit. It goes with the job."

"Photographer?"

"I'm a writer, too, I'm afraid."

"Okay, then—at least I know what I'm up against. But let's take it slow. We've got a whole lot of time, I think, to get acquainted."

"You're right," he said, thinking to himself that his interviewing technique might have gotten a bit rusty. "Why don't we just go back to the photo tips and start over?"

He quickly ran down a few pointers for her on taking photographs at sea, especially in the peculiar light so far south, then headed back to his cabin. *Take your time,* he reminded himself, *let your subjects open up on their own.* At the door to his cabin, he remembered that he'd been told to dress appropriately for dinner, and he knew he'd have to dig out his least wrinkled flannel shirt, slip it under the mattress, and lie down on it for a while.

CHAPTER SIX

June 20, 1854, 6 p.m.

IT WOULD HAVE BEEN an altogether typical night for Sinclair Archibald Copley, lieutenant in the 17th Lancers, had it not concluded in such an unforeseen way.

It began about six, with several rounds of écarté in the barracks, at which Sinclair lost the sum of twenty pounds. His father, the fourth Earl of Hawton, would not be pleased at another request for funds—he had sworn, after buying Sinclair the army commission, that he would offer no more help. But rather than suffer any damage to the family name, he had already quietly settled an outstanding bill with Sinclair's tailor, then another with the Oriental proprietor of a dubious establishment in Bluegate-fields, where Sinclair had indulged in what the earl decried as "depraved behavior." He could hardly refuse one more small request, certainly not from a son who might well be dispatched any day to fight the Russians in the Crimea.

"What would you say to dinner at my club?" Rutherford asked, raking in his winnings. "As my guests, of course."

"That's the least you can do," said Le Maitre, the other loser for the night. Because of his surname, he was known to his friends as Frenchie. "It's my money you'll be spending."

"Now, now," Rutherford said, stroking his extravagant side-whiskers, "let's not quarrel about it. What do you say, Sinclair?"

Sinclair wasn't eager to go to the Athenaeum just then, either. He had a small indebtedness to several of the members there, too. "I'd prefer the Turtle."

"The Turtle it is, then," Rutherford said, lumbering up from his chair—they had all done a fair amount of drinking while gambling—"and perhaps a late visit to Mme. Eugenie?" He winked broadly at Sinclair and Le Maitre, while stuffing their pound notes into the pocket of his scarlet pelisse. He was in a good mood, and rightly so.

The three of them careened out into Oxford Street, sending several civilians scurrying out of their way, and splashed through the muddy London thoroughfares. At the corner of Harley Street, where a Miss Florence Nightingale had recently founded a hospital for indigent gentlewomen, Sinclair stopped to watch as a pretty young woman in a white bonnet leaned out to close the shutters on a third-story window. She saw him, too—his epaulettes and gold buttons gleamed in the dusk—and he smiled up at her. She ducked her head back inside, and the shutters closed, but not before he thought he'd seen her smile back.

"Come along!" Rutherford cried from down the street. "I'm famished."

Sinclair caught up to his companions, and together they made their way to the beckoning globe of the Turtle tavern. A wooden placard, depicting a bright green turtle standing, improbably enough, on his hind legs, swung over the door, and Sinclair could hear the roar of many voices and the clattering of cups and cutlery from inside.

The door banged open as a fat man in a top hat spilled out, and Rutherford held it wide for Sinclair and Le Maitre to enter.

Long trestle tables ran the length of the low-ceilinged room, and a crackling fire burned in the vast stone hearth. Waiters in grease-spattered vests moved among the diners with platters of roasted chicken and slabs of bloody roast beef. Customers banged empty beer mugs on the wooden tabletops to signal the need for replenishment. But Sinclair was neither hungry nor thirsty.

"Rutherford, give me back a fiver."

"What for? I already said I'm buying."

"I'm going out back."

Nearly all the taverns had a fighting pit out back, but the Turtle's was especially well attended. With a bit of luck, Sinclair would be able to win back what he'd lost at cards.

"You're incorrigible," Rutherford replied, while obligingly providing the five-pound note.

"I'll join you," Le Maitre said, and Rutherford looked shocked.

"You're leaving me to dine alone?"

"Not for long," Sinclair said, as he drew Le Maitre by the arm toward the rear door of the tavern. "We'll be back with our winnings."

Behind the tavern there was a filthy alley, littered with bones and offal, and beyond that an old stable that had been converted to gaming use. It was insufferably warm and fetid inside; gas lamps burned from iron stanchions, illuminating the mob that crowded around the fighting pit—a square about fifteen feet on each side, and perhaps four feet deep.

The pit boss, bare-chested and sporting a tattoo of the Union Jack across his back, was standing in its center, announcing the next bout. The sand in the floor of the pit was wet with blood and spittle and littered with scraps of mangled fur.

"We got Duke, a black and tan," he shouted, "and we got Whitey! If you will make way, gentlemen, you will be afforded the opportunity of seeing these fine beasts before placing your wagers!"

The crowd parted, opening crooked avenues for two men with pit bulls on short chains, their muzzles tied with rope. The dogs strained ferociously at their leashes as they moved toward the lip of the pit, and it was all their masters could do to keep them from leaping inside, or going after each other.

"Duke, he hails from Rosemary Lane," the boss announced, "and Whitey, why Whitey's the pride of Ludgate Hill. Two fine champions, gentlemen, and a right even match. So place your bets!" he cried out. "Place your bets, if you please!"

He stepped up out of the pit and rolled a barrel to its rim.

"Have you seen either of them fight?" Frenchie asked, leaning close to Sinclair's ear to be heard over the crowd.

"Yes, I've won on Whitey," Sinclair replied, while raising his hand to a passing bookmaker. "Five on Whitey!"

"Make it ten!" Frenchie threw in.

The bookmaker tipped his cap—as they were clearly gentlemen, he would not insist on the cash in advance—and turned to an old drunk pulling at his sleeve.

"Last call, gentlemen," the boss called out as he pounded a fist on the closed barrel at the rim of the pit. "Place all bets!"

There was a sudden flurry of cries and raised hands as the dogs' masters removed the ropes from their muzzles. The dogs barked furiously, foam flying from their lips. Then a bell rang, the pit boss shouted, "All done!" and everyone's eyes turned toward the barrel. The boss yanked off its lid, and with his foot tipped it over.

A swarm of rats, black and brown and gray, tumbled out and fell in a frenzied torrent into the pit. They righted themselves quickly and ran in all directions, some nipping at each other, others scrabbling at the wooden boards that lined the pit. Several actually managed to leap out, but the laughing gamblers booted them back in again.

The dogs went into a frenzy at the sight of the rats, and their masters had no sooner unhooked the leads than the dogs sailed into the pit, jaws snarling and claws bared. The white one was the first to make a kill, grabbing a fat gray rat and biting clear through it.

Sinclair clenched a fist in triumph, and Frenchie shouted, "Good work, Whitey!"

Duke, the black and tan, quickly evened the score, shaking a brown one like a rag until its head flew off. The rats scurried to the sides of the pit, clambering over each other's backs in their rush to escape. Whitey lunged at the one on top of a pile and tossed it into the air. The rat landed on its back and before it could turn over Whitey had lunged for its belly and ripped it open with one swipe.

There was a huzzah from Whitey's supporters in the crowd.

And so it went for the full five minutes. Blood and bone and bits of rat flew everywhere—Sinclair always made it a point to stand well back so that his uniform would remain unmarred—but at some point Whitey seemed to lose his enthusiasm for the kill and decided to eat his prey. That was not good training, Sinclair thought; while the dog should be kept hungry before a bout, enough to keep its instinct for blood alive, it should not be so starved that it stopped to consume the quarry.

"Get up, Whitey!" Frenchie shouted, as did many others, but the dog remained on all fours munching the dead rodents scattered around its paws. Duke, meanwhile, continued about his grim business.

Sinclair could see his money evaporating even before the bell rang and the boss called out "Time, gentlemen!" The dogs' masters leapt into the pit, landing between the dogs and among the few maimed rats still crawling about, half-alive.

The pit boss looked to his fellow judge—a dirt-covered urchin holding the brass bell—and announced, "It's Duke, gentlemen! Duke of Rosemary Lane has carried the day with a baker's dozen."

There was a happy clamor from Duke's supporters, and the passing of notes and coins among the mob. The bookmaker in the cap appeared before Sinclair, who grudgingly handed him the fiver. Frenchie did the same.

"Won't Rutherford gloat," Le Maitre said.

Sinclair knew he was right, but he had already put the loss out of mind. It was always best not to dwell on misfortune. And his thoughts, as it happened, had already turned in a decidedly more pleasant direction. As he joined the raucous throng heading back to the tavern, he was thinking of that fetching young woman he'd seen, in the crisp white bonnet, closing the hospital shutters.

CHAPTER SEVEN

November 30

FOR DAYS the sky had been filled with a swirling cloud of birds, following the *Constellation* as it headed south toward the Antarctic Circle. And Michael had set up his monopod—a Manfrotto with a trigger grip for quick, automatic adjustment—on the flying bridge to get as many good shots of them as he could. In his cabin at night, he'd been reading up on them, too, so he'd know what he was looking at.

Now—even if it didn't make them any easier to catch in flight—he could at least begin to tell them apart.

Nearly all of the birds were tube-nosed, with bills that contained salt-excreting glands, so that didn't help much. Nor did their color scheme, which was almost unrelievedly black and white. But the different species did exhibit unique flight patterns and telltale feeding methods, and that made the job a bit easier.

The diving petrels, for instance, were small and chubby, and shot above the sea with fast-beating wings, punctuated by short glides; often they went right through the crest of a wave, before plunging down to capture a bit of krill.

The pintado petrels danced with their webbed feet across the top of the water itself.

The southern fulmars, gunmetal gray, would allow themselves to stall in the wind, then fold their feet and drop, head last, into the sea, like a scaredy-cat jumping off a high dive.

The Antarctic prions plowed through the surf using their broad, laminated bills like shovels, filtering plankton from the water. Their cousins—the narrow-billed prions—flew more languidly, leaning down to pluck nimbly the occasional prey from the top few centimeters of the sea.

The snowy white petrels—the hardest to see against the foam and spray of the turbulent ocean—caromed around like pinballs, darting this way and that, their sharp little wings even touching the icy water to gauge the shape and drift of the swells.

But the king of them all—soaring on high like a ruler calmly surveying his realm—was the wandering albatross, the largest of all the seabirds. Even as Michael rooted around in his waterproof supply bag for a new lens, one of them had roosted on the helicopter tarp on the lower deck, and several more were keeping time with the ship, flying at the height of the bridge. Michael had never seen any creature travel with such beauty and economy of motion. With a wingspan of over three meters, the ashy white birds—with bright pink beaks and blackened brows—barely seemed to exert themselves at all. Their wings, Michael had learned, were a miracle of aerodynamic design, feeling every tiny shift in the wind and instantly adjusting an entire suite of muscles to alter the angle and sweep of each individual feather. The bones themselves weighed almost nothing, as they were partially filled with air. Apart from the brief spells when an albatross might alight to nest or mate on an Antarctic island, the bird lived its whole life in the air, borrowing the power of the changeable winds and using it, through some prodigious feat of navigation, to circle the entire globe, again and again.

No wonder sailors had always revered them and, as Captain Purcell later explained over dinner one night, "regarded them as a symbol of good luck. Those birds have a better global navigational system in their heads than we've got in the wheelhouse."

"I had a few of them keeping me company today," Michael said, "while I was up on the flying bridge."

Purcell nodded as he reached for the bottle of sparkling cider. "They can adjust their dip and their speed to the velocity of the ship they're following."

He refilled Dr. Barnes's glass with the cider. As Michael had learned on his first night aboard, when he'd innocently asked for a beer, no alcohol was allowed on U.S. Navy or Coast Guard ships.

"A friend of mine, a Tulane ornithologist," said Hirsch, "radio-tagged an albatross in the Indian Ocean and tracked it by satellite for one month. It had traveled over fifteen thousand kilometers on a single foraging expedition. Apparently, the bird can see, from hundreds of meters up, the bioluminescent schools of squid. When the squid come up to the surface to feed, the bird goes down."

Charlotte, taking one of the serving bowls from its rubber pad, paused and said, "This isn't calamari, is it?" and everyone laughed. "I mean, I'd hate to deprive some hungry albatross."

"No, that's one of our cook's specialties—fried zucchini strips."

Charlotte helped herself, then passed it to the Operations officer—Ops, for short—Lieutenant Kathleen Healey.

"We serve lots of fresh vegetables and fruit on the way out," Captain Purcell observed, "and lots of canned and frozen on the long way back."

The ship suddenly swerved, as if taking a step sideways, then swerved back again. Michael put one hand on the rubber strip that went all the way around the rim of the table and the other on his cider glass. He still hadn't gotten used to the ship's constant rolling.

"The ship is shaped sort of like a football," Kathleen said, looking utterly unperturbed by the turbulence. "In fact, she's not really designed for calm seas; she hasn't even got a keel. She's designed to move smoothly through brash ice and bergs, and that's when you'll be glad you're on her."

"We've been lucky so far," the captain said. "We've had a high-pressure area over us—meaning low seas and good visibility—and we've been able to make good progress toward Point Adélie."

But Michael could hear the hesitation in his voice, and so could the others. Charlotte was holding a zucchini strip on the end of her fork.

"But?" she asked.

"But it looks like it's dissipating," he said. "On the cape, the weather can change very quickly."

"We're gradually moving across what's called the Antarctic Convergence," Lieutenant Healey put in. "That's where the cold bottom water from the pole sinks beneath the warmer water coming up from the Indian and Atlantic and Pacific Oceans. We're traveling into much more unpredictable seas, and less temperate weather."

"Today was temperate?" Charlotte said, before snapping the zucchini strip off her fork. "My braids froze so hard, they felt like jerky." She said it with a laugh, but everyone knew that it wasn't really a joke.

"Today will feel like a heat wave before we're done," the captain said as he held out the big bowl of pasta primavera. "Anyone for seconds?"

Darryl, who'd passed on the appetizer—shrimp cocktails—immediately reached out. Despite his size, they had discovered that he could eat them all under the table.

"I'm only trying to prepare you," the captain went on, "for what's coming."

———————

His warning came true even sooner than he might have expected. The winds had been picking up steadily, and the ice, drifting their way in chunks the size of train cars, was lumbering past in even-more-massive blocks; when some became impassable, the ship did what it was designed to do and plowed right through them. With dinner done, and the sun still hanging motionless above the horizon, Michael went out to the bow to watch the grudge match unfold between the oncoming bergs and the pride of the Coast Guard's cutters.

Darryl Hirsch was already out there, bundled up with only his eyeglasses poking through the red woolen ski mask that covered his entire head and face.

"You've got to watch this," Hirsch said, as Michael joined him at the rail. "It's positively hypnotic."

Just ahead lay a tabular slab of ice the size of a football field, and Michael felt the *Constellation* pick up speed as it rammed directly into the center of the snow-covered pack. The ice at first didn't give an inch, and Michael wondered just how thick it was. The engines groaned and roared, and the hull of the ship, rounded for just this purpose, rode up onto the surface of the glacier, and let its own weight—thirteen thousand tons—press down. A crooked fissure opened in the ice, then another, shooting off in the opposite direction. The cutter pressed forward, bearing down the whole time, and suddenly there was a great splintering and cracking of the ice. Massive shards reared up on either side of the prow, rising almost as high as the deck Michael and Darryl were standing on. Instinctively they stepped away from the railing, then suddenly had to lunge for it again to keep from tumbling all the way back to the stern.

When the shards subsided, Michael looked down over the rail and saw the pieces slipping away to the sides, before being sucked under the ship, on their way toward the giant screw propellers—three of them, sixteen feet in diameter—at the other end; there, they'd be chewed and chopped into manageable size, before drifting off in the ship's wake.

But what probably surprised Michael the most was the underside of the ice. What looked white and pristine on top did not look at all that way when broken and upended. The underbelly of the ice was a disheartening sight to see—a pale, sickly yellow that reminded Michael of snow a dog had peed on.

"It's algae," Darryl said, intuiting his thoughts. "That discoloration on the bottom." He had to raise his voice to be heard over the crunching of the ice and the rising winds. "Those bergs aren't solid ice—they're honeycombed with brine channels, and the channels are filled with algae and diatoms and bacteria."

"So they live under the ice?" Michael shouted.

"No—they live *in* it," Darryl shouted back, looking vaguely proud of them for their resourcefulness. The ship plunged forward again, then dipped, and even in this strange light, Michael could see that Darryl was starting to look a little green at the gills.

After Darryl hurriedly excused himself to go below, Michael got tired of trying to keep his own footing and headed down to the wardroom, which was usually a hive of activity at night, with card games going and some DVD blaring on the TV. (The choices ranged from Bruce Lee and Jackie Chan to professional wrestling and the Rock.) But there was nothing going on; the crew, he assumed, must have been called to various duties. He ducked his head into the gym—a cramped exercise room tucked into the bow, separated from the icy ocean only by the bulkheads. Petty Officer Kazinski was on the treadmill in a pair of shorts and a tight T-shirt that read "KISS ME—I'M COAST GUARD!"

"How can you stay on that thing?" Michael asked, as the ship rolled again.

"No better time!" Kazinski said, clutching the handrails and keeping up a brutal pace. "It's like ridin' a bronco!"

A small TV monitor overhead carried a live feed from the bow. Between the drops of water and foam that spattered the outside lens, Michael could see a grainy, black-and-white picture of the heaving sea, bobbing with slabs of ice.

"It's getting rough out there," Michael said.

Kazinski glanced up at the monitor without breaking stride. "Gonna get a lot worse before this one blows over—that's for sure."

Michael was glad Darryl wasn't there to hear that. But personally, he was pleased. To have passed through the deadliest stretch of sea on the planet without encountering a storm would have been like going to Paris and missing the Eiffel Tower.

With his hands outstretched toward the walls of the corridor, he stumbled back toward his own cabin and opened the door. Darryl wasn't in his bunk, but the door to the head was closed and Michael could hear him in there, throwing up everything he'd eaten.

Michael slumped onto his own bunk and lay back. *Fasten your seat belts,* he thought, *it's going to be a bumpy night.* Kristin had often used that old Bette Davis line when they'd found themselves stranded somewhere precarious as the sun went down. What he would have given to have her there with him now, and to hear her say it just one more time.

The plywood door unstuck itself and Darryl, bent over double, staggered out and sprawled on his bunk. When he noticed Michael, he mumbled, "You don't want to go in there. I missed."

Michael would have been surprised if he hadn't. "Did you really have to have seconds tonight?" he said, and Darryl, wearing only his long johns, gave him a wan smile.

"It seemed like a good idea at the time."

"You gonna be okay?"

The ship suddenly lurched again, so violently that Michael had to grab the bed frame bolted to the floor.

Darryl turned a deeper shade of green and closed his eyes.

Michael leaned back against the interior wall, still gripping the frame. Yes, it undoubtedly was going to be a rough night, but he wondered how long a storm like this could blow. Would it last for days? And how much worse would it get? How much worse, for that matter, *could* it get?

He picked up one of his Audubon books, but the boat was pitching and rolling far too much to read; just trying to focus made him nauseous. He stowed the book under the mattress. And the roar of the engine and propellers, there in the aft quarters of the ship, was louder than it had ever been. Darryl was lying as still as a mummy, but huffing and puffing.

"What'd you take?" Michael asked him. "Scopolamine?"

Darryl grunted yes.

"Anything else?"

He held up one limp wrist. It had an elastic strap, thicker than a rubber band, wrapped around it.

"What's that?"

"Acupressure band. Supposed to help."

Michael had never heard of that one, but it didn't look like Darryl would swear by it, either.

"Want me to see if Charlotte's got something stronger?" Michael asked.

"Don't go out there," Darryl whispered. "You'll die."

"I'm just going up the corridor. I'll be right back."

Michael waited for a momentary lull, then got to his feet and out the door. The long corridor, tilting to one side and then the other, looked like something out of a carnival fun house. The fluorescent lights flickered and buzzed. Charlotte's cabin was about at midships, maybe a hundred feet away, but it was slow going, and Michael had to keep his feet broadly spaced.

He could see a telltale ribbon of light under her door, so he knew she was awake when he knocked.

"It's Michael," he called out. "I think Darryl could use some help."

Charlotte opened the door in a quilted robe with a Chinese motif—green and gold dragons, breathing fire—and woolly slippers on her feet. Her braided hair was knotted in a ball atop her head. "Don't tell me," she said, already reaching for her black bag, "he's seasick."

By the time they got back to the cabin, Darryl had curled himself into a ball. He was so small—maybe five-foot-four, and skinny as a rail—that he looked like a kid with a tummy ache, waiting for his mom.

Charlotte sat down on the edge of the bed and asked him what he'd already taken. When he also showed her the acupressure band, she said, "No telling what some people will believe."

She bustled in her bag and pulled out a syringe and bottle. "You ever heard of Phenytoin?"

"Same as Dilantin."

"Ooh, you do know your drugs. Ever taken it?"

"Once, before a dive."

"I hope not too soon before a dive." She readied the syringe. "Any bad reaction?"

Darryl started to shake his head no, then thought better of shaking anything unnecessarily. "No," he mumbled.

"What's it do?" Michael asked, as she rolled up one of Darryl's sleeves.

"Slows down the nervous activities in the gut. It's a seizure med, and, technically speaking, it's never been approved for seasickness." She swabbed a spot with alcohol. "But divers like it." She readied the syringe, then had to wait again as the ship took what felt like a series of body blows. "Hold real still," she said to Darryl, then plunged the needle into the freckled skin of his upper arm.

"Give it about ten minutes," she said, "and you ought to start feeling the effect."

She slipped the used needle into an orange plastic sleeve and the bottle back into the bottom of her bag. For the first time, she looked around and seemed to take in the cabin. "Man, it looks like I did get the best room on board. I didn't believe it when the Ops told me that, but now I do." She wrinkled her nose at a sudden gust from the head. "You boys ever heard of Lysol?"

Michael laughed, and even Darryl faintly smiled. But when she'd gone, Michael started pulling on his parka, boots, and gloves.

The cabin was foul and stifling, and the action outdoors was too tempting to resist.

Darryl rolled his head to one side and fixed him with a baleful glare. "Where," he croaked, "do you think you're going now?"

"To do my job," Michael said, slipping a small digital camera deep inside his parka; the batteries could die quickly in the cold. "Anything I can do for you first?"

Darryl said no. "Just call my wife and tell her I loved her, and the kids."

Michael had never really asked him about his family. "How many have you got?"

"Not now," Darryl said, waving him away. "I can't remember."

Maybe the drug was working faster than expected.

Michael left the light on in the cabin and made his way carefully down the corridor, then up through the hatchway, and he was just about to continue on to the bridge—he thought he could probably get some decent shots by leaning out a porthole or doorway—when he saw, through the sliding door, an apparently seamless picture of gray sea and gray sky, a panorama in which the horizon was unrecognizable and the world was reduced to a scene of flat, inarguable desolation.

He could visualize the finished shot already.

Putting up his hood, he fumbled for his camera with his gloved hands, and let it hang just below his neck. He had to use both hands to pull back on the door handle, and when it slid open even a few inches, the wind reached in and grabbed him by the collar. This was probably, he realized, a very bad idea, but then sometimes his best shots had come from his worst ideas. He pulled harder, then slipped through the crack, the door sliding shut again the second he let go.

He was on the deck, just below the bridge, with ice water sluicing down around his feet, and the wind pummeling him so hard that tears were whipped out of his eyes and his forehead burned. He wrapped one arm around a metal stanchion and pulled off one glove with his teeth, but the ship was heaving too much to frame a shot. And each time he tried, some part of the boat got into the picture. He didn't want that. He didn't want anything identifiable, anything concrete, to intrude on the image. He wanted a pure, almost abstract picture of empty, disinterested, all-powerful nature.

He waited for the ship to roll on the coming swell, then lunged for the next handhold, a steel armature that housed one of the lifeboat rigs. From there, looking out over the rail, he'd have nothing to worry about—except for the freezing salt spray that dashed into his face and doused the camera. He snagged one arm through the rail, as he had before, and raised the camera. But just then, the ship was canted at a forty-five-degree angle, and all he could get was the turbulent sky. He slipped a foot or two forward, waiting for the roll to correct itself, raising the camera. His fingers were already freezing, and he found that he couldn't open his mouth to breathe without the wind taking his breath away. He tried one shot—still at too much of an angle—and was about to try another when a bullhorn directly overhead blared, "Mr. Wilde! Get off the deck! Now!"

Even in the roaring wind, he could make out the voice of the Ops, Lieutenant Healey.

"Right now! And report to the captain!"

Before Michael could even turn around, he saw the sliding door opening and Kazinski, in a waterproof jacket over his running shorts, reaching out to him with a yellow life preserver. "Just grab it!" Kazinski shouted, and Michael, slipping the camera back into the top of his parka, fell back to the stanchion, then put his gloved hand out toward the preserver; his other hand was almost completely numb.

Once Michael had hold of it, Kazinski reeled him in like a fish, slammed the sliding door latch back, then stood there, brushing off the ice-cold water and shaking his head in dismay. "All due respect, sir, but that was truly a numbnuts thing to do."

Michael did see his point.

"The captain's up on the bridge. If I were you, I'd be prepared to have him tear me a new one."

At the moment, Michael just wanted the feeling back in his fingers. He wiped the hand briskly back and forth on his pant leg, but the cloth was so wet it didn't help much. He unzipped his parka, and shoved his hand inside, into his armpit.

Kazinski gestured at the stairs leading up to the bridge, as if it were the way to the gallows. Maybe, Michael thought, it was.

He went up them slowly, and as soon as he entered the brightly lighted bridge, Captain Purcell swiveled in his chair and said, "What the *hell* do you think you were doing out there? Are you out of your fucking mind?"

Michael shrugged and finished unzipping his coat, letting the flaps fall open. "Probably not the best idea," he offered, knowing how feeble it sounded, "but I thought I might get some great shots for the magazine."

The other two officers seated in front of the navigation consoles stifled their amusement.

"I'm used to some pretty harebrained stunts from the scientists I have to ferry around down here," Purcell said, "but I figure they're so smart, they're entitled to act stupid sometimes. You, I can't figure out at all. You're no scientist, and you're sure as hell no sailor."

Ensign Gallo, who was standing at a silver wheel mounted on a freestanding console, said, "Barometric's falling again, sir."

"What to?" Purcell barked, swiveling back in his chair and adjusting the headset that had slipped askew while he was chewing out Michael.

"Nine eighty-five, sir."

"Jesus, we're in for it tonight." His eyes scanned the glowing screens and dials, the sonar, the radar, the GPS, the fathometer, all of which showed a constantly changing and multicolored stream of data.

A spattering of hail clattered against the square windows on the westward side, and the ship heaved like a great hand had just slapped it. Michael snatched at one of the leather straps that dangled from the ceiling and hung on tight; he'd already heard tales of seamen who had been flung from one end of the bridge to the other and broken arms and legs in the process. He wondered if his public flogging was over, or if he was supposed to wait around for more.

Despite the roar of the sea outside, the slashing of the rain and the howling of the winds that seemed to be coming from all directions at once, the atmosphere in the bridge quickly returned to the tranquillity of an operating room. The flat white light panels in the ceiling cast a cold even glow around the blue walls of the room, and the officers all spoke to each other in low, deliberate tones, their eyes fixed on the instrument arrays before them.

"Port engine, full forward," the captain said, and Lieutenant Commander Ramsey, whom Michael had met a couple of times, reached for a short red-handed throttle. He repeated the captain's words as he executed the order.

Then, Ramsey nodded discreetly toward Michael—who was still standing around like a kid who'd been haled into the principal's office—and said offhandedly to Purcell, "If Mr. Wilde is no longer needed here, sir, perhaps he should join the Ops in the aloft con? It's impossible to fall overboard from there, and he might like to see how the ship is steered."

Purcell blew out a breath of disgust, and without turning around, said, "If he does fall out, tell him he can float all the way back to Chile before I turn this ship around."

Michael didn't doubt it, and he took it as his cue to step toward the spiral stair that Ramsey gestured at, and swiftly start climbing.

"How'd you like some company, Kathleen?" he heard Ramsey say into his headset, but he didn't slow up to find out if he wasn't welcome. He went straight up until he was well out of the bridge, and found himself standing on a platform in a virtually black funnel, with only a steel ladder leading higher. The ship juddered, and his shoulders crashed against the rounded wall; he felt like he was in the chimney of the house in *The Wizard of Oz,* the one that got picked up by the tornado and spun all around. Up above, at least twenty or thirty feet, he could see a blue glow, a lot like you'd get off a TV screen, and he could hear the beeping and hum of machinery.

He put his boot on the bottom rung of the ladder and slowly started to climb. When the prow of the ship came up, he was slung backwards off the ladder, and when the ship righted itself, he was flung forward again; once, he narrowly missed knocking out his front teeth, and he had a sudden terrible flash of having his dental clearance revoked. The rungs were cold and clammy, and he had to grip each one firmly before reaching for the next. As he went up the last few, he saw first a pair of black, rubber-soled shoes, then a pair of blue trousers. He hauled himself up the rest of the way, and when the ship seemed level for a second or two, clambered to his feet.

The Ops was holding steady to a smaller version of the wheel down below, her stern expression illuminated by a GPS screen and a couple of other scopes that Michael couldn't identify. Her eyes were set straight ahead and her jaw was locked; a headset clung to her short brown hair. The aloft con itself—the modern-day equivalent of the crow's nest—was barely big enough for the two of them, and Michael tried not to breathe down Kathleen's neck.

"Going out on deck was a very bad idea," she said, reminding Michael that she was the one who'd busted him. "We're clocking winds of over a hundred miles per hour."

"Got it," he said. "The captain happened to mention it, too." Then, hoping to change the subject, he said, "So you're up here, all alone in the driver's seat?" On all sides, there were reinforced windows, equipped with Kent screens—whirling discs powered by centrifugal force to throw off water like windshield wipers—that provided an unobstructed, 360-degree view of the boiling ocean all around. Behind him, on the aft deck, one side of the helicopter tarp had ripped loose and was flapping like an enormous, dark green bat's wing.

If only he'd been able to get some decent shots of all this...

"When visibility is as limited as it is now—with such high seas," she said, "control of the vessel is often passed to the aloft con."

Michael could see why. Everywhere he looked, the vista was in violent motion, the gray sea heaving and churning for miles, with great blocks of jagged ice bobbing and sinking and slamming into each other. Waves higher than any he had ever imagined rushed at the prow of the ship, crashing down on the bow deck and sending a freezing spume into the air. The spray flew as high as the windows of their aerie.

And all of it—the mad, seething sea and the roiling sky above it, the black specks of birds driven like leaves before the screaming wind—were bathed in the unnatural light of the austral sun, a dull copper orb stubbornly fixed on the northern horizon. It was as if the whole tumultuous picture were lighted from below by a giant lantern that was burning its last few drops of oil.

"Welcome to the Screaming Fifties," the Ops added, in a slightly more congenial tone. "Once you get below fifty degrees latitude south, that's when you hit the real weather."

The cutter's prow went up, as easily as if it had been lifted from below, until it was pointing nearly straight up at the shredded storm clouds racing across the southern sky. Kathleen clung to the wheel, her feet braced far apart, and Michael tried to steady himself on the handrail. He knew what was coming . . . because what went up must come down.

Moments later, the crest passed under them—he could feel the swell of it tingling in his feet—and once gone, the ship teetered, then dropped like a stone skittering down the side of a steep hill. Through the front of the conning tower, Michael could look straight down into a massive trough, a dark cleft as wide as a ravine, but with nothing in it but a watery bottom that seemed to recede even as the ship raced headlong into it.

Kathleen said, "Aye, aye, sir," into the headset and notched the wheel to the right. Michael could taste the pasta he'd had for dinner. "Depth, one thousand five hundred meters," she confirmed to the captain below.

The ship plunged down, down, then stopped, then spun—with water rising up in sheer walls all around it—before turning to starboard. Even there, easily ninety feet above the deck and twice as far from the diesel turbines, Michael could hear the engines revving and roaring, the propellers turning—sometimes in nothing but air—as the ship tried to forge its own course through the ice-strewn minefield that engulfed it.

"If you're a praying man," the Ops said, sparing her first glance directly at Michael, "do it now." She twisted the wheel again to the right. "You're passing over the wrecks of no less than eight hundred ships and ten thousand sailors."

The ship charged toward an iceberg that suddenly loomed up before it like a triton.

"Shit, I should have seen that," Kathleen muttered, and a moment later, said, "Yes, sir," into her headset. "I do see it, sir. I will," she added, twisting the wheel.

"Hope I didn't distract you," Michael said over the pelting sleet and wind. "If it's any comfort, I didn't see that coming, either."

"It's not your job," she said. "It is mine."

Michael fell silent, to let her concentrate, thinking instead of the graveyard that lay below him, the wreckage of hundreds of ships—schooners and sloops, brigs and frigates, trawlers and whalers—mauled by the ice, broken by the waves, ripped to pieces by the searing wind. And he thought of the thousands of men who had fallen into the raging, empty, endless maw, men whose last sight might have been the masts of their ships snapping like twigs, or a slab of glistening ice tumbling over their heads and plunging them down—what had she said, one thousand five hundred meters?—toward the bottom of a sea so deep no light had ever penetrated it.

What exactly lay right below them, many fathoms under their hull, frozen to the floor of the ocean for all eternity?

The ship careened suddenly from one side to the other. The Ops spun the wheel back to the right and said, "Hard starboard, sir!" to the captain down below. Michael saw the wave, too, gathering force and coming at them like a wall, spreading its wings to either side, lifting chunks of ice the size of houses, and blotting out even the deadening light of the constant sun.

"Hold on tight!" Kathleen barked, and Michael braced himself against the walls, his legs straight, his feet spread. He had never seen anything so large move with such velocity and force, carrying everything—the whole world, it seemed—before it.

The Ops tried to turn the boat so that it would miss the brunt of the wave, but it was too late and the wave, no less than a hundred feet high, was too huge. As it rushed toward the cutter—a streaming wall of angry gray water, rising and widening every second—something else—something white, no, black—something out of control, caught in the storm's unbreakable grip—rocketed toward them even faster. A second later, the window shattered with the sound of a shotgun blast, and shards of ice sprayed the compartment like flying needles. Kathleen screamed and fell away from the wheel, knocking into Michael, who tried to grab her as she slid to the floor. Freezing water pelted his face, and he shook it off, to see— alive and cawing—the bloodied head of a snow-white albatross lying atop the wheel. Its body was wedged against the broken window, its twisted wings splayed uselessly to either side. The wave was still surging over the boat, and the bird clacked its ruined bill, flattened like a boxer's nose. Michael was staring straight into its black unblinking eyes as Kathleen huddled on the floor, and the blue light of the flooded console screens sputtered and went out.

The wave passed, the ship groaned, rolled one way, then back in the other, and finally righted itself.

The albatross opened its mangled beak one more time, emitting nothing more than a hollow rattle, and then, as Michael tried to catch a breath, and Kathleen moaned at his feet in pain, the light in the bird's eyes went out like a snuffed candle.

CHAPTER EIGHT

June 20, 1854, 11 p.m.

THE SALON D'APHRODITE, known to its regular clientele simply
as Mme. Eugenie's, was located on a busy stretch of the Strand, but
back from the street. A brace of lanterns always hung from the gates
of the porte-cochere, and so long as they were lighted, the salon was
open for business.

Sinclair had never known them to be out.

He was the first to step down from the hansom cab, followed by
Le Maitre and then Rutherford, who had to pay the cabbie. Thank
God he was of a rich, generous—and just now drunken—nature, as
he would also have to pay for their privileges of the house. Mme.
Eugenie could occasionally be persuaded to extend credit, but it
was at a usurious rate of interest, and no one wished to be hauled
into court for an outstanding debt to the Salon d'Aphrodite.

As the three of them mounted the stairs, John-O, a towering Jamaican with a pair of gold teeth in the front of his mouth, opened
the door and stepped to one side. He knew who they were, but he
was paid in part never to say so.

"Good evening," Rutherford said, rather thickly, "is Madame at home?" As if he were paying a call on a society acquaintance.

John-O nodded toward the parlor, partially concealed by a red velvet drape; Sinclair could hear the sound of the pianoforte, and a young woman singing "The Beautiful Banks of the Tweed." With the others in tow, he moved toward the light and gaiety. Frenchie lifted the drape to one side, and Mme. Eugenie looked up from a divan, where she was seated between two of her girls.

"Bienvenue, mes amis!" she said, quickly rising. She was like an old bird, with bright new feathers; her skin the texture of leather, her dress an elaborate green brocade studded with rhinestones. She came forward with her hands extended, a gaudy ring on every finger. "I am so glad you have come to call."

As Le Maitre guffawed, Sinclair sank gratefully onto a well-cushioned ottoman; he wasn't feeling much steadier on his feet than his companions. The room was spacious—it was once the exhibition hall of a bibliographical society, but as there had been too few bibliophiles to keep the house solvent, Mme. Eugenie had swooped in and snapped it up for a song. The bookshelves held knick-knacks—busts of Cupid and silk flowers in chinoiserie vases. A large oil painting, badly rendered, of *Leda Seduced by Zeus* hung above the hearth.

The studies and workrooms upstairs had been converted to more private and intimate use.

At present, Sinclair counted perhaps half a dozen of the *femmes galantes* circulating around the parlor, in clinging or revealing costume, and an equal number of customers, lounging about on the sofas and chairs. A servant asked him if he would care to have a drink, and Sinclair said, "Gin, yes. And one for each of my friends."

Rutherford said, "Make mine a whiskey," and threw him a cautionary look that said: *If I'm to pay for all this, I'll bloody well have what I want.*

Sinclair knew he was only going deeper into trouble, and debt, but sometimes, he reflected, the only way out was down. And there was still a ways to go.

Frenchie, he noted, was already entangled with a raven-haired harlot in jeweled slippers.

"That you, Sinclair?" someone asked, and Sinclair could guess whose voice it was. Dalton-James Fitzroy, a fool of the first water, whose family's lands adjoined his own. "My lord, Sinclair, what are you doing here?"

Sinclair turned on the ottoman, and saw Dalton-James Fitzroy, his bulky rump parked on the piano bench, beside the singing girl. Now that the girl turned, Sinclair saw that, despite her gangly frame, she couldn't be more than twelve or thirteen years old, with a simple country face.

"I thought you'd been hounded out of town by your creditors," Fitzroy said. His pudgy cheeks were gleaming with sweat, and Sinclair steeled himself not to rise to the bait.

"Evening," he simply replied.

But Fitzroy was determined. "How will you pay the apothecary if you catch a dose here tonight?"

This time, he was saved the trouble of answering at all by Mme. Eugenie's intervention, who rushed to the defense of her establishment. She fluttered between them, saying "*Messieurs,* my companion ladies are clean as whistles! Dr. Evans, he inspects them *régulièrement.* Every month! And our visitors," she declared, sweeping one hand around the room, "are *la crème de la societé.* Only the finest gentlemen, as you may see for yourself." Wagging one bejeweled finger at Fitzroy, playfully but with meaning, she said, "Shame on you, sir, in front of these agreeable ladies, to be so rude."

Fitzroy took his chastisement in the spirit of irony, bowed low over the piano keyboard, and begged forgiveness. "Perhaps it is best that I sheathe my sword and depart the field," he said, which was rich, Sinclair thought, coming from a coward like Fitzroy—always full of bluster until the army came calling for recruits.

He stood up, his silk waistcoat straining at its seams, and clutching the girl's hand walked unsteadily toward the main stairs.

"John-O," Mme. Eugenie called out, "please show our guest to the Suite des Dieux."

The girl cast a frightened eye back toward Sinclair, of all people. But he could see—under her rouge and makeup—just how young and inexperienced she was. And he could not resist one sally.

"Why not have a woman?" he taunted Fitzroy.

Two of the other gentlemen in the room laughed.

Fitzroy stopped, teetering, but did not turn. "*Chacun à son goût,* Sinclair. You, above all people, should know that."

As Fitzroy left the room with his reluctant prize, Mme. Eugenie came to Sinclair, clucking her tongue. "Why are you so quarrelsome tonight? It is not like you, my lord." Sinclair was not a lord, not yet, but he knew that Mme. Eugenie liked to flatter her customers that way. "That is bad form, and Mr. Fitzroy has paid well for this privilege."

"What privilege?"

Mme. Eugenie reared back as if astonished at his stupidity. "This young girl is a flower that has never been plucked."

A virgin? Even in his inebriated state, Sinclair knew that that was the oldest con in the trade. Virgins commanded a premium price not only because they were, by definition, safe as houses, but because they were also reputed to be able to cure—through vigorous use—several of the amatory infections. It was all balderdash, of course, and Sinclair would normally have put the whole business out of mind already—what concern was it of his, after all?—were it not for that stricken look in the young girl's eye. She was either such an accomplished actress that she belonged on center stage at Covent Garden . . . or else it was genuine. There was no law against prostitution, and the age of consent was twelve; girls of her tender years were, quite legally, corrupted every day. Fitzroy had no doubt spent twenty-five or thirty pounds for the privilege.

"Come now," Rutherford cajoled him. "That fat bastard's going to be your neighbor for years to come. Don't begin a fracas now."

Mme. Eugenie winked at one of the other women, with bright red hair spread across a pair of creamy, well-exposed shoulders, who artfully drew Sinclair off the ottoman and onto a loveseat beneath a picture of a nymph fleeing a satyr. The servant appeared with the gin.

Frenchie had taken the country girl's place at the pianoforte, and was playing, as well as his own compromised condition would allow, a lugubrious version of something by Herr Mozart.

The redhead introduced herself as Marybeth, and tried to engage Sinclair in conversation, asking first about his regiment, then where they might be posted, before expressing deep concern— somewhat premature, in his view—for his continued safety. But all the while, Sinclair could only think of that girl, with the coltish frame and the frightened eyes, being dragged up the stairs behind John-O and his golden teeth.

Sinclair had had a sister once. She'd died about that age, of consumption.

"That's quite enough of that," one of the other men called out to Le Maitre. "Give us something with a bit of a song to it. If I wanted to attend the Lyceum, I'd be off with my wife."

A round of laughter and applause followed, and Frenchie, bowing to public opinion, launched into a sloppy rendition of "My Heart's in the Highlands." He had finished with it, and played another number just then sweeping the Strand, when Sinclair heard a cry from upstairs.

Everyone else scrupulously ignored it—though Frenchie did pause for a second, and Marybeth took sudden pains to adjust the buttons and collar of Sinclair's shirt. An elderly gent with a matronly brunette on his arm continued his slow ascent of the stairs. When the song ended, Sinclair listened more closely, and even though the Suite des Dieux was a full floor above, he could hear a muffled cry, and the sound of something falling to the floor.

"The *table d'hôte* has just been replenished," Mme. Eugenie said, clapping her hands together. "Please, gentlemen, enjoy *le canard aux cerises* and oysters on the half shell."

Several of the guests roused themselves—Rutherford among them—and made their way toward the buffet in the next room. But Sinclair neatly disengaged himself and went toward the stairs. As luck would have it, John-O was just then welcoming a trio of inebriated men about town, taking their cloaks and hats, and Sinclair was able to mount the stairs unobserved.

The suite was on the second floor, just above the porte-cochere; Sinclair had occupied it himself once or twice. And he knew that its door—like all the doors in the Salon d'Aphrodite—was not locked while occupied. Mme. Eugenie had long since discovered that exigencies of the trade required her, or John-O, to have immediate— if judiciously employed—access to any chamber.

He kept his feet to the carpet runner as he went to the door, and quietly put his ear against the wood. There were two small rooms, he knew—an antechamber with a few sticks of maple furniture, and a bedroom with a massive, canopied four-poster. He could hear the rumble of Fitzroy's voice, in the bedroom, and then a low sob from the girl.

"You will," Fitzroy said, his voice raised.

The girl cried again, repeatedly calling him sir, and it sounded as if she were moving slowly, warily, about the room. A vase, or bottle, smashed on the floor.

"I'll not pay for that!" Fitzroy said, and Sinclair heard the whistle of a whip cutting the air, and a scream.

He threw open the door and ran through the antechamber to the bedroom. A bare-chested Fitzroy was standing, his white trousers still on, with one suspender hanging down; the other suspender he held in his hand.

"Sinclair, I'll be damned!"

The girl was naked, holding a bloodied sheet around her. All of her powder and rouge had run down her face in a flood of tears.

"You've got a bloody nerve to break in here!" Fitzroy said, moving toward his clothing thrown on the settee. "Where's John-O?"

"Put your things on and get out."

Fitzroy, his belly hanging down like a market sack, said, "It's you who'll be leaving."

He fumbled in his jacket, and pulled out a silver-plated derringer, the kind a cardsharp might carry. Sinclair should not have been surprised. The girl, seeing her chance, ran past them both and out of the room.

The sight of the gun did not diminish Sinclair's determination. Rather, it inflamed it. "You bloody fat coward. If you aim that thing at me, you'd better plan to use it." Sinclair took a menacing step forward, and Fitzroy fell back toward the windows.

"I will," he cried. "I will use it!"

"Give it to me," Sinclair growled, throwing out one hand.

Sinclair took another step, and Fitzroy, closing his eyes, shot the gun. Sinclair heard a loud pop, the sleeve of his uniform ripped away, and an instant later he felt a wetness—his blood—running down his arm.

He lunged at Fitzroy, glass crunching beneath his boots. Fitzroy flailed at him with the gun, but Sinclair was able to grab it and yank it from his grip. Fitzroy twisted, looking for somewhere to run, but where could he go?

Sinclair heard the heavy tread of John-O running up the main staircase, and Fitzroy must have heard it, too.

"John-O!" he shouted. "In here!"

He leered in victory at Sinclair, and Sinclair, in a blind rage, whirled him around, snatched him by the seat of his trousers, ran him three paces toward the closed windows, and hurled him straight through the glass. Fitzroy, screaming in terror, tumbled out and landed with a huge thump and a rain of shattered glass a few feet below, atop the bricks of the porte-cochere. The horses of a carriage parked beneath it whinnied in alarm.

John-O stood stunned in the bedroom door, as Sinclair turned around, a bloody patch of his sleeve flapping loosely from his left arm.

"Please advise Madame," he said, brushing past the Jamaican, "to send me the bill from her glazier."

Rutherford and Le Maitre, along with several others, anxiously awaited him at the bottom of the stairs.

"Good God, you've been shot?" Rutherford exclaimed, as Sinclair descended the stairs.

"Who was it?" Frenchie insisted. "Was it that blackguard Fitzroy?"

"Take me to that hospital we passed," Sinclair said. "The one on Harley Street."

Rutherford and Frenchie looked puzzled. "But that's for indigent women," Rutherford said.

"Any port in a storm," Sinclair replied.

It might yet be possible, he thought, to salvage something from this night.

CHAPTER NINE

December 1, 11:45 a.m.

THE STORM RAGED for hours, and only let up by late morning the next day. The damaged aloft con had been abandoned and sealed off for the duration of the voyage.

Dr. Barnes had helped the ship's own medic to remove the ice and glass shards from Lieutenant Kathleen Healey's face, but her eyes were still severely compromised and Charlotte thought she should be taken back to civilization—and a first-rate ophthalmologist—as fast as possible.

"She could permanently lose the sight in one or even both of her eyes," she told the captain in his private cabin. Purcell didn't say anything, but looked down at his shoes, thinking hard, and when he looked up again a few seconds later, he said, "Start packing."

"Come again?"

"I'd planned to get you closer to Port Adélie before launching the chopper, but I think we can make it from here."

Charlotte really didn't like the sound of that "I think."

"We'll just have to jettison some of the provisions and supplies, in order to lower the cargo weight. Then we can board you and Mr. Hirsch and Mr. Wilde, with your gear, and take off from here. The chopper should be able to carry just enough fuel to drop you there, and then get back to us while we're already heading back north. Lieutenant Ramsey!" he called out as the officer passed through the corridor outside.

"Sir?"

"Prepare the helicopter. Who are our pilots on this trip?"

"That would be Ensigns Diaz and Jarvis."

"Order them to fuel it up and be ready to deliver our three passengers to Point Adélie ASAP."

"From here, sir? Won't—"

But the captain cut him short, completed his instructions, then dismissed him. Returning his attention to Charlotte, he asked if she'd tell Wilde and Hirsch to get a move on, too.

"How long should I tell them they've got?"

The captain glanced at his watch, then said, "Let's shoot for 1300 hours."

Charlotte still had to do the quick math—that meant 1 p.m. And that meant she had about fifty-five minutes.

Darryl she knew where to find—he was still lying in his cot, less green than he'd been the night before, but still a color no human being should ever be. When she told him the news, he closed his eyes, clearly willing himself to get up, and did.

"You gonna be all right?" she asked, watching him move, like a sleepwalker, toward his bags.

"Uh-huh," he said. "Go on, get Michael."

"You know where?"

"Where else? On deck."

Charlotte did not have time for a concerted search—she had her own stuff to get together—but she quickly went up on the main deck, looked toward the bow, and saw nothing, then looked aft, where several crewmen were wrestling the dark green tarp off the helicopter fixed to its raised pad. The wind was still strong, and the tarp whipped around like a monstrous cape. Getting a photo of the undertaking was Michael.

"Did you know we're supposed to be on that helicopter," she said, "in less than an hour?"

"Yep," he said, still kneeling to get the shot he wanted. "The crew told me. Most of my stuff never came out of my duffel. I'm ready to go in three minutes."

"Aren't you Mr. Smarty Pants," she said. "Well, I got things to do. When you go below for your stuff, make sure you bring Darryl with you. That boy still doesn't look all that steady on his feet."

As Charlotte headed below, Michael finished taking a couple of shots, then hastily stowed his gear. He had finally gotten his sea legs, and could pretty well anticipate—and correct for—the rolling and rocking of the boat. But he wouldn't be sorry to leave it. Ever since his stroll on the deck the night before, not to mention his disastrous visit to the aloft con, he'd felt himself to be persona non grata and had studiously avoided bumping into any of the senior officers. Even Petty Officer Kazinski had looked at him like a bad-luck charm. When the accident had happened, he'd done everything he could think of for Lieutenant Healey, helping her down the ladder like a fireman—which meant staying on the outside and one step below her—then going back up top to try to remove the dead albatross and somehow seal the conning tower window. But there wasn't much he could do—the bird's body was so tightly wedged into the broken window, with the edge of the Kent screen slicing into its breast like a scalpel, that he decided it was best to leave it where it was. At least that way there was something to keep the battering waves from flooding the con again.

No, he wouldn't be sorry to leave the boat and get to Point Adélie. That's where he could begin his work in earnest.

After the tarp was removed, Michael, who'd been on a pretty fair number of helicopters in his time, could see that it was one of the Dolphin class, a sturdy, twin-engined, single-rotor chopper that was routinely used for missions like drug interdiction, ice patrol, and search and rescue. Like the ship they were on, the helicopter was painted red, a common safety measure in icy climes where a spot of color could make all the difference between discovery—and survival—and being lost forever. As he looked on, several seamen began to run fuel lines and prepare the craft for departure; a couple of others began to off-load some crates. They reminded him of a pit crew at a NASCAR race, each one of them going about his business with practiced hands and almost no words exchanged. He collected his camera gear and went back down to his cabin.

Darryl was slumped on the edge of his bunk, gnawing on a protein bar.

"Why don't you go to the mess?" Michael said, stuffing his shaving kit into his duffel, "and get something warm? They've got sloppy joes going."

"Can't," Darryl replied.

"You can't make it?" Michael said. "I could go get you one."

"Can't, because I don't eat meat."

Michael stopped packing.

"You haven't noticed?" Darryl said.

And now that Michael thought about it, it struck him that no, he *hadn't* ever seen Darryl eat any meat. Lots of fruits and veggies, tons of bread, cheese, crackers, corn chowder, cherry pie, spinach soufflé. But no burgers or pork chops or fried chicken.

"For how long?"

"Ever since college, when I majored in biology."

"What's that got to do with it?" Michael asked.

"Everything," Darryl said, rolling the foil down another inch on the protein bar. "Once I started to study life in earnest—in all its countless permutations and manifestations—and I saw that all of it, no matter how large or how small, had one thing in common, I couldn't find it in my heart to interfere anymore."

Michael thought he got it. "You mean the urge to live?"

Darryl nodded. "Every species, from the blue whale to the fruit fly, will struggle, with every fiber of its being, to preserve its own existence. And the more I studied them, even the single-celled diatoms, the more beautiful they all appeared to me. Life is a miracle—an absolute fucking miracle—in every form it takes, and I just never felt right again about taking any of it unnecessarily."

While Michael was not about to give up his baby back ribs or his porterhouse steaks, he did understand Darryl's point of view. But there was one thing he didn't get.

"So why haven't you mentioned it before? In the Officers' Mess, or the wardroom? They could have made you vegetarian plates or something."

Darryl gave him a long look. "Do you know what sailors, and military types in general, think of vegetarians?"

Michael had never considered the question, and Darryl could see that.

"I'd be better off telling them that I was a child molester."

Michael had to laugh. "What are you going to do at Point Adélie? Try to keep it a secret again?"

Darryl shrugged, finished the protein bar and crumpled the foil into a tiny ball. "I'll cross that bratwurst when I come to it." He got up from the bunk and started pulling a sweater over his head. "As for the other scientists there, they won't notice a thing or care either way." His head popped up again out of the hole. "Give a glaciologist a fresh ice core to inspect, and he's the happiest man on the planet. As long as you don't mess around with their experiments, scientists couldn't care less what you do."

With that, Michael had to agree. He'd covered a few of those guys—a primatologist in Brazil, a herpetologist in the Southwest—and they lived, totally absorbed, in their own weird little worlds. At Point Adélie, there'd be a prize collection of them.

When Darryl had finished his packing, they dragged their bags up to the aft deck, where Michael could see that the pilots had already boarded the chopper and were going through some routine instrument checks. Petty Officer Kazinski showed up, carrying Dr. Barnes's bags; she was right behind him, in her long green down coat, pulling her braided hair into one big knot.

Captain Purcell approached them before boarding, but he seemed to be addressing everyone but Michael. "On behalf of the United States Coast Guard, I'd like to wish you well on the remainder of your journey to Point Adélie. We're glad to have been of service, and look forward to helping out again whenever we're needed."

Charlotte and Darryl thanked him profusely, they shook hands, and finally the captain looked directly at Michael. "Try not to get into any trouble between now and then, Mr. Wilde."

"I hope Lieutenant Healey is okay. Could you keep me posted on her progress?"

"I'll do that," the captain said, in a tone that made it clear he would not.

A couple of seamen came up, gathered their bags, and started to load them into the cargo hold.

The captain glanced off to the west, then added, "Better get going. We've got more weather on the way." Then, he gave a short wave toward the helicopter pilots, turned, and headed back to the bridge.

Michael followed Charlotte and Darryl into the side door of the chopper, ducking his head and flopping into a seat on the far side, next to a big, square window. The choppers were designed to afford maximum visibility, and it would give him a great view the whole way. Darryl, perhaps purposely, sat on the inside, next to Charlotte. The cabin was warm, and after Michael had quickly shed his coat and gloves, he strapped himself into the over-the-shoulder seat harness. Then, just as the pilots switched on the rotor, and the whole craft began to vibrate and hum, he put on the noise-deadening headphones, with intercom mike attached. A seaman slapped and latched the side door shut. There was a short aisle between the passenger compartment and the cockpit, and through it Michael could see the pilots—Diaz and Jarvis, as he'd learned from the sailors who'd removed the tarp—flicking overhead switches, checking dials and computer screens. It looked like a compressed version of the bridge on the ship.

The helicopter teetered on the platform, like a teenager in high heels, before suddenly gaining confidence—and power—and lifting straight up into the air, pointing toward the stern. Then, as the ship moved away beneath it, it banked to the southwest and swerved away. The last thing Michael saw, peering out, was the demolished window of the aloft con. The dead albatross had been removed, and a makeshift cover of wood, crisscrossed with aluminum bands and duct tape, had been used to seal the hole.

Below him was the Weddell Sea—named after the Scottish sealer, James Weddell, who was among the first to explore it in the 1820s—and the water was thick with floating ice and immense, seemingly stationary glaciers. From above, Michael could see straight down into the glaciers' jagged crevasses; when the light was right, and a ray of sun just happened to hit at the proper angle, the inner ice glowed a bright neon blue. And when the light had passed, it was as if the electricity had just been turned off, and the crevasse became again a frightening scar, a black suture on a dead white face.

There was a crackling sound in the headphones, then Ensign Diaz came on to introduce himself and advise everyone that their flying time would be roughly one hour. "We hope it's a smooth ride," he said, "but by now you know the score down here."

Michael couldn't help glancing at Darryl, who'd already had enough turbulence to last him a lifetime, but his headphones were off, and he was blissfully asleep, his mouth open, his head listing toward Charlotte's ample shoulder. Charlotte had on her big round shades, and was looking down at the sea with a pensive expression.

Michael could guess at some of what she was thinking. When you were flying over the vast, barren waste of the Antarctic wilderness, it was hard not to dwell on some things—the insignificance of your own tiny life, the possibility, at any time, of one minor mishap leading to a series of events resulting in death or disaster. Despite the explorers and whalers and sealers who had plied these dangerous waters for centuries, the Antarctic continent was still the most untouched by humankind. Its very inhospitability was all that had saved it. When the economic cost of killing the remaining whales for oil and baleen had become too great, the industry had finally ground to a halt. When the fur seals had been so decimated by ruthless predation—hundreds and hundreds of thousands wantonly slaughtered on the ice, the mothers dead, the pups left to starve—that grim business, too, had gradually ceased to flourish. Wherever humans had set foot, the carnage had been so brutal, so extraordinary, and so quick that the very thing making the killers rich was nearly eradicated in a hundred years' time.

The goose that laid the golden egg had been killed, over and over and over again.

But the icy fastness of the South Pole had, ultimately, worn out all its would-be invaders and made itself impervious to all but the most tentative intrusions. There were scientific bases and research stations, like Point Adélie, scattered around the shores of the Southern Ocean, but they were like little black pebbles on a vast white beach. Tiny dark specks in a world of blue sea and crystalline peaks. And most of them, as Michael had learned at his dinners in the Officers' Mess, were less about the quest for knowledge than they were about making a claim on the land—and the limitless mineral resources that might lie beneath it.

"The Antarctic is the only continent on earth with no nations on it," the Ops had pointed out over dinner one night, "and to keep it that way, the Antarctic Treaty was drawn up in '59. The treaty declares the Antarctic—which means any ocean or land south of sixty degrees—to be an international zone. Nuclear-free. Forty-four nations have signed on."

"But that hasn't stopped the squatters," Darryl had said, piling the potatoes au gratin onto his plate. "Come one, come all."

Lieutenant Healey had smiled ruefully at that. "You're right. Many nations, including some unlikely newcomers like China and Peru, have set up so-called research stations. It's their way of asserting their rights to participate in any discussions about the Antarctic—or any exploitation of its resources that might later occur."

"In other words, they're just getting in line, like us," Darryl said, "for whenever the free-for-all really gets under way." He shoveled another mouthful of potatoes into his mouth, and before quite swallowing it, added, "And it will."

Michael had no doubt he was right, although looking out the window at the frozen panorama below and the sun, squatting like a fat bronze ball on the horizon, it was hard to envision that coming cataclysm. The endless ice, and the rolling sea, looked as impervious as they did eternal.

To the west, he could see the first signs of the storm front the captain had hinted at. Wispy gray clouds were filling the sky and starting to fly in their direction, like strips of a shroud being torn by invisible fingers. The ocean, too, was starting to stir, the gentle swells growing higher, the waves frothing white. Flocks of seabirds were driven before the rising wind.

Darryl had come awake, and was sitting up straight; apparently, the seasickness was at long last behind him, and his skin, though pallid as any redhead's, was at least no longer green. He grinned at Michael and gave him a thumbs-up. Charlotte was studying a folded map in her lap.

In the cockpit, Michael could see Diaz and Jarvis conferring, surveying their scopes and monitors, and a few seconds later the helicopter gained altitude and, if he wasn't mistaken, speed. It was impossible to make out much but a vast undifferentiated tableau of ice below. And for the next twenty minutes or so, the chopper seemed bent on nothing but getting to its destination as quickly as possible. Michael wondered if the storm front wasn't advancing faster than they'd expected.

He put his head back and closed his eyes. He, too, was pretty tired; sleeping on board an icebreaker hadn't been easy. Between the constant rumbling of the engines and the grinding of the screws as they pulverized the passing growlers—chunks of ice as big as buses—not to mention the dank, dark quarters (he could still smell the odor of mildew on his clothes), it was doubtful he'd gone for more than a couple of hours without being jarred awake, or, more than once, heaved out of his bunk and onto the floor. No matter what his quarters were like at Point Adélie, he looked forward to sleeping in a bed that wasn't rocking, where the deadliest ocean in the world wasn't hammering away at him from just a few feet away, dying to get in.

He wondered if there had been any change in Kristin's condition. It was odd to be so out of touch, so far removed, in every sense, from all the concerns of his ordinary life. It was true that he'd been taking a sort of sabbatical from his friends, his family, his work; after the accident, he'd just kind of holed up with his misery, letting the answering machine field his calls and AOL keep track of his e-mails. But he knew that if anything dire occurred, he'd find out; the world—or at least Kristin's little sister—would breach his walls and get word to him, one way or the other. But where he was headed, regular communication of any sort was bound to be difficult, and his ability to respond in any meaningful way was nil. He could hardly race to a bedside, or worse, a cemetery, from the most inaccessible part of the planet, thousands of miles away.

The terrible thing about that, if he was being completely truthful with himself, was that it came as a relief. Ever since he'd embarked on this journey, he'd felt a lightening of his load, a reprieve from feeling he was forever on call. For months, he'd felt suspended, on a round-the-clock watch, unable to move forward without constantly looking back. There was something to be said, even if he couldn't say it, for the imposition of physical barriers. They had a nice way of taking things out of your hands.

The chopper was buffeted by the wind, and without moving his head, Michael cracked open one eye. The scene outside had changed entirely. The wispy clouds had become a ghostly army, scudding across the sky. And even the ocean, far below, was almost completely cloaked by a swirling fog. The lines between sea and sky, ice and air, were becoming increasingly obscured, and Michael knew that this was one of the greatest hazards in the Antarctic—the whole universe, in a matter of minutes, could be reduced to a glaringly white photon soup. Ships foundered and explorers plummeted into unseen crevasses. Pilots, unable to orient themselves, crashed their planes into glacial peaks or straight down onto the pack ice.

"Guess you can tell," Ensign Diaz said over the intercom headsets, "we've got some headwinds coming at us."

Michael sat up in his seat and glanced over at his traveling companions. Charlotte was folding up her map and putting it away, and Darryl was craning his neck to see out her window.

"But we're almost at Point Adélie. We're tracking the coastline, and coming in from the northwest. If the fog breaks, you should be able to see the old Norwegian whaling station, or maybe even the Adélie rookeries." He clicked off, but then, a few seconds later, came back on again. "Ensign Jarvis has asked me to advise you that our ground time will be minimal, so please be prepared to depart the craft as soon as you are advised that it is safe to do so. Don't wait for your bags and gear—they'll be transferred for you." Then he clicked off again and stayed off.

Michael tightened the laces on his boots, and gathered up his coat and hat and gloves, even though he couldn't put them on again until he was out of the shoulder harness. The chopper was slowly losing altitude—he could feel it even if he couldn't see it—and cutting through the fog. Occasionally, a patch of rocky shoreline would become visible, and once or twice he saw great black swarms of penguins, massed on a snowy plain. Then he caught a glimpse of a patchwork of abandoned wooden buildings, the colors of soot and rust; what looked like a steeple poked up from the fog. But it was hard to say for sure, as the chopper was skimming along so quickly, rising and falling on the powerful air currents, bucketing from side to side. A few minutes later, it came up over a low ridge, slowing down and turning, the rotors whirring louder than ever. Michael leaned close to the window to look down; the chopper's blades were shredding the mist below, and through it he could see a man in a hooded orange parka wildly waving and sliding around on the ice. Splotches of gray and brown surrounded him, some of them moving, skittering across the snow and ice, others disappearing as if they'd spontaneously evaporated. The helicopter hovered, but a gust of wind hit it hard and set it rocking in the air. In the cockpit, Diaz and Jarvis were hunched over their controls; Diaz was speaking rapidly into his microphone.

The man below vanished from Michael's field of vision, then ran back across it, his arms still waving. The chopper rocked again, an air horn blasted twice, then, slowly, the aircraft descended. When its blades touched the ice, there was a grinding noise that reminded Michael of cracking open one of those old-fashioned ice-cube trays, and under it came the sound of the man in the orange parka shouting. He skidded past the window—Michael caught a glimpse of a bearded, weather-beaten face under dark goggles—and then he heard the gradual sigh of the rotors winding down. The pilots were flicking off switches and shucking their own seat belts.

Michael did the same.

Diaz turned around, and called out, "Last stop!"

Jarvis had already climbed out, and was yanking on the latch to the passenger compartment. The door jerked open, and a blast of Antarctic air blew like a gale into the cabin. Charlotte was still wrestling herself out of her seat harness, and Darryl was doing his best to help her.

"All ashore that's going ashore!" Jarvis shouted, extending a hand to Charlotte, who finally freed herself and stepped out gingerly onto the ice. Darryl tumbled out after her, and Michael followed.

The orange parka guy was shouting at the pilots, something about seals, Weddell seals, and pups. Michael was still a little deaf from the roar of the chopper, and much of what the guy was saying was snatched up and blown away before he could quite make it out.

Michael moved away from the helicopter, as several other men in parkas and goggles ran toward the tail of the helicopter, where Jarvis had already thrown open a cargo bay. Michael saw pallets of supplies sliding out, but then he almost lost his footing and had to focus again on where he was going. Where *was* he going? There was no sign of the research station, and the ice, he suddenly discovered, had holes in it, roughly a few feet wide. He stopped, and he could see that there was something on the ice, something red and pulpy and wet, and the orange parka man was shouting again, though now Michael could actually hear some of it.

"The Weddell seals, they're whelping here! Right now! Watch where you're going!"

Charlotte and Darryl, arm in arm, were frozen in place.

"Holes in the ice!" he cried, pointing at several spots around them. "They've chewed breathing holes in the ice!"

A few yards off, almost indistinguishable against the ice, Michael saw a pup. Then two. White, but smeared with blood, their black eyes open. A mother lay beyond them, like a gray barrel.

And then, as he watched, another seal—bigger, darker, fully grown—put its head down into a hole, and somehow managed to slither through.

"Keep going!" the guy in the orange coat shouted. "Get off the ice!"

Someone from the station, a guy with a frozen handlebar moustache, was guiding Charlotte and Darryl forward. Michael inched in the same direction, but sometimes the fog made it hard to see as far as your own feet. And the ice, slick under the best of circumstances, was even harder to navigate on, wet with blood and littered with afterbirth. When, finally, he felt the grit of rock and lichen under his boots, Michael breathed a sigh of relief. A burst of wind dispelled a patch of fog, and he saw, on a low rise not more than fifty yards away, a handful of muddy gray, prefab structures, raised a few feet above the permafrost, and huddled together like the ugliest college quad in the world. An ice-rimed flagpole stood in the center, with Old Glory snapping in the freezing wind.

The guy in the orange parka came up behind him and said, "We call it the garden spot of Antarctica."

Michael stamped his cold, and bloodstained, boots.

"But I've got to warn you," he went on, in a thick Boston accent, "it's not always this pretty."

PART II
POINT ADÉLIE

"And a good south wind sprung up behind;
The Albatross did follow,
And every day, for food or play,
Came to the mariners' hollo!

In mist or cloud, on mast or shroud,
It perched for vespers nine;
Whiles all the night, through fog-smoke white,
Glimmered the white Moon-shine."

"God save thee, ancient Mariner!
From the fiends, that plague thee thus!—
Why lookst thou so?—With my crossbow
I shot the ALBATROSS!"

The Rime of the Ancient Mariner,
Samuel Taylor Coleridge, 1798

CHAPTER TEN

December 2 to December 5

THE FIRST FEW DAYS at Point Adélie were difficult to sort out. Not only because so much was going on, but because there was no sense of the time passing. With the sun perpetually shining, its rays beaming through the cracks in the blinds at night, the only way to tell what time it was at all was to look at your watch, or perhaps ask someone, if you were still confused, if that was 11:30 in the morning or 11:30 at night. Followed by, what day of the week? It wasn't as if you could check the morning newspaper, or the TV listings for that night. All the ordinary markers by which you measured and regulated your life—when you went to bed or when you got up, what time you exercised at the gym or attended the yoga class, when you left for work or came home—were all useless. It didn't even matter whether it was a weekend or a weekday, since you weren't very likely to find a date, or go to the movies, or sleep over, unexpectedly, at someone else's place, or have to take the kids to a soccer practice. All of it was moot. You were in a time and a place where none of that quotidian stuff mattered. In the Antarctic, everything existed in a free-floating state, and you either learned to impose your own kind of order on it—any kind of order—or you slowly went bonkers.

"The Big Eye is what we call it," Michael was informed over his first meal in the commons. (That college quad notion had even extended to some of the nomenclature at the camp.) The guy in the orange parka and goggles, who'd turned out to be the research station's Chief of Operations—Murphy O'Connor, by name—had eaten with the new arrivals, and taken that opportunity to run down some of the camp's rules and regulations, among other things.

"If you work too hard, for too long, you lose all track of time, and before you know it you're walking around with the Big Eye." He made his eyes bulge out in his face, while sucking in his cheeks, making himself look gaunt and demented.

Charlotte smiled, and Darryl laughed, as he ladled another pile of baked beans onto his plate.

"Won't be so funny when you get it."

Darryl stuck the serving spoon back in the beans.

"For a little guy, you sure can shovel it in," Murphy observed.

Michael wondered if Hirsch would take offense at that, but Murphy's manner was at once so plainspoken and open-handed that Darryl didn't seem to mind at all.

"So," Murphy resumed, "try to stick to some kind of schedule while you're down here. Make it up yourself, but try to keep on it. The kitchen's always open—you can always rustle up a sandwich—but if you flip out, we don't have a psych ward on the premises." He glanced over at Charlotte. "Unless Dr. Barnes is planning to open one."

"Not if I can help it," she said.

Then he proceeded to offer them a long list of other Point Adélie pointers, including the most important of all.

"You never leave the base alone," he said, staring at each one of them to emphasize the point. His eyes were big and brown, behind aviator-style glasses that barely cleared the black stubble covering his chin and cheeks. "A year ago, we had a guy—a geologist from Kansas—who just wanted to go out and grab a few quick specimens. Went out alone, didn't leave word where he was going," and at this, Murphy raised a cautionary finger, "and we didn't find him for three days."

"What happened?" Michael asked.

"Went down a crevasse and froze to death." He shook his head sadly and sipped his coffee from a mug with a picture of a penguin on it. "Sometimes you can't see the crevasses for shit." He pointed back in the direction of his office. "That's why we've got a blackboard in the hall; if you are leaving the base, you write down who's going, where you're going, and when you're planning to return."

Michael had already seen the board—the last entry said something about a ground terrain exploration in Dry Valley One.

"And when you get back—safely—check it off on the board. I do not appreciate having to do a bed check to make sure everybody's tucked in for the night." He paused, then smiled at the thought of something. "You'd be surprised what I find."

Michael couldn't imagine anything too salacious. Looking around the commons, which was sparsely populated just now, there were a couple of tables where the service personnel were sitting— all youngish men in blue uniforms—and a couple of others where the scientists were concentrated. It wasn't any harder to spot them there than it had been to pick out Darryl at the Santiago airport. They were a small eccentric crew, one with a long gray ponytail and wire-rimmed specs halfway down his nose, and a couple of stout blond women with broad shoulders who looked like bit players in some Norse legend. Murphy must have been following his gaze, because he said, "We call the scientists beakers."

Michael got it. Beakers, as in lab equipment.

"But they don't mind. They call us grunts."

"And you don't mind?" Charlotte said.

"We sure as hell do," Murphy said, in mock protest, "but we are slow to take offense." Then, more seriously, he said, "We all have to rely on each other down here, and we all know it. Without us grunts running the place, keeping the diesel generators going and the lights on, and the meals cooked, and the U-barrels removed—that stands for urine, by the way; all human waste has to be contained and transported out of the Antarctic—the beakers wouldn't be able to get a thing done. And without them . . ." he paused, as if unsure how to complete the thought. "Oh, yeah, without them, the rest of us wouldn't be stuck out here in the back of beyond in the first place."

"Sounds like the perfect arrangement, if you ask me," Darryl said.

"Spoken like a true beaker," the chief said. "Now, get settled in your quarters for the night. Tomorrow, you've all got a long day at snow school."

Charlotte and Darryl and Michael exchanged puzzled looks.

"And don't forget to bring your mittens."

Murphy moved on to join his grunts at their table—several of them had turned around to get a better look at the newcomers—and Michael and Charlotte and Darryl were left like the new kids in the high-school cafeteria. The beakers were absorbed in their own conversations, or ate intently with their heads hung low over their plates of franks and beans and corn bread (one had a sheaf of computer printouts spread across the table in front of him).

"Weird, isn't it?" Michael said, indicating the scientists. "We're now in a universe where they're the cool kids."

Darryl laughed and said, "I've waited for this my whole life. If you'll excuse me," he said, getting up, "I believe I heard someone say 'isopod' over there."

As Charlotte and Michael looked on, Darryl fearlessly traversed the linoleum floor and made a seat for himself at the picnic-style metal table where the blond women, wearing untucked flannel shirts, were debating something. For several seconds, the conversation seemed to stall, and Michael started to wonder if he should go and rescue his friend. But then Darryl said a few things Michael couldn't make out, hands were shaken, credentials loudly declared, and as if he had passed some secret initiation process, Darryl was immediately welcomed into the club. For the next ten or fifteen minutes, Michael and Charlotte gave him time to bond with his new buds, then got up and dumped their trays. Michael caught Darryl's eye, and Darryl quickly wrapped up some entertaining anecdote about a nematode—to much laughter—before rejoining them.

"Great bunch," Darryl said, as the three of them buttoned up for the brief journey back to their quarters.

"You looked like you were a hit," Michael said.

"It was a new crowd," Darryl replied, with a modest shrug, "so I could trot out my best material."

Once they stepped outside the commons module, which also housed the chief's office, they had to cross about a fifteen-foot-long, exposed wooden walkway. The modules were like wide railroad cars, laid out in a big square, with braided red nylon ropes strung along both sides of the connecting walkways. Michael knew that the ropes were there for more than helping you to keep your balance; in the event of a whiteout—and he'd been caught in one—the ropes could provide the only means of finding your way to refuge; even if that refuge was only a foot or two in front of you, you might not know it. Men had died in polar climes, frozen to death just yards from their unseen tents.

In the next module over, where the infirmary was located, Charlotte had that rarity, a single room, if you could call it that. It was a tiny cell about eight feet by ten feet, and it had been occupied, until the moment their helicopter arrived, by the previous medical resident. Judging from the posters on the wall, he'd been a fan of three things: surfing, sailing, and Jessica Alba. But he was now on his way back to the world, by way of the Coast Guard Cutter *Constellation*. Charlotte's bags were still on the bunk.

"That's some décor," Michael said, poking his head in.

"Never occurred to me to pack my own posters."

"Next time you'll know," Darryl said.

"Next time," Charlotte said, "I won't be here."

Michael and Darryl were in the next module over, reserved for the beakers and other transient types—and they had to share a room not much bigger than Charlotte's. There was one narrow window, more of a louver really, and a two-tiered bunk bed, with flimsy blackout curtains around each berth; the floor was covered with the kind of industrial-strength carpeting, in maroon and yellow, that you might see in a hotel banquet room. But the single closet, behind a slatted plywood door that had trouble remaining on track, revealed a surprising bounty inside.

"Whoa," Michael said, "check this out."

Darryl looked over.

"Either the previous tenants left us a lot of presents..."

"Or the NSF has made damn sure we're properly outfitted." Darryl pulled out the sleeve on one of the two orange anoraks hanging on the bent rod. "I wondered why they kept asking for my sizes on the application forms."

In addition to the two anoraks, their hoods lined with coyote fur, there were two goose-down parkas, wool shirts, and wool "wind pants," with enough pockets to carry a whole hardware store. On the shelf above, Michael found and handed down to Darryl polypropylene underwear designed to wick sweat away from the body, furry mittens big enough to wear gloves inside of them, wool socks, leather gloves and liners, and, finally, woolen ski masks to cover the head and neck and most of the face.

"It's like Christmas!" Darryl said, examining the various items as Michael handed them out.

"And we're not done yet."

On the floor, there was an assortment of boots, all neatly aligned and separated by size. There were bunny boots—two layers of rubber, with insulation in between; soft, Eskimo-style mukluks; and fireman's boots, tall and black, for water work and wet ground.

"Looks like they've thought of everything," Darryl said.

"Yeah," Michael agreed, surveying the cache. "I'm just wondering where they've parked our snowmobiles."

The communal bathroom was at the far end of the module, and was blissfully unoccupied when Michael took a hot shower— "Limit yourself to three minutes when bathing!" the sign warned— and padded back down the hallway. It, too, was done in the same carpeting as the rooms—they must have gotten it at a fire sale, Michael thought, when some Holiday Inn had suddenly gone out of business.

As soon as he got back to his room, and closed the door, he could hear the low snoring from behind the curtain in Darryl's lower berth. The floor was still littered with all their new clothing. Michael adjusted the black blind that came down over the slot that passed for a window, turned out the light, then climbed up to his own bed, where he plumped the foam-filled pillow against the headboard. A slant of cold sun still penetrated the room. He pulled the bed curtains closed, and by the time he put his head back on the pillow, he was already half-gone. Eight hours later, he awoke in the same position he'd fallen asleep in and, for the first time in months, he could not remember a single thing about his dreams. For that, he was deeply grateful.

———————

Snow school was mandatory for all newcomers to the base. It was overseen by a lanky young guy named Bill Lawson, who wore a cotton kerchief, pirate-style, over his head. Michael thought he might have seen *Pirates of the Caribbean* one too many times. A civilian employee of the Navy, he taught the course as if it were a self-esteem seminar. When Michael was the first to demonstrate that he knew how to build a fire from scratch, Lawson said, "Way to go, Michael!"

And when Darryl got his tent erected in under ten minutes, Lawson let loose with a "Props to you, Darryl!" and more props when he was able to dismantle and stow it back on the sled in even less time.

Charlotte, who was failing to win any of the survival skills tests, was looking more and more disgruntled. It was plain that she was used to being the star pupil and that she didn't welcome the lectures on hypothermia and frostbite either. Those were topics she'd clearly already mastered, and while Lawson was talking, she would stare off into the middle distance, at the icy plains that surrounded the base on three sides and the ragged ridge of the Transantarctic Mountains, a muddy brown in those places where the snow had been blown away by the unrelenting winds. She looked even un-happier when Lawson announced that they'd be spending the night outdoors.

"In a tent?" Charlotte said. "My room isn't much, but at least it's got a bed, thanks."

Lawson pretended to take it in good humor—or maybe, Michael thought, the guy really was impervious to any negativity—and said, "No, no tents. We'll be building our own igloos!" For a second, Michael thought Lawson was going to clap his hands in joy.

"Well, if that's how things are done at the South Pole," Darryl started to say, before Lawson corrected him by saying, "Pole. Just pole."

None of them entirely understood.

"No one says *the* South Pole down here," Lawson explained, "or even *the* pole at all. It gives you away as a newcomer, or a tourist. Just say, for instance, 'We're going to pole next week,' and you'll sound like an old hand."

While they all silently tried mouthing the new locution, Lawson produced four serrated ice saws from his rucksack, handed them out, and proceeded to show the class how to cut blocks of snow and ice from the ground as if they were slicing up a wedding cake. Then he went about demonstrating the proper method of stacking the blocks atop each other, though slightly cantilevered, in order to fashion a kind of sloppy dome. Even though the temperature was in the low twenties, Lawson was sweating profusely by the time he was done, and stood back to admire his little Taj Mahal.

"Didn't you forget something?" Charlotte asked.

"You must mean the door," Lawson said, grinning. His teeth were as white as Chiclets. "I was just taking a breather."

Then, with the saw, a shovel, and often his mittened hands, he started burrowing into the ground like a beaver. Chips of ice and snow, pocked with the occasional bit of gravel, flew behind him as if he were a wood chipper. As Michael watched in wonder, he dug a shallow, and very narrow, tunnel that ran down through the snow, then up into the igloo. Casting the shovel aside, he got down on his belly, and gradually, his whole body disappeared, one segment at a time, into the earth, until, finally, his boots, too, wriggled out of sight. Michael crouched down at the open end of the tunnel, and called out, "Everything okay in there?" and Lawson's voice, sounding winded and sepulchral, came back, "Snug as a bug in a rug."

Charlotte looked like she'd like to squash that particular bug.

But when he reemerged, he managed to cajole them, under his close supervision, into making their own snow dome. Although he guided their every move, he insisted that they do the manual labor every step of the way, unaided. "You've got to *know* how to do this—and *believe* that you can do this," he said, hovering above them as they chopped the blocks of snow. "It could make the difference between life and death."

The close proximity of death, Michael reflected, was becoming a frequent refrain at Point Adélie.

That night, instead of repairing to the commons for dinner, they huddled behind an ice wall they'd built with the leftover materials from the snow dome, and thanked God for the NSF gear they'd found in their closets. They ate field rations that Lawson had brought along; they weren't labeled MREs, or Meals Ready to Eat, but Michael suspected that they came from the same fine kitchens that supplied the U.S. military. Michael's can said corned beef hash, but with his eyes closed, he wasn't sure he would have been able to identify it as such. When they were done eating—a quick and cold business—Lawson passed a plastic bag around and every scrap of refuse was gathered up and tossed inside.

"Out here, we leave nothing behind," he said. "Whatever humans bring in, we take out."

The base itself was maybe a half mile off, and downhill; its bare white lights, illuminated even in the constant sunlight, were just visible by the shore of the Weddell Sea. Charlotte was looking off at them as if they were the lights of Paris. When the wind blew their way, they could faintly hear the howls of the sled dogs in their kennel.

"You sure we can't call it a night?" she said to Lawson. "I mean, we know how to build igloos now. Do we really have to sleep in 'em?"

Lawson cocked his head, and said, "I'm afraid so; we're just following the chief's orders. Ever since that beaker—excuse me, I mean the geologist from Kansas—got lost and died out here, Murphy's required a full day and night of snow school for all new arrivals."

Darryl stood up and slapped his arms around himself to get the heat going. "So, who's sleeping where?" he said. "It looks like one of the dorms will have to be coed."

"Right you are," Lawson said, in keeping with his apparent philosophy of complimenting them on anything, no matter how obvious, that they uttered. "Michael, why don't you share with me? I made this first one with extra leg room."

Each one of them picked up a subzero, synthetic-fill sleeping bag from the sled, said good night, and while Michael waited for Lawson, flashlight in hand, to squirm his way inside, Charlotte, in her great big green parka, waited for Darryl to go into the other one.

"Least he won't get seasick in there," Michael said, and Charlotte just nodded. Her eyes were fixed on the hole in the snow as she held the rolled-up sleeping bag.

On a hunch, Michael said, "Don't even think about trying to walk back to the camp. It isn't safe."

She glanced over at him, and he could tell he'd read her mind—or at least her inclination.

"Come on in, anytime," Lawson called out in a muffled voice.

"See you in the morning," Michael said, before scrunching down, pushing the sleeping bag into the hole, and crawling in.

It wasn't a long tunnel, but it was a tight squeeze. Lawson was, like Michael, over six feet tall, but the guy was built like a rubber band, and Michael wished that he'd provided just a little more leeway. The ceiling grazed his head every inch of the way, and to make any progress he had to dig the tips of his boots into the snow, then shove himself forward with the front of his body supported on his elbows. He didn't suffer from claustrophobia but that would have been a terrible time to develop it; his entire body was stuck in the snow, his lips were wet with flakes, and the sleeping bag he was pushing ahead of him blocked out nearly all the light from Lawson's flashlight. When it finally popped through, it was like a new world; Lawson shoved the bag out of the way and helped pull Michael in.

"Best thing about it," Lawson said, "is that you don't need a fridge."

Michael crawled in and got to his knees; the roof was only a few feet high, but the walls—firm and already slicked with ice from the condensation of their breath—were wide enough apart that, if he let his feet protrude into the tunnel entrance, he'd be able to lay out his bag to its full length. Lawson had covered most of the floor with insulated sleep mats.

But it was the light inside that truly stunned him. The flashlight beam was angled upward, and it sent twinkling rays of light in all directions. The walls seemed to glow with a glistening blue-white sheen, and a few errant flakes of snow, fallen from the roof, idly turned in the air, like diamonds on display. Michael felt like he was caught inside a snowball.

"The roof will drip a bit during the night," Lawson said as he shimmied down into his own sleeping bag, "especially around the blowholes. It's nothing to worry about, but I'd suggest you drape the waterproof flap of your bag over your face."

Lawson lay back, and loosely threw his own flap over his head. "Like this," he said, his breath puffing up the fabric.

Michael unrolled his bag, and even though he managed to bang his head on the ceiling three or four times during the process, laid it out. He took off his boots, leaving on the wool socks and boot liners, then scrunched his parka, as Lawson had done, into a pillow. But the hardest part was squinching himself down into the bag with so many other layers of clothing still on. In the closed space of the snow dome, he got a good whiff of himself, and it wasn't a pleasant smell. He wedged himself down, a little at a time, until his feet hit the bottom of the sack. Lawson had already stuck the end of his own bag into the tunnel, but there was just enough room left over for Michael to extend his legs without playing footsie. He put his head back on the balled-up parka and stared up at the curved ceiling, wondering if the whole thing might not cave in at any second. Instead, a big single drop of ice water dangled from the roof, then landed with a splat on his stubbly chin. He'd been shaving less and less in recent days, in anticipation of just such events as these, when any protection, even whiskers, might come in handy. He brushed the droplet away with the back of his glove, then fumbled for the sleeping bag flap to drop over his face.

"Lights out?" Lawson muttered.

"Right," Michael replied, and groped for the flashlight lying between them. He found it, flicked it off, and the dazzling snow globe vanished in an instant, replaced by a blackness and a stillness as profound, Michael could not help but reflect, as the grave.

CHAPTER ELEVEN

June 21, 1854, 1:15 a.m.

ELEANOR AMES HAD been employed at the Establishment for Gentlewomen during Illness, located at No. 2 Harley Street, for only less than a year, but it was a sign of Miss Nightingale's confidence in her that she had been appointed the night nurse. Although it meant staying awake until dawn, Eleanor was honored, and pleased, to have that responsibility. And, truth be told, she enjoyed the relative tranquillity of the night hours. Apart from having to administer the occasional medication, or change a soiled poultice, her duties were largely spiritual in nature; some of the patients, restless and distressed at the best of times, became even more so after dark. Their private demons seemed to descend as the night wore on. And it was Eleanor's task to keep these demons at bay.

Already she had looked in on Miss Baillet, a governess who had lost her position in Belgravia after a violent seizure had afflicted her, and Miss Swann, a milliner who was suffering from a high but utterly inexplicable fever. The rest of the night she had simply patrolled the wards, making sure that all was well, and tidying up the

dispensary. As superintendent, Miss Nightingale had made it abun-
dantly clear that the hospital was to be spotlessly clean and orderly
in every way. She insisted upon fresh air being let into the wards (or
as fresh as you could get in London), especially at night; she was
equally adamant that all beds be made up daily, fresh linen bandages be applied to every wound, and well-prepared, nutritional food
be served at every meal. In many circles, Miss Nightingale's ideas
had been greeted with skepticism, or a shrug—even the doctors
who cared for the patients seemed to think it all irrelevant, though
harmless. Eleanor, however, had come to embrace the Nightingale
ideals, and was proud to be among the young women—and at nineteen, she was among the youngest—to have been accepted into the
hospital's training program.

Locking up the dispensary (particularly the laudanum, which
was much in demand as a sleeping draught by certain patients), she
caught a glimpse of herself in the glass of the cabinet. Her dark
hair, so tightly pinned under the white bonnet, had begun to come
undone, and she had to stop to tuck it under again. If Miss Nightingale came down from her rooms on the top floor and found her
night nurse looking disheveled, she would not be pleased. And for
all her tender solicitude toward the patients, Miss Nightingale was
not someone by whom you wished to be reprimanded.

Eleanor turned down the gas lamp and went out into the hall.
She was about to go upstairs and straighten the solarium—Miss
Nightingale was a great believer in the restorative power of sunlight—
when she happened to glance toward the front door. Through its
glass panels, she thought she saw a coach stopping, directly in front
of the steps. As she watched, she saw three men stepping down,
and, to her surprise, mounting the stairs. Did they not know that visitors were only allowed during the afternoon hours?

Apparently not, because even as she moved to forestall the
sound—she did not wish any of the patients to be unnecessarily
awakened—she heard the front bell tinkling, and almost at the same
moment a fist hammering on the wooden portion of the doors. She
saw a muttonchopped face peering in, and heard a voice call out,
"Assistance? May we have some assistance?"

Just as the fist was raised again, she unlatched the door and
threw it open. A big man with a florid face—the one who had been
demanding assistance—looked suddenly abashed, and said, "Please

pardon our intrusion, Miss, but we have a companion in need of attention." That companion, also in a red cavalry uniform, was holding his hand over one arm, while another soldier held him by the elbow, as if to steady him.

"This is a hospital for women," Eleanor said, "and I'm afraid—"

"We're aware of that," the florid man said. "But this is in the nature of an emergency, and we did not know where else to turn."

She could see blood seeping from a wound on the blond soldier, who suddenly looked familiar to her. Why, he was the same man who had stared up at her a few hours earlier, when she had leaned out to close the shutters.

"There is no physician on the premises," she said. "And there won't be until tomorrow morning."

The big man looked back at his companions several steps below, as if unsure what they wanted him to do next, and the wounded man said, "My name is Lieutenant Sinclair Copley. I've been injured while helping a woman to ward off an attacker."

Eleanor vacillated on the front step; what would Miss Nightingale wish her to do? She did not dare to awaken her—after all, wasn't she, Eleanor, the night nurse, in charge?—but she also felt it incumbent upon her to offer a wounded man some help.

"In short," the lieutenant said, "I've been shot and require someone to attend to the wound." He had ascended the steps and, in the feeble glow of the streetlamp, he looked imploringly into her eyes. "Could you not at least examine the arm and see if you have some remedy on hand until I can consult a surgeon in the morning? As you see," he said, removing his hand and revealing the blood-caked sleeve of his uniform, "something must be done to stanch the flow."

She remained in the doorway, irresolute, until the big fellow, apparently losing heart, said, "Come on, Sinclair, Frenchie. I know an apothecary in the High Street, and he owes me a favor." He turned his back on Eleanor and clumped down the stairs, but the blond man stayed where he was. Eleanor had the distinct impression, though a blush rose in her cheek for even thinking such things, that he had come here expressly so that she might care for him.

She stood to one side and swung the great door open behind her. "Please be careful to make no noise. The other patients are sleeping."

She locked the door behind them, then ushered them down the wide and chilly hall—all the windows being left open—and into the receiving suite. It was something of a cross between a parlor and a surgery, with armchairs, tasseled lamps, and a desk in the front room, and in an alcove at the rear a leather-topped examination table, stuffed with horsehair, a white linen screen, and a locked bureau containing medical instruments and a small cache of medicinal supplies.

"I'm Captain Rutherford, by the way," the big man said, "and this other fine gentleman is Lieutenant Le Maitre, generally known as Frenchie. All of the Seventeenth Lancers."

"Pleased to make your acquaintance," Eleanor replied—she could tell from their uniforms and their manner of speaking that they were wellborn men of means—"but I must ask you again to keep your voices low."

Rutherford nodded, put a finger to his lips in confirmation, and retired to one of the armchairs. He turned up the lamp on the table, adjusted the wick, then pulled out a packet of cigars, offering one to Le Maitre. Striking a lucifer off the bottom of his boot, he lighted the two cheroots and the men sat back contentedly.

"Go to it," Rutherford whispered, whisking his hand toward Eleanor and the alcove. "We don't want him to die here; the Russians want a shot at him first."

Frenchie guffawed, then slapped a hand over his mouth.

"Don't mind them," Sinclair said, softly. "They left their manners in the barracks." He stepped toward the examining table and began to remove the jacket of his uniform. But the blood had stuck the cloth to the skin, and he winced as he tried to free it. Until that moment, Eleanor had not had a chance to give her full consideration to just what she was doing. She could think of at least three rules she had already broken. But the sight of the lieutenant trying to separate the bloody fabric from the wound suddenly seemed to snap her into the moment. She said, "Stop. Let me do that," and, hastily unlocking the bureau, took out a pair of tailor's scissors and snipped away at the sleeve until a larger opening allowed her to pull the cloth away from the skin and gently remove the torn jacket.

Which she did not know what to do with.

The lieutenant laughed at her temporary confusion, took it from her hand, and tossed it onto a coatrack behind her, which she had completely forgotten was there. Then he took a seat on the edge of the leather table.

The billowy white linen of his shirt was also torn and bloody, but she would not think of having him take off the shirt. Instead, she used the scissors to slice the sleeve open from below his shoulder to above his wrist. It was fine fabric, that she could tell, and she regretted having to cut it. But what disconcerted her more was his steady gaze; while she tried to focus all her attention on revealing the wound, she felt that he was studying her, from her green eyes to the dark brown ringlets of her hair, escaping, yet again, from under the white bonnet. She knew that she had begun to blush again, and though she would have liked to will the blood back down from her cheek, there was nothing she could do.

Once the shirtsleeve had fallen open, she was able to see that the flesh had been torn away, but the bullet did not appear to have penetrated the bone, or even the muscle very deeply. It was hard for her to know, as the hospital never saw wounds of that particular nature, and even when somewhat similar injuries did occur—one elderly lady had been accidentally pierced by a fireplace poker—the surgeon seldom if ever allowed a nurse to assist in any significant way.

"What do you think?" the lieutenant asked her. "Will I live to fight another day?"

Eleanor was not used to being spoken to in such a playful way, much less by a man to whom she was in such close proximity . . . and whose bloody arm was exposed. An arm that *she*, in fact, had been the one to expose.

Instead, she briskly turned to the bureau, removed a clean cotton rag and a bottle of carbolic acid, and began to daub at the wound. The blood had largely caked, and it came off in flakes, which she deposited in an enameled basin atop the bureau. As she did so, the wound was gradually more revealed to her, and she could see that the skin had been sufficiently broken that stitches would be required for it to knit properly together again.

"Yes," she finally said, "you will live, but I hope not to fight again." She fetched a fresh cloth. "You will need to see a proper surgeon, though."

"Why?" He glanced down at his arm. "It doesn't look so bad to me."

"The wound will need to be closed, and that will require stitches—the sooner, the better."

He smiled, and though she knew he was ducking his head to try to catch her eye, she kept her gaze averted.

"Is tonight too soon?" he said.

"As I've said, at this hour there is no doctor here."

"I meant you, Miss . . . ?"

"Ames," she said. "Nurse Eleanor Ames."

"Can't you do it, Nurse Eleanor Ames?"

Eleanor was nonplussed. No one had ever suggested such a thing. A woman—even if she was a nurse—mending the bullet wound of a soldier, under no one's aegis but her own? She felt her face turn as scarlet as his uniform.

Lieutenant Copley laughed. "It's my arm, and if I believe you can do it, why shouldn't you?"

She glanced up, into his face, and saw a great, gleaming smile, tousled blond hair, and a fine, pale moustache—the kind you might see on a young man determined to make himself look older.

"But I'm only a nurse, and not yet done with my probationary training."

"Ever sewn a garment?"

"Many times. But this is—"

"And could you do any worse than the regiment's surgeon, whose specialty is pulling teeth? At least, unlike our good Dr. Phillips, you're not drunk." He touched her hand and said, in a conspiratorial tone, "You're not, are you?"

Despite herself, she had to smile. "No, I'm quite sober."

"Then good. And we certainly don't want the wound festering all night." He yanked the sleeve free from his wrist and bunched it up at his shoulder. "Now, what do you say we begin?"

Eleanor was utterly torn between her certainty that she was violating her responsibilities and a desire, growing every second, to do something that, in her heart, she felt that she could do. Regardless of the surgeons' routine dismissals, she had seen enough of their handiwork—often cursorily done—to know that she could match it. But what would Miss Nightingale say if such a gross breach of medical protocol ever came to light?

As if he'd read her mind, the lieutenant said, "No one will ever know."

"A Lancer's word is as good as his bond," Rutherford called out from his chair, and Frenchie immediately gestured for him to lower his voice.

Sinclair waited expectantly, his arm bared, a half smile creasing his lips, and when Eleanor poured some water into the basin and began scrubbing her hands with a bar of lye soap, his smile broadened. He knew he had won.

Rutherford got up from his chair, withdrew a silver flask from under his pelisse, and held it out to Sinclair. When Eleanor saw it, she said, "We do have chloroform, and ether." Which she was very hesitant about administering; this she had never done, and she feared the consequences of a misapplication.

But Rutherford said, "Pshaw! Brandy's the thing. Enough of it, and I've seen men sleep through a leg being taken off."

Sinclair took the flask, tipped it toward his benefactor, then took a healthy swig.

"Again," Rutherford said.

Sinclair did as instructed.

"There you go," Rutherford said, patting him on the shoulder and turning toward Eleanor. "The patient awaits."

She turned up the gas lamps in the wall sconces and began to withdraw from the bureau drawers the implements she would need—catgut and a sewing needle—then asked Sinclair to lie back on the table so that she could better see the wound. Her hands were shaking as she threaded the sutures through the needle, and Sinclair put out his own hand, on top of hers, and said, in a calming voice, "Steady."

She swallowed and nodded twice, then continued, slowly and deliberately. She bent low to study the skin, then decided on a plan of action: She would begin at the bottom of the wound, where the skin was most separated, pinch it together, put the needle through, and then, as if completing a hem, stitch upward. It would take, she estimated, no more than eight to ten stitches...though she knew it would prove quite painful for the lieutenant. She would have to work as speedily as she could.

"Are you ready?" she asked.

He had thrown his other arm behind his head, and was resting as if he were lying on a riverbank in June. "Quite."

She touched the needle to the skin and hesitated several seconds before she could bring herself to put it through. She felt his muscles flex, saw the arm go taut, but he didn't say a word. She knew that he was loath to appear anything but stoic in front of his companions... or, she suspected, in front of her. She drew the flap of skin from the other side closer, put the needle through that, too, and then, as if holding a pinch of salt between her fingers, held both together as the needle came back in the other direction. She had seen patients, in the midst of painful procedures, often look away, as if focusing on some idyllic, faraway vision, but his eyes, she could tell, were fixed— in that same way—upon her.

She drew the needle through again, and again, and again, and the wound gradually closed, until it was more of a puckered scar running several inches up his arm. When she had finished, she tied off the knot, but rather than biting it off, as she would have done with ordinary thread, she used the tailor's scissors to cut it short. Finally, she glanced up at his face; his forehead was gleaming with sweat, and the smile wavered on his lips, but he had not flinched.

"That should hold," she said, turning to dispose of the leftover suture. She gently coated the skin with the carbolic acid once more, then took a clean bandage from the bureau and wrapped it tightly around the arm. "You may sit up, if you like."

He took a deep breath, then, without leaning on his right arm for support, sat up. For a second, due to the effects of the surgery, the brandy, or both, he swayed from one side to the other, and Frenchie and Rutherford quickly stubbed out their cigars and came to steady him.

And that was how Miss Florence Nightingale found them.

She stood like a pillar of rectitude in a long, hooped skirt, with her black hair perfectly and severely parted down the middle, her pale hands crossed in front of her. Her dark eyes, under high up-lifted brows, flitted from the soldiers, who appeared no doubt inebriated, to the night nurse, her bonnet askew, her hands wet with water and carbolic acid, then back again. It was as if she were trying to make sense of an elephant in her parlor.

"Nurse Ames," she said at last, "I expect an explanation."

Before Eleanor could summon a single word to her parched lips, Rutherford stepped forward, hand extended, and introduced himself as a captain in the 17th Lancers. "My friend here," he said, gesturing toward Sinclair, "was injured in the act of defending a woman's honor."

Frenchie put in, "Quite nearby."

"And we required immediate assistance. Your Miss Ames has rendered it, and in a thoroughly professional manner."

"That is for me to decide," Miss Nightingale said, frostily. "And were you gentlemen unaware that this is an institution devoted solely to the care of gentlewomen?"

Rutherford looked over at Frenchie and then Sinclair, as if unsure how to answer that one.

"We were," Sinclair said, managing to step down onto the floor. "But as my regiment leaves for the east in the morning, we had no time to seek out an alternative."

Rutherford and Frenchie appeared happy with that improvisation.

And even Miss Nightingale seemed mollified, somewhat. She swept into the alcove, and closely examined the newly stitched wound.

Eleanor was quivering in fear, but when she glanced at Sinclair, he winked at her.

"And are you happy with the result of this...unorthodox procedure?" she said to Sinclair.

"I am."

She straightened up, and without looking yet at Eleanor, said, "As am I." She then turned toward Eleanor, and said, "It appears to have been expertly done."

Eleanor took her first full breath in minutes.

"But we cannot have this sort of thing here. The reputation and public standing of this hospital is in constant review. I will require a full account, in writing, by eight o'clock in the morning, Nurse."

Eleanor bowed her head in assent.

"And if you gentlemen have now received the care you required, I will have to ask you to leave."

Rutherford and Frenchie made quick to fetch their cigar butts, and then, with Sinclair slung between them, made their way out into the hall. Miss Nightingale held the front door open for them, with Eleanor hanging back behind. But as they stopped at the bottom of the stairs, Miss Nightingale stepped forward, her long skirts swaying, and said, "Be careful, young men, and come back safe."

From her limited vantage point, Eleanor could only see Lieutenant Copley, his blond hair shining beneath the streetlamp, his scarlet jacket draped around his shoulders. But he was smiling up at her. She suddenly felt a twinge of concern—quite unexpected, and surprising in its intensity—at the thought of his imminent departure for the battlefront.

CHAPTER TWELVE

December 6, 3 p.m.

WHILE ANYONE IN HIS RIGHT MIND would have despaired at the very sight of the marine biology lab at Point Adélie, Darryl Hirsch was beside himself with joy. The floor was a concrete slab, the walls were prefab, triple-insulated plastic, the ceiling was low, and the whole place had the musty, briny smell of old fish and spilled chemicals.

But it was his alone, and he had no one looking over his shoulder as he conducted whatever experiments and studies he chose. For once, he didn't have that highly paid and traitorous flack, Dr. Edgar Montgomery, trying to poke holes in his research and find reasons—as he had successfully done more than once—to have the funding curtailed. This lab, with its bubbling tanks and hissing air hoses, was Darryl's own private fiefdom.

And as far as the necessary equipment went, the National Science Foundation had outfitted the lab with pretty much everything he needed, from microscopes, petri dishes, and pipettes, to respirometers and plasma centrifuges. The large round tank in the center of the room, open at the top, was called the aquarium; it was four feet deep, wide enough to float a rowboat in, and divided like a pie into three compartments. The division was critical since many aquatic specimens had an unfortunate tendency to eat each other. At the moment, the tank held some enormous cod, and someone had handprinted a sign that read: "For Cod's sake, pet me!" The sign hung from the tank, but Darryl knew what a dumb, and dangerous, prank that was. Cod could be very aggressive fish, rising up and snapping at anything from a camera to a human hand. He removed the sign and tossed it in the waste barrel.

Against two walls, there were long metal dissecting tables, and above them rows of shelves which held the smaller tanks, with pale purple lights and strange creatures—sea spiders, urchins, anemones, scale worms—crawling around inside, or suctioning themselves, like the starfish, to the glass.

Darryl spent the better part of the first week just inventorying everything he had, organizing the lab, reviewing his files, orchestrating his plan of attack. What he wanted to do, as soon as possible, was to dive. He wanted to capture his own specimens—most notably the icefishes of the Channichthyidae family—and bring them to the surface alive; that was often the hardest part, as deep-sea creatures who lived under such frigid conditions were extremely sensitive to changes in pressure, temperature, and even light. He had already alerted Murphy O'Connor to his needs, and the chief had assured him that everything from the ice auger to the dive hut would be up and running, just so long as he filled out all the necessary NSF paperwork in advance. The man was a bit rough around the edges, and a stickler for the rules and regulations, but Darryl did feel he'd be someone he could work with.

On a table by the door Darryl had found a Bose one-piece audio system, nicer than anything he had at home, and an eclectic collection of CDs. He did not know whom to thank—the NSF? some previous marine biologist?—but he was grateful, nonetheless. Just then he had on Bach's E major Partita—Bach and Mozart were the best to help concentrate the mind, he had long since determined—and perhaps that was why he didn't hear the knocking on the door. He did feel the blast of cold air, though, and when he looked up from the slide he was preparing, he saw Michael drawing back his fur-lined hood, then zipping open his parka. A camera, on a heavy cord, swung from his neck.

"What were you shooting?"

"Lawson and I went out to the old Norwegian whaling station. I thought I'd get some good atmospheric shots."

"And did you?" Darryl asked, laying the paper-thin slice of algae across the slide, then slipping it under the microscope's lens.

"Not really. Too *much* atmosphere this morning. The light is bouncing around off the fog, and it's impossible to get a focus on anything."

"Let me know when you're planning to go out there again. I want to come."

Michael laughed. "Yeah, sure you do." He lifted his chin at the fish tanks and specimen jars. "This is your idea of paradise. I'll never get you out of here."

Darryl raised his shoulders, as if to concede the point, before adding, "Not completely true. Weather permitting"—which is something that preceded virtually every statement in the Antarctic—"I'll be stepping outside tomorrow morning."

Michael sat back on a lab stool and brushed some snow off his sleeve. "Really? Where to?"

"Davy Jones's locker," Darryl said with a dramatic flourish.

"You're diving?"

"I assume so," Darryl said. "I didn't see any submersibles lying around, did you?"

"In search of what?"

That was a big question, and Darryl didn't have an easy answer. It was what he had come all that way to investigate. "There are about fifteen kinds of Antarctic fish," he said, deliberately skipping the Latinate names, "that can survive in conditions that no other species can. They can live in freezing waters, in total darkness for four months at a time. They have no scales, and they have no hemoglobin."

"So in other words their blood is—?"

"Colorless. Exactly. And even their gills are a pale translucent white. What's more, they carry a kind of natural antifreeze, a glycoprotein, that keeps ice crystals from forming in their circulatory systems."

."And you're going to catch some of these fish?" It was plain from his tone that Michael found everything he was hearing bizarre, to say the least.

But Darryl was fairly used to that. "Catching them isn't really very hard. When they swim, it's very slowly, and most of the time they just sit on the bottom, waiting for some hapless krill or smaller fish to wander by."

"How would they feel about my wandering by?"

"You want to come with me?" He could see from the smile on Michael's face that he meant it. "Do you know how to dive?"

"Certified on three continents," Michael said.

"I'll have to check with Murphy and make sure that it's okay."

"Don't bother," Michael said, springing off the stool. "I'll do it." He was out the door before he'd even finished zipping up his coat, and Darryl wondered if he'd just made a smart call or an utterly insane one. Did Michael have any idea what he was getting into?

But Michael did know. Whenever a new challenge presented itself, and he felt even that slightest flicker of hesitation—sometimes confused with the instinct for self-preservation—he immediately overruled it. The adrenaline rush was what he lived for—and these days, he knew no better counteractive than that to the depression that was always, subtly, tugging at his sleeve. If he let his mind wander, it would invariably, by Byzantine routes he could never have traced, find its way back to the Cascades . . . and Kristin. And it was only by losing himself in some extreme challenge, or tortuously wrestling his thoughts in another direction, that he could find any real peace.

The night before, when he'd found himself descending into that bottomless pit, he'd mustered up his courage and called her younger sister's cell phone. Though he was a world away, the base had a powerful satellite hookup, courtesy of the U.S. military, and apart from brief bursts of static and a telltale delay, the connection was pretty good. Karen sounded amazed.

"So you're calling from the South Pole?" she'd said.

"Not exactly, but damn close."

"And are you freezing to death?"

"Only when the wind blows . . . which is always."

There was a silence on the line, while the words made their way to her—and they both wondered what to say next.

Michael finally broke the impasse by asking, "Where are you right now?" and Karen laughed. Damn, it was so much like Kristin's laugh.

"You won't believe this," she said, "but I'm at the skating rink."

Michael could instantly picture it. "Are you in the Skate and Bake?" That was the coffee shop attached to the rink.

The connection faltered, then came back as Karen was saying "... hot chocolate and a bear claw."

He could see her in his mind's eye, in a bulky cable-knit sweater, in one of the tiny booths.

"Alone, or are you on a hot date?"

"I wish. I've brought along a book on William Rehnquist. That's my hot date."

Michael wasn't surprised. Karen was every bit as bright and blond and pretty as her older sister, but she'd always been something of a loner. And even though plenty of guys asked her out—and she sometimes went—she never went out with anyone for very long. It was as if she put up books as a barrier to intimacy, a way of steering clear of emotional entanglements.

They talked for a bit about her classes, and whether or not she'd have time to work at the Legal Aid clinic, then she turned things back to Michael's adventures on the way to Point Adélie; he told her about the voyage on the *Constellation*, and getting to know Darryl Hirsch and Dr. Barnes. When he described the albatross crashing through the windscreen of the aloft con, she said, "Oh, no! That poor bird!" and Michael had to laugh, ruefully. It was just what Kristin would have said—her concern for the bird immediately superseding any worry about the people involved.

"Don't you care about what happened to me?" he said, feigning exasperation.

"Oh, yeah, that, too. Were you okay?"

"I lived, but the Ops officer got hurt, and she had to be taken back to civilization."

"That is too bad." There was a pause, or else it was just a transmission delay. "But I really do worry about you, Michael. Don't do anything too dangerous."

"Never do," he said, then regretted it instantly, because it had brought them around, at last, to the one thing they had both been avoiding . . . and the one occasion when he had indeed let something dangerous, and foolhardy, happen.

Karen must have felt it, too, because she said, "Not much new with Krissy, I'm afraid."

Michael had expected that.

"But my parents are very big on this new stimulation and arousal program. They bang wooden blocks together next to her ear, or shine a flashlight right into her eyes, on and off and on and off. The worst is they put a drop of Tabasco sauce on her tongue— I know for a fact that Krissy hated Tabasco—to see if it would make her swallow, or spit."

"Did it?"

"No . . . and even though the doctors and nurses all encourage my folks to keep on trying, I think it's all just to give them a sense that they're doing something."

Michael could really hear—even over the thousands of miles— all the resignation and sorrow in her voice. Karen was just not a sentimentalist, or a believer. Mr. and Mrs. Nelson were Lutheran, and went to church regularly, but their daughters had long since abandoned the faith. Kristin had defied their parents outright and made sure that every Sunday morning she was off kayaking or rock climbing somewhere, but Karen had simply let things slide, tactfully, until they stopped asking her to go and she stopped having to come up with excuses. And that same gulf was evident when it came to Kristin's predicament. Her parents, despite what all the tests might show, would keep on battering away, while Karen would look hard at the CT scans, discuss the latest findings with the doctors—frankly and plainly—and come to her own conclusions.

Michael knew what those conclusions were. And after they'd hung up, he found that he couldn't sit still—not an uncommon problem for him—or even stay indoors. He put on his heavy-weather gear, and his deep green eye goggles, and went outside, alone. The chief was strict about the buddy system—you were never to go very far unaccompanied, or without entering your itinerary on the blackboard, but Michael intended to stay close to the base . . . and he definitely did not want company.

A hard wind was blowing, the American flag snapping so hard it sounded like gunshots. Michael made a trip around the encampment, which was laid out in a rough square; there were the main modules—the administration and commons, the dorms and infirmary—then upslope, and lying just outside the central quad, the outlying structures. These were the labs—marine biology, glaciology, geology, botany—and the equipment sheds. The base had snowmobiles, boats, graders, all-terrain vehicles called Sprytes that looked like Jeeps with tractor treads, and God knows what else, all housed in tin-roofed shacks with double doors closed by unsecured padlocks. Who was going to steal anything? Where would you go with it? In a separate shed, with a hard-packed earth floor, covered with straw, there were a dozen huskies with bushy gray fur and ice-blue eyes. Sometimes at night, their howls would mingle with the constant wind, and swirl, like the cry of forlorn spirits, around the outside of the dorms.

As Michael passed by the narrow windows of the rec hall, he could just make out the sound of the upright piano. He looked inside and saw one of the grunts—a guy whose name he thought was Franklin—barreling his way through a ragtime number, while Betty and Tina, the sturdy glaciologists, swatted a Ping-Pong ball back and forth with the regularity of a metronome. Both of them, he'd learned, had winter-overed—meaning, they'd stayed at the base over the long, dark austral winter, when the sun never shone and the fresh supplies seldom came and the outside world might as well have been another planet. You actually earned a medal for doing that, and he'd seen one on Murphy's lapel, too. It was a badge of honor, a kind of street cred, that the grunts and the beakers alike all respected.

But once he turned the corner of the rec hall, the wind suddenly hit him full in the face, so hard that he could lean into it, almost falling, and yet be kept standing. He picked his way carefully across the loose scree, the wind tearing at his clothes, and down toward the icy shore. It was never clear where the ground ended and the ice entirely took over, but it hardly mattered. It was all rock hard and equally unforgiving. In the distance, he could see a flock of penguins skittering down a frozen hill, then sliding on their bellies into the freezing waters. With a mittened hand, he fumbled for the drawstring on his hood and pulled it so tight that only his goggles remained uncovered. The sun, as cold and silver as an icicle, hovered slightly higher in the sky than it had the week before, making its slow but inexorable progress toward the southern horizon, and oblivion. The temperature, the last time he'd checked, was twenty below zero ... but that didn't take into account the infamous wind-chill factor.

A gray-and-white blur shot past his face, and he instinctively raised a hand against it. A second later, it shot past again. It was a skua, one of the scavenger birds of the Antarctic, and he realized he must be standing too close to its nest. Knowing that the birds always aimed for the head, the highest point of any intruder, he lifted one arm above his hood and, as the bird buzzed his mitten, looked around. He didn't want to step on anything. A few yards behind him, there was a tiny hillock, which afforded some protection from the raging winds. The skua's mate was tending to two chicks there. She had a live krill in her beak, one she must have just plucked from the water. Its many legs were still waving wildly. Michael stepped a few paces back, and the papa bird, apparently satisfied by his retreat, returned to the nest.

The two chicks were both crying for the food, but one was larger than the other, and every time the little one chirped, the bigger one whipped round and pecked at it. Each time that happened, the littler bird was driven farther from the protection of the nest, but the parents seemed completely unperturbed. The mother dropped the krill from her hooked bill and, while the little chick looked on forlornly, its sibling snatched it up and wolfed down the entire thing.

Michael wanted to say, *Come on already, share and share alike,* but he knew that no such rules were in play here. If the little chick couldn't fend for itself, its parents would simply let it starve. Survival of the fittest, at its most unadorned.

The little chick made one last try at returning to the nest, but the bigger one flapped its wings and pecked again, and the little chick retreated, its head down, its pale gray wings clutched tight around its body. The mama and papa stared impassively in the other direction.

And Michael took his opportunity. He stepped forward, and before the baby bird, not yet fully fledged, could scuttle away, he bent down and scooped it up between his mittens. Only its white head and the black buttons of its eyes poked out from his hands. The papa bird screeched, but not, Michael knew, at his kidnapping the chick; it was only because he'd come too close to the nest and the fat heir apparent.

"Get lost," Michael said, holding the baby chick close to his chest. Then he turned around, the wind at his back, and let it blow him halfway up the slope and toward the warmth of the rec hall. What, he wondered, would Kristin have named the little foundling in his mitts?

CHAPTER THIRTEEN

July 6, 1854, 4:30 p.m.

ASCOT. For Eleanor, it had always been just a word, the name for a place she would never get to see. Not on her meager salary, and certainly not unaccompanied.

But there she was, leaning close to the wooden rail as horses—the most beautiful she had ever seen, with gleaming coats, colorful silks draped beneath their saddles, and white cloths wrapped around their lower legs—were led from the paddock to the starting gate. All around her, and in the grand pavilion above, thousands of people—more than she had ever seen in one place in her whole life—were shouting and milling about, waving racing calendars and arguing loudly about things like sires and dams, jockeys and muddy tracks. Men drank from flasks and puffed on cigars, while women—some of them, she felt, of rather dubious aspect—paraded about, showing off their costumes and twirling pink or yellow parasols in the sun. Everyone was laughing and gabbling and clapping each other on the back, and all in all it was the merriest, and noisiest, scene she had ever been a part of.

She felt Sinclair's eyes upon her a moment before he spoke. "Are you enjoying your day?"

She blushed at how transparent she probably was to him. "Yes," she said, "I am," and he looked quite pleased with himself. He was dressed in civilian clothes, a deep blue frock coat and crisp white shirt with a neatly tied, black silk cravat. His blond hair curled just over his collar. "May I suggest a rum punch? Or some cold lemonade?"

"No, no," she quickly said, thinking of the additional expense. He had already paid for a private carriage to take them all the way to the racecourse, and for admission to the park—for three. Eleanor, for the sake of propriety, had not wanted to travel alone with the young lieutenant, and he had been very gracious about inviting the nurse with whom she shared a room at the boarding-house—a Miss Moira Mulcahy—to join them for the afternoon. Moira, a chubby Irish girl with a wide smile and an outgoing, though occasionally coarse, nature, had been only too quick to accept.

And she accepted the offer of a drink with the same alacrity.

"Oh, sir, I would quite enjoy a lemonade," Moira said, barely taking her eyes from the grandstands behind them, where a teeming multitude had gathered for the most celebrated race of the afternoon, the Ascot Gold Cup. "This sun is positively"—she paused, as if looking for the most aristocratic way of saying it—"parching." She smiled broadly, happy at her choice, and Sinclair excused himself to go and fetch the drink. Once he was gone, Moira nudged Eleanor with her elbow, and said, "That chicken's already in the pot."

Eleanor professed incomprehension, but as with most of Moira's aphorisms, the point was plain.

"Haven't you seen the way he looks at you?" Moira scoffed. "Or, to be sure, the way he looks at naught else? And such a gentle-man! Are you sure he's not a lord?"

Eleanor was not sure of much. The lieutenant was still a man of mystery in many ways. After she had stitched his arm at the hospital, a box of raspberry marzipan had arrived for her the next day, with a note addressed to "Nurse Eleanor Ames, My *Sweet* Angel of Mercy." Miss Nightingale had intercepted the package at the door, and when she passed it along, it was with a distinct expression of disapproval.

"This," she had said, "is what comes of precipitous conduct," as she swept back toward the garden, where she cultivated her own fresh fruits and vegetables. But Eleanor was hard-pressed to see the crime, and Moira didn't even pause long enough to look for one. She had pulled the lavender ribbon off the box, tucking it into her pocket—"it's too beautiful to waste, and you don't mind, do you, Ellie?"—and then waited, bouncing on the balls of her feet, for Eleanor actually to open the box. When she did, Moira dug right in, while Eleanor simply marveled at the smooth beauty and the sweet fruity aroma of the candy. The lid of the box, which she held in her hands as if it were a fine painting, had a gold fleur de lis stamped upon it, and the words CONFECTIONS DOUCE DE MME. DAUPIN, BELGRAVIA. No one had ever sent her candy before.

A few days later, Lieutenant Sinclair had sent by messenger a note, asking when it might be convenient for him to call upon her, but she had had to reply that, apart from Saturday afternoon and evening, she received no time off; on Sunday morning, at 6:30, she again resumed her usual duties at the hospital. To which he had replied that he would request her company, then, on the Saturday next, at noon. He said he would brook no denial, and Moira, who'd read the note over her shoulder, said she should by no means offer any.

A bugle sounded, and Moira said, "Look, look, Ellie!" as the horses were rounded up and settled into place behind a long, thick rope that was stretched between two poles on either side of the oval track. "Is the last race about to begin?"

"It is," Sinclair said, reappearing through the crowd, with two glasses in hand. He gave one to Moira, and one to Eleanor. "And may it please you, ladies, I have taken the liberty of entering a wager on your behalf." He gave Eleanor a paper chit, with several numbers scrawled on one side, and the name "Nightingale's Song," on the other. Eleanor did not entirely understand.

"The name of the horse," he said, as Moira leaned closer to see, "seemed especially lucky, don't you think?"

"How much have we wagered?" Moira gleefully asked, though Eleanor wished she hadn't, and Sinclair said, "Ten pounds . . . to win."

They were both aghast at the very idea of wagering ten pounds on anything. Their salaries were fifteen shillings a week, and one meal a day courtesy of the hospital commissary. That you might lose ten pounds, in a matter of minutes, on nothing but a horse race, seemed well-nigh incomprehensible. Eleanor knew that to her family—a barely solvent dairyman with five children and a long-suffering wife—it would be worse than that; it would be sinful.

Moira, in a quieter voice now, said, "And what do we win, if she does?"

"At the present odds, thirty guineas."

Moira nearly dropped her lemonade.

A portly man in a red cutaway strolled past the starting line, then up to the top of the judging scaffold, draped in red and gold velvet; a Union Jack rippled from a very tall flagpole behind him. "Ladies and gentlemen," he announced through a speaking trumpet in stentorian tones, "we are now honored to welcome you to the running of Her Majesty's first Ascot Gold Cup!"

There was a chorus of huzzahs and hooting and clapping that momentarily perplexed both Moira and Eleanor. Sinclair bent toward them and said, "Traditionally, this race has been known as the Emperor's Plate, after Czar Nicholas of Russia."

They immediately understood.

"But given the situation in the Crimea," Sinclair added, "the race has been renamed this year."

The clamor died down, and the bugle sounded again, a trill of rounded notes aimed at the topmost balconies in the pavilion, and the horses paced impatiently, as if anxious to stretch their long legs and run at last. The jockeys stood high in their stirrups to keep their weight off the horses' backs until the last possible second, with their whips tucked under their arms, the silken sleeves of their jackets billowing out in the afternoon breeze. The portly man in the cutaway pulled a pistol from his cummerbund and raised it in the air. Two stable hands untied the rope wrapped around the poles and threw it in a coil onto the grass. The jockeys fought to maintain control of their steeds and keep them behind a chalk line in the dirt.

"Riders, prepare!" the judge called out. "And on the count— one, two..." and instead of saying three, the gun fired, and the horses, bumping and jostling for position, stumbled or leapt forward onto the open track. There was a brief skirmish, as each horse and jockey vied for position, and then they were galloping off.

"Which one is ours?" Moira cried, jumping up and down at the rail. "Which one is Nightingale's Song?"

Sinclair pointed at a chestnut filly, currently running in the middle of the pack. "The crimson silks."

"Oh, she's not winning!" Moira cried in despair, and Sinclair smiled.

"It's not even the first furlong," Sinclair advised, "and there are eight in all. There's plenty of time for her to catch up."

Eleanor took a drink of her lemonade and hoped to appear composed . . . but inside she was as excited as Moira. She had never wagered on anything, even if it *was* with someone else's money, and until then she'd had no idea what that might feel like. But now she knew, and it felt oddly—wonderfully—exhilarating. The idea that thirty guineas was at stake—which, if she won, she would surely return to Sinclair, their rightful owner—was enough to make her head spin.

And again, she could tell that Sinclair had intuited her excitement. In her feet, she could still feel the vibration of the thundering hooves, and from the grandstands she could hear a chorus of voices cheering and jeering and crying out instructions that no jockey would ever hear.

"Keep to the inside rail!"

"Use the bloody whip!"

"Whatcha waiting for, Charger!"

"Ascot," Sinclair confided to Eleanor, "is a hard track."

"How so?" To Eleanor it looked like a wide and inviting oval, with a center expanse of deep green grass.

"The dirt is hard-packed. It takes a great deal out of the horse, more so than Epsom Downs or Newmarket."

But unlike those racecourses, which Eleanor had never heard of, this one had the royal imprimatur. When she had come through the towering, black wrought-iron gates, she had noted the golden crown mounted in relief at their crest, and it was as if she were entering Buckingham Palace itself. There were rows of concession stands, selling everything from barley water to toffee apples, and all manner of customer, from well-dressed gentlemen with their ladies on their arm, to scruffy young boys hawking and shilling—and once, she could swear, stealing—from the carts and stands. Sinclair, with Eleanor on one arm and Moira on the other, had navigated through the crowds with absolute assurance, and taken them to this spot, which he assured them provided the best viewing of the race.

It certainly seemed so to Eleanor. The horses were rounding the first curve, and together they made a beautiful blur of black and brown and white, colored by the shimmering costumes and silks of the jockeys. The summer sun beat down on the field, and Eleanor had to fan herself—and beat away the persistent flies—with a program Sinclair had purchased for her. He stood close, much closer than any man would customarily stand to her, and it seemed only in part due to the pressing crowd. Moira was leaning halfway over the railing, her plump arms planted on either side, calling out encouragement to Nightingale's Song.

"Move along!" she cried. "Move your arse!"

Eleanor stole a glance at Sinclair, and they shared a private smile. Moira turned, abashed.

"Oh, do forgive me, sir! I forgot myself."

"It's quite all right," Sinclair replied. "It wouldn't be the first time such a sentiment was uttered here."

Indeed, Eleanor had already heard far worse, and working in a hospital—even one that was dedicated to the care exclusively of women with some breeding—had inured her to both grisly sights and desperate oaths. She had seen people whom she knew would have been perfectly upright and respectable if she had met them in the normal course of their lives, reduced to violence and rage. She had learned that physical anguish—and sometimes merely mental perturbation—could warp a person's character out of all recognizable shape. Meek seamstresses had screamed and writhed and forced her to tie their hands with bandages to the bedposts; a governess, from one of the finest houses in the city, had once ripped the buttons off her uniform and hurled a dirty bedpan at her. A milliner, from whom a tumor had had to be removed, had scratched her arms with sharp nails and cursed her in language Eleanor thought only sailors might use. Suffering, she had learned, was transforming. Sometimes it elevated the spirit—she had seen that, too—but more often than was generally admitted it simply ran roughshod over its helpless victims.

In words as well as in actions, Miss Florence Nightingale had taught her that lesson. "She is simply not herself," Miss Nightingale would say, overlooking whatever transgression had just occurred.

"Look! Look, Ellie!" Moira cried. "She's gaining! She's gaining!"

Eleanor looked across the racecourse, and yes, she could see a flicker of crimson, like a tiny flame, beating its way, slowly but surely, toward the front of the pack. Only two other horses—one black, one white—were running ahead. Even Sinclair seemed excited by the turn of events.

"Good show!" he shouted. "Nightingale, come on! Come on!" He squeezed Eleanor by the elbow, and she felt as if her whole arm—no, her whole body—was galvanized. She could barely focus on the race at all. Sinclair's hand stayed where it was, though his eyes were on the horses charging around the far post.

"The white one, she's faltering!" Moira called out with glee.

"And the black one looks fagged, too," Sinclair said, rapping his own rolled-up program nervously on the rail. "Come on, Nightingale! You can do it!"

There was something so boyishly charming about Sinclair just then—the rapt enthusiasm, the pale moustache made nearly transparent by the direct sun. Eleanor had not failed to notice the attention he drew from other women; when they had come through the crowd, parasols had twirled brightly, as if their owners were hoping to catch his eye, and one young woman, on the arm of an elderly gent, had gone so far as to drop a handkerchief in his path—which he retrieved and returned, with a half smile, while moving on. Eleanor had become more and more conscious of her own attire, and wished that she, too, had something more colorful, or stylish, or becoming to wear; she had but this one fine dress, and it was a rather somber forest green, of ribbed taffeta, with old-fashioned gigot sleeves. It buttoned firmly up to her throat, and on a day like this especially, she might have wished for something that bared at least a bit of her neck and shoulders.

Moira had simply opened the collar of her own dress—a peach-colored affair that neatly matched the color of her hair and complexion—and was even then pressing the cool but empty lemonade glass against the base of her throat. Still, she looked about to faint from the mounting excitement.

The horses were barreling around the near side of the oval track, and the white one had indeed faltered. Its jockey was whipping it mercilessly, but the horse was falling farther behind every second. And the black one, a frisky colt, was simply holding its own, hoping to make it to the finish line without any greater exertion. Nightingale's Song, however, was not spent at all; indeed, the horse seemed only then to be stretching itself to its utmost. Eleanor could see every sinew and muscle in its legs pumping and its head bobbing up and down as the jockey, sitting uncustomarily far forward on its withers, spurred it on, the chestnut mane flying into his face.

"By God," Sinclair cried, "she's going to do it!"

"She is, isn't she?" Moira exulted. "She's going to win!"

But the black colt hadn't given up yet. As often happened with racehorses, this one suddenly felt himself being beaten—saw out of the corner of one eye the contender keeping pace—and unleashed a last burst of energy and drive. They were in the final furlong, virtually nose to nose, but something in Nightingale's Song, some reserve that had still been held in check for this critical moment, was released, and as if she had been borne forward by some sudden wind, she burst ahead of the colt, the crimson silks rippling like flames along its flanks, as she flashed across the finish line, streaming with sweat, and the judge on the scaffold waved a golden flag back and forth and back and forth.

There was a tumult in the crowd, cries of disappointment from the losing horses' bettors, but here and there a whoop of joy and astonishment. Eleanor gathered that Nightingale's Song had not been favored to win, which, even she knew, was what stood so much to their advantage. She studied the paper chit in her hand, and as Moira danced in place, from one foot to the other, Sinclair took it from her.

"Will you allow me to go and collect your winnings?"

Eleanor nodded, and Moira simply beamed. Paper chits, torn in half by the losing bettors, wafted like confetti from the grandstands and swirled in the air overhead. As Eleanor and Moira looked on, three of the jockeys walked their winded horses to the circle beside the judging scaffold. Each of them took off his colorful silk jersey, and one of the stable hands tied it loosely to the rope of the flagpole. Then the silks were raised—a yellow one at the bottom, a purple one in the middle, and at the very top, signifying its win for all to see, the crimson-and-white colors of Nightingale's Song. Eleanor felt, silly as it seemed, a surge of pride, while Moira seemed utterly beside herself at the prospect of her newfound riches.

"I'll not tell my father about the whole of it," she said, "or he'd surely come to town and beat it out of me."

At least Eleanor knew that her father would do no such thing.

"But I will tell my mam I come into a bit o' luck, and send some home to ease her days. The good Lord knows she do deserve it."

Eleanor was still resolved to return her share to Sinclair—after all, she hadn't wagered so much as sixpence out of the small sum she carried in her faded velvet reticule. When he came back, he stuffed a handful of coins and notes into Moira's mesh handbag, then waited for Eleanor to open her own. She declined.

"But it's yours!" he said. "Your horse came in, at very favorable odds!"

"No, it was your horse," Eleanor said, "and your money." She could see that Moira wanted no part of this nobility, and she was sorry if it made her friend uncomfortable.

Sinclair paused, the money in hand, then said, "Would it make you feel any better if I told you I'd made my own packet, too?"

Eleanor hesitated, as Sinclair dug into the side pocket of his trousers, withdrew a wad of pound notes and playfully shook them at her. "You two," he said, gallantly including Moira, "are my lucky charms."

Eleanor had to laugh, as did Moira, and she could no longer argue when he opened her purse and slipped her winnings inside. It was far more money than she had ever possessed at one time, and she was glad to have the lieutenant there to help guard it.

Dark clouds from the west were only beginning to obscure the bright sun as they sauntered back toward the high main gates. They were just passing through them when Eleanor heard someone cry, "Sinclair! Did you have a winning day?"

As she turned, she saw the two men who had accompanied Sinclair to the hospital that night, only now they were not in uniform, but in handsome civilian attire.

"By Jove, I did!" Sinclair replied.

"Then, in that case..." the big one—Captain Rutherford—said, extending his hand palm open, "you won't mind settling accounts?"

"Are you sure you wouldn't rather consider it an investment and leave it where it is, to seek some future gain?"

"A bird in the hand," Rutherford replied, smiling, and Sinclair dutifully slapped some of the cash from his pocket onto the open hand.

"But forgive me," Sinclair went on, taking one step back in order to effect the introductions all around. Le Maitre's companion, a Miss Dolly Wilson, nodded—her face was almost entirely obscured under her wide-brimmed garden hat, garlanded with burgundy and mauve flowers—and Sinclair then asked, "Are you all traveling back to town? I was going to hire a carriage, but perhaps we could make the journey together."

"Capital idea," Rutherford replied, "but I've already got a coach waiting, in the Regent's Circle. Plenty of room for all."

Eleanor glanced at Moira, who looked both thrilled and fearful—this day, for both of them, was taking so many unexpected turns that she herself began to feel as if she were riding a wild horse galloping off across the fields.

"Then right this way," Rutherford declared, brushing out his muttonchops with the tips of his fingers, "for time and tide..."

"Wait for no man," Moira piped up, always anxious to complete a saying, and Eleanor noted that Rutherford gave her an appreciative glance—a glance that lingered, most notably, on the glimpse of creamy bosom afforded by her unbuttoned bodice.

"Right you are, Miss Mulcahy," he said, offering her his arm. "May I escort you?"

Moira appeared flummoxed for a moment—a man of Rutherford's stature, wearing a pearl-gray cutaway coat, offering his arm to someone of her social position—but Eleanor gave her a discreet nudge and she slipped her hand onto his arm, and out they all went.

The coach was a brougham, with a family crest—a lion rampant on crossed shields—drawn by a sturdy pair of Shire horses with bay coats. Until that moment, Eleanor had been unsure of the world she had entered, but this—the family coach, the easy way the men all had with money (though her lieutenant, she guessed, was overly profligate with his)—decided the matter. Both she and Moira were swimming in waters way over their own heads.

The interior of the coach was upholstered in Morocco-finished leather, with its fine pebble grain, and stowed beneath the seats there were lap robes, also embroidered with the family crest. The footrests were of polished mahogany and the front wall—just behind where the coachman sat—housed a small window, like a trap, with a tasseled handle. And though the captain had assured them there would be plenty of room, there was not, what with Rutherford being such a large man and Moira possessing such an ample figure. Room also had to be made for Miss Wilson's striking hat. Sinclair, very courteously, offered to sit between Eleanor and Moira so that they might gaze through the open windows and enjoy the passing view.

They were traveling through a largely rustic landscape, the Ascot racecourse having been built, in 1711, on the fringes of Windsor Great Park, in a natural clearing close to the village of East Cote. The green fields were dotted with sheep and cows, and the farmers and their families, going about their chores, often paused to watch Captain Rutherford's impressive coach rumble by. A boy with a heavy pail in each hand stood stock-still, staring, and Eleanor could well imagine his awe; she had felt it herself, at the sight of such coaches going by, and wondered, as he was no doubt doing, what it was like to be inside of one . . . to be a wealthy landowner, or born aristocrat, who traveled, and lived, in such a manner. When her eyes met, for just an instant, with the dumbstruck boy's, she felt such a welter of emotion—at first she simply wanted to explain to him that she wasn't in fact one of those fortunate few, that she was merely a simple farm girl by birth, ordained to live a life much like his own—but then, a curious thing happened. She inclined her head slightly, as she imagined an aristocrat would do, and felt in her breast a thrill of delight, and pride, and deception. She felt the way she had when she'd worn a princess costume—as a little girl, at a country fair—and thought the townspeople had mistaken her for the genuine article.

"Winning always whets my appetite," Sinclair declared. "What would you all say to a buffet supper at my club?"

Le Maitre—or Frenchie, as Eleanor now recalled—said, "Perhaps we should go to my club? Given certain circumstances, regarding Mr. Fitzroy," he added, raising one eyebrow at Sinclair, who brushed it off.

"Pshaw! Nothing to fear from that quarter," Sinclair said, even though Fitzroy had been demanding satisfaction ever since he'd been thrown through the brothel window. "What would you say to some cold meats, cheeses, and a much finer port than anything Frenchie's club could provide?"

Eleanor didn't know what to say—events were galloping on again, with her barely clinging to the reins.

When no one lodged an objection, Rutherford declared it a fine idea and rapped hard with his knuckles on the trap behind his head.

When it opened, and the coachman's head leaned down, Rutherford said, "Pall Mall—the Longchamps Club."

The coachman nodded, the trap was closed, and the carriage wheels rattled loudly over a wooden bridge.

Eleanor, her shoulder pressed close against that of Lieutenant Copley, sat back on the plush seat and wondered how this marvelous dream might end.

CHAPTER FOURTEEN

December 7, 8 a.m.

THE FIRST THING IN THE MORNING, as soon as he was dressed and before he'd even had his coffee, Michael checked on his baby skua, whom he'd named Ollie, after another unfortunate orphan, Oliver Twist.

It hadn't been easy deciding what to do with him (or her, as there was really no easy way to determine its gender at that point). But adult skuas were devious birds, and had a nasty way of preying on the weak—he'd seen a pair of them work to distract a penguin mother from her brood, just long enough for one of them to snap up a chick, drag it away, and rip it, screeching, limb from limb. They just might do the same with Ollie if the bird didn't grow a bit and get its wings.

But after consultation with several of the others at the base, including Darryl, Charlotte, and the two glaciologists Betty and Tina, it was decided that the best place for Ollie was in a protected environment, but still somewhere outdoors.

"If you raise him in here, he'll never be able to fend for himself,"

Betty had said, and Tina had vigorously agreed. To Michael, with their blond hair braided into coils atop their heads, they looked like a pair of Valkyries.

"But if you kept him in the core bin behind our lab," Tina had suggested, "he could have the best of both worlds."

The core bin was a rough enclosure behind the glaciology module, where the ice cylinders that they had not yet had time to cut up and analyze were stacked like logs on a graduated metal rack.

"I just unloaded a crate of frozen plasma," Charlotte said, "and we could use the empty box to give the little guy some cover."

It was sounding more and more like a grammar-school class working together on a biology project.

Charlotte retrieved the crate and they tucked it into a corner of the enclosure, then Darryl went next door and brought back some dried herring strips he used to feed his own living menagerie. Even though he—she?—was clearly starving, the baby bird didn't immediately take the food. He seemed to be waiting for the bigger bird to descend from somewhere and peck him away. He'd already been programmed, as it were, to die.

"I think we're all standing too close," Darryl said, and Charlotte agreed.

"Just leave the strips near the crate, and let's go in," she said, with a shiver.

They had all gone back to their separate rooms, fallen into the uneasy sleep of people with no day or night to mark their time, and in the morning Michael had immediately gone to check on his ward.

The herring strips were gone, but had Ollie been the one to eat them? Looking around the frozen ground, where wisps of snow skidded around like wispy white feathers, he couldn't see Ollie either. He lifted his dark green eyeshades away from his face, knelt down, and peered into the back of the crate. Charlotte had left some of the wood shavings, used to cushion the plasma bags, inside the box, but snow and ice had already blown into it, too. He was just about to give up when he saw something black and shiny as a pebble tucked into the far corner. It was the bird's tiny unblinking eye, and now that he looked more carefully, he could make out the tiny gray-and-white fluff ball of its body. Curled up, the bird looked like a dirty snowball.

"Morning, Ollie."

The bird stared at him, with neither fear nor recognition of any kind.

"You like the herring?"

Not surprisingly, Michael got no reply. He took out of his pocket two strips of bacon that he'd smuggled out of the kitchen on his way to the core bin. "I hope you're not keeping kosher," he said, leaving the bacon just inside the crate. He saw Ollie's eyes flick, for just an instant, to the food. Then Michael stood up and headed back to the commons for his own breakfast. It was dive day, and he knew it would be important to fuel up before taking what the grunts and beakers alike referred to as "the polar plunge."

Darryl was already halfway through a stack of blueberry pancakes, smothered in maple syrup, and a pile of veggie sausages, when Michael sat down. Lawson was sitting across the table. Contrary to any fears Hirsch might have had, his vegetarian status had done nothing to undermine him among even the grunts. In fact, nobody had turned a hair. As Michael had quickly learned, eccentricities of any sort were as common in the Antarctic, and as blithely accepted, as penguins squawking. People came to pole—Michael always had to remind himself to say it that way—to do their own thing. In the real world, they'd already been cast as loners, oddballs, and kooks, only down here nobody cared. Everybody had his own quirks to deal with, and being a vegetarian didn't even rate on that scale.

"The first year that you come down here," Lawson confided, speaking for the government personnel, "you do it for the experience."

Michael could buy that.

"The second year," he went on, "you do it for the money."

"And the third year," he said, grinning, "you do it because you're no longer fit for anything else."

There was some uneasy laughter, except for one of the grunts, Franklin, the ragtime piano player, who swiveled toward them and said, "Five years, man, I've come down here for five years in a row. What the hell's that make me?"

"Beyond repair," Lawson said, and they all laughed, including Franklin. The put-down was the lingua franca of base life.

After powering through his own breakfast, though with a lot less

coffee than usual—"You really don't want to have to pee once you
get into a dry suit," Lawson had advised him—Michael went back
to collect his camera gear. He sealed up his Olympus D-220L in its
watertight Ikelite housing, made sure it had a brand-new battery,
and said a silent prayer to the god of technical fuckups. Hundreds
of feet under the polar ice cap was no place for even a minor glitch
to crop up.

Like just about anything in the Antarctic, a dive was a complicated production. The day before, Murphy had sent a work crew
out onto the ice with a huge auger, mounted on the back of a
tracked vehicle, to bore two holes through the ice. The first hole,
which would be covered by the rudimentary dive hut, was the hole
the divers would use to get in and out of the water. The second hole,
maybe fifty yards away, was the safety hole, just in case anything
from shifting ice to aggressive Weddell seals made the first one temporarily inoperable. (Weddell seals could get very territorial about a
nicely drilled breathing hole.)

Murphy also insisted, den mother that he was, that anyone diving get a once-over from Dr. Barnes first. Michael had to prop himself up on the edge of her examining table, let her examine his
throat and nasal passages, clear out his ears, take his blood pressure.
It was odd, having to let someone whom he'd come to regard as
simply a friend treat him suddenly in a professional capacity. He just
hoped she wouldn't have to give him the hernia test, by holding his
testicles and having him cough.

She didn't. Nor did she seem the least bit uncomfortable in this
different role. Charlotte, he discovered, could put on the dispassion-
ate face of the physician and go about her duties in a purely clinical
manner. Not that it stopped her, when the exam was done and she
had declared him fit as a fiddle, from asking, "You sure you want to
do this?"

"Absolutely."

She was taking her stethoscope off and slipping it into a drawer.
"Going under that ice, in a face mask and all that gear . . . you don't
have any claustrophobia?"

From something in her voice, he suddenly had the thought that
she was talking about herself, not him.

"No. Do you?"

She tilted her head to one side, without looking him in the eye, and he thought back to the snow-school night, when they had had to sleep in the hand-carved domes.

"How'd you make it through the igloo training?" he asked.

"Darryl didn't tell you?"

"Tell me what?"

"That boy *can* keep a secret," she said appreciatively. "I never did go inside."

Michael was puzzled. "Tell me, please, that you did *not* go back to camp, by yourself." He was appalled at the thought of such recklessness.

"Nope. I slept in eighteen layers, inside the sleeping bag, with just my feet inside the tunnel. I was afraid if I wedged any more of me in there, Darryl might suffocate inside."

Once he knew about her phobia, and how she'd toughed it out without ever letting on, he admired her even more.

And Darryl, too, for being able to keep her secret.

"I'll be on the walkie-talkie all day," Charlotte said, "if you need anything out there."

He expected no less.

"Now you and Darryl be careful, and watch what you're doing. And don't you let Darryl boss you around too much."

"I'll tell him you said so." Then he started piling on all the outdoor gear again and left the infirmary for the dive site.

To get there, he had to board a Spryte—a humble cross between a tractor and a Hummer, which in turn dragged a Nansen sledge weighted down with some of the extra diving equipment. Darryl sat beside him, looking like a kid on his way to Disneyland. Their caravan made slow progress on the ice, and it was about ten minutes before Michael saw the prefab dive hut, built along the lines of a garden shed, sitting out in the middle of nowhere, with a black-and-white flag flying. The hut itself was an improbable pink, like a pale summer rose, and a couple of the base personnel were piling up fresh snow all around its foundation to keep out any wind; its floor actually rested on cinder blocks a foot or so above the ice.

Darryl craned his neck out the side of the Spryte as they approached, and his fingers drummed nervously on his knees. They would have to undress, then suit up for the dive inside the hut, because once you were encased in all the waterproof gear, you would pretty much suffocate from the heat unless you were quickly able to immerse yourself in the ocean; the open water itself, regardless of the depth or season, kept to a fairly steady 33 degrees Fahrenheit.

It looked like Franklin, whose handlebar moustache was all you could see poking out from under the furry hood, who waved them to a halt.

"Nice day for a swim," he said, jerking open the cranky door of the Spryte. Darryl tumbled out first, slipping on the slick ice, and Michael followed, as Franklin started to off-load some of the gear from the sledge. They went straight into the hut, which felt like walking into a kiln after being outside. Space heaters were mounted on metal brackets, and an impressive rack of gear hung from cluttered racks along all four walls.

But most noticeable was the round hole, maybe six feet in diameter, sitting like a big Jacuzzi in the center of the floor. A steel grid had been placed over its top to prevent any accidental or premature entries, but Michael couldn't help but gaze down into it, into the deep blue water, frazzled with shimmering ice platelets, that awaited him below.

Calloway, a wry fellow with a pronounced Australian accent, said, "G'day, mates, I'll be your divemaster for today's activities." From what Michael had heard from Lawson and others, Calloway wasn't really an Aussie, but had adopted the persona as a ploy to get girls, many years ago, and somewhere along the way had forgotten to give it up. "Now, let's strip down to our skivvies and get started. There's a lot to do."

That turned out to be the understatement of the year; Michael had dived many times before, and was used to the lengthy process of suiting up, but this outdid anything he'd ever been through before. Under Calloway's expert instruction, he and Darryl first put on expedition-weight polypro long underwear, and over that a Polartec thermal jumpsuit. On their feet, they wore the U.S. Antarctic program's own issue socks, and Thinsulate nylon shell booties. Darryl, at that point, looked suspiciously like a red-haired elf.

Calloway next handed them each a light purple dry-suit undergarment to haul on over all the underclothes.

"Bit warm in here, eh?" Calloway said, flapping open the front of his flannel shirt.

"You can say that again," Michael agreed.

"Bit warm in here, eh?" Calloway dutifully repeated.

Michael had had to get used to the sophomoric sense of humor that prevailed at Point Adélie, or, in his experience, at any remote camp where men tended to congregate.

Next up was the dry suit itself, which Calloway held up like a fashion designer showing off his latest creation. "State of the art, mates. TLS Trilaminate. Much lighter than the compressed neoprene jobs, and it won't retain the surface moisture either."

It was hard to imagine, as Michael struggled into yet another layer, to believe that it was lighter than anything else. He was already feeling like the Michelin man, and this was before they got to what would surely be the most constricting step of all—the protection of the head and face.

Calloway was digging in a duffel bag Franklin had brought in, then extracting two black Henderson ice caps—full-face hoods that left room only around the eyes and lips; a thin strip of neoprene ran above the mouth aperture. Pulling the balaclava on, Michael felt like a burglar. And over it, he knew, would come the attached latex hood. Calloway had to help him drag the hood over the top of his head, and down to the top of the orange dry suit, where it snapped closed like a suction cup, effectively turning him into a big human sausage in a complete orange casing.

"Can you turn that down?" Darryl said, lifting one bulky arm toward the nearest heater. "I'm dying."

"No problem, mate, shoulda done it sooner." He flicked off both heaters. "A few more minutes, and you oughta be out of here," he said, encouragingly. He helped both men on with their mountaineering glove liners, then their three-fingered rubber dry gloves, followed by their weight harnesses (without being weighted down properly, Michael knew, a diver could bob upside down until he drowned). Finally, he hoisted onto each of their hard-shell backpacks a ScubaPro ninety-five-cubic-foot, steel oxygen tank with twin regulators. Michael could barely move.

"Any last words," Calloway said, "before the face masks go on?"

"Hurry," Darryl gasped.

"Remember—no dawdling down there. You've got one hour, maximum."

He was referring, Michael knew, both to their air supply and to a human being's ability, even under all the gear, to withstand the extreme temperatures.

"The nets and traps are already down?" Darryl asked, as he wrestled his wide rubber fins over his booties and onto his feet.

"Sent 'em down myself, not two hours ago, tied to the lines from the safety hole. Good luck with the fishing."

"Before we forget," Michael said, "I'll need that."

He gestured at the underwater camera that had been all but forgotten in the heap of discarded clothes.

"Right you are," Calloway said, retrieving it. "If you see any mermaids, get me a snap."

With that, their face masks were fitted snugly into place, their regulators tested for oxygen flow, and Darryl got a clap on the back from Calloway. While Michael was stepping into his own fins and attaching the flashlight to his waist belt, Darryl lifted the safety grate away from the dive hole, and he was already gone when Michael turned back around. Calloway gave Michael his own clap on the back, a thumbs-up sign, then he followed suit, feetfirst, down the rabbit hole.

The ice cap there was about eight feet thick, and the auger had cut a hole that was wider at the top than the bottom. It was a lot like sliding down a funnel, and Michael felt his feet break through a thin scrim of icy crystals that had already recongealed since Darryl's dive. He plunged through, surrounded by a cloud of sparkling ice and bubbles, and it took a few seconds for the water to clear enough for him to see.

He was hanging suspended about a dozen feet below the dive hole, in a blue world that seemed as lacking in limits as it did in dimensions. He could see, it seemed, forever, and he knew it was because the waters, particularly at that time of the year, were as free of plankton, or any particulate matter, as any on the globe. The sunlight only dimly illuminated the ice cap, which made the safety hole above stand out like a beacon radiating sunbeams downward. A trio of long lines, with plastic pennants on them, hung down from the lip of the hole and into the unseen depths.

And though he had braced himself for the shock of the icy

water, Michael was pleasantly surprised. The gear that had left him feeling unbearably clumsy and hot up top was quite comfortable down below. The water not only made it easier to move, but it cooled the outer layers, and he felt himself positively relieved to be in the Antarctic Sea; no wonder Darryl had ducked in so quickly. But he also suspected that what felt cooling at the moment would be chilling soon, and frigid before the hour was up.

Glancing down, he could see Darryl's fins already propelling him downward toward the benthic regions. Clearly, Hirsch was not about to waste any of the time he had. The waters themselves were undisturbed and almost entirely free of any currents or tides that could, in some seas, stealthily move a diver far from his starting point. It was a great blue quiet kingdom, in which all Michael could hear at first was the intrusive clattering of his own regulator.

The seafloor sloped away from the area where the dive hut had been erected, and Michael began to follow its gradual descent. Glaciers had scoured the bottom, leaving massive striations in their wake, and dropping boulders that had been picked up miles away and strewn there like marbles. As he came closer to the floor, he could begin to see the myriad life-forms that populated even that seemingly barren landscape. The mud bore the telltale spirals and squiggles of mollusks and crustaceans, sea urchins and brittle stars; limpets clung like pale streamers to the algae-covered sides of the rocks, while starfish—some of them heaped atop each other— silently prospected for clams in the ooze. A sea spider, big as Michael's hand with the fingers spread, stood on a pointed pair of its eight legs, aware of his approach. Michael hovered in the water, raised his camera and took several shots. The creature appeared to have almost no body, just a rust-colored head and neck with two pairs of eyes; the segmented posterior sections were so reduced that they melded into the long legs. But Michael knew that the sea spider's proboscis was a deadly device, which it employed to probe the sediment for its sponge and coral prey. Once it had pierced its quarry, the proboscis then sucked up the fluids and flesh of its victims in one long and lethal kiss. As Michael swam by, the sea spider was buffeted by the wave from his fins, and toppled over in slow, underwater motion. As he turned, he could see it indignantly scrambling to its spiky feet again, ready to impale any unfortunate passerby.

Darryl was below, with a net in one hand and his other hand on a rock the size of a basketball. When Michael came closer, Darryl indicated, with a tilt of his head and a gesture, that he wanted Michael to tip the rock over. Michael let the camera dangle from his neck while he used both hands to push the rock first one way, then the other. When it finally rolled over, a swarm of tiny amphipods, the size of a fingernail, their antennae waving and their many legs pumping, scurried out, many of them landing in the net, which Darryl expertly turned inside out before transferring them to a transparent Ziploc bag. Darryl gave Michael a thumbs-up—as much as could be done, given the thickness of the gloves—then waved good-bye and Michael took the hint. Darryl really didn't want any extra commotion around him while he was trying to collect his samples and make his observations.

Nor did Michael want to be so encumbered. He had his own job to do, his own discoveries to make. He loitered above a clump of what looked like worms, each a yard long, as they writhed atop some nearly consumed carrion, and took some more photos that he would later on ask Darryl to explicate. The light was beginning to fade as he swam farther below the surface and the seafloor gradually yielded to a field of icy pressure ridges, like a gigantic sheet of crumpled white paper. From one side, a dark shape suddenly flashed into view, and as Michael peered through his face mask he saw a pair of big nacreous eyes, surrounded by a brush of long black whiskers, looking back at him.

It was one of the Weddell seals, the deepest-diving mammal apart from the minke whale in these waters, and he knew it would do him no harm. As he lifted his camera, the nictitating membrane that protected the cornea contracted, and the whiskers extended out like an opened fan. *Ready for your close-up,* Michael thought as he clicked off a series of shots.

The seal, five or six feet long, flicked one of its flippers and shot past him, looking back the whole while. It loitered then, as if waiting for this strange new acquaintance to catch up, before sailing off again.

Okay, Michael thought, *I'm game.* These, he thought, could be some terrific, and even amusing, shots for his article. He used his fins to take off after it, and the seal—a young one if he was any judge, with a sleek, undamaged coat and white unbroken teeth—retreated farther into the depths. Michael's oxygen tank hissed and burbled as he followed the seal around a rotten berg the size of a cabin cruiser, then over a rocky outcropping matted with brown and red algae.

The sea was truly opening up beneath him, and he sensed that if he wasn't careful, he would go too far. He clung to his vision of the sloping floor, and in the gloomy light provided by a break in the ice above, he saw something that looked entirely out of place. It was rectangular, too neatly so, and even encrusted with ice, it looked like a trunk of some kind. The seal spun in a lazy circle around it, almost as if it had been leading him here all along.

Oh my God, Michael thought, *sunken treasure? It can't be. Not here. Not at the South Pole.*

He worked his fins and rapidly drew near. Even with all the exertion, he was beginning to feel the cold seeping through the many layers of his clothing. He stopped just above it, waving his arms lazily in the freezing water. And under all the ice, under the clinging limpets and sea urchins and starfish that festooned its sides—one of the ivory-colored starfish had even spread itself out on top like a skeletal hand—he could see that it was definitely a trunk, and that its lid had fallen open. By instinct, he took out his camera and reeled off half a dozen shots.

The seal did a quick arabesque above him.

Michael went deeper, until he could actually look inside the trunk; a frozen cascade of ice spilled out, like crystal coins, but mixed in with them he could detect a hint of something darker. Plum-colored. Glistening.

He swept his gaze from left to right, scanning the seafloor. To one side, the sea descended to a bottomless black, to the other he saw—perhaps a few hundred yards off—a sheer wall of ice that clearly went from high above the cap to a depth he could never approach. Between his present location and the looming glacier, he saw something else, also plum-colored, covered with an icy sheen, but lying on the seabed. He took the flashlight off of his harness belt and aimed the beam in its direction.

It was a bottle . . . it had to be. A wine bottle.

Michael swam down, and with his three-fingered glove brushed the sediment away from its neck. An urchin, attached to its base, opened and closed its mouth—a mouth was really all it was—thinking that something edible might be in reach. Michael used the tip of the flashlight to scrape it off. Ice coated the bottle from top to bottom, but under it he could see a scrap of what once had been a label, altogether illegible. He tried to prize the bottle from the seafloor, but it was not about to be plucked so easily. He would have to use both hands. He carefully balanced the flashlight between two chunks of ice moored to the bottom, inadvertently disturbing a scale worm that looked like a broken rubber band several feet long— and that then undulated off in search of calmer quarters—before trying again. To loosen the grip of the mud and ice, he had to rock the bottle carefully—the last thing he wanted to do was break an artifact that might have survived for God knows how many years. Eventually, it broke free—he felt exactly as if he had just won a delicate tug-of-war with the ocean floor—and he turned it all around in his hands, admiring it.

Before he suddenly spotted one more, a dozen yards off, even closer to the glacial wall.

Perhaps he had found a treasure trove! Thoughts of fortune certainly crossed his mind—how couldn't they?—but more than that, it was the scoop! Wait till Gillespie back in Tacoma got a load of this! A photojournalist, on assignment from *Eco-Travel Magazine,* discovering a sunken chest hundreds of feet below the Antarctic ice cap. From there on in, Michael would be able to write his own ticket.

He stuck the bottle in a mesh bag attached to his harness, and sailed closer to the ice cliff. The seal seemed to hold off, drifting along on his back and looking at him down the length of his own sleek belly.

The closer he got to the glacier, the colder the water suddenly got; it reminded Michael of the impossibly cold katabatic winds that rushed down the sides of glaciers on land and gusted across the polar plains. He shivered in his suit, and glanced at the diving watch clamped to the outside of his wrist. He would have to turn around soon, very soon, and come back later.

The second bottle was wedged beneath a rock, and he decided to leave it where it was. His regulator hissed, and he realized that he had not been breathing normally—the excitement had been getting to him, and he'd not been paying attention. The slanted wall of the massive glacier rose above him like a sheer white cliff—not so different from one that he'd encountered on a tragic day in the Cascades—and fell away forever under his feet. Its walls were gouged and scarred, like a fighter who'd been in the ring far too many times. He ran his hand across it, feeling, even through the thick glove, the rough and ancient power of it, a mountain of ice that could slowly but inexorably demolish anything in its path.

And then his breath did stop—entirely.

Beneath his fingers, he saw . . . a face.

He shoved himself away, in shock and confusion, a cloud of air bubbles trailing away.

With his arms and legs treading water, he stayed in place. The Weddell seal came back to play, but Michael paid no attention to it.

He could not have seen what he knew he had just seen. He looked around for Darryl, but all he could make out was an orange speck in the far distance, tending to a trap that was being hauled up the line to the safety hole.

He turned back toward the glacier, his heart hammering in his chest—he had to get a grip, or he'd do something stupid and wind up drowning before he ever got to tell anyone about what he'd found—and turned the flashlight on the mottled ice.

From there, he could see very little.

But when he allowed himself to move closer, he saw again something emerging from under the mask of ice . . . and when he went closer still, he could see it even more plainly.

A frozen face, with a crown of auburn hair, and a chain—an iron chain?—wrapped around its throat. There was a smudge of blue and black under the ice, where her clothes must be, and quite possibly some other form nestled close behind the one he was looking at. But it was all too difficult to discern or separate out in the dim glacial waters.

He brushed the ice gently—reverently now—with his glove, and put his face mask closer to the wall.

In the beam of the flashlight, he looked into the ice, where, like Sleeping Beauty imprisoned in an icy fortress, he saw a young woman's face, staring out . . . but not in repose.

Nothing like it.

Her eyes were open, wide open—eyes so green that even here

he was stunned by their brilliance—and so was her mouth, in a final scream. A violent shiver racked his body and a warning alarm sounded from his oxygen tank. He drifted back, barely able to accept what was happening, until he was far enough away that the ice clouded over and its terrible treasure was again concealed.

CHAPTER FIFTEEN

July 6, 1854, evening

WHEN THE BROUGHAM RUMBLED across Trafalgar Square and into the refined precincts of Pall Mall, where the finest gentleman's clubs had all come to roost, Sinclair had the coachman stop at the corner of St. James's, rather than in front of the main entrance to the Longchamps. It was there that the side entrance was located, and it was only through the more humble door that any woman was ever allowed to pass.

The coachman stepped down smartly, unfolded the carriage steps, and helped the ladies to disembark. The gas lamps that lined the street (Pall Mall had been the first such district in London to be so graced, in 1807) were just flickering on against the encroaching dark.

Inside the marble vestibule, a liveried servant—Bentley, if Sinclair recalled his name correctly—awaited, but when he saw Sinclair an uncertain look crossed his face.

"Evening, Bentley," Sinclair crowed, in his most affable manner. "We've had a winning day at Ascot!"

"I'm pleased to hear it, sir," Bentley replied, casting his eye over the assemblage.

"And what we need now is refreshment."

"Indeed, sir," Bentley replied, without volunteering anything more.

Now Sinclair knew that something was awry. His debts, he suspected, had risen to the point where the board of governors had posted his name as being in arrears, and his club privileges had been suspended.

While the ladies were no doubt blissfully unaware of any problem—too busy marveling at the way the evening light came through the stained-glass oriel window—Sinclair knew that Rutherford and Frenchie must have guessed at the problem already. Rutherford looked ready to escort them all back to his coach, and on to the Athenaeum, where he belonged.

"Bentley, may I have a word?" Sinclair said, drawing the nervous servant aside. Once they were out of earshot, Sinclair said, "Have I been posted? Is that it?" and Bentley nodded.

"A bookkeeping mistake," Sinclair said, regretfully shaking his head, "nothing more. I'll straighten it out in the morning."

"But sir, until then, I have been instructed—"

Sinclair put up a hand and Bentley immediately fell silent. Reaching into his pocket, Sinclair extracted a wad of bills, peeled off several, and handed them to Bentley. "Give this to Mr. Witherspoon in the morning, and have him put it toward my account. Will you do that?"

Bentley, without counting or even looking at the money, said, "I will, sir, of course."

"Good man. For now, what my companions and I require is a cold supper and colder champagne. Can you have something served up in the stranger's coffee-room?" Though hardly the most appealing room in the massive old club, it was the only place where women were permitted at all. Bentley said that he could arrange it, and Sinclair returned to his guests.

"Right this way," he said, showing the ladies down a short corridor and into what was in fact an annex that the club had built to accommodate its growing membership. The room was untenanted at present, though a servant quickly appeared to draw the long, red velvet curtains and light the wall sconces. There was a vast, rough-hewn stone hearth at one end, surmounted by a stuffed elk's head, and an array of worn leather seats, sofas, and oaken tables.

The ladies seated themselves in a small conversational grouping beneath the main chandelier, their tired feet resting on a faded Oriental rug.

"Shall we have a fire?" Sinclair asked his guests, but everyone declined.

"Good Lord, haven't you sweltered enough today?" Rutherford said, taking the seat closest to Moira, who was still fanning her throat and shoulders with the Ascot program. "I'm praying for rain."

A storm had been threatening the whole way back from the racecourse, but it had not yet broken. Sinclair, too, appreciated the cool of the room after the long, hot ride in the carriage.

A pair of servants bustled in, and soon one of the round tables was set for six, with yellow damask napery, glittering crystal, and a gleaming silver candelabrum. When everything was ready, Bentley nodded toward Sinclair, who seated Eleanor directly to his right, and Moira on his left. Frenchie and Dolly, who had at last removed her garden hat to reveal a cascade of black ringlets, completed the circle. She was a pretty girl, no more than twenty or twenty-one, but wore a rather heavy layer of makeup to conceal what appeared to be smallpox scars.

Once the champagne had been poured, Sinclair raised his fluted glass and declared, "To Nightingale's Song—our noble steed and generous benefactor!"

"Why do you only share your *losing* hunches with me?" Frenchie said, winking at the memory of the pit-bull match, and Sinclair laughed.

"Perhaps my luck has changed," he said, turning ever so slightly toward Eleanor.

"To luck, then," Rutherford said, weary of all the words, and draining his glass all at once.

Eleanor had had champagne just once before in her life, when the town's mayor had celebrated his election with the farmers and tradesmen, but she was sure that it was meant to be drunk slowly.

She lifted the glass, and the cold froth of the bubbles almost made her sneeze. Even the glass was cold, and the wine, when she tasted it on her tongue, was sweet and surprising. She took only a sip, then gazed at the glass, with its bubbles rising, and it reminded her of the bubbles one would sometimes see under the thin ice that covered a stream. There was something very nearly mesmerizing about it, and when she took her eyes away, she saw that Sinclair was amused at her concentration.

"It's for drinking," he said, "not contemplation."

"Hear, hear," Rutherford said, commandeering the bottle to refill his own glass, and then Moira's. He leaned very far over her as he poured, and Moira obligingly leaned back in her chair to afford him more room, and a better view.

Eleanor, who had often wondered what the interior of such impressive clubs might be like, was somewhat let down by the reality. She had imagined far more sumptuous surroundings, rich with gilding and ornamentation and fine French furniture beautifully upholstered in silks and satin. The room, large though it was and with a high, beamed ceiling, felt much more like a comfortably appointed hunting lodge than a palace.

Under Bentley's close supervision, a series of cold dishes—veal tongue, mutton with mint jelly, duck in aspic—were brought out, and the men regaled their companions with stories of the brigade and its exploits. All three were members of the 17th Duke of Cambridge's Own Lancers, first formed in 1759, and as Rutherford proudly declared while holding a scrap of duck aloft on his fork, "Never far from the cannon fire since!"

"In the thick of it more often that not," Le Maitre added.

"And soon to be so again," Sinclair said, and once more, Eleanor felt an unexpected pang. The situation in the east was worsening—Russia, under the pretext of a religious conflict in the ancient city of Jerusalem, had declared war on the Turkish Ottoman Empire, and defeated the Turkish fleet in the Black Sea. It was feared, as Rutherford explained to the ladies, that "if we don't stop the Russian bear on the land, he will soon be swimming in the Mediterranean Sea." Any such challenge to the British command of the seas, it was universally understood, had to be nipped in the bud.

Eleanor grasped only some of this, her knowledge of foreign

affairs—and even geography—being slight; her education had been limited to a few years at a local academy for girls, where the emphasis was on etiquette and deportment rather than more intellectual matters. But still, she could see the eagerness and the enthusiasm with which her male company were looking forward to the prospect of battle, and she marveled at their bravery. Frenchie had removed from his pocket a silver cigarette case, on which was emblazoned the emblem of the 17th Light Brigade. It was a Death's Head, and beneath the crossed bones were unfurled the words, "Or Glory." It was passed from hand to hand, and when Eleanor received it, she instinctively recoiled and gave it quickly on to Sinclair.

A platter of cheeses, then sweets, were served, along with what was surely the third—or was it the fourth?—bottle of champagne. Eleanor just remembered hearing the popping of several corks over the course of the meal, and when Sinclair offered to fill her glass again, she placed a hand over it.

"No, thank you. I'm afraid it's already gone to my head."

"Perhaps you'd like to take some air?"

"Yes," she said, "that would probably be well advised."

But when they excused themselves and stepped to the portico door, they could see that the rain had finally arrived. The pavement was wet and shining in the light of the gas lamps, and as Eleanor looked on, a pair of gentlemen in top hats and black capes bolted from a hansom cab and up the steps of the equally grand clubhouse across the street.

"These houses are quite beautiful," she said, craning her neck to see the façade of the Longchamps. There were great rounded columns, made of a cream-colored limestone, and an exquisitely carved bas-relief of a Greek god, or perhaps an emperor, above the imposing double doors.

"I suppose you're right," Sinclair said, affecting nonchalance. "I'm so accustomed to it, I hardly see it anymore."

"But others do."

He lighted a cigarette and gazed out at the rain. A weary dray horse, drawing a wagon of beer kegs, slowly clip-clopped by, the wheels rumbling over the wet cobblestones. He blew out a puff of smoke, then, struck by inspiration, said, "Would you like to see more?"

Eleanor wasn't sure what he was proposing. "I didn't bring an umbrella, but if you—"

"No, I meant more of the clubhouse."

But Eleanor knew it wasn't allowed.

"There's a quite marvelous tapestry, a Gobelins, in the main hall, and the billiards room is the best in Pall Mall."

Seeing her uncertainty, he said, leaning close with a mischievous smile, "Oh, yes, I see your natural reluctance, and it *is* quite forbidden. But that's why it will be such fun."

Would it? All day long Eleanor had felt like she'd passed through the looking glass and was moving in a realm she didn't fully understand, and this was just one more instance of it.

"Come on," he said, taking her hand like a child inviting another to play. "I know a way."

Before she knew it, they had reentered the club, passed back down the corridor from the stranger's coffee-room, then crept up a back stairs that she suspected only the servants were to use. Sinclair inched a door open, then put a finger to his lips as two men in white tie, holding brandy snifters, ambled by.

"Not even if the Admiralty ordered you to?" one asked, and the other said, "Particularly if the Admiralty ordered it," and they both chuckled.

Once they'd gone, Sinclair opened the door wider and escorted Eleanor through. She was standing at one end of a narrow mezzanine, overlooking a vast entry hall with alternating white and black marble tiles. A dual staircase swept up on either side, and at its apex hung a huge antique tapestry, depicting a stag hunt. It was faded, but must have once been done in brilliant purples and blues; a ragged gold fringe lined its edges.

"It's Belgian," Sinclair whispered, "and quite old."

Still clutching her hand—no one had ever held it so long, or so possessively, and she still did not know how she should have responded to such conduct—he drew her on, offering her a glimpse of a cardroom, where several men were so focused on their game that none so much as looked up at the opening of the door; a sumptuous library with satinwood bookcases standing twelve feet high, all lined with leather-bound books; a trophy room with various silver plates and cups and a veritable menagerie of stuffed animal heads staring off, glassy-eyed, into eternity. Three or four times they had to duck into alcoves or behind closed doors to avoid being seen by a passing servant or member of the club, and on one such occasion Sinclair whispered to her, "That buffoon with the belly is called Fitzroy. I've thrashed him once, but I fear I shall have to do it again."

When Fitzroy had passed, stifling a belch with the back of his hand, Sinclair drew her out of hiding again. "This way," he said. "Just one more."

They were on the third story, and she could hear a hard but unfamiliar clacking sound, as Sinclair led her up a narrow, carpeted stair, and into a velvet-curtained recess. He held his finger to his lips again, then, finally releasing her hand, parted the curtains a few inches.

They were standing on a tiny balcony, with an elaborately scrolled black iron rail; below them there were half a dozen billiards tables, spread like a deep green lawn across the wainscoted gallery. Just two of the tables were in play, and the men at one were only in their shirtsleeves, their suspenders hanging down; Eleanor blushed at the sight. One of the players stroked a white ball and it rolled smoothly across the table, striking a red ball, before gently nestling against the bumper.

"Well played," his opponent said.

"If only life were a billiards table," the first one replied, pausing to rub something on the end of the stick.

"Ah, but it is. Weren't you told?"

"Must have been on furlough that day."

"Like most," the first one said with a laugh.

Was this how men talked, Eleanor thought? Was this how they conducted themselves in private? She was both fascinated and embarrassed; she wasn't supposed to be there, she wasn't meant to see, or hear, any of this. Though she didn't dare speak, for fear of being overheard, she looked at Sinclair. He turned toward her, and in the confines of the balcony, concealed behind the barely parted curtains, she could feel the intensity of his gaze. She lowered her own eyes—why had she allowed herself to drink that second glass of champagne; her head still felt light from it—but then she felt his finger touching her chin, raising it, and she allowed her face to rise. He was bending toward her; she was aware chiefly of his pale moustache. And then, though she was sure she had given him no improper encouragement, his lips were touching hers...and she did not resist. Her own eyes closed, she could not have said why, and for several seconds time seemed to stop altogether—everything seemed to stop—and it was only when a victorious whoop went up from one of the billiards players below—"That's the game, Reynolds!"—that she took a half step back, her lips tingling, her face on fire, to look again at the young lieutenant.

CHAPTER SIXTEEN

December 8. 10:00 a.m.

"NOT POSSIBLE, not possible, not possible," Murphy was saying as he strode down the corridor and into his cluttered office in the administration module. Michael was close behind, with Darryl lending support.

"It's not only possible," Michael insisted yet again, "I saw it, with my own eyes. Right in front of me!"

Murphy turned around and said, in a tone meant to convey sympathetic concern, "Look, this was your first time diving in polar waters, right?"

"What's that got to do with it?"

"It can be an overwhelming experience, and that goes for a lot of people, not just you. The water temperature, the ice cap above, the unfamiliar critters—you said yourself you had a close encounter with a Weddell seal."

"Are you suggesting I mistook a seal for a woman frozen in the ice?"

Murphy paused, to let things cool down.

"No." Then, "Maybe. You probably weren't keeping track of your time, or your oxygen levels. I'm sure you've heard of rapture of the deep—maybe you had a touch of it down there. I had a guy who swore he saw a submarine, and it turned out to be a nice big pressure ridge. You were just lucky you came to your senses and got out while you could. And as for you," he said, speaking to Darryl, "you should have been keeping better tabs on him. You were dive buddies—that means keeping an eye on each other and staying close."

"Point taken," Darryl said, looking sheepish. "But the fact remains, he brought up the wine bottle. It's in my lab now, thawing. You can't deny that the bottle exists."

"It's a big leap," Murphy said, falling into his high-backed swivel chair, "from a frozen wine bottle to a woman—wrapped in chains yet—stuck inside a glacier."

Michael hated to add this, but he felt that he had to. "And she might not be alone."

"What?" Murphy exploded.

"There might be someone else frozen with her."

Even Darryl, who hadn't heard that part, hesitated.

"Is that all of them then?" Murphy replied. "Or maybe they were all getting off a bus, and the bus is frozen inside the glacier, too."

There was a temporary standoff while Murphy unrolled an antacid and popped it into his mouth.

"You got pictures of the seal?"

"Yes," Michael said, knowing where he was going.

"And the sea spider? And the scale worms? And the trunk the bottle came from?"

"Yes."

"So why no pictures of the ice princess?"

"I was too scared." The words were like ashes in his mouth, and even as he'd been hauled up into the dive hut, he had wondered how—at the most crucial moment in his career—he could have failed to get a photo. The shock, coupled with the urgent necessity to surface, had just been too great. And though he knew it was a pretty good excuse, he still felt an unrelenting disappointment in himself—a disappointment that could only be cured by going back down again.

"Why don't we just settle this the easiest way possible?" Michael said. "Let me go back to the scene of the crime."

"It's not that easy."

"Why not?" Michael asked, as Darryl chimed in with, "I'll go, too."

Murphy looked from one of them to the other. "You may think that we're off in the middle of nowhere, with nobody looking over our shoulders, but you're wrong. Every single thing we do here, I have to write up and report to the NSF, or the U.S. Navy, or the Coast Guard, or, believe it or not, NASA. See that?" he said, pointing to an unwieldy tower of papers and forms stacked in wire bins on his desk. "That's just one week's worth of crap I've got to fill out and file. And every dollar of what we do has to be accounted for. You know what it cost to send that auger out onto the ice, and prep the dive hut, and prime all the gear?"

"I'm sure it's plenty," Michael said, "but that's why we need to do this quickly. Everything's still in place. I can go down tomorrow—and with a little help from Calloway, and the right equipment, we can even get the body out of the glacier somehow. Jesus," Michael said in exasperation, "this could be a monumental find."

"Don't you mean a monumental story for your magazine?" Murphy retorted.

There was nothing more to say for the moment. Murphy chewed on his antacid, and Michael and Darryl exchanged a long frustrated look.

Murphy blew out a weary breath. "Where's Calloway?"

"I saw him in the rec hall," Darryl said.

"Tell him to get over here," Murphy said, busying himself with some papers on the desk blotter. "Now."

Michael knew enough not to say another word. And so did Darryl.

The wine bottle rested in a small tank of tepid seawater, on the counter in Darryl's marine lab. With its icy coating gone, the label was revealed, but the ink had been so smudged that it was nothing but a blur. Darryl peered into the tank, as if watching a live specimen that might surprise him at any moment, and Michael paced up and down, wondering what else he might need to do to persuade Murphy.

"Give it a rest," Darryl advised him. "He's a bureaucrat, but he's not stupid. He'll come around if he hasn't already."

"And what if he doesn't?"

"He will, trust me." Darryl sat back on the stool and looked at Michael. "I'll tell him I need to go down again to collect more samples—he can't refuse a beaker—and at that point, what's the difference if he lets you go down, too?"

Michael considered it, but he was afraid it wasn't fast enough. "What if she's gone?"

"Gone?" Darryl said, incredulously.

"I mean, what if I can't find her again?"

"A glacier that size isn't going anywhere soon," Darryl replied, "and I know exactly where you were. I can orient it from the dive and safety holes."

Down deep, Michael felt the same way. Something told him he'd be able to find the girl again, no matter what.

He came back to the table and studied the bottle in the tank. "When do you think we can take it out?"

"What? You need a drink?"

Michael laughed. "I'm not that thirsty. What do you think it is?"

"I think it's wine."

"But is it sherry or is it port? From France, or Italy, or Spain? And what century—the nineteen hundreds? The eighteen hundreds?"

Darryl had to ponder that. "Maybe if we can bring up the chest you saw, that will help date it." He paused. "The girl might help, too."

Despite their friendship—or maybe because of it—Michael had to ask the question. "You do believe me, don't you? That I saw her, in the ice?"

Darryl nodded. "I'm the guy who studies sponges a thousand years old, and fish that don't freeze in freezing water, and parasites that purposely drive their hosts crazy. If I'm not your guy, who is?"

———————

Michael took what comfort he could from Darryl's show of support— and Charlotte, too, had assured him that she would vouch for his mental health—but the night, nevertheless, was a long one. He ate a big meal of chicken, black beans, and rice—it was as if he could never get his inner furnace hot enough to banish the chill of the polar sea from his bones—and tried to distract himself in the rec room. Franklin was banging away at a Captain and Tennille song, until Betty and Tina tired of their nightly Ping-Pong game and decided to watch a DVD of *Love Actually* on the big-screen TV. A couple of the other base staff, playing gin rummy in the corner, groaned when the movie came on.

Michael ducked outside to the core bin to check up on little Ollie. The light in the sky was faint, obscured by a thickening scrim of clouds, and the wind was blowing especially hard. He had to kick some snow away from the crate and, as always, he had to look hard to find Ollie tucked away in the back. He knew Charlotte was right—that if he took the bird inside, it would never adapt to its natural life again—but it wasn't easy to leave him out there. The temperature was already at fifteen below zero. He took his paper napkin from his pocket and shook out the shreds of chicken and a big ball of rice that he'd smuggled out of the commons. He pushed them into the crate, on top of the wood shavings, said, "See you in the morning," to the little gray head staring out at him, and went back to his room.

Darryl was already asleep, the bed curtains drawn around his lower berth. Michael got ready for bed, taking a Lunesta first; he had enough trouble sleeping under normal circumstances, and the present situation was anything but. He did not want to turn into one of those guys who staggered around the base like a zombie, suffering from the Big Eye. He turned out the light and climbed up into his bunk in a T-shirt and a pair of boxer shorts. He checked his fluorescent watch—it was ten o'clock sharp—when he pulled the bed curtains closed and tried to relax enough to let the sleeping pill do its job.

But it wasn't easy. As he lay there in the dark, the bed curtains enclosing him like a coffin, he could only think of the dive...and the girl in the ice. Her face haunted him. He rolled over and punched the foam pillows a couple of times, hoping to get more comfortable. He could hear Darryl gently snoring down below. He closed his eyes, tried to concentrate on his own breath, on letting the tension flow out of his muscles. He tried to think of something else,

something happier, and his thoughts of course turned to Kristin ...
to Kristin before the accident. He remembered the time they'd
entered a couples-only chili-eating contest, and won first prize ...
and the time a cop had caught them going at it in a parked car and
threatened to give them a ticket ... or the time they'd flipped their
kayak three times in as many minutes in the Willamette River.
Sometimes it seemed like they'd always been taking on challenges,
or getting into scrapes, together. They'd been friends as well as
lovers, and that was why losing her had opened such an achingly
huge hole in his heart.

The events that led to the catastrophe, in retrospect, were so
small, so incremental. He kept thinking that if only one little thing
had changed, one little thing had been done differently, the outcome would have been completely altered. If they hadn't assumed
that the climb on Mount Washington would be such a cakewalk,
they would have planned their expedition better. If they'd set out on
schedule instead of arriving at the trailhead later than expected,
they wouldn't have been in such a hurry to get cracking. If they'd
taken the time to study the route diagrams, they wouldn't have
wound up on such a treacherous part of the cliff face just as dusk
was beginning to fall. And if he had only held her back, just a little,
none of it would have happened.

But reining her in was something he hated to do ... and something that Kristin would never tolerate even when he tried.

They were dressed for Alpine climbing, in light clothes, and carrying a minimal amount of gear—enough for one overnight on the
mountain. And Kristin thought she'd spotted the perfect perch on
which they could spend the night—a flat ledge that jutted out like a
card table another fifty yards or so above their heads. Michael volunteered to go first, with Kristin belaying him from below, but she
said it would be safer to have him do the belaying. "I'm not sure I'm
up to stopping you in the middle of a free fall," she'd said.

But Michael had known that wasn't really it. Kristin always
wanted to be the one who forged ahead first, who planted the flag
that others would then aspire to reach.

They'd roped up, and Michael had driven a couple of nuts and
cams into a jagged seam in the rock that zigzagged its way all the
way up to the ledge. The climbing guidebook showed this very
seam, though to Michael's eye the real thing looked a lot less direct

than it did in the diagram. And the rock, to his consternation, seemed more friable. As he'd hammered in the hardware, flakes and grain of the stone had come away too quickly and easily. He'd mentioned it to Kristin, who was already moving, like a spider, up the cliff, but she'd sort of brushed it off, and he hadn't made a federal case of it. One more thing that he wished he could do over.

It was getting late in the day, but the view was perhaps more extraordinary than ever. For much of the early climb, they'd just been hiking through a pine forest, then scrambling over mild slopes of consolidated pumice. But the climber's trail had disappeared under the snowpack, and for the past couple of hours they'd been working the rock itself, searching for toeholds, finger grips, fissures sufficient to hang on to for a few seconds and catch a needed breath. Even though the temperature was still mild, the air was thinner, and the afternoon sun was sending its long beams over the crests of neighboring Mount Jefferson and Three-Fingered Jack. Far, far below lay Big Lake, and the parking lot where they'd left his Jeep.

A spray of loose stone rattled down the cliffside and Michael looked up, shading his eyes with one hand. He could see Kristin's legs, in stretch fleece shorts, scraping at the wall, then one of her feet catching hold on a tiny protuberance. Of just such little bits of luck were successful ascents made.

"You okay?" he shouted.

"Yep." Then he heard her hammer driving home a nut.

He adjusted the 10.5 mm rope around his shoulder, and bit into a high-protein bar. He could hear his mother's voice telling him he'd spoil his appetite for dinner.

"There's a seam here, and somebody's already left a hex in it!" she called down. There was nothing like coming upon free hardware.

"You think it's secure?"

He could see her tug at it. "Yeah, it is—must be why they left it."

And again, a distant alarm bell had gone off in his head; he made it a point never to trust anyone else's work—especially when it was someone he'd never even met. But he did not insist that Kristin replace it. He was anxious, too, to reach that ledge and start setting up for the night; it promised to be a very romantic sunset.

She'd placed another of her own nuts into the crooked seam, and started inching up again. He made sure she had just enough slack, and he could see her groping for a handhold, when suddenly something went awry.

"Damn!" he heard her mutter, and a second later even more of the rock came scuttling down the cliff and pattered on the top of his helmet. Dust blew into his eyes, and before he could do anything to clear his vision, the rope went loose—terribly loose—and he heard a pinging sound—nuts and pitons and hexes popping out of the rock—and Kristin screaming as she hurtled past. Instinctively, he had braced himself, clutching the rope, but the rapidity of her fall was too much—the anchor-pieces he'd hammered in held for no more than an instant before jerking free, the rope around his shoulder had fastened like a tourniquet, and he'd been whipped around, half-blind, just in time to see Kristin swinging headfirst, like a wrecking ball, into the cliff below. Her scream had stopped dead, and even as he felt his shoulder pop out of the socket in a blazing shot of pain, he'd managed, though he still could not imagine how, to arrest his own fall. He'd been dragged to the very edge of the narrow strip he'd been standing on, and lying flat, hanging on to the lifeline, all he could hear was the creaking of the rope and the grinding of the rock that was fraying it.

How long he stayed that way, he could never tell. And he had only the vaguest recollection of looping the rope around a block of stone, then running it through a fresh piton, hammered home with his one good hand. He called down to her, but there was no reply. He dug into his gear, found the emergency whistle, and blew on it as loudly as he could, but the sound simply echoed off the surrounding cliffs.

Before he could even think about hauling her up, he had to attend to his left shoulder, and with no one there to help, he would have to try to knock it back into place on his own. With the rope secured, he considered his options, and the only one looked like a flat wall of stone behind him. He lined himself up parallel to it, then—after taking a deep breath—bashed himself up against it. The arm exploded in pain, but it did not fall back into the socket. He dropped to his knees and vomited the remains of the high-protein bar he'd eaten. When he could stand up again, he wiped his mouth with the back of his right hand, then took another look at the side of the cliff. There was a section where the wall swelled, like a pregnant belly, and he thought that it might be possible, if he could stand the pain, to use that swell to massage the shoulder back. He approached it gingerly, trying to gauge the best way to use it, but he also knew that he had to move fast. Kristin was still swinging at the end of a rope, above a thousand-foot fall to the pine trees below.

He braced himself against the rock, laid his shoulder on it, and pressed hard—then harder; he could hear the popping and grinding of the joint, as the parts sought to regain their proper places, and though the pain was excruciating, he kept thinking only of Kristin, and pressed up, then down, then sideways. With each motion, he felt the parts realigning, until, like the pieces of a puzzle all of a sudden falling into place, he heard the shoulder click back to where it belonged. He gasped several times, and waited, terrified, to see if it would hold...but it did. His entire body was drenched in sweat.

He took a swig of water from the bottle in his backpack, then began the laborious process, a few inches at a time, of hauling Kristin up to the ledge. He had tried calling to her again and again, but ominously there had been no answer. He prayed that she had only been knocked unconscious and would come to her senses soon. But when her head appeared above the rim, and he saw that even the yellow safety helmet had been pulverized as if by a giant mallet, he knew that things were bad. Very bad indeed.

Once he had her body all the way up, he unfastened her harness and removed her backpack, which had ripped open in the fall; everything, including their cell phone, had spilled somewhere far below. He checked her heartbeat and her breathing, then unfurled his sleeping bag and laid it over her. He felt his own body going into a kind of delayed shock, and he stopped to take four Tylenol from their first-aid kit, then tried to eat another protein bar to keep his energy levels up. But his mouth was so dry he could barely chew, and he wound up just breaking it into pieces and washing them down with sips of water. He debated trying to give Kristin some water, but he was afraid of making her choke. Instead, he simply elevated her head on a mound of dirt and gravel he'd gathered, and waited.

The last rays of the sun were tingeing the Western Cascades a pale pink, and Big Lake, far below, was as black as obsidian. He remembered thinking that it was a beautiful sight, and that Kristin should really sit up and enjoy it. She loved sunsets, especially when she was off in the wilds somewhere; she used to say that she slept better under the stars than she did at the four-star hotels where her family sometimes stayed. The stars that night were out in profusion.

But the temperatures were dropping.

Michael made a windbreak out of whatever loose rocks he could assemble, then tucked his nylon jacket carefully around Kristin's head, leaving her shattered helmet in place. Her face was blissfully unmarred, and she looked peaceful. Not in pain. And for that at least he was grateful. Until the first light of dawn, when it would be possible to begin the descent, he would just have to stifle his own fears, hunker down and try to keep her as warm as possible. For what it was worth, he blew on the whistle one more time, and as the sound faded away among the surrounding peaks, he scrunched up next to her under the sleeping bag, and whispered in her ear, "Don't worry—I'll get you home. I promise I'll get you home."

CHAPTER SEVENTEEN

December 9, 1 p.m.

DARRYL FELT A LOT LIKE an astronaut who'd just been told he couldn't take his space shot.

"But I feel fine," he repeated as he watched Dr. Barnes make another note on his chart.

"That's not what your body temp indicates," she said. "You're still suffering some hypothermia from yesterday's dive, and I'm not letting you go down today, no matter what you say."

As Darryl had predicted to Michael, the chief had indeed authorized another dive, to retrieve the sunken chest if nothing else. And as for the ice princess, he'd said they should bring her up, too, if she wanted to come.

"But you're letting Michael go," Darryl now complained to Charlotte in a last-ditch appeal.

"Michael is fine," she said, "and besides, if Michael leapt off a bridge, would you do that, too?" She laughed, scrawled something else on his chart, and Darryl knew that he wasn't going to get anywhere with her.

He buttoned his shirt up and hopped off the examination table. In his heart, he knew that Charlotte was right—he *was* still feeling the effects of the dive. No matter how much hot tea he drank, and how many pancakes smothered in syrup and butter he ate, there was still some spot at his core that remained chilly. Last night, he'd slept under every blanket in the room, and at around 3 a.m. he'd awakened, nonetheless, with his teeth chattering.

"Killjoy," Darryl said, as he left the infirmary. In the hall outside, he bumped into Michael, just coming back from delivering his own medical clearance papers to Murphy's office.

"You coming?" Michael asked, and Darryl had to give him the bad news.

Michael looked surprised. "You want me to talk to her for you?" he said, nodding at Charlotte's office.

"Wouldn't do any good. The woman is made of stone. You just go out and make the discovery of a lifetime without me—I'll be in the lab guzzling your bottle of wine. It ought to be safely thawed by now."

Michael clapped him on the shoulder and loped off down the hall. Darryl pulled on his parka and his hat—even the shortest excursions, from one module to another, required protection from the elements—and, after a quick stop in the kitchen, headed back to the marine biology lab.

Although he had a lot of more important things to do, the bottle of wine was waiting for him, right in front of his lab stool, and he did find the damn thing strangely intriguing. True, it wasn't going to make his name or his reputation in the scientific community, but how many times did you get the chance to study some historic artifact? He felt like the guys who scraped the encrustations from the *Titanic*'s dishes just to see the doomed ship's name appear again. And this bottle had a good chance of being far older than anything from the White Star line.

He reached into the tank, filled with room-temperature seawater, and lifted out the bottle. Illegible shreds of the label hung down into the water. When he held it up to the light and tilted it, he could see the liquid sloshing around inside. Plenty of wine left—and possibly aged to perfection—for a victory toast that night. All he would need for his routine tests were a few drops. And it would be nice to know—if he ever did submit a small piece on the find to a scholarly journal—what kind of wine it had been.

The cork had held, reinforced as it had been by a quick and durable coating of polar ice. He took out the corkscrew that he'd just borrowed from the commons kitchen, but he was afraid to just insert it into the bottleneck and start drilling away. He wanted to go slow, and make sure the wine remained as uncontaminated as possible. First, he secured the bottle in the vise attached to the counter; the clamp was normally used on reluctant bivalve shells. After a quick survey of the lab and its instruments, he selected a scalpel freshly sterilized in the autoclave and used it to cut away the remnants of the red sealing wax around the tip of the bottle. When had the wax been applied, and by whom? A French peasant in the time of Louis XVI? An Italian winemaker during the Risorgimento? A Spaniard, perhaps, and contemporary of Goya?

He placed the waxy bits in a pile to one side, then inserted the tip of the scalpel between the cork and the bottleneck and began gently to cut around the edge. He wanted the cork to be as loose as he could make it before employing the corkscrew. When the circle had been completed, he put the scalpel aside and stopped just long enough to put the triumphal march from *Aida* on the Bose audio system; then, to its opening flourishes, he placed the mechanical corkscrew to the cork and began to turn the handle. There was a moment of resistance, followed by a smooth entry—so smooth that Darryl was afraid the cork was going to disintegrate, after all. But the corkscrew eventually made it all the way through, and its lateral wings began to rise as the cork came up and out in one sustained motion. There was even an audible pop as the cork broke entirely free.

Success, Darryl thought, as he bent down to inhale the first fumes of this vintage wine ... and immediately recoiled.

If he'd been wondering if the wine would still be even remotely drinkable, he would wonder no more. The odor was vile. He gave it a few seconds to dissipate, then, pricked by curiosity, put his nose to the bottle again. It wasn't just a bad aroma—and it wasn't just wine that had long ago turned to vinegar. The scent was something else, and it was something that, to a biologist, was disturbingly familiar.

His brow furrowed, and he opened a counter drawer to remove and prepare a clean slide. _____

"All right, mates," Calloway was saying in his manufactured Aussie accent, "I want you to listen carefully to what I'm about to say and do exactly what I tell you."

Suited up once more in the suffocating dive suit, and with Bill Lawson dressed just the same, Michael was not about to argue with anything. He just wanted to get into the water as quickly as possible.

"You've got dual tanks today, but that still gives you a max— max, I say—of ninety minutes. And given the exertion of sawing through submarine ice, probably a fair bit less than that. Any difficulty with the saw, and you come up, pronto! Got that?"

Michael and Lawson nodded.

"That means, any tear in your suit, no matter how small, and you come straight up. Any tear in your skin—anything that leaks blood—and you come up even faster. We've seen leopard seals around the dive hut today, and you know they're not your friends."

Michael did know—the Weddels were frisky but harmless; their close cousins, distinguishable by their large reptilian heads, were not. A Weddell would play with you, but a leopard, with its immense curving mouth, would bite.

"If you have to, defend yourselves with the ice saws."

Each of them had been equipped with a fifty-two-inch-long Nils Master ice saw; it wasn't necessarily the most precise ice-cutting instrument, but with its wing-nut design and razor-sharp teeth, angled inward like a shark's, nothing could cut through underwater ice faster.

"Michael, you know where you're going, right? So you'll go down first and lead the way. Bill, you take the net and salvage line and follow."

Michael was nodding the whole time while he inched in his fins toward the beckoning ice hole. A cool bloom seemed to rise up off it and into the overheated dive hut, and he noted that its diameter had been enlarged.

"That's it then, mates," Calloway said, slapping Michael on the shoulder to indicate it was time to go. "Masks on, feet in the deep freeze."

Michael sat at the edge of the hole, then slipped down the icy funnel and into the sea. He didn't have to go in search of the sunken chest; an earlier dive team had already gone down and retrieved it, and he'd seen a team of huskies dragging it back on a sledge toward the base camp. A big guy named Danzig was mushing them, and as he passed Michael, he raised one hand in salute. Word had quickly spread around the compound that Michael had made a pretty unusual find, and even if the ice princess didn't turn up, his stock had definitely risen.

Michael knew that she *was* going to turn up.

After orienting himself in the water, and waiting for Lawson to take the plunge, Michael turned away from the dive and safety holes and swam off toward the glacier wall that appeared in the distance. Much as he regretted it, he did not have his camera with him; Murphy had forbidden it. "I don't want you mucking around with photography down there," he'd said. "You have limited time, and if you're right about what you saw"—he still hadn't been willing entirely to concede the point—"you're going to have your hands full helping Bill to cut through all that ice." With his saw in one hand and a flashlight in the other, Michael propelled himself through the water like a seal, undulating his body and working his fins for all they were worth. Still, it was harder work, and more time-consuming than he thought, just to reach the glacier. It was difficult to gauge distances underwater, and especially so there, where the ice cap cast a pall over everything. Once in a while, a break in the ice might let some direct rays of sunlight penetrate the depths, creating a shaft of gold aimed straight at the black and benthic regions below, but otherwise the ocean water was a very pale and clear blue, like an early-morning sky in summer.

And his glove was leaking—not a lot, not so much to be dangerous, but enough to make things uncomfortable already. The glove was the one noncontiguous part of the suit, and as such, no matter how tightly you tried to seal it, there could be a certain amount of penetration. The linings underneath it absorbed the moisture as it leaked in, eventually bringing it to body temperature, but in the meantime it was a numbingly cold reminder of just what a hostile climate he was traveling in.

He slowed up in the water and turned to make sure Lawson—the ever-cheerful Boy Scout leader—was still with him. He could see his face mask glittering in the water, the sharp tip of his ice saw, and the salvage line playing out behind him; it was tied to his harness and tethered up top to a 200-hp winch behind the dive hut. The line, normally used for dredging up oil barrels and sunken wreckage, had two thousand yards on it and could withstand a couple thousand pounds of weight. Michael turned around again and continued toward the glacier. As it loomed above him, and below, he felt a note of hesitation, even fear, that he had not felt the first time. Then, he had been unaware of what the ice held. Now, he not only knew, but he was there to steal it. The walls of ice seemed more defensive now, like the walls of a fortress erected by some ancient god of sea and ice, and Michael felt like a soldier about to try to breach them.

There was even a low murmur of noise, a crackling and grinding, from the ice itself. He hadn't noticed it before. But the immense glacier was moving, it was always moving, though so slowly it could not be seen, and only seldom heard. Michael drew closer to the wall, and now he knew that the hard part was about to begin. The wall was vast, and finding the body was a question not only of longitude but of latitude. He could roughly gauge the section of wall where he had seen it, but at what depth? He would have to travel both up and down the wall, and that could take time. He motioned at one large area with his arm, and indicated to Lawson that he should begin to scout the glacier there. Michael himself moved thirty yards off, and to orient himself took one long look back at what was called the down line—it extended from the safety hole, far, far away, and there were colored pennants attached to it for better visibility. He tried to recall if this was the angle he'd had on it the day before. But he couldn't remember at all. He had been so shocked that he'd just paddled away backwards, in a burst of bubbles and flapping fins.

What he did remember was the quality of the light, and that, he decided, would be his best clue. The weather today was much like the day before, and the unchanging sunlight—if he could just remember how bright, or dim, it had been when he discovered the body—could steer him in the right direction. The water and the light was not the pristine blue that he was inhabiting now, so he deflated his suit and allowed himself to sink, staying close to the wall, a dozen yards or so. He swept the flashlight across its rough mottled surface in even strokes, back and forth, while looking for anything—

a fissure in the rock, an unusual formation—that might trigger a memory. But so far, he saw nothing.

What he did notice was the creeping cold, colder than the water even a little ways off. The iceberg gave off a freezing breath that made him have to wipe his mask with the back of one glove. It also made him wonder what it could possibly be like to be a captive of that ice for decades, even centuries. To be absorbed, suspended, immobilized—like one of Darryl's specimens floating in a jar of formaldehyde—forever. Lifeless, but immaculately preserved. Dead, but not gone.

And he thought then of Kristin, lying perfectly still in her hospital bed in Tacoma.

He raked the tip of the saw against the glacier, and slivers of ice immediately came loose, like the skin curling off a potato. Another drop or two of frigid water seeped into his glove.

He went lower still, and the light grew dimmer, more like the quality of the light that he recalled. He swam from one side to the other of a wide swath, gradually working his way down, until something in the ice looked different—a spot where it didn't sparkle quite so brightly in the concentrated beam—and he went straight for it.

The closer he got, the darker and colder the water became, but his heart was beating fast. He waved his arms and fins slowly to keep his position, and surveyed the wall. There was indeed something buried here (there had been moments, though he confessed them to no one, when he, too, had wondered if he'd imagined it all) and he quickly waved his flashlight beam at Lawson, still a considerable distance above him, to catch his attention. Then he swam even closer, peered in at the ice . . . and saw her face staring out at him.

But it was—and it was not—what he remembered. He had remembered a look of utter horror on her face, eyes wide and mouth shaped in a scream . . . but that was not what she looked like now. Although it was impossible—and he knew he would never try to explain this part of it to Murphy O'Connor—her eyes were level, and her mouth composed. She looked not like a person in extremis, but instead like someone in the midst of a mildly troubling dream. Someone who would soon awaken.

Lawson swam down toward him, the salvage line trailing behind, and when he, too, saw the face in the ice, he held still in the water, taking it in. All along, Michael knew Lawson had been secretly dubious, wanting to believe what Michael had said but well aware of the tricks that deep-sea diving can play on the mind. But this was no trick, and now he would know that for sure. If they were going to extricate her, they would have to get to work fast—there were at least several inches of ice covering her, and covering whatever else there might be clinging close behind her.

Lawson placed his saw against the ice, about five or six feet down, and indicated that he would be cutting laterally there. He lifted the tip of Michael's saw, and made a horizontal cutting motion about three inches above the woman's head. The plan was to leave just enough leeway to be safe, but no more than that—a block of ice with a body inside was going to weigh a ton as it was.

Michael tucked his flashlight back into its belt loop and let the jagged teeth of the saw bite into the ice. He drew the blade toward him, like drawing the bow on a violin, and a thin groove opened. He pushed it back and the groove deepened, translucent slivers of ice peeling away. It would be a long job, but the saw seemed up to it. The hard part was making sure that he kept his body, and his fins in particular, angled away from Lawson, who was working below.

It was also important to keep his eyes on the deepening groove and not let them stray to the face in the ice. Looking at her could make his blood run cold, and the iron chain wrapped around her neck was the stuff of nightmares. He tried to regulate his breathing and listen not to his own thoughts but to the hissing of the regulator, and the occasional groan or sputter from the ice. It crossed his mind, in the strange way that he knew humans anthropomorphized everything, that the glacier was in pain, that it could feel the bite of the saw cutting into it, that it was fighting to hold on to its frozen prize.

But it would not win. Michael made steady progress up top, and when he felt that he'd gone deep enough, he turned to making a vertical incision. Gradually, both he and Bill were cutting a box around the figure, and around the other shape—also human, or something else entirely?—that lurked behind. Michael saw Lawson check his dive watch, then hold up a hand with bulky fingers spread, twice, to indicate that they should cut away whatever else they could for ten more minutes. After that, it would be up to the winch to do the rest.

Lawson removed a dagger-sharp piton from his harness kit, and with steady blows drove it into the back of the ice block they'd been carving. Then he drove several more. The idea was simply to create enough of a fracture plane behind the block that a sudden and powerful tug would tear the whole piece loose. When he had the pitons in, he unfurled the net, wrapped it as best he could around the chopped block, and secured it with several more pieces of Alpine hardware—the same sort that Michael routinely used on mountain climbs. When that was done, and he had clamped all the hardware to the unbreakable salvage line, he gave the line three hard tugs, waited, then gave it three more.

Michael and Lawson back-paddled a few yards off and waited for the winch to kick in. The first thing they saw was the salvage line, which had shown almost no slack, suddenly straighten out like an arrow; Michael could hear a high-tension thrumming in the water, and a second or two later, he saw the ice block budge. It inched forward, then stopped; he could hear the cracking and grinding of the ice. It was like sliding a block out of a gigantic pyramid, and he suddenly had a terrible vision of the whole ice wall crumbling down around him. He moved farther back and inflated his suit to rise a few yards higher in the water.

The winch must have pulled again, because the ice block came forward on one side, then the other, almost like a penguin waddling across snow. Again, it stopped, still clinging precariously to its frozen perch, before issuing a mighty agonized groan and toppling forward, away from the iceberg, and swinging free above the bottomless sea. Lawson quickly swam toward it, and even as the winch began to haul it up and toward the dive hole, he attached himself like a limpet and knotted the back portion of the net for added safety. Michael, stunned, was quickly left behind, as he watched the block of ice, the size and shape of a big refrigerator, drifting away, with Lawson holding on and hitching a ride. The glove on Michael's left hand was leaking again, leaving his wrist feeling like an ice-cold iron bracelet had been bound around it. His air tank beeped a warning, and with his ice saw at the ready in case of a leopard seal attack, he followed the trail of bubbles up from the depths and toward the bluer waters above.

From below, the ice block looked like a crystal ornament, something that might twinkle on a Christmas tree, as it sailed back up out of the void and into the living world . . . carrying its strange and petrified cargo.

CHAPTER EIGHTEEN

August 8, 1854

SINCLAIR SAT HIGH ASTRIDE HIS HORSE, Ajax, in full uniform and regalia, his peaked black helmet, modeled on that of the Polish lancers, at a slight tilt to provide some protection from the glare of the sun. A dozen other lancers were in a neat line to either side of him, and all the way across the drill field—a distance of no less than several hundred yards—an equally perfect line of cavalrymen were arrayed, also in everything from glittering gold epaulettes to tasseled sword knots. Sinclair knew, as did they all, that they were often mocked as dandies because of the richness of their apparel— mandated by their commanding officer—but he was also confident that if they were ever fortunate enough to see battle, they would prove that they were much more than that.

The horses pawed the patchy ground, apprehensive about what was coming; all morning, the 17th had been doing lance exercises and circling-the-haunches drills, requiring close formation and precision riding. But now the lances had been discarded, and when the cornet sounded, the riders were to engage in mock, hand-to-hand combat, using blunted wooden swords. Sinclair wiped a trickle of sweat from his brow with the back of his hand, then dried his hand on the chestnut mane of his horse. Ajax had been with him since he was a colt, first at the family's country estate in Hawton, then in the regimental stables in London. As a result, there was a rapport between the horse and rider that the other soldiers could only envy. While the others were struggling to teach their mounts the most basic commands and maneuvers, Sinclair had perfect control of his own and could—sometimes with a gentle twitch on the reins, sometimes with just a word—make the horse do his bidding.

The trumpeter stepped up on one of the fence rails, raised the gleaming instrument to his lips, and played, three times in rapid succession, the rousing line that called the cavalry to charge. The horses whinnied and neighed, and Winslow's mare, directly to Sinclair's right, raised his head and forelegs, nearly throwing Winslow off altogether.

Sinclair, like the others, drew his wooden sword in one swift, almost silent motion and raising his right arm straight, shouted, "On!" to Ajax, while nipping at the horse's flanks with the jangling spurs. The horse burst forward like a racer on the Ascot track and the ground thundered as the entire line of cavalry rushed to meet the line coming at them. Somewhere in the opposing force, Le Maitre and Rutherford were riding, but the dun-colored horse coming most directly at Sinclair was ridden by Sergeant Hatch, a superb horseman in his own right and a veteran of the India campaigns. Hatch held the reins down low, a sign of confidence in his ability to control his mount, and his saber was held steadily aloft. He would pass, Sinclair judged, to his left, which meant they would be exchanging blows while pivoting in their saddles.

Sinclair held his legs tight to the sides of the horse as the turf exploded under the horses' hooves, and now he could even make out Hatch's face—the man was grinning, showing off his white teeth and thick moustache, in a face made permanently tan by years in the Punjab sun. The commanding officers, most of whom had never seen combat, often disdained the "India men"—men who had not been able to purchase higher commissions and who had actually served in the Gwalior Campaign, or fought alongside the Bengal Light Cavalry in battles at Punniar or Ferozeshah—but to Sinclair it was an admirable, and enviable, thing. To have seen combat! To have engaged, and killed, an enemy soldier! What could be grander than that?

Hatch was bearing down on him now—with all the joy of a veteran soldier about to teach a neophyte, in gold braid and cherry-colored trousers, a lesson or two about the manly art of war. He screamed, "Huzzah!" as their horses nearly collided, and his wooden sword whirled in the air. Sinclair's went up to meet it, but the force of the blow made his sword and his arm, too, shudder all the way to the shoulder. The clatter of the wood caused the horses to whinny and buck in fear, but Sinclair was able to keep control of Ajax using the pressure of his own legs and one firm hand on the reins. Hatch's horse bared its teeth, as if it, too, had lessons to teach, and Ajax pulled his head away. Hatch leaned back in his saddle and aimed another blow, this time his blade sliding down the length of Sinclair's sword with a deadly scratching noise, stopping just short of the handle guard.

The horses bumped sides, like rolling battleships, and parted. But Hatch wheeled around behind, and as Sinclair twisted in his seat, the saber flew again; Sinclair ducked and felt the top of his helmet knocked askew. The strap suddenly jerked off his chin, and the hat tumbled down into the melee of hooves. Hatch's horse trotted in front of Ajax, and Hatch himself taunted Sinclair by tapping the tip of his sword on the baldric from which his opponent's empty scabbard hung.

"Dance, my Russian bear," Hatch said, pretending to treat him like their foreign foe. "Dance!"

But Sinclair was in no mood for jokes, or ridicule. While all around him, other soldiers wheeled and clashed and battled, he touched his spurs to Ajax's left flank, and the horse moved forward; without his helmet on, Sinclair could actually see better, and as Hatch prepared for Sinclair to come to his right, Sinclair tugged on the reins and Ajax immediately altered his course. Sinclair swung his sword, and Hatch had just enough time to fend off the blow. But rather than drawing back, Sinclair struck again, the blow glancing off the edge of Hatch's saber and nearly taking off the man's nose. The dun-colored horse neighed and kicked out. Hatch reared back in his saddle, virtually standing in his stirrups, to get out of reach of another swing, and when Sinclair had passed, he drove his horse headfirst into Ajax's flanks. Before the horse could turn, or Sinclair could right himself in the saddle, Hatch had looped his reins on his pommel and with his hand now free reached out and grabbed Sinclair by the fur collar of his pelisse, dragging him off his horse altogether. Sinclair slid down the horse's flanks, his equipment clanking, his shoulder harness slipping loose, and thumped down onto the broken soil, rolling free as nimbly as he could of the flying hooves all around him. There was dirt in his mouth, and the remnants of his helmet were crushed flat.

The bugler sounded an end to the conflict, and as the combatants separated, some laughing, others licking their imagined wounds, Sinclair looked around; three or four other men were also lying in the dirt, one with a bloody or broken nose, another with a gash in his leg from a caught spur. All looked less than pleased with themselves. As Sinclair struggled onto all fours—his cherry trousers sporting a great hole in one knee—he saw a pair of black boots striding up and saw a gnarled, brown hand extended.

"You can't always expect your enemy to fight fair," Sergeant Hatch said, helping to lift Sinclair off the ground. He bent down, picked up the black brim of Sinclair's helmet, knocked the dust off it, and ceremoniously handed what was left of it to him. "But that was a fine bit of riding—you held your horse well."

"Not well enough, apparently."

Hatch laughed, and though he was probably no more than eight or nine years older than Sinclair, his face folded itself into a thousand tiny brown lines, reminding Sinclair of a parchment map, and making it very hard for Sinclair to hold a grudge.

"We India men," he said, boldly appropriating what was generally considered a slur, "are so used to fighting scoundrels that we've learned to fight like 'em." He paused, and the smile left his face. "Which is why you must, too."

Sinclair was mildly surprised—he was so unaccustomed to hearing anything but the most high-minded sentiments about warfare, espoused by officers drawn from the aristocracy and whose battle experience was generally nil, that to listen to such advice seemed almost treasonous in itself. War was regarded as a courtly game, played by an elaborate set of rules that all gentlemen adhered to, whatever the cost. But here was this battle-hardened veteran, telling him that it was a struggle with brutes who would just as soon manhandle you off your horse than engage in proper swordplay.

As they led their mounts off the field, Sergeant Hatch offered a few more pointers on the most recent theory of equitation, presented by Captain Nolan of the 15th Hussars—"If your horse kicks at the spur, it's a sign your weight is too far forward; if he capers, it means the weight is too much on the haunches"—and they were waiting in file to pass through the gate when a rider, Corporal Cobb, the flanks of his horse streaming with sweat, charged up to the fence, waving a sheaf of papers at the lancers.

"They've come!" he shouted, his horse rearing back on his hind legs. "The orders from the War Office!"

The men stopped in their tracks.

The corporal gained control of his mount, then rising in his saddle to make himself better seen and heard, announced that "By order of Lord Raglan, Commander in Chief of the British Army of the East, the 17th Duke of Cambridge's Own Lancers shall depart on the tenth of August, aboard Her Majesty's Ships *Neptune* and *Henry Wilson*, for the port of Constantinople; there, under the supervisory command of Lieutenant-General, Lord Lucan, they shall aid in the taking of Sebastopol."

There was more to the announcement, and Cobb went on reading, but Sinclair could hear nothing of it over the cheers and hollering of his fellow dragoons. Many of the men threw their helmets into the air, others brandished their wooden swords; several shot off a round on their pistols, frightening the horses. Sinclair, too, felt his blood racing in his veins. This was it, at last! He was going to war. All the drilling, and training, and mucking about in the barracks, was finally going to come to something! He was going to go to the Crimea and help rescue Turkey from the depredations of the Czar. He thought of a cartoon he'd seen in the paper that morning—it showed the British lion in a bobby's hat, tapping the rampaging Russian bear on the shoulder with a nightstick and saying, "Now, now, I shall have no more of that!" He heard himself shouting, too, and saw Frenchie astride the fence, leading a dozen men in a raucous chorus of "Rule, Britannia, Britannia, rule the waves!" He turned to Sergeant Hatch to clap him on the back, but stopped short when he saw his face.

Unlike all the others around him, Hatch was not exulting. He did not look afraid, or reluctant in any way, but he did not look to be champing at the bit, either. He had a half smile on his lips as he surveyed the pandemonium around him, and in his eyes there was a serious, even faraway expression. It was almost as if he could see their destination, and perhaps their fate, in his mind's eye, and Sinclair's own spirits suddenly grew more sober. Still, he said, "It's a great day, Sergeant Hatch, is it not?" and Hatch nodded, and placed a hand on his shoulder. •

"You'll never forget this day," he said, in a tone more solemn than it was jubilant.

"Bri-tons," Frenchie and his chorus were singing out, "never, never, never will be slaves!"

Another hand seized Sinclair by the elbow, and when he turned it was Rutherford, his muttonchops fairly bristling with the news. His face was red with shouting, and he could only shake Sinclair with delight.

"By God," he sputtered at last. "By God we'll show 'em a thing or two!"

And Sinclair immediately fell in with his mood. He turned away from Sergeant Hatch and threw himself again into the happy madness. He deliberately led Ajax off, holding tight to his reins; he wanted to slag off any doubts or hesitation. This was a time for celebration, for camaraderie, and he wanted no part of warnings or admonitions. Hatch had reminded him of a poem, by that fellow Coleridge, the one where the wedding guest is stopped by an ancient mariner, who insists on telling him a dire tale. Sinclair wanted no dire tales that day—he wanted the promise of glory and the opportunity of valor. And finally, it appeared, he would most certainly have them!

But the tenth of August was only two days away, and there would be a great deal to do in the time remaining. No doubt all their uniforms and weapons and tack would have to be organized, polished, cleaned, and inspected; their mounts would have to be readied for the long voyage aboard the navy frigates—or would the army commandeer a fleet of the new steamers, to make the trip in much less time?—and affairs in London, of any nature, would have to be wound up, too.

Which meant he must consider how to break the news to Eleanor. Indeed, he was due at her boardinghouse that afternoon. He had promised to take her to Hyde Park, where the Crystal Palace had so recently stood. He had hoped to make a day of it, having a stroll under the stately elms that filled the park, but unless he was sorely mistaken, his entire brigade would be confined to the barracks until their departure. He would have to make his exit right away and hope to be back again before he was missed in all the commotion.

He took Ajax to the stables and once he was in his stall, made sure to give him a double ration of oats and hay. Running his hand down the white blaze on his muzzle, he said, "Shall we cover ourselves in glory?" Ajax lowered his chestnut head as if assenting. Sinclair patted him down with a cloth to wipe away the sweat from his strong, well-muscled neck, then left the stables by the rear gate, where he had less chance of being seen.

He'd have liked to change his shirt, or at least wash up a bit, but the risk of being forestalled was too great. He hurried to the Savoy Hotel, where he knew he'd find a hansom cab or two waiting; he hired the first one he spotted, and called out his destination while leaping into the seat. The coachman flicked his whip and the carriage took off through the busy, dirty streets at a brisk pace, while Sinclair caught the first deep breath he'd had since hearing the news and debated how he would relay it all to Eleanor. He'd hardly had time, for that matter, to digest it himself.

His father, the earl, would probably be pleased; it would place Sinclair out of reach of the gambling dens and music halls and other expensive amusements of London, and, if he didn't get his head blown off, return him to England with a reputation as a soldier instead of a wastrel. But ah, if only the earl knew where Sinclair was headed at present—to the humble quarters shared by a pair of impecunious nurses, on the top floor of a dilapidated boardinghouse. It would make the old man shudder, that much Sinclair knew, and if he were to be completely honest with himself, he would have to admit that he derived a certain enjoyment from that fact. The earl had been forever parading one plain aristocratic lady after another past him, hoping that Sinclair would find one of them sufficiently enticing, but Sinclair was a man who had always known what he wanted, instantly, and what he wanted was Eleanor Ames. He'd known it the moment he saw her closing the hospital shutters.

When the cab arrived on Eleanor's street, Sinclair directed the driver to the boardinghouse, then tossed him some coins while stepping down. "If you wait, you'll have the fare back again!" he cried.

The front steps were cracked, and the vestibule door had no lock. As Sinclair entered, he could hear a dog forlornly barking behind one flimsy door and a man bellowing about something at the end of the front hall. There was a musty smell on the stairs, which grew worse as he ascended, and as there was only one small window on each landing, it also grew darker. His boots made the floorboards creak, and as he approached Eleanor and Moira's door, he saw some feeble sunlight spill into the narrow hall. Moira was holding the door open a few inches, waiting to see who it was, but once she had ascertained that it was Sinclair, she seemed to crane her neck to look behind him.

"Good afternoon," she said, the disappointment evident in her voice. "You've come all on your own, then?"

She must have been hoping he'd bring Captain Rutherford along; Sinclair knew that they had seen each other on several occasions, though he also knew that Moira set greater store by those meetings than did Rutherford.

"Eleanor's in the parlor."

From previous occasions, Sinclair knew that the parlor simply referred to the tiny portion of the room that faced the street, and which was separated from the remainder of the room by a modesty curtain concealing the bed that Eleanor and Moira had to share. Eleanor was standing by the window—had she been looking down, waiting to see him arrive?—in the new pale yellow frock that he had, after some cajoling, persuaded her to accept. Each time they'd met, she'd worn the same simple forest-green dress, and though it was becoming on her, he longed to see her in something more gay and stylish. Though he knew nothing of ladies' fashion, he did know that the bodice of the new dress was more generously cut, allowing for a glimpse of neck and shoulder, and the sleeves were not so puffed out as to obscure the line of her slender arms. He had been walking with Eleanor down Marylebone Street one afternoon, and he had seen her eye linger on the dress in the store window. He sent a messenger the next day to purchase it and deliver it to her at the hospital.

She turned toward him, blushing but pleased to let him see her in her new finery, and even in the sooty light of the London afternoon, she looked radiant. "I don't know how you knew," she said, gesturing at the dress. A border of white lace lay like new-fallen snow across her bosom.

"And we only had to take it in by an inch or two," Moira said, bustling about behind the curtain. "She's a regular dressmaker's form, this 'un." She reappeared, gathering a shawl around her ample shoulders and carrying a mesh sack. "I'm off to the market," she said, "and shan't be back for at least the half hour." She all but winked at them before closing the door behind her.

Sinclair and Eleanor stood alone, still somewhat awkwardly. Sinclair wanted to take her in his arms, and beautiful as the dress was, divest her of it as quickly as possible . . . but he would not do that. Despite the inequality of their positions in society, he treated her as he would any of the wellborn young ladies that he met at the country-house balls or formal dinners in the city. For his more base appetites, there was always the Salon d'Aphrodite.

But instead of coming to him, Eleanor remained where she was, studying his face. "I fear I haven't thanked you for the dress yet," she finally said. "It's a very beautiful present."

"On you, it is," Sinclair said.

"Would you like to sit down," she said, indicating the two hard-backed wooden chairs that filled the entire space allotted for the parlor, "or shall we go out?"

"I'm afraid I haven't much time for either," he said, fidgeting in place. "Truth be told, I'm in breach of orders just being here."

———————

At that confession, Eleanor's curiosity immediately turned to concern. She had already noted that he was full to bursting, with what she did not know, and she also observed that he was dressed in uniform, with dirt caked on his boots and his complexion ruddy with exertion.

Had he broken a military regulation of some kind? She had guessed, over the past few weeks, that the young lieutenant was no stickler for protocol (hadn't he shown her, a woman, the inner sanctums of the Longchamps Club?), but she did not imagine him committing some serious wrong. Her fears were allayed only by the broad smile that flitted around his lips.

"Why? What orders are you defying?"

Sinclair clearly couldn't hold it in any longer, and he suddenly told her the news—the joyous news—that his regiment had been called into action.

And Eleanor found herself smiling, too, and feeling his excitement, as if it were contagious. For some time, the streets of the city had been filled with demonstrations, some protesting the march to war, but others loudly beating the drum for it. The papers had been filled with terrible stories of the atrocities visited upon the helpless Turks, and the dangers of the Russian fleet sweeping into the Mediterranean and posing a threat to the long-standing British supremacy on the seas. Conscription gangs had been tromping through the backstreets and alleyways, rounding up any reasonably able-bodied men—and some who were not—for Her Majesty's infantry. Even the boy who tended the coal bin and stoked the furnace at the hospital had been enlisted.

"When will you be going?" Eleanor asked, and when he told her, the full impact of the news suddenly struck her. If he was leaving the day after next, and he was already in contravention of the orders to remain at the barracks and camp, then this would be their last encounter, their last few minutes together before he sailed for the Crimea. The thought occurred to her, despite everything that she felt had passed between them in the previous weeks, despite any bond that might have been formed, that she truly might never see him again. And it wasn't only the dreaded prospect of war, and the inevitable chance of death, that terrified her; it was also the knowledge that had haunted her from the night she'd attended to his wounded arm. The knowledge that they did indeed inhabit utterly different worlds, and that if it weren't for that unlikely encounter, their paths would never have crossed. Sinclair, after his time overseas, might not return to London at all—he might go back to his family's estate in Nottinghamshire. (Although he was still quite circumspect about his background, she had gathered enough about it, from comments dropped by Le Maitre or Captain Rutherford, to know that it was rather impressive.) And even if he did return to London, would he choose to pick up again with a penniless nurse rather than the grand ladies who moved in his own social circles? Would this little adventure of his—and that was how she sometimes thought of it, in the darkest part of the night, when Moira's constant turning in the bed kept her awake—would it still hold sufficient appeal for him to overrule all questions of practicality and decorum?

As if reading her mind, Sinclair said, "I'll write to you as soon as I can."

And Eleanor suddenly had a vision of herself, sitting in the chair by the sooty window, holding a letter, creased and worn by its long journey from the east.

"And I will write to you," she replied. "Every day."

Sinclair took a half step forward, as did she, and suddenly they were in each other's arms, her cheek laid flat against the rough gold braid that adorned the front of his uniform. He smelled of dirt and sweat and his beloved horse, Ajax; he'd escorted her once to the regimental stables and let her feed the horse a handful of sugar. She clung to Sinclair for several minutes, neither of them saying a word. They didn't need to. And when they kissed, it held a bittersweet and valedictory note.

"I must go," he said, gently disengaging.

She opened the door for him and watched as he hurried down the steps without looking back, the thunder of his boots echoing up the stairwell. If only opportunity had allowed, she thought, if only he'd had just a little more time, she would have liked him to see her outside, in the afternoon light, wearing the new yellow dress.

CHAPTER NINETEEN

December 9, 5 p.m.

AS MIGHT HAVE BEEN EXPECTED, news of the amazing underwater discovery had threatened to sweep through the camp like
wildfire, so Murphy—notified by walkie-talkie from the dive hut—
had immediately imposed an executive order. Michael heard him
barking instructions at Calloway to admit no one else onto the ice,
or anywhere near the hut. He also ordered everyone in earshot to
zip their lips until further notice.

"Wait for Danzig and the dogs to get there," he said before signing off.

By the time the ice block was safely stowed on the back of a
sledge, Danzig and his dog team had pulled to a stop fifty yards off.
The huskies lay down on the snow and ice and watched the proceedings warily.

"Jesus H. Christ," Danzig said, striding up to the sledge and
marveling openly at the thing—the frozen woman—contained in
the ice. He paced slowly around the ponderous block, and Michael

could tell he was already making some quick calculations about how best to transport it.

"That there, mates," Calloway said, "is the weirdest thing I've ever seen come up, and let me tell you, I've seen plenty of weird stuff."

"No shit, Sherlock," said Franklin, who'd been assisting on the dive.

Michael could barely believe they'd done it. He had hastily taken off his diving gear, wrapped himself in more layers of dry clothing than ever before, and was sipping from a thermos of hot tea; still, he had the occasional shiver, and he knew he was suffering from a touch of the predictable hypothermia.

Lawson asked Danzig if they should call for a Spryte, or if he thought his dogs could pull the block back to camp.

Danzig, who always wore a good-luck charm of walrus teeth around his neck, laid one huge hand on the ice and with the other rubbed his chin. "Once we get it started, we can do it," he declared. There was little that Danzig thought his dogs couldn't do, and he was always looking for ways to prove that modern technology had nothing on the reliable, old-fashioned methods that had been good enough for Roald Amundsen and Robert Falcon Scott.

While Danzig took care of unhooking his dogs from the one sledge and attaching them to the other, Michael rubbed his wrist, where the dry-suit seal had leaked. It ached the way a bad sprain would. Franklin and Calloway were still gawking at the woman in the ice—and when one of them laughed, and made some coarse joke about waking Sleeping Beauty with a kiss she'd never forget— Michael took a tarp from the dogsled and threw it over the ice. Franklin looked at him oddly for stopping the show, but as Michael secured the tarp with a couple of pitons, Danzig glanced at him knowingly, and asked, "Did the chief tell you anything about where he wanted to put her?" He sounded vaguely like a funeral director asking a family member about the recently deceased.

"Not a word." For Michael, it was strange even to be asked. He wasn't a scientist, and he wasn't even one of the grunts. He occupied some middle ground, some ill-defined territory, and yet he had already come to be regarded as the rightful advocate for the woman retrieved from the deep.

"Well, she shouldn't be moved directly inside," Danzig said, thinking out loud, "because if the thaw was too rapid, it might do some damage."

Yes, Michael could see the wisdom of that.

"So it might be a good idea to keep her in the core bin, behind the glaciology lab. Betty and Tina could even use some of their tools to cut away the excess ice."

"Sure," Michael said, "that sounds fine." He was glad to have someone there who was thinking more clearly than he was.

There was a commotion among the dogs, and Danzig hollered, "Hey!" and moved off to put a stop to it. The huskies were a rambunctious lot—Michael had already seen them in action more than once—but usually they obeyed any command as soon as it was given. Only this time, several of them were struggling at their leads, backing away from the block of ice, and their pack leader, Kodiak—a massive dog with eyes like big blue marbles—was actually barking and snarling. Danzig was using a firm but even voice, coupled with hand signals, to quiet the dogs down, but even he looked surprised at the rebellion.

"Kodiak!" Danzig finally shouted, repeatedly shaking the dog's lead. "Down!"

The dog stayed on his feet, barking madly.

"Down! Kodiak—down!"

Danzig had to put a hand on the dog's squirming neck and press him toward the ice. Once down, he held him there, impressing his authority. The other dogs, though still whining, gradually took the cue and quieted down. Danzig unsnarled some of the harnesses and leads, then stepped onto the back of the sledge, and shouted, "Hike!"

The dogs jerked forward to get the sledge sliding, but not with their customary exuberance, and the sledge hardly budged. Two or three of them were still trying to look behind them, as if afraid of something coming up close behind, and Danzig had to snap the reins and shout his orders again and again.

Michael wondered if the load was simply too great.

"Hike! Hike!" Danzig shouted, and the dogs again leapt forward, this time getting the runners sliding on the ice. As the sledge gained momentum, it went more smoothly, until the dozen huskies were racing in unison, and the slab of ice, with its frozen cargo, was on its way back toward the base. While Calloway closed up the dive hut, Michael hitched a ride on Franklin's snowmobile, and they followed the barking dogs back to camp.

No matter how long Michael stood there, head down, the hot water running off his scalp and down his body, he felt like there was still some part of him, deep inside, that still harbored another shiver or two. When the steam in the shower room had achieved epic proportions and he could hardly see his hand in front of his face, he shut off the water and rubbed himself down briskly with the fresh towels that were always in abundant supply. He had to take special care with his shoulder, the one he had dislocated in the Cascades. It still gave him trouble from time to time, and diving in such heavy gear, in frigid waters, hadn't helped. He used the towel to wipe clear a section of the fogged mirror, then disentangled some of his long black hair. He'd taken care of nearly everything before leaving Tacoma, but getting a haircut had slipped his mind. So it was looking more shaggy than usual. He could, he supposed, get it cut—one of the base personnel doubled as a barber—but it didn't seem like anyone else at Point Adélie cared a whole lot about personal appearance. Betty and Tina stomped around in men's clothes, with their blond hair hastily gathered into loose clumps, and most of the men looked like they'd just stepped out of a cave. Nearly all of them had beards, moustaches, even long woolly sideburns that hadn't been seen since the Civil War. Ponytails were popular too, especially among the balding beakers like Ackerley, the botanist who was so seldom seen outside his lab that he had earned the nickname "Spook." As for Danzig, in addition to his necklace of walrus teeth, he wore a bracelet of bones and a pair of pants he'd made himself out of reindeer hide. Michael was reminded of a joke he'd heard from a single woman he'd met in a bar when he was on assignment in Alaska: "The odds are good," she'd said, surveying all the men, "but the goods are odd."

Before heading over to the commons—man, could he use a hot meal about now—he ducked into the SAT-phone room and called his editor, on his home line. In the background, he could hear a basketball game on TV, but when Gillespie knew it was Michael, and not some phone solicitor, the game went off immediately and he said, "You okay? Everything okay?"

Michael took a second to savor what he was about to tell him, then said, "Better than okay. Are you sitting down?"

"No, and now I don't plan to. What?"

And then Michael told him, in as calm and deliberate a manner as possible—he didn't want Gillespie thinking he'd gone off his rocker at the South Pole—that they had found a body, maybe even two, frozen in an iceberg, and that, furthermore, they had recovered them. Gillespie had remained silent the whole time that Michael had been talking and he stayed silent now, too. Michael had to finally say, "Are you there?"

"You're not joking?"

"Not joking."

"This is for real?"

Michael heard a timer go off on a microwave.

"Totally. And did I mention that I'm the one who made the discovery?"

It sounded like Gillespie had dropped the phone on a counter. Michael could dimly make out, through the static, a series of whoops and hollers. When Gillespie picked up the receiver again, he said, "Oh my God. This is phenomenal. And you've got photos?"

"Yes, and I'll get more."

"Michael, I'm telling you, if this is for real—"

"It is," Michael assured him. "I saw the girl with my own eyes."

"Then this is going to get us a national magazine award! If we handle this right, we could triple our subscription base. You could go on *Sixty Minutes*. You could get a book deal, and maybe even sell some movie rights."

He went on for another minute or so, during which time the reception occasionally broke down, and Michael had to wait patiently for it to return. But when the line cleared, and he could explain that the phone was operational only for certain hours every day and that someone else was waiting to use it, Gillespie let him go; it sounded like he needed a stiff drink, anyway. And Michael was going to keel over if he didn't get to the commons.

Once there, he filled his plate with chili con carne, steam coming off it, and corn bread, and sat down with Charlotte Barnes. She nodded approvingly at his plate, and said, "Follow that up with some hot cherry cobbler."

"I just might," Michael said, digging in at last. "I haven't seen

Darryl all day. I hope he's not sulking because you wouldn't let him dive today."

"No, I think he got over that pretty quick. He's been holed up in his lab."

Michael picked up a piece of corn bread, slathered it with chili, and shoved the whole thing in his mouth.

"I do want you to raise your core temperature," Charlotte said, "but please don't make me do the Heimlich maneuver. It's really pretty gross."

Michael slowed down, and when he had finished chewing and swallowing, he said, nonchalantly, "So, have you heard about the dive today?" He wasn't sure if Murphy had included her in the inner circle yet and didn't want to give anything away.

Charlotte sipped her coffee, and nodded. "As chief medical officer at the base, he thought I should know...everything."

"I'm glad he did," Michael said, relieved, "but I don't think there's much you'll be able to do for her."

"He wasn't worried about her," Charlotte said. "He was worried about you. He was afraid you might want to talk to me about it and I'd think you'd flipped out."

"I haven't, have I?" Michael said, and Charlotte shrugged.

"Too soon to tell. But you still think there's two of them? One in front and one in back?"

"I couldn't tell for sure—it could be her cloak, or maybe just some kind of shadow or occlusion in the ice. We left a thick slab of ice in back, just to be on the safe side, so once Betty and Tina have carved away some of the excess, we'll finally know one way or the other."

Behind Charlotte, Michael saw a hand wildly waving. He tilted to one side and saw Darryl, with his own tray in hand, making his way across the commons. He plopped himself down on the bench next to Charlotte, and said to Michael in a conspiratorial tone, "Congratulations! I just visited Sleeping Beauty in the core bin, and I can report that she is resting quite peacefully."

Michael felt a vague discomfort—not only at the jocularity, but at the very notion of her being asleep. He couldn't forget that Kristin's parents thought she, too, was simply sleeping.

"But you know," Darryl said, as he spread a whole bowl's worth of grated parmesan over a plate of spaghetti, "once Betty and Tina have done what they can do with the trimming, the best way to preserve the specimen would be to move it to the marine biology lab." He said it so casually that Michael could tell he'd been thinking about it long and hard.

"Why?" Michael asked.

Darryl shrugged, again too offhandedly. "It needs to be thawed slowly, and ideally in local seawater. Otherwise, you could inflict some damage, or it could disintegrate. I could empty out the aquarium tank—those cod aren't even my experiment—and lift the partitions. Then we'd be able to get the whole block of ice, or whatever remains of it, into a cool bath. We could melt it down very slowly, under controlled laboratory conditions."

Michael looked at Charlotte for her expert opinion—after all, at least she was a doctor—but she seemed as much at sea as he was. "But why are you asking me, anyway?" Michael finally said. "Shouldn't all this be Murphy O'Connor's call?"

"He just runs the place," Darryl replied, "and generally tries to stay clear of all the scientific issues. And like it or not," Darryl said, raising a forkful of hanging spaghetti, "you're Prince Charming in this scenario. How do *you* think we should bring her back? With a kiss?"

It was hard for Michael to think of himself as Prince Charming in this, or any, scenario, but he *was* starting to feel that if anyone was going to protect Sleeping Beauty's interests, whatever those might be, it might just as well be him.

"If you think that's what's best," Michael said, "I guess I do, too."

Darryl, a bit of spaghetti dangling from his lip, looked very pleased. "Good call," he said, sucking up the loose strand. "Especially in view of what I'm going to show you both after dinner."

Michael and Charlotte exchanged a look.

"I haven't told anyone else yet," he added, "and I'm not sure if I plan to. We'll see."

With the mystery sufficiently deepened, Michael and Charlotte simply had to wait for Darryl to finish his meal. Michael filled the time with cherry cobbler, as did Charlotte, who followed hers with a decaf cappuccino. "Six months from now," she said, pouring a sugar packet into her cup, "they're gonna have to fly in a cargo plane just to carry my fat ass back to civilization."

Later, in the marine lab, Darryl flew around the place setting things up while Michael and Charlotte stripped off their parkas and gloves. Even the short trips from one module to another required protection from the elements; thirty seconds outside and exposed skin could be frost-nipped.

Darryl dragged two more stools over to the counter, where a microscope with a dual eyepiece and a video monitor stood. "I've got to say one thing for the National Science Foundation," he said. "They don't skimp. This microscope, for instance, is an Olympus CX, with fiber-optic technology. The video monitor's got five-hundred-line resolution." He gazed at the equipment with genuine fondness. "I wish I had this kind of setup back home."

Charlotte, who could barely stifle a yawn, exchanged a look with Michael, and Darryl must have caught it. Like a magician pulling a rabbit out of a hat, he produced the wine bottle, the cork sticking up from the top, and said, "Dr. Barnes, perhaps you would care to do the honors."

Twisting the cork back out, she said, "I hope you're not planning to drink this stuff."

"Not after you've seen what I have."

With another flourish, he handed her a clean pipette and said, "Could I ask you to remove a few drops of the liquid from inside this bottle?"

Both Michael and Charlotte wrinkled their noses at the smell from the bottle, but she did as she was asked.

"Now, leave a drop on one end of this slide."

The moment she had let one drop of the viscous fluid touch the slide, Darryl expertly drew another slide across it, leaving a deep purple smear that was thicker at one end and thinner at the other. Then he took an eye dropper and let several drops of alcohol fall on top of it. "In case you were wondering," he said to Michael while closely attending to his work, "we're fixing the smear." He glanced up at Charlotte. "Remind you of med school?"

"That was too long ago," she said.

He continued to narrate the proceedings as he let the slide dry, then applied something called Giemsa stain. "Without the stain," he explained, "many of the features would be impossible to see."

"Features of what?" Charlotte asked, a note of irritation creeping into her voice. "Merlot? Cabernet sauvignon?"

"You'll see," Darryl said.

Even Michael was getting antsy. It had been a very long day, his wrist still ached from the cold, and all he wanted to do was get into bed with the covers over his head. He needed time to process what he had done, and what he had seen, and he knew that he was starting to make some unhealthy connections between Kristin back home and the so-called Sleeping Beauty here. He knew it, but he still couldn't stop it. Maybe all he needed was a solid eight hours in the sack.

But Darryl was still chattering away, about stains and smears and something else, called Canada balsam, and Michael finally had to interrupt the flow long enough to say, "Okay, Darryl, enough with the hocus-pocus. You ready yet?"

"Not really. If this were being done by the book, we'd first let it set overnight."

"Fine," Michael said, starting to get up, "then we'll come back tomorrow."

"No, no, wait." Darryl mounted the slide under the microscope, and after examining it himself and adjusting the focus several times, he got up off his stool and invited Charlotte to have a look. Wearily, she moved over, bent her head down, then stayed very still.

Darryl appeared gratified.

She fiddled with the focus knob again, then finally leaned back, a puzzled look on her face.

"If I didn't know better," she began, but Darryl put up a hand to stop her.

"Let Michael have a look first."

Michael now assumed the center seat, and when he looked down through the binocular eyepiece, he saw a pink, particle-filled field; most of the field was dotted with free-floating circles. Some of the circles were round and fairly uniform in size and shape, though slightly depressed in the middle, like cushions that had been sat on. Others were larger, grainier, and more misshapen. Michael was no scientist, but for this you didn't have to be.

"Okay," he said, "it's blood." He looked up from the microscope. "You put blood in the wine bottle. Why?"

"Oy," Darryl exclaimed, throwing up his hands. "You *were*

underwater too long. I didn't put anything in the wine bottle. Or on the slide. That's why I had you two come here and do the experiment for yourself. To see what I saw. That wine bottle, as you call it, is filled with blood. And I'll bet that the others that came up in that trunk are filled with it, too."

Neither Michael nor Charlotte knew what to say.

"The perfect little circles you saw," Darryl went on, "are red blood cells—erythrocytes. The bigger ones are leukocytes, or white cells. Some of the tiny matter you see between them is what we call neutrophils."

"Those are a kind of phagocyte, right?" Charlotte said. "They eat bacteria and die."

"Exactly—med school is coming back to you, I see."

"Don't be a smart aleck."

"But there are a lot more neutrophils than there ought to be," Darryl added.

He let that sink in, but when no one jumped to the next step, he said, "Which means that before this blood ever went into the bottle, it was tainted."

"How? By what?" Michael asked.

"Offhand," Darryl said, "I'd say it came from seriously sick or injured people. People with wounds, perhaps, that were seeping pus."

Suddenly Michael understood the especially putrid odor from the bottle—the "wine" wasn't only ancient blood, it was polluted ancient blood. But why would it ever have been bottled up and transported, like treasure, in a chest?

"Forgive me," Charlotte said, "but it's been a long day. What are you suggesting, Darryl? That some ship, from God knows when, was carrying a cargo of bad blood, all neatly packed away in trunks, to the South Pole?"

"It's unlikely the ship was actually heading for Antarctica," Darryl said. "It was probably driven off course, and who knows how long the ice has been moving the debris southward? Ice moves, you know."

"But why?" Michael asked. "What possible use could there have been for it, anywhere?"

Darryl scratched his head, leaving a tuft of red hair sticking out on one side. "You've got me there. Bad blood is of no use to anyone, unless it was being used in some sort of inoculation experiment."

"Aboard ship?" Michael said.

"Hundreds of years ago?" Charlotte chimed in.

Darryl threw up his hands in surrender. "Don't look at me, kids! I don't have the answers, either. But I do find it hard to believe that the bottle, the trunk, and the body—or bodies, if it comes to that—aren't all connected somehow."

"I'll give you that," Michael said. "Otherwise, it would be just about the most amazing coincidence in maritime history."

Charlotte looked to be in agreement, too.

"And once we're able to do so," Darryl said, "I think it would be worth seeing if I could draw a viable blood sample from Sleeping Beauty."

"To prove what?" Michael asked.

Darryl shrugged. "A match?"

"With what?" Michael said, in some exasperation; he felt like he wasn't following. "With diseased blood from a bottle? Are you saying she was saving her own old blood in bottles, as a keepsake?"

"Or is it something else?" Charlotte put in. "Are you suggesting that she was keeping a ready supply of this stuff on hand for some weird medicinal purpose?"

"Sometimes, in science," Darryl said, looking from one to the other and trying to calm the waters, "you know just what you're looking for, and you know where to find it. Other times, you don't know, but you just keep turning things up and following every lead."

"Sounds like some strange leads to me," Michael said, feeling oddly defensive about the whole thing.

"Can't argue with you there," Darryl admitted.

Charlotte blew out a breath and headed for her coat and gloves. "I'm going to bed," she said, "and I'd advise both of you to do the same."

But Michael suddenly felt almost too weary to get up. He stayed where he was, studying the mysterious black bottle.

"Michael," Charlotte said, as she zipped up her coat, "get some sleep. Doctor's orders." Turning to Darryl, she said, "And you, put a cork in it."

Darryl gestured at the bottle.

"You know what I mean."

CHAPTER TWENTY

Early September, 1854

THE HORSES. It was the terrible toll taken on the horses that drove
Lieutenant Copley nearly mad.

His beautiful Ajax, along with eighty-five others, had been
driven down into the hold of Her Majesty's Ship *Henry Wilson*—a
small, dark, and unbearably foul place—where almost no advance
preparations had been made. There were no stalls constructed, no
head collars, only tethering ropes, and even on a calm sea, the
horses brushed up against each other, stepping on their neighbors'
hooves, struggling to lift their heads clear of the herd. But once the
ships of the British fleet had hit the gales in the Bay of Biscay, the
horses went wild with fear. Sinclair, along with many of the other
cavalry officers—the ones who were not laid up with fevers or seasickness—were down in the hold, standing at their horses' heads,
trying desperately to calm and control them. But it was not possible.
Each time the vessel rolled, the poor panicked beasts were pitched
forward against the manger, whinnying in terror and stamping their
feet on the creaking, wet boards. Cascades of water flooded down

from the hatches, rivers of it sloshed around their legs, and every time one of the horses fell, it was the devil's own business to get him righted again. When Ajax went down, tumbling in a heap atop Winslow's horse, it took several soldiers and sailors to get them separated and standing once more. Sergeant Hatch, the India Man, seemed to be down in the hold at all times—Sinclair wondered if he ever slept or went up on deck for a breath of air that didn't stink of dung and blood and moldering hay—but even he was unable to stem the losses. Every night horses died—of broken bones, panic, and heat prostration (there was almost no ventilation belowdecks)—and were unceremoniously thrown overboard the next day. All the way to the Mediterranean, the British fleet had left a trail of bloated, floating carcasses in its wake.

And Sinclair, though he knew he was only a young unproven lieutenant, could not help but wonder why the army had not requisitioned steamers to make the voyage. From what Rutherford had told him (and Rutherford's father had been a lord of the admiralty under the Duke of Wellington), a steamer could make a trip in ten to twelve days that it would take a sailing ship a month or more to do. Even if it had taken a fortnight to round up enough steamships, so much of this appalling damage could have been avoided, and the troops—with their horses, in decent condition—could have arrived on the Turkish shores, ready to do battle, sooner than they would arrive now.

But no such thoughts appeared to have occurred to the command, nor to the throngs of onlookers who had attended the army's departure. When Sinclair marched aboard the transports, in the company of the Light Brigade, the Heavy Brigade, the 60th Rifles, and the 11th Hussars, he too had been caught up in the gay atmosphere at the docks. The war, everyone believed, would be so brief that it might be over before some of them had even had the chance to use their lance or sword or rifle; the Russians, it was said, were such a lackluster fighting force that most of them had to be forced onto the field at gunpoint. Le Maitre had told Sinclair that the Russian infantry's rifles were dummies, made of wood, like the swords the brigade used in its field exercises. As a result, many of the English officers had received permission to bring their wives along on the mission, and the ladies were outfitted in their finest, most colorful dresses. Some brought their own maids and favorite horses with them. As Sinclair scanned the crowds lining the docks and quayside, searching for a spot of pale yellow, he saw cases of wine, bouquets of flowers, and straw baskets filled with hothouse fruit being brought aboard. Hundreds of people were holding pennants of the Union Jack, others were wildly waving caps and bonnets and lace handkerchiefs, and a military band was playing martial tunes. The sun was shining brightly, and he could hardly wait for the adventure before him to unfold.

"Moira tells me it's unlikely Miss Nightingale will give them leave," Captain Rutherford said, leaning on his elbows at the rail and divining what Sinclair was looking for.

Sinclair glanced at his companion, whose brow was gleaming with sweat.

"I told her that this Miss Nightingale was no patriot, then," Rutherford concluded, taking his fur pelisse from his shoulder and laying it across the rail.

Sinclair had never quite understood what bond existed between the captain and Miss Mulcahy. While his own connection to Eleanor Ames was in itself unusual—and, as anyone would have told Sinclair, held no promise in practical terms—Rutherford's attachment to the buxom, earthy nurse Mulcahy was stranger by far. Rutherford came from a very prominent family in Dorset—he was destined for a peerage—and his family would be appalled at this liaison. Yes, it was, of course, understood that cavalry officers had their pick of the ladies in town, and that they often indulged in reckless, even unwholesome, affairs, but it was also understood that the young men would eventually come to their senses, especially on the eve of a great foreign expedition. It was the perfect time, and the perfect means, to cut the cord. It was one of the signal advantages to being in the army.

But behind Rutherford's bluster, Sinclair thought he had detected an oddly sentimental streak. He was not a man comfortable in the salons to which he was regularly invited, or around women in general—Sinclair had once seen him clumsily upend a punch bowl on a young lady to whom he was being introduced. He much preferred the life of the barracks, with its bawdy talk and camaraderie, and there was something about Miss Moira Mulcahy, for all her working-class ways, that appealed to him. Indeed, if Sinclair had to hazard a guess, it was that very *lack* of refinement that appealed to him ... coupled, of course, with her bountiful bosom, always and ever on display. It occurred to Sinclair that he might be better off trying to spot an expanse of creamy flesh in the dockside mob than the new yellow dress that Eleanor might accompany Moira in.

Lord Cardigan, commander of the 11th Hussars, could be seen on horseback, in all his finery, surrounded by aides-de-camp, bellowing out orders. He was a vain, handsome man, with a full russet moustache and side-whiskers, and he rode erect in the saddle. But he was known for his hot temper and his fanatical devotion to protocol and foolish points of honor; indeed, he had created a scandal at an officers' mess, the repercussions of which haunted him still. Lord Cardigan insisted that only champagne might be served at his table, and not the black bottles of porter that many of the soldiers, particularly those who had served in India, enjoyed. When a general's aide requested Moselle, which was placed on the table in its own black bottle rather than being decanted first, Lord Cardigan mistook it for porter, exploded into a rage, and insulted a captain of the regiment. Before the affair blew over, all of London had heard about it, and laughed. Lord Cardigan could not attend the theater, or even walk his Irish wolfhounds down the streets of Brunswick Square, without hearing the occasional catcall of "black bottle!" The men under his command particularly resented it, and often fell into brawls when so taunted.

Though the 17th Lancers of the Light Brigade were nominally under the command of Lord Lucan, Cardigan's stubborn brother-in-law, Lieutenant Copley suspected that they, the hapless soldiers, were actually pawns in a bitter family rivalry.

"Here," Rutherford said, to a passing naval officer, "may I borrow that?"

The navy man, perhaps so bowled over by the richness of Rutherford's costume that he was unable to determine a particular rank, immediately relinquished the telescope he carried, and went on about his duties.

Rutherford raised the telescope and scanned the crowd, from the top of the High Street to the bottom of the loading ramps. There was the unending tramp of the soldiers' feet, the neighing and huffing of the horses, the vagrant notes of the Inniskilling anthem, played by the military band and blown out to sea on the swirling winds. An order was shouted out, relayed around the decks several times, and dozens of sailors began rounding up the stragglers, among whom quick embraces and mementoes were exchanged with family and well-wishers; the heavy ramps were sealed off, then hauled aboard the boats. Dockhands unknotted the thick mooring ropes and threw their loose ends aside. But Rutherford's search had apparently come up empty-handed.

"I shall have a word with this Florence Nightingale when next I see her," Rutherford said in a huff.

"Let me try," Sinclair said, taking the telescope in hand. He lifted it, and spotted first the sight of a horse's rump—Lord Cardigan's horse, as it happened—traveling back toward town. The great lord, scuttlebutt had it, would follow the troops later, in the more comfortable accommodations afforded by a French steamer.

But Sinclair was having no more luck than Rutherford. For a moment, he thought he saw Frenchie's lady friend, Dolly, but the size of the bonnet made it too hard to be sure. Even Frenchie had become separated from his friends in the melee, and was presumably lost somewhere on the crowded deck of the *Henry Wilson*. Sinclair saw a little boy, holding his mother's hand and smiling bravely, and another who was far more intent on trying to catch an injured sparrow that was hopping between the wheels of a commissary wagon.

More orders were shouted, and a dozen sailors scrambled up the rigging, loosing the sails and letting them unfurl with a great flapping noise. The ship creaked and groaned, like a great stiff giant coming to life, and a ribbon of brackish water now ran between it and the dock. Sinclair swung the telescope from one end of the harbor to the other, stopping once at a yellow parasol, and again at what turned out to be a yellow placard advertising a show in Drury Lane.

"I wonder when we shall see our first fight," Rutherford said. "I hope it's not some skirmish, all close quarters and no chance to use the lance properly." The lance had been a relatively recent innovation, modeled, as were their uniforms, on the Polish lancers who had so distinguished themselves at Waterloo.

Sinclair muttered his assent, while continuing the search. He was just about to give it up—the lurching and swaying of the vessel made it difficult to hold any image still—when he saw an open wagon rumble down a side alley, and two figures, one in yellow, one in a white apron, jump off its end and run toward the docks. With one hand, he held on to the railing and with the other trained the telescope on the running girls. The one in front was Eleanor, clutching her nurse's hat, and Moira, holding her skirts up and away from her ankles, lumbered behind.

The *Henry Wilson* was now a hundred yards or more from the dock, and the flag flying from its stern obscured his view. But he could tell that the girls' eyes were trained, and their steps directed, toward one of the other transports leaving the dock. Eleanor, he could see, had stopped a man in uniform, and after a few hasty words with him, she had taken Moira by the arm and turned her instead toward the dock from which the 17th Lancers' ship had just departed.

The flag rippled and snapped in the gathering sea breeze, and Sinclair shouted to Rutherford, "They're there! Coming toward the dock!"

Rutherford craned his neck over the bulwark railing, and Sinclair tucked the telescope under one arm and waved in wide, sweeping motions.

More sails cascaded down from the topmasts and the ship instantly pitched forward, gaining speed. The land was being left behind, and the people on it were being quickly reduced to specks.

Sinclair lifted the telescope one more time, and found the bright spot of yellow one last time. He willed her to look in his direction— she seemed to be staring toward the bulging sails for some reason— and just as the ship plunged into the first of the waves to skirt the breakwater, casting a mist of chilling spray over everyone on the decks, he thought she had indeed turned her green-eyed gaze toward him. Or at least he chose to think so.

The weeks that followed were the most miserable in Sinclair's young life. He had enlisted in the army to ride for glory and, truth be told, for the chance to parade around town in the dashing uniform of a cavalryman, but not for this—not to be imprisoned in the stinking bowels of an overcrowded ship. Not to eat cold salt pork and mealy biscuits—once you were done plucking out all the weevils, there was nothing left but a handful of crumbs—day after day, and to spend night after night in a wretched, dark hold, fighting to keep his terrified horse from dying. He thought longingly of his London life, his card games and dog fights and evenings at the Salon d'Aphrodite. (Throwing Fitzroy through the window had become the stuff of regimental legend.) When the ship's steward served him out his pitiful daily ration of rum, he thought of the fine port at the Longchamps Club, and cold champagne. When the first mate—a commoner, no less—upbraided him for smoking a cigar belowdecks, he thought of the rich humidor kept in the company barracks—not to mention the riding crop he would have liked to use on the man who had just dared to speak to him like that. The army, despite the occasional chafing he'd felt at its myriad rules and regulations, had served him well till then . . . but with every hour aboard the filthy, pitching vessel, something was changing in him. In his breast, he felt a growing resentment, a sense of having been cheated, misled.

He could see the spirits of his friends being dampened, too. Frenchie, once so quick to whistle a tune or make a joke, lay in his swaying hammock, green as a cricket pitch, clutching his stomach. Rutherford, ordinarily full of bluster and noise, spoke less confidently, when he spoke at all. Many of the others—Winslow, Martins, Cartwright, Mills—moved about the ship like ghosts, their faces ashen, their clothing soaked, and while the air on deck was undoubtedly fresher, there was the constant spectacle of dead horses—and increasingly men, too, who had fallen to dysentery, colic, or some other affliction—being dragged to the gunwales and tossed, like refuse from a dustbin, into the churning sea. A career in Her Majesty's navy, now that he had been able to see it so closely, was something Sinclair could not fathom.

The only one who seemed to weather it all was Sergeant Hatch, the India man who was scorned by the senior staff and officers. Sinclair knew that his fraternizing with the man made him a bit suspect, too, and Rutherford had gone so far as to warn him not to make the friendship so plain, but Sinclair found that Hatch's company anchored him in a way. Hatch had long ago accepted his lot, in life and in the army; he knew what was thought of him, what was required of him, and how to go about doing it. And while he was sufficiently cognizant of their respective stations not to seek out Sinclair, he always seemed, in his own reserved way, to be glad to see him when they did meet—especially as they were both great admirers of Captain Lewis Edward Nolan, whose theories of horse training had lately begun to be widely appreciated. What had long been done with the whip and spur, Nolan accomplished with a kind word, a soothing gesture, and a lump or two of sugar. His methods, chiefly developed in Austria where he had served under the Archduke, were making their way through the British, and reputedly even the American, cavalry, and it had been a point of honor to return him to England's own service. He was now attached to the 15th Hussars, and traveling, as were they all, into the Black Sea.

"I saw the man himself," Sergeant Hatch observed, as he held out a handful of barley for his own charger, Abdullah. As with nearly everything else, the fleet had sailed without enough forage for the horses, so that in addition to their other torments, the animals were nearly starved. "There now," Hatch said to his horse, as its tongue lapped his hand, desperately searching for more. He stroked its muzzle. "No more till tomorrow."

"And was he the finest rider you've ever seen?" Sinclair asked. "I'm told that no one can hold a candle to Nolan."

Sergeant Hatch smiled, and said, "He was only reconnoitering with Lord Raglan's aides-de-camp, so it would be difficult to say."

Sinclair felt, as he often did with Hatch, that he sounded like a boy.

"But yes, he did have a very natural way with his horse. Almost no motion in his hands or feet, but the animal always knew what was wanted of him."

Abdullah stretched his lean neck out and nudged Hatch on his shoulder, hard, and Hatch stepped back. "Maybe we ought to go up," he said, uncharacteristically. "If we stay down here, the poor thing will try to eat my epaulettes." He said it as if it were a joke, but they both knew that it was not.

As they clambered up on deck, they had to step over the bodies of several feverish soldiers—the infirmary, such as it was, had long ago been filled—and they heard a splash as another body, in a canvas shroud, was heaved overboard. When the first casualties of the journey had been consigned to the deep, the Dead March in Saul had been played by a few members of the military band. But once the numbers had grown, and the burials at sea had become such a commonplace event, the officers had curtailed that practice. As

Sinclair had overheard the ship's captain confide to an aide, "Morale is low enough already, and I shall go mad if I hear that damned tune again."

Hatch and Sinclair found a few square feet of deck, where they could sit with their backs against a mast while Hatch filled his pipe with a sweet-smelling tobacco he'd become accustomed to in India. Winslow sauntered past and gave Sinclair an odd look. Sinclair glared back.

Hatch noted the exchange, and said, "You do yourself no favor, Lieutenant, consorting with the likes of me."

"I'll consort with whomever I please."

Hatch lit his pipe. "They don't like to be reminded."

"Of what?"

"That they have not been blooded yet." He took a puff on the pipe, and the strange aroma of the weed wafted into the air. "And, I suppose, of Chillianwallah."

Even Sinclair had not known that Sergeant Hatch had served in that battle—one of the British cavalry's worst disasters. From the scandalous reports that circulated at the time, a brigade of light cavalry had advanced, without taking the precaution of sending skirmishers out to scout the terrain, against a powerful Sikh army in the foothills of the Himalayas. Suddenly confronted by a formidable array of enemy horsemen, the squadrons in the center of the front line had either balked, or received orders to retreat—it was never clear—and wheeled around, only to collide with the ranks behind them. The Sikhs, famous for taking no quarter, raised their razor-sharp kirpans and charged. In the general confusion that embroiled the British forces, two British regiments, and their Bengali counterparts, turned tail and fled, overrunning their own gun batteries at the rear, and sacrificing, along with hundreds of lives, three regimental colors. Though the action was five years in the past, the memory of it smarted still.

"That's why I keep this under my shirt," Hatch said, lifting a chain from which dangled a silver military medal stamped PUNJAB CAMPAIGN, 1848–9. He dropped it back out of sight. "Every man who survived that day is looking for the chance to redeem himself."

There was a cry from the crow's nest, carried down to them on the wind, which was picked up and echoed by several of the naval officers on deck. Sinclair and Hatch quickly got up and went to the starboard rail; the men who could stand were jostling for elbow room as a hazy mist over the water dissipated, revealing the rolling shoreline of the Crimea, and a flotilla of British ships that had already arrived and anchored there. As the *Henry Wilson* furled its topgallants and royal sails, and glided into the tranquil waters, Sinclair could hear the occasional bugle call in the distance and see the glitter of weaponry on the beach; the disembarkation had already begun, and Sinclair felt a quickening of his own blood. From what he could discern on the cliffs above, the Crimea was a land of vast, gently undulating steppes, devoid of trees or shrub, and consequently ideal for cavalry maneuvers. He longed to bring Ajax up out of the hold and let him graze on the pastures there and run free on the seemingly serene hills.

It was only when the ship grew closer, and the anchor chains were loosed, that Sinclair noticed something else, something bobbing about in the waters of the bay. At first he took it for some form of aquatic life—were there seals here? or dolphins?—until one of the shapes, sinking and rising like a buoy, was drawn toward the bow of the *Henry Wilson*. As he watched, it slowly made its way along the length of the ship, caught in the swirls and eddies, bumping against the wooden hull, then spinning away. And he saw suddenly that it was the head and shoulders of a soldier in his sodden red tunic. The lifeless head lolled from one shoulder to the other, the cheeks were hollow, the glassy eyes stared. And then it was gone, past the stern, moving out to sea.

But there were many others, bobbing about like hideous red apples in a barrel.

A sailor standing at the rail next to Sinclair crossed himself. "It's the cholera," he muttered. "They're too dangerous to bury, or burn."

Sinclair turned to Hatch, whose teeth were firmly clenched on his pipe.

"But . . . this?" Sinclair asked.

Hatch took the pipe from his lips. "They're weighted down before they're thrown overboard," Hatch said, "and they're meant to sink. But sometimes the weights aren't enough."

"And they do swell up," said the sailor in a sober voice. "That's when they come back, some of 'em, for a last look about."

Sinclair looked out over the busy harbor, where ships and

transports were being unloaded and troops ferried to shore in white rowboats, where flags rippled in the ocean breeze and bayonets glistened in the bright sunlight . . . and then down again at the terrible flotsam rising and falling on the whitecapped waves.

"What's the name of this place?" he said, sure he would never forget it, and the sailor chuckled mirthlessly.

Touching a finger to his brow before turning away, the man said, "It's called Calamita Bay."

CHAPTER TWENTY-ONE

December 11, 1 p.m.

BETTY SNODGRASS AND TINA GUSTAFSON were sometimes thought to be sisters. Both were "big-boned gals," as they often joked with each other, with blond hair and wide-open faces. They'd met at the University of Idaho's renowned Glaciological and Arctic Sciences Institute, and that was probably the first place, though certainly not the last, where they'd been dubbed the ice queens. Glaciology was generally considered the toughest, most rigorous, most hard-core specialty in all the earth sciences, and that was undoubtedly what had interested them both in pursuing it. They wanted nothing wimpy, or soft, or feminine; they wanted something that required sheer physical stamina and guts. If you wanted to be a glaciologist, you weren't going to be spending much time on the beaches of Cozumel.

And they'd gotten what they wished for.

At Point Adélie, they lived a spartan life in the great outdoors, drilling core samples, storing them in their underground deep freeze—kept at a steady 20 degrees below zero—or, if they needed the compressed ice to relax a bit, in the core bin, before analyzing the samples for isotopes and gases that would indicate changes in the earth's atmosphere over time. And along the way, they'd become expert ice carvers—the best, they liked to think, in the business. Betty sometimes kidded Tina that if things didn't work out in glaciology, they could always make a living doing ice sculptures for weddings and bar mitzvahs.

With Michael's find they had their work cut out for them. The massive ice block chopped out of the underwater glacier stood upright, midway between the stack of cylindrical ice cores ranged on the rack and the wooden crate, marked PLASMA, that housed Ollie, the baby skua. To provide a windbreak, there was a sheet metal fence, about six feet high, all around the pen. But that was it— no roof, no floor, just the gray sky above and the frozen tundra below.

From force of habit, Betty and Tina had put on bright white "clean suits" over their cold-weather gear—ice cores were notoriously easy to contaminate—although they didn't have such fears about the specimen before them. That ice had already been compromised in a hundred different ways, from the saws that had cut it out of the iceberg to the dive hut where it had been hauled up out of the depths. And anyway, if you were looking to date it, you were going to get much better evidence from the body inside; even now, with several inches of ice still needing to be cut away from the front, Betty could see the vague shape and style of the clothing the woman wore—and it reminded her of various *Masterpiece Theater* series she used to watch as a girl. She thought she could even detect the dull glow of an ivory brooch on the woman's breast.

She tried not to look into her eyes as she worked the hand drill, the saw, and the pick. It was too unnerving.

Tina was working on the back of the block, using the same tools, and as usual, they were talking about something else entirely—the recent changes in the NFL—when Tina stopped and said, "They were right."

"About what?" Betty shaved another slice of ice away.

"There is a second person in the ice. I can see him now." Betty came around back, and she could see him, too. His head was pressed against the back of the woman's, and the same iron chain was wrapped around his neck; he had a pale moustache, and appeared to be wearing a uniform of some kind. Betty and Tina looked at each other, and Betty said, "Maybe we should stop."

"Why?"

"This might be bigger than we can handle, down here. It might be the kind of thing that ought to be sent up to, say, the NSF labs in D.C. Or even back to the U. of Idaho."

"What—and miss our chance to make history?"

Michael, laden down with gear—cameras, a tripod, a couple of lights—didn't have a hand free to bang on the sheet-metal panel that served as a gate to the core bin, so he had to simply kick it with his foot. He'd heard Betty and Tina talking behind it—one of them had just said something about history—and when Betty pulled it back, he said, "Sorry I didn't call ahead."

"That's okay. We love company."

"*Living* company," Tina added, portentously.

But Michael was so intent on his first task that he failed to pick up the hint. Instead, he laid a few things on the ground, then immediately went to the crate in the corner of the pen. He got down on his knees and looked inside—Ollie was so used to him by then that he actually got to his feet and waddled forward. Michael removed the strips of bacon he had just taken from the commons and held one out. Ollie cocked his fluffy gray head—he was looking more like a gull every day—studied it for a moment, then took a quick peck.

"Whoa, you almost got my finger there." Michael placed the other strips at the edge of the box, then stood up. But when he saw the apprehensive looks on Betty and Tina's faces, he stopped and said, "Don't look so worried—skuas can eat anything."

Betty said, "It's not that."

And then he followed Tina's gaze, toward the block of ice. "Holy smokes," he said, stepping closer. "I was right."

The man was still buried in the ice—if she was Sleeping Beauty, then had this been her true Prince Charming?—and Michael had the immediate impression that the man had been a soldier; there was a hint of gold braid around the chest area.

And he also experienced the oddest feeling—a sense of comfort, that she had not been alone all this time.

"Don't make another cut," he said. "I need to make a photo record of this stage in the process."

He quickly assembled some lights and mounted them around the block. It was a bitterly cold and gray day, and the lights suddenly turned the ice into a glittering beacon.

"Betty and I were just talking," Tina ventured, "and we were thinking that something as extraordinary as this maybe ought to be kept intact."

Michael was so busy figuring out his game plan—what would be the best way to capture the image of what lay inside the ice?— that he didn't acknowledge her words. The play of light and shadows, not to mention the problems with reflections off the ice, was going to be murder. But that was part of the challenge. He lifted his green goggles up on top of his woolen hat and took a light reading.

"Michael," Betty said, "maybe we should slow down and think this through."

"Think what through?" Michael said.

"The process of extracting these bodies. This job might require extensive lab facilities—and, say, X-ray and MRI capabilities—that we don't have down here."

"Darryl's convinced that he's got all the equipment and facilities he needs," Michael said, though he was given pause. Was he rushing headlong into this? Inflicting damage to what could prove to be a truly miraculous discovery?

"It isn't just a question of removing them safely," Tina added. "That's easy. It's preserving them afterwards that's hard."

Wouldn't Darryl know what to do? And wasn't the whole Antarctic basically just a vast deep freeze? Even if the bodies were taken from the ice, couldn't they be kept sufficiently cold to keep them from deteriorating?

Whatever the answers to those questions were, right then he had work to do. The find wasn't just a boon to *Eco-Travel*—it was also the sort of thing that national magazine awards were made of. He had to pay attention and not muck it up. Before backing off, Joe Gillespie, his editor, had actually given him grief that he'd come back without any pictures from his tragic misadventure in the Cascades. Sometimes Michael suspected that the scoop was all that counted with Gillespie.

Once Michael had decided on the right cameras and equipment, he took a series of shots through the ice—first of the man, whose face was still largely concealed, then of the woman. Capturing the quality of the ice, without losing too much to the reflections and refractions, made the work extremely tricky, but Michael liked that. The good stuff was always the hardest to get. At his behest, Betty and Tina went back to work and he took a couple of dozen shots of them, as they shaved or cut away more of the ice, and one or two of Ollie, who'd waddled over to see if the ice shavings littering the ground were edible.

The wind was really picking up, and the sheet-metal fence, though firmly planted, was rattling so loudly it was hard to talk over it. Michael had to shout at Tina and Betty just to get them to move to the right or the left, into the light or out of a shadow, and he quickly sensed he was making them uncomfortable. The ice queens weren't the kind of people, he suspected, who relished publicity or having their pictures taken. "Just one more," he said to Betty, "with the hand drill about six inches higher." It was obscuring the face of Sleeping Beauty.

Betty obliged, holding the drill in place while Michael hastily adjusted a light that the wind had blown out of position. The full illumination was falling on the ice, and he moved closer to pick up as much detail in the shot as possible. Whether it was from the extra wattage, or the work that Betty had been doing all morning, the face of the woman came into fuller view than ever before. Michael could see the auburn hair caught beneath the rusted chain, the glimmer of a white pin, and the emerald gleam in her eyes. Her expression was the one he remembered from the second time he'd found her underwater, and he marveled that he could have thought it had changed. Funny, what tricks the memory could play on you. He ran off a couple of shots, but his own shadow was falling into the frame, and he had to lower his shoulder and move a few inches to one side. He focused another shot, and even as he did so, he could swear that something had changed again. He had a great eye for detail—his photography teachers had always remarked on it, and so did his editors—and he knew that something in the image was different. Something tiny, something ephemeral. But as he shifted position again, he saw it happen—he saw the pupils of her eyes contract.

He lowered the camera, then looked at the digital images he had just recorded. Back and forth, from one to the other. And though the change was infinitesimal, he could still swear it was there.

"Found you!" he heard Darryl call out, over the windy rattling of the metal fence. "You've got a call on the SAT phone—someone named Karen! They're holding it for you." Darryl took in the work that Betty and Tina had done on the ice block. "Wow! You've made a lot of progress."

Michael nodded, and said, "Leave everything just the way it is. I'm coming back."

"I don't think you should leave the lights on," Betty said.

She was right. Michael tucked his camera back inside his anorak, then, before heading for the administration module, flicked them off. The block of ice instantly went from a shimmering pillar to a somber monolith.

CHAPTER TWENTY-TWO

December 11, 3 p.m.

"I'M SORRY," Karen was saying, "did I take you away from something important?"

"No, no, I always want to hear from you. You know that." But his heart was in his mouth every time that they did talk on the SAT phone. It was very unlikely she was bringing him good news. "What's up?"

With his foot, he pushed the door to the communications room closed, and hunkered forward on the armless computer chair.

"I just thought I'd let you know that Krissy's leaving the hospital, so you don't need to try calling there anymore."

For a second, his spirits lifted—Kristin was going home?—but there was nothing jubilant in Karen's tone, so he asked, "Where is she going?"

"Home."

Now he was puzzled again. That was a good sign, wasn't it? "The doctors think she's improved enough to go home?"

"No, not really, but my dad does."

That sounded about right. Mr. Nelson was not one to let professionals get in the way.

"He thinks they're not doing enough for her—enough physical therapy, enough cognitive stuff—and he's decided to hire all his own people and just have them come to the house, where he can monitor them."

"Who's going to run the car dealerships?"

"Don't ask me. This is his big idea, and we're all just along for the ride."

That, too, sounded like the family dynamic; Kristin had been the only one who ever actively refused to go along. And though Michael did not doubt for one minute Mr. Nelson's love for his daughter, he also saw this as a way—a final, irrefutable way—for him to gain control over her again, entirely.

"When is this happening?"

"Tomorrow. But they've been making the arrangements—for hospital beds, ventilators, round-the-clock nurses—for the past week."

"So," Michael said, absentmindedly rubbing his left shoulder, "she's going to be back in her old room. That might be good for her."

"Actually, her old room is upstairs—I don't need to tell you that," she said, with a wry laugh, "and it's too hard to get everything up there. So we're converting the family room instead."

"Oh, right. That makes sense," he said, a burst of static suddenly interfering with the connection. He was trying to sort through it all—was this a good idea, or just a desperate one? Even with nurses coming and going at all hours, how could her parents and her sister really oversee her recovery?

A recovery that Michael had understood, from the doctors, to be impossible.

Lord knows he had tried to believe in it. For the whole of that long, cold night in the Cascades, and for much of the next day, he had forced himself to think only optimistically; he had willed himself to believe that she would wake up and come around again, just as soon as he got her back down the mountain. At daybreak, he'd crawled out of the sleeping bag he'd shared with her all night and rubbed as much feeling back into his own limbs as he could. He had a big purple bruise on his thigh, where he'd been lying on a carabiner, and his left shoulder still ached. He unwrapped another PowerBar and wolfed it down. As he looked up at the dawn sky, he could see a private plane buzzing by overhead. For the hell of it, he waved his arms, shouted, and even blew his whistle, but the plane didn't bank its wings to signal that they'd seen him, much less return for another look. It disappeared to the west, and the only sounds remaining were the cries of birds and the rustling of the wind.

Kristin had not reacted in any way to the whistle or the shouts. He bent low over her, felt for her pulse and checked her breathing. It was low, but steady. He had two alternatives—he could wait where he was and hope that some other climbers would come by— or he could try to move her down the mountain on his own. He glanced again at the horizon. There were clouds coming in, and if they brought rain or fog, then nobody else would be climbing that day. No, he would just have to do it himself, with an elaborate system of ropes and jerry-rigged pulleys. He could lower Kristin maybe ten or fifteen yards at a time, then climb down, redo all the ropes, and try it again. If he could just make it down far enough, he might bump into some casual hikers, or even get close enough to Big Lake that the sounds of his emergency whistle would carry to some boater—provided, of course, that the wind was right.

He gathered up all the gear that hadn't fallen off the cliff, or spilled out of the backpack, and started making his plan. There was another ledge, no bigger than an ironing board, about twenty-five or thirty feet below, and he thought he could maneuver Kristin down onto it. He knew he had to be careful with her head and neck, but for the life of him he couldn't figure out a way to stabilize them; he had nothing firm to use. He would have to take his chances.

It took the better part of an hour to rig up a system and tie Kristin's limp body into it—and another hour just to get the two of them down onto the ledge. By then, Michael was soaked in sweat and covered with a thousand cuts and scratches. He sat on the ledge, one hand on Kristin's leg—if only she would show some sign of consciousness, if only she could talk to him for even a few seconds—while the other held his canteen. He drained the last few drops. A few pieces of rock, disturbed by their recent descent, crumbled down onto their precarious aerie.

The dark clouds were coming closer.

He looked down, at the tops of the pine trees and the waters of

Big Lake, and he knew that this system would not work. It was taking too long, and he did not dare keep her out on the mountain for another night. He decided to go for broke. Shedding every ounce of unnecessary equipment, and stripping down to his climbing shorts and T-shirt, he strapped her to his back, with her arms dangling down at her sides, her crushed yellow helmet resting on his own shoulder, and started climbing down. Either he would make it to the bottom and carry her out of the forest below, or they would die together, falling out of the sky.

All the way down, he whispered to her. "Now, hang on," he'd say. "I've just got to find a toehold." Or "Don't let this worry you, but I think my shoulder is starting to separate again." Or "What would you say to a nice big steak at the Ponderosa? You're buying." Her head would loll around his shoulder, and sometimes he could feel her warm breath on his neck, but that was enough—he knew that she was with him, that she was alive, that he would get them out somehow. By late afternoon, the storm clouds had completely filled the sky, but they hadn't burst. There was only a faint mist in the air—its coolness actually felt good—and an occasional drop or two of rain. "Please, God, do me one favor—hold the rain till I get off this damn mountain."

And God had kept his part of the bargain. Michael had made it across the slope at the foot of Mount Washington and into the shelter of the pine forest before all hell broke loose. Thunder clapped and sheets of rain poured out of the sky. Briefly, he knelt on the wet earth, breathing in the rich scent of the pine needles, letting the rain wash over him. He had used it to wash the grime off Kristin's face, and wet her lips with it. Her eyelids quivered when the droplets fell on them. But otherwise, there was no sign of life.

He tried to pick her up again, but all his limbs were quivering with exhaustion and he could barely move. He didn't care. He pulled Kristin up into his arms and leaned back against the trunk of a tree, his face lifted toward the branches above, and lay there, for how long he never knew. When he stirred again, soaking wet and shivering, it was dark. The rain had stopped, and a full moon was out. He draped Kristin across his back once again, and staggered in the moonlight back toward the Big Lake parking lot, where he'd left his Jeep. When he broke out of the trees—filthy, wet, and bleeding, with an unconscious girl on his back—he saw two young guys in U. of Washington sweatshirts, unloading a pickup truck. They watched him coming toward them as if he was a Sasquatch. "Help," he mumbled. "We need help."

And then, according to the two frat brothers, he had passed out cold.

———————

The moment Darryl had seen the two figures in the ice, he knew it was time for him to step in. Enough of the ice had been cut away— or melted away by Michael's lights—that he could actually see, when he crouched in front of the block, the pommel of a sword at the man's side. Its gold tassel was frozen in an upside-down position.

"You've done great work," he said again to Betty and Tina, "but let's get this inside my lab now and finish the job."

Michael had gone for the phone, but Betty and Tina acted as if they wanted to wait for his verdict. "Michael will be back in a few minutes. Let's talk about it then."

But Darryl was no fool, and he knew what was afoot. Give scientists—even glaciologists, why should they be any different?—a taste of something really extraordinary, and they'll never let go. So much of science was routine lab work, endless experiments, blind tests, statistical breakdowns, that when they found something groundbreaking, something that had come out of nowhere—and that, in addition, had the potential to make some headlines in the outside world—there was a natural reluctance to let go.

He had to work fast, and decisively. He scurried back toward the equipment sheds, where the snowmobiles and Sprytes and augers were kept, and rounded up Franklin and Lawson, who were already privy to the find. He brought them back with an industrial dolly, the ones they normally used to transport drums of diesel fuel, and while Betty complained that Darryl was moving too fast, and Tina fretted about the scientific integrity of the specimens, Darryl had his two recruits throw the tarp back over the substantially di- minished ice block, then tip it back onto the dolly. Carting it around the corner, they pushed it up the ramp that led into the safe harbor of the marine biology lab.

"Now what?" Franklin said, looking around at the cluttered space, packed with hissing oxygen tubes, clattering instruments, and tanks filled with alien creatures bathed in lavender light.

"I want it in there," Darryl said, stepping to the large aquarium tank. Earlier, he had removed the subdividers, emptied out the old water, scrubbed the tank from top to bottom, and refilled it with fresh seawater. It was now one large tub. He'd taken the resident cod out to a hole in the ice and slipped them through. If they were still part of someone else's experiment, then they should have been so labeled. Through the ice cover, he could dimly make them out as they slithered away—along with a darker form, swiftly approaching. No doubt a leopard seal who had suddenly spotted his lunch buffet. Life in the Antarctic was a precarious business.

Franklin moved the dolly to the lip of the tank, and Lawson stepped into the water; wearing his trademark kerchief on his head, he looked a bit like a buccaneer about to wade out to his prize.

"You know the water displacement's gonna wet your floor, right?" Franklin said, and Darryl replied, "That's why we've got the floor drains. Go ahead."

With Lawson bracing it from inside the pool, and Darryl helping Franklin to tilt it forward gently, the ice block slowly made its way over the rim of the pool, then, as Lawson jumped back, it completed its descent, splashing into the water and sending, as Franklin had predicted, a wave of temperate salt water sloshing onto the floor and over the tops of their boots. As the tarp drifted free, the ice seemed to float and settle for a few minutes, with the two figures lying back to back, before the ripples in the tank subsided and the block became still.

His prize, at last.

Franklin took a long look at it, then said, "I wouldn't want to work in here alone with that."

Lawson, stepping out of the tank drenched, looked like he felt the same way.

But Darryl wasn't bothered in the slightest. His eyes were riveted on the slab of ice, which now rested, horizontally, in the pool; the seawater rose enough to cover nearly all of it. If his calculations, based on the thickness of the ice and the temperature gradient in the aquarium, were correct—and his calculations generally were—the bodies would float entirely free in just a few days. Cool, but still intact and well composed.

Once Franklin and Lawson had gone, he closed up shop. There wasn't much he could do in there immediately; the most important thing was to go out and check some of his underwater nets and traps, and see what fresh examples of the antifreeze fish—as the marine biology crowd referred to them—they might yield. You never knew when, or how, the additional specimens might come in handy.

Before leaving, he turned off the overhead fluorescents, but the lab still glowed in the lights from the tank and the aquarium, radiating a pale purple that pervaded the steel-and-concrete space, and only failed to reach into the farthest and darkest corners. He pulled on his coat and gloves and hat—God, it got to be a nuisance after a while, all this dressing and undressing—and opened the door to a blast of freezing wind. Closing it firmly behind him, he tromped down the icy ramp and off toward the shore.

Inside the lab, the various denizens of the tanks, ranged all along the walls and shelves, went on about their quiet, confined, and ultimately doomed lives. The sea spiders stood up on their spindly hind legs and used several others to probe the glass. The worms moved through the water, spooling and unspooling like ivory ribbons. The starfish spread themselves flat, suctioning themselves to the walls of their prison. The big-mouthed, nacreous ice fish swam in endless tight circles. The hoses burbled, the space heaters hummed, the wind howled around the outside of the module.

And the slab of ice in the aquarium slowly, imperceptibly, melted. Little by little, the cool water circulating in the tank eroded the thickness of the ancient ice. Occasionally, there was a crackling sound, as the seawater found a minuscule fissure and rushed to fill it. Tiny, almost invisible striations appeared here and there, like scratches on a mirror. Air bubbles surfaced and popped. The black PVC pipes that brought the freshwater into the tank and removed the same amount of water that had now been cooled by the melting ice kept the temperature at a steady thirty-nine degrees. In a day or two, the ice would become thin enough to see through clearly, thin enough to let in the faint purple glow of the lab . . . so thin the block might begin to split and crumble.

And then the ice would have to relinquish, however grudgingly, everything it still held captive.

CHAPTER TWENTY-THREE

December 13, 12:10 p.m.

RIDING IN A DOGSLED was actually much more comfortable than Michael would have imagined. The cargo shell of the sled was a hard, molded polymer plastic, much like a kayak, but you rode a few inches above its bottom, cradled in a sort of hammock. Even when the dogs ran over a rough patch in the ice, or hit a bump, you were cushioned by all the cold-weather gear you had on. The snow and ice whizzed past on either side, as Danzig, standing straight on the runners behind Michael's head, shouted encouragement to the dogs—the last dogs, as Michael had learned from Murphy back at the base, in the entire Antarctic.

"Dogs have been banned," Murphy'd explained. "They were passing on distemper to the seals. This is the last team still in operation, and the only way we could grandfather them in was by claiming they were part of a long-term study." He'd rolled his eyes. "You have no idea of the paperwork, but Danzig wouldn't let it go. They're the last dogs at the South Pole, and Danzig's the last of the mushers."

Even from his less-than-ideal vantage point, Michael could see how perfectly the pack ran together, pulling at the harness, following Kodiak's lead. He was amazed at the speed and the power they could muster. At times, they just seemed a blur of gray-and-white fur, bobbing and heaving like the painted horses on a carousel, and the sled seemed to soar behind them. Even without Danzig's occasional cry of "Haw!" for left, or "Gee!" for right, the dogs knew exactly where they were going—they were heading for the old Norwegian whaling station, about three miles down the coast; Danzig made this their regular exercise run. He had suggested Michael might want to come along—"while your Sleeping Beauty melts"—to photograph the abandoned outpost. Michael had decided to take him up on the offer. He'd visited the marine biology lab earlier in the day, but there was nothing much new to photograph, and Darryl had assured him it would be another day or two before any big change occurred.

"Better safe than sorry," Darryl had said of the slow process, and Michael agreed.

But watching ice melt, he'd discovered, was about as interesting as watching grass grow.

The last time Michael had tried to make this trip to Stromviken, he'd been drowned in a thick fog that made taking photos impossible. Today, in contrast, it was bitterly cold—twenty-five below zero—but clear. And the light—the constant, unyielding light—gave the air a strange, pellucid quality. Things that were far away could look much closer than they were, and up close things could look like they were almost under a magnifying glass. The Antarctic air and light made taking pictures—crisp, clear, and properly exposed pictures—even more of an intellectual challenge than ever.

Michael's arms were folded over his chest, with his camera nestled under his parka.

"How do you like it?" Danzig shouted, leaning down toward him, his walrus-tooth necklace brushing the top of Michael's hood.

"Sure beats the bus!"

Danzig patted him on the shoulder and leaned back again. He could never show off his dogs enough.

But it was difficult for Michael to see much, especially straight ahead, so the first intimation he had of the old whaling station was off to his right—the rusting hulk of a Norwegian steamboat, beached on the rocky shoreline. The pier beside it had long since collapsed, crushed by the ebb and flow of the ice. At its bow, pointing inland rather than out to sea, was the harpoon gun—a Norwegian invention—which had once fired a lacerating spear about six feet long, and loaded, in later years, with explosives. The fleeing whale, hit between the shoulder blades if the gunner was good, would dive for cover, only to have the bomb detonate inside it, ripping apart its heart and lungs.

That was if the creature was lucky. If the gunner was off, or the strike wasn't lethal, the battle could go on for hours, as the whale breached, bleeding and spouting, and more harpoons were launched. A massive winch, pulling on the cables, provided a further drag, and as the animal—first humpbacks, then right whales, and finally, as even those began to disappear, the more difficult to catch rorquals—grew weaker, it was gradually reeled in, like a shark, until it could be gaffed with sharpened hooks and stabbed to death at will.

This particular whaling station had operated, off and on, since the 1890s, until finally closing down in 1958 and leaving everything, from locomotives to firewood, behind. Supplies that were worth bringing in were too difficult and costly to bother taking out again. Not that the Norwegians even then had entirely given up whaling; like Japan and Iceland, they continued to assert their customary prerogative to hunt whales, and when this was mentioned in passing over dinner one night in the commons, Charlotte had thrown down her fork in disgust and said, "That's it—I'm getting rid of every Norwegian thing I own." Darryl had asked her what that would entail and on reflection she said, "I guess I'll have to throw out this reindeer sweater."

"Don't be too hasty," Michael said, plucking out the label and laughing. "See? It's made in China."

Charlotte had breathed a sigh of relief. "It *is* awfully warm."

As the dogs pulled the sled up a slight, icy rise, Michael got his first crystal-clear look at the camp, which, hard as it was to believe, was even drearier than Point Adélie. From the jetty where the boats pulled in with their catch—sometimes as many as twenty at a time, often pumped up with air to keep the carcasses afloat— wide ramps led to a crazy quilt of half-buried railroad tracks; a locomotive, gone black and red with rust, hauled the dead or dying whales to the flensing pan. That was the broad yard where the whalers took out their sharpened flensing knives and began to slice the blubber and tongues away in great, bloody strips. The tongues especially, huge and ridged with muscles, contained hundreds of gallons of oil.

It was there, now, that Danzig called out to the dogs, while pulling back on the reins; as he nimbly dismounted from the runners, the sled ground to a halt. The sudden cessation of the whooshing of the blades left what seemed a curious silence, until Michael listened again and heard the polar wind rattling the corrugated steel walls of the storehouses and moaning through the timbers of the wood-and-brick structures that had long preceded the metal ones. He clambered out of his berth in the sled, with Danzig giving him a hand, and stood up on the frozen mud of the yard. On all sides, and up the hill, he was surrounded by ramshackle buildings of obscure purpose, and he thought, not surprisingly, of a ghost town he had once photographed in the Southwest.

But this felt worse somehow. This felt like a killing ground, and he knew that the tundra he was standing on had once been ankle deep in blood and guts. The blackened rails rose, like a roller-coaster track, straight into the dilapidated building a few hundred yards up the hill; mechanized carts had carried the desirable parts of the whale into the processing facilities, while the rest of the bones and offal had been shunted off to the guano pits and the reeking shoreline, where clouds of birds, shrieking with delight, had descended upon the still-steaming piles.

As Michael fumbled to collect his tripod and waterproof equipment bag—it was too cold to take off his gloves for more than a few seconds—Danzig set the snow hook, like the emergency brake on a car, to keep the dogs from dragging away the sled. Then, for extra security, he tied the snub line to an iron skip wagon, missing two wheels and upturned on the frozen earth. Kodiak, watching him closely with his marble-blue eyes, sat back on his haunches, waiting.

"I'm going to give them their snack now," Danzig said. "This is their favorite part of the trip."

A couple of the wheel dogs, the ones who ran closest to the sled, pranced in place, already licking their chops as Danzig pulled a stiff burlap sack from the handlebars.

"I'll pass," Michael said, as Danzig took out several knotted ropes of beef jerky.

Danzig laughed and said, "Don't say I didn't offer."

Picking his way across the rusted tracks and over the icy, wind-scoured earth, accompanied only by the yips of the pack and the cawing of some skuas—drawn no doubt by the dogs and the jerky—Michael thought that this might well be the most desolate place he had ever seen.

The ice block slowly continued to disintegrate in the tank, until small chunks were breaking off, much sooner than might have been expected... almost as if something inside the block were exerting pressure from within. One jagged piece, the size of a baseball, broke off the bottom of the block, just below the spot where the toe of the man's boot could now be seen, and floated free. It drifted on the water, until it got closer to the PVC pipe that was draining the water from the tank and keeping it level; there, it was sucked into the mouth of the hose, where it stubbornly lodged.

Gradually, the water in the tank, replenished by the other pipe, rose, but as it did, it ran up into the topmost fissures and invisible brine channels, like blood rushing to fill untraceable veins and cap-illaries. An ear, put to the ice, would have heard a sound like static, as the ice crackled and crumbled... and a sound, too, of something else. Of scratching. Like nails on glass.

The beach at Stromviken was not like any other Michael had ever surveyed. It was a massive boneyard, covered with gigantic skulls and spines and gaping jaws, all bleached to a dull white by the punishing wind and the austral sun. Some were the remains of whales that had been slaughtered at Stromviken, others were the residue of whales that had been butchered at sea by so-called factory ships, their carcasses thrown back into the ocean and even-tually washed up here. Lying among the bones and rocks, sunning themselves in the cold glare, was a handful of elephant seals, who paid no attention to the man in the bulky parka and green goggles, pointing the camera in their direction... just as they had paid no attention to the men who had come there years before, who had then gone about slaughtering them as indiscriminately as the whales.

But unlike the whales, the elephant seals, with their trunklike noses and brown bloodshot eyes, had been easy to catch and kill. On land, they were clumsy and moved slowly. Sealers had only to walk right up to them, punch them on the nose, and when the animals reared back on their flippers in surprise, thrust a lance several times through their heart. Sometimes it would take the better part of an hour for the animal to bleed out, but once the bulls were rounded up and killed, the sealers could move on methodically to slaughtering the cows, still protecting their young, and then, if they weren't too small to bother with, the cubs. The skinning was the hard part; it took four or five men to properly flay a fully grown elephant seal, then to separate the thick yellow blubber from the flesh beneath. Most of the seals, hunted nearly to extinction, yielded one or two barrels of oil apiece when the boiling was done.

Although Michael knew they posed no threat to him, he approached them warily, not wanting to cause any undue disturbance. He wanted shots of the seals at leisure, not in alarm, and besides that, the creatures did smell pretty awful. The main bull, distinguishable only because of his enormous size, was molting, his shed hair and skin spread around him like a fouled carpet, and the cows, belching loudly, weren't much better. He stepped up onto a low-lying ventifact—a stone carved into a strange shape, almost like a top hat in this case, by centuries of wind—and framed his first shot. But it was hard enough to stand erect in the unceasing wind without trying to hold a camera steady; he would have to set up a tripod and do it the right way.

As he dug around in his bag, the bull seal roared, and Michael could smell its breath, reeking of dead fish. "Jesus, have you ever heard of mouthwash?" Michael said, as he set the tripod down on a relatively level patch of the rocky beach.

Water from the aquarium began to seep over the edge of the tank and drip onto the concrete floor, where it ran in rivulets toward the floor drains. The marine biology lab, like all the modules, was raised above the ground on cinder blocks, and the water simply coursed down some steel funnels and out onto the icy land below.

The block of ice was now no thicker than a deck of cards in some places, its prisoners obscurely visible within. The first spot entirely to give way was at the bottom, where the chunk had fallen off and blocked the PVC pipe. The toe of a black leather boot protruded from it now, glistening like onyx.

The melting continued, and a crevice appeared right down the center of the block; the bodies locked inside were like the flaw in a diamond, a strange imperfection in a giant crystal . . . and when the crevice widened and suddenly split, it was as if the ice itself were rejecting them. The halves of the ice block fell away on either side, and the seawater washed over the bodies of the soldier and the girl like a baptism. They were exposed to the air, bathed in the lavender light of the lab, and for several seconds they simply lay still, side by side, bobbing on the ice.

The flaking chain yoked around their throats and shoulders held them together until, corroded by the centuries of ice and saltwater, it disintegrated and slipped to the bottom of the tank.

———————

Sinclair was the first to draw a breath. Half air and half water, it made him cough.

Then Eleanor coughed, too, and an uncontrollable shiver ran the length of her body.

What little ice was still supporting them began to give way, and Sinclair's boots searched for the bottom of the tank . . . and found it.

He stumbled, swaying like a drunkard, to his feet, and quickly took hold of Eleanor's cold hand. Dripping wet, he raised her up from the chunks of floating ice. Her eyes were dull and unfocused, her long brown hair plastered to her cheek and forehead.

Where, he wondered, *are we?*

They were standing in a vat of some kind, filled with salt water up to their knees, in a place he could find no words for. No one else was there; the only living things he could see were strange creatures swimming in glass jars—jars that gave off a pale purple light and a soft hissing sound.

He looked at Eleanor. She raised her hand slowly, as if she had never done so before, and her fingers instinctively went to touch the ivory brooch on her bosom.

He sloshed to the rim of the tank, then over it. He helped her down onto the floor, water sluicing down all around them.

"What is this place?" she asked, trembling, as he gathered her into his arms.

Sinclair didn't know. For her sake, he hoped it was Heaven. But from his own experience, he feared it was Hell.

PART III
THE NEW WORLD

"They groaned, they stirred, they all uprose,
Nor spake, nor moved their eyes;
It had been strange, even in a dream,
To have seen those dead men rise."

The Rime of the Ancient Mariner,
Samuel Taylor Coleridge, 1798

CHAPTER TWENTY-FOUR

December 13, 4:20 p.m.

MICHAEL WAS STANDING in the bow of the scuttled whale catcher when he picked up an ice-covered life preserver and, despite a couple of now-illegible letters, read the name of the ship off it; it had once been the *Albatros,* and it had sailed out of Oslo. But there were no albatrosses effortlessly soaring overhead now—only skuas and pretrels and squat, white sheathbills, all lured by the arrival of the dogsled and looking for handouts.

From his vantage point, right behind the harpoon gun, Michael could gaze down at the beach, where the elephant seals had cooperated nicely for their photo op, and up the icy hill, past the warehouses and boiling rooms and flensing yards, to the uppermost structure in the station. It was an old wooden church, with patches of white paint still clinging to the walls and a cross, knocked askew, high atop its steeple. He used the zoom to take some long-distance shots, but it would be worth a closer visit later on.

He'd already explored the bowels of the ship, which in some ways looked like it had been abandoned for years—rusted panels, broken windows, warped stairs—but in other ways looked as if it had been tenanted the day before. On a galley table, a fork and knife were still neatly crossed on a tin plate. A bunk bed was made up with a striped woolen blanket and a white sheet, folded back at the top. In the wheelhouse, a frozen cigar butt rested on a windowsill. Even the harpoon gun, mounted on a raised steel platform like a machine-gun turret, looked as if it could still go about its deadly work—if it could be aimed. Michael had tried to make it swivel, and tried again, but the entire assembly was frozen solid.

"Hey, watch where you point that thing," he heard Danzig call out from the beach below. He was standing in the petrified jaws of a blue whale.

"It's not loaded," Michael replied.

"That's what they all say." Danzig, walrus teeth hanging down around his neck, his beard blowing in the wind, stepped out of the jaws like some Norse god choosing to walk among men. "You get what you came for?" he asked.

"Some of it. Why?"

"Because I need to get back."

Michael was on board with that. For the past few hours, no matter how hard he had tried to forget the block of ice in Darryl's lab, it had never been far from his thoughts. Was he missing some great shot?

"I'm expecting a call from my wife," Danzig added.

Danzig had a wife? It struck Michael as funny in a way—so banal, so ordinary—coming from such an original specimen as Danzig.

Danzig must have guessed as much from Michael's hesitation, because he said, "It's not impossible, you know."

"But when do you see her?" Michael called back, even as he gathered up his equipment and stored it all in the bag. "I thought you lived here."

"Not *all* the time," Danzig replied.

"Where is she?" Michael asked, then said, "Wait. Tell me when I get down there."

When he joined Danzig among the bones on the beach, Danzig said, "Miami Beach," and Michael inadvertently laughed.

"What's wrong with that?"

"It's not that. It's just not what you'd expect."

"Which would be?" Danzig said, as they turned back toward the dogsled.

Michael only had to think for a second before replying, "Valhalla."

For the first few minutes, Sinclair and Eleanor simply accustomed themselves to breathing again. And then to moving. And finally to being alive . . . though where—and when—they had no idea.

It was Eleanor who discovered the source of the heat in the room, a metal grate of some kind, glowing orange along the baseboards. She bent down in her wet clothes, trying to see the fire inside or smell the burning of tinder or gas, but she heard only a distant humming and smelled nothing at all. Still, she huddled close and whispered urgently for Sinclair to come near.

Instinctively, they had both been whispering.

"It's a fire," she said. "We can dry our clothes."

Sinclair helped her remove her sodden shawl, and they draped it across a stool he drew close. Then she took off her shoes and laid them in front of the grill.

"You, too," she said. "Before something happens . . ." What that something could be defied the powers of her imagination altogether. She did not know if they were among friends or foe, in Turkey or Russia or, for that matter, Tasmania. She could hardly be sure, even now, that they were actually alive.

But there wasn't time to dwell on any of it.

"Take off your jacket," she said, "and your boots."

He shrugged the uniform jacket off, and Eleanor spread it out. She put his boots beside her shoes. He unfastened his sword and, though keeping it close at hand, let it rest with the wet clothing.

Then, they huddled close in front of the heat, staring into each other's eyes, and silently wondering what the other knew or understood . . . or remembered.

Eleanor feared that she could remember too much. For so long—how long?—it was all that she had done . . . just dreamt and drifted and remembered everything.

Over and over again.

But what she was thinking of, with the clothes drying and her arms gathered tight around her own knees, was the night she had sat before the hearth, just like this, with Moira, in their cold room at the top floor of the boardinghouse in London...on the night that Miss Nightingale had announced her intention to travel, with a small company of willing nurses, to the Crimean battlefront.

Sinclair coughed, his cold white hand raised to his mouth, and Eleanor stroked his brow with her own stiff fingers. It was second nature to her at that point—she remembered doing this for so many of the wounded soldiers, lying in agony at the hospital barracks in Scutari and Balaclava. Sinclair looked up at her now, his eyes red-rimmed and wild, and said, "But you? Are you..." and then, for want of a better word, "well?"

"I am..." she said, not knowing what else she could say. She was alive, apparently. Beyond that, she wasn't sure of anything. She was as lost as he was, chilled to the bone, in spite of the remarkably consistent heat from the grate. And weak, too—from ordinary hunger, as well as the unspeakable need.

It crossed her mind that she could die again...and soon...and she wondered if it would feel any different this time.

It could not be worse.

Sinclair's gaze swept around the room, and she followed it. A thing that looked like an enormous spider was trying to clamber out of a square jar, filled with water and a pale purple illumination. There were long counters, like trestle tables, with basins, like flower sinks, in them. A black metal apparatus, with a white box beside it, sat before a stool, and next to that, she saw, just as Sinclair must have done, a wine bottle. He was already springing to his feet.

He picked up the bottle, rubbed the label against the billowing sleeve of his white shirt, then examined it more closely.

"Is it?" she asked.

"I can't be sure," he said, twisting the cork out. He put his nose to the top, then recoiled.

And so she knew it must be.

In his stockinged feet, he padded back to her and placed the open bottle between them, like a papa bird bringing an offering to the nest. He was waiting for her to take it, but she couldn't. It was too horrible to have awakened, after how long, from a dream—a nightmare—only to be plunged right back into it once you'd been restored to life. The bottle stood before her as a grim reminder, a memento mori. It represented death, but at the same time—if she was desperate enough to want it—life. She could smell the vile odor of its contents, and she wondered: Was that the very bottle he had raised to her lips on board the *Coventry*? If it was, then how had it come to be here, in this strange place, now? Had one of the sailors thrown it, too, into the heaving sea, after she had been chained to Sinclair? After...

Her mind stopped dead, like a team of horses suddenly reined to an abrupt halt. She could not think of it; she could not allow herself to. She had governed her thoughts for so long, she could not stop doing it now. She had to guide them, control them, even chastise them, like unruly children, if they went too far astray. To do anything else would be an invitation to madness.

If, that is, she had not already gone mad.

"You have to," Sinclair said, urging the bottle on her.

But Eleanor was not so sure. "What if," she ventured, "after all this time..."

"What?" he snapped, his eyelids drooping, then snapping open again. "What if, after all this time, everything has changed?"

"It's possible, is it not, that—"

"That what? God's in his heaven again, and we're safe as houses, and Britannia rules the waves?"

There was a fire in his eyes again now. All that time, in the ocean, in the ice—*no*, her mind said, *do not think of it, do not let it in*—had done nothing to dampen his ardor, or his anger. That wicked flame, lighted in the Crimea, still burned. He was not the Lieutenant Copley who had sailed off for glory. He was the Lieutenant Copley who had been found, covered with mud and blood, lying among the dead and dying on a moonlit battlefield.

"Shall I try it first?" he said, his face ruddy in the orange glow of the grate, and when she didn't answer, he raised the bottle, tilted his head back, and took a swig. His Adam's apple bobbed as he swallowed, then bobbed again as the liquid tried to come back up again. He sputtered, gasped, then put the bottle to his lips again and forced some more of it down. When he dropped the bottle back into his lap, his light brown moustache was stained the color of a bruise.

"There," he said, "right as rain." He smiled, and his teeth, too, were stained. He pushed the bottle toward her.

"What we need," she said, her eyes nonetheless drawn to the bottle, "is food. And water. Clean water, fresh food."

Sinclair scoffed. "Spoken like a true Nightingale. And we shall have those things. But you know, as well as I do, that right now you need something more."

In her heart, she knew he was right . . . or at least that he *had* been right. But wasn't it possible that this curse had been lifted? Wasn't it possible that, in addition to whatever strange miracle had released them from their bondage, another one had been performed, too? That this dreadful sustenance, sitting before her, was no longer necessary?

"We don't know where we are," Sinclair said, softly. "And we don't know what awaits us out there." He was speaking in his most reasonable voice, but Eleanor had become used to such sharp changes. Even in his letters home, she had detected them.

"I believe we must take our opportunities when and where we find them," he said, pointedly glancing down at the bottle.

Eleanor had to shift her position on the floor, so as to warm and dry a different section of her dress. She worried about how long they would be able to stay there without being discovered. "Couldn't we just take it with us, wherever we have to go?"

"Yes," he replied, his temper, she could tell, mounting. "But it was taken away from us once, was it not? It could be taken away again."

He was right, of course . . . and she recognized as much. But still her spirit rebelled.

Either to prove his point, or because he craved another draught, Sinclair grabbed the bottle and drank again. This time, he was able to manage several swallows before slamming the bottle back to the floor and letting a dark rivulet run from the corner of his mouth.

She found herself transfixed by the deep crimson line touching his chin. He had done that, she knew, deliberately. Her throat, parched already, felt as rough as a dusty road, and she could feel the muscles in her neck straining. Her palms, which she had just gotten dry, were damp again with perspiration, and so, she feared, was her brow. Her temples began to throb, like a distant drumbeat.

"The least you can do," he said, "after all this time, is to kiss me."

His blond hair, though wild and twisted on his head, gleamed with a fiery light in the glow of the strange heater. The collar of his white shirt lay open at the neck, and a drop from the bottle had landed there, too. God help her, but she wanted to lick the spot away. Her tongue involuntarily pressed at the back of her teeth.

"As your friend Moira might have said," he pressed, "will you not do it for auld lang syne?"

"I will not do it for that," Eleanor finally answered. "But I will do it . . . for love."

She leaned forward, as did Sinclair, and with the bottle between them, their lips met—at first chastely, but then, when his parted, she could taste it, the blood, in his mouth.

He put his hand to the back of her head, wound his fingers through her long, tangled hair, and held her there. And she let him—let him hold her, let him ensnare her. She knew that was what he was doing. She let him unite them again as they had been united so long before. She let him do all of it, because it had been so long since she had felt something like this . . . so long, truly, since she had felt anything at all.

CHAPTER TWENTY-FIVE

December 13, 6 p.m.

ON THE TRIP BACK, Michael begged, and Danzig agreed, to let him drive the dogsled. After a few rudimentary pointers, Danzig clambered into the cargo shell—it was even a tighter squeeze than it had been for Michael—and said, "Ready?"

"Ready," Michael replied, adjusting his goggles and pulling his furred hood tighter around his face. Then, gripping the handlebars and making sure his feet were planted on snow and not ice, he shouted the order—"Hike!"—that Danzig always used. The dogs, perhaps unaccustomed to his voice, at first didn't move; Kodiak actually turned around and looked at him questioningly.

"You've got to do it with some authority," Danzig said. "Like you mean it."

Michael cleared his throat—now he felt like he was auditioning for the dogs—and shouted, "Hike!" while giving a sharp jerk on the mainline.

Kodiak, in the lead position, whipped around and jumped

forward; the other dogs, taking their cue, started to pull, as Michael ran behind, pushing the handlebars.

"Jump on!" Danzig warned him, and just as Michael got his boots onto the wooden runners, the sled gathered momentum and took off across the snow and ice. Danzig had taken the trouble to point it in the right direction, so Michael didn't have to worry about making a turn, but the task was already harder than he had imagined. As smooth as the surface might look, it was filled with bumps and cracks and stones, and he could feel the shock of each one radiating up his legs. It was all he could do to keep his balance and stay on the runners.

"Loosen up!" Danzig cried over his own shoulder, and Michael thought, *Easier said than done.*

Still, he tried to let his shoulders fall and his arms bend a bit, and he willed his knees to unlock.

"If you want 'em to go straight ahead," Danzig advised, though Michael had a hard time hearing him over the wind battering at his hood, "shout 'Straight ahead!' "

Okay, that one wouldn't be hard to remember.

"And if you want 'em to go slower, pull back on the lines and shout, 'Easy!' "

Michael had no idea how fast they were actually going, but the impression of speed was incredible. As he clung to the rubberized handlebars, the icy landscape went flying by on either side. When he'd been hunkered down in the shell, it had been quite different; he'd been warm and protected, and everything had been seen from just a few feet off the ground. But standing up, with the wind smacking his face and rippling at his sleeves—the sound reminded him of the snapping flag at Point Adélie—it was both exhausting and invigorating. A cloud of ice crystals, thrown up by the paws of the running dogs, stung his lips and spattered like rain on his goggles. Carefully, he raised one glove, swiped the crystals away, then grabbed for the handlebars again.

But as he began to feel the rhythm of the team and became accustomed to the swooshing movement of the sled, he began to relax. He could look beyond the bushy heads and tails of the dogs and off into the distance. The base was still too far off to be seen at all, and that was just as well. What he saw instead was simply a limitless continent of snow and ice and permafrost—larger, he knew, than Australia, but so desolate that it made the great outback look crowded. The sled was clinging to the shoreline, which comparatively teemed with life, but just a few miles inland, the seals no longer frolicked, the birds ceased to fly, and even the modest lichen disappeared from sight. It was a desert, as bereft of life—in fact, as hostile to it—as anyplace on the planet. Humans had found a way to reach the South Pole; they could fly over it, they could plant a flag, they could take some measurements, but they could never really claim it. No one could really stay there, and only a madman would want to.

The coppery sun was hanging like a watch fob, in an empty sky. Time had become as fluid for Michael as it did for everyone in the Antarctic—he'd already used up nearly half of the time on his NSF pass, but the days simply flowed into each other like a running stream. He had to check his watch constantly, but even then he couldn't always tell if it was a.m. or p.m. There were several times when he had gotten confused, and occasions when he had suddenly had to part the blackout curtains around his bunk, stagger into the hall, and confirm whether it was night or day with the first person he saw. Once it had been Spook, the botanist, who was seldom seen outside his lab—or "the flower shop," as it was known to the grunts—and together they had agreed it was afternoon, when it actually turned out to be the dead of night. They'd gone to the commons and been surprised to find it so empty. That was when Michael had looked at Spook more closely and seen the telltale signs of Big Eye—the glassy stare, the slack, though oddly bemused, expression.

It was also when he'd started regulating his own sleep cycle with Lunesta or lorazepam—whatever he could get the good Dr. Barnes to prescribe for him that night.

"There's an old saying," she'd advised. "If one person tells you that you look tired, don't worry about it. But if two people tell you that you look tired, lie down."

"What are you telling me?"

"Lie down—and take it easy."

Michael knew that he'd been pushing it—photographing everything, making endless notes in his journal, trying to master all the polar skills from igloo construction to, right now, dogsledding—but he was conscious of the limited time he had at Point Adélie, and he didn't want to overlook anything. On New Year's Eve, the supply plane would carry him back out, and he didn't want to find himself back in Tacoma, wondering why, for instance, he hadn't taken some photos inside the old Norwegian church—already he was planning to get back there—or how he'd failed to solve the mystery of Sleeping Beauty and Prince Charming.

Even now, he knew, the block of ice was slowly thawing. He'd have to go and see it as soon as they got back to base and get some more photos of that stage in the transformation. It was funny, but that was how he'd come to think of it—as a metamorphosis. The ice was the chrysalis, from which the two lovers would emerge—for lovers, he felt certain, was what they must have been. Who else would have been so yoked together, with coils of chain, and consigned to a watery grave? He tried to imagine the scenario, any scenario, that would make sense of it all. Were they captured and thrown into the sea by a jealous husband? Or was it done at the orders of a spurned wife? Had they violated some code of conduct— a code of the sea, or, given the gold braid on the man's uniform, of the military? What crime could they have committed that such an awful crime would have been committed in turn against them?

The dogs made a wide circle to skirt some uncommonly high sastrugi—windblown ridges of snow and ice—and Michael was reminded again that the dogs knew the route better than anyone. And they were heading home, to their comfortable kennel, with its straw-lined floor and food bowls. All he had to do, most of the time, was hang on to the handlebars and stay on the runners. He hadn't heard a peep out of Danzig, and he had the distinct impression that the man was asleep, his chin resting on his chest, his hood gathered close around his face. Whether that was a sign of his confidence in Michael, or in the dogs, wasn't clear, but Michael hoped he could make it all the way back to the base without waking him.

Far off on his left, out on the ice floes, he saw a tiny red light flash, and a few minutes later he saw it again—the beacon, he realized, on top of the dive hut. Michael had witnessed some of the traps being hauled up from the bottom, several of them containing stunned and gasping fish, with translucent gills and white eyes, and he'd watched as Darryl transferred the ones that had survived the trip to specimen buckets. But how, he wondered, could such a confirmed vegetarian and animal rights activist do this kind of work?

"Rationalization is the key," Darryl had said. "I tell myself that, by studying the few, I can save the many. The first step in getting the world to conserve natural resources is to remind the world that they are imperiled." He'd lifted one dead fish by its tail and gently deposited it in a separate bucket, packed with ice. "And if I work fast, I can still get an interesting blood sample, even from this one."

As the sled drew parallel to the dive hut, the dogs turned inland, several of them yelping in gleeful anticipation. The blades swished through the snow as the sled surmounted a low hill, and now Michael could see the camp. The various modules and sheds and storehouses looked, from here, like the Lego blocks he'd played with as a kid, strewn about in only the rudest semblance of order. A collection of black and gray structures, with huge yellow Day-Glo circles painted on their roofs so that the camp could be spotted by the supply planes in the long, dark austral winter.

Hard as it was to live there in the summer, with the unending light, Michael could barely fathom how anyone withstood a winter at the South Pole.

Danzig stirred in the shell and raised his head. "We there yet?" he mumbled.

"Almost," Michael said.

Now he could see the American flag, so stiffened by the wind that it looked flat.

"But since you're awake," Michael said, "what do you say to get the dogs to stop?"

"Try whoa."

"*Try* it?"

"It doesn't always work. Pull back on the lines, hard, and step down on the brake." Michael glanced down at the metal bar, with two claws, that served as the brake, and prepared to step on it as soon as the sled got within a hundred yards of the kennel. He didn't anticipate a swift stop.

From the ocean side, he could hear the distant roar of a snowmobile, and he couldn't help but compare it to the smooth, natural whooshing of the sled. As a photographer—somebody who relied

upon all the latest gizmos—he knew he was in no position to throw
stones at technology. Hell, if it hadn't been for airplanes, he'd never
have gotten here, and if weren't for digital cameras, he'd be fumbling with a lot of frozen, broken, and scratched film. But the noise
of the snowmobile, which looked like it would arrive back at the
base just about as he did, was an intrusion nonetheless, like a power
mower breaking the perfect quiet of an August morning. He wondered, as he watched it zip across the ice like a black bug skittering
across a tabletop, if Darryl was on board, loaded down with fresh
specimens.

The kennel was at the back of the station, beyond the quad
where the dorms and administration modules were set up, back
where the labs butted up against the equipment sheds and generators. Even though the generators were placed as far away from the
dorms as possible, there were still many nights, if the wind was
down, when Michael could hear their constant thrumming. When
he'd complained about it at breakfast one morning, Franklin had
said, "Worry about it when you *don't* hear that racket."

The dogs cut a narrow path past the ice-core bins and the
botany lab, past the garage where the Sprytes and snowmobiles and
augers were housed, and on toward the kennel, across a winding
alley from the marine biology lab. Michael shouted "Whoa!" to almost no effect, and pressed with both feet on the brake. He could
feel its steel claws digging into the permafrost and slowing the speed
of the sled, but they weren't slowing it enough for a soft landing. He
shouted again and leaned back, with all his weight, on the mainline, until he saw the brush bow, at the front of the sled, lift an inch
or two, and the dogs gradually wind down. Kodiak stopped straining against the harness and fell into a trot, and the others immediately followed suit. The blades coursed almost silently across the
snow and ice, until the sled pulled up to the kennel—an open shed
with a hayloft above, illuminated by a glaring, white light. From the
happy reaction of the dogs, it looked to them like the Ritz.

"Nice job, Nanook," Danzig said, hoisting himself up and out
of the shell. "What's on the meter?"

———————

Sinclair had heard the sled arriving—the barking of the dogs, the
runners cutting through the snow. But he didn't dare to open the

door to see what was out there—for all he knew, a guard might be posted right outside.

There were no proper windows, either, but he did see a narrow glass panel running just below the flat ceiling, close to the door, and he quietly drew a stool over to it. He stepped up on the stool—his socks, still damp, squishing on its seat—and tried to peer outside. The noise of the dogs was quite close. But the window was so encrusted with snow and ice, he could barely see anything. On his side of it, however, there did appear to be a handle of some kind—like a crank—and when he turned it, the bottom of the window lifted, pushing some snow out of its way. He cranked it again, and now he had a couple of inches through which he could see. The blast of wind, despite the narrowness of the aperture, was forbidding.

He saw an ice-packed alley, with a team of wolfish dogs prancing through it. There were two men on the sled—one, in a bulky, hooded coat, was driving, and the other, wearing a necklace of bones around his neck, was riding in the carriage. The sled ground to a halt inside a wide-open barn—brightly lighted, even though it appeared to Sinclair to be midday outside—and the man in the sled clambered out. Sinclair could not hear what the men were saying. But his attention was drawn instead to the back of the dog pen.

His chest was there. The one that had contained the cache of bottles.

The men pushed their hoods back and lifted some sort of heavy dark spectacles from their eyes. The driver was young—maybe Sinclair's own age—tall, with longish black hair; the other man, with a full beard and wide Slavic cheekbones, was older and stocky. Neither of them wore anything that suggested a uniform, or national allegiance, of any kind, but that was little help. Sinclair had known soldiers, so weary and so encumbered with gear, that by the time they arrived at the front, they looked more like a band of hooligans than Her Majesty's own.

The bearded man was untying the harness lines—Sinclair was reminded of his own horses and carriages, back at his family's estate in Nottinghamshire—while the driver filled a stack of bowls with food from a sack. One by one, the dogs were tied to stakes, spaced a few feet apart; their eyes were riveted on the bowls as the young man dispensed them. While the dogs devoured their meals, the bearded man hung his overcoat on a wall hook—he had some other coat on underneath it—where Sinclair saw a motley assortment of other garments, hats and gloves and even a pair of those green spectacles, also hanging.

More and more, he knew that he would have to raid that barn. There was food (even if it was only considered fit for dogs), there was clothing . . . and there was his chest.

"What do you see?" Eleanor whispered.

"Our next objective."

He climbed down from the stool and began to put his own clothes back on.

"Are they dry yet?" Eleanor asked. "If they're not dry . . ."

He lifted his saber out of its scabbard—it stuck for a second, before sliding free—then slid it back in again. He hoped he would not have to draw it, but it was best to know, that if things came to such a pass . . .

"What do you want me to do?" Eleanor asked, her voice not only soft but weak. He knew she hadn't really tested her strength yet—for that matter, neither had he—but he wondered if she would be fit to travel, as they would no doubt have to do, and especially in what appeared to be the same hostile climes they had last encountered.

"I want you to get dressed again," he said, undraping her shawl from the stool where it had been drying, "and come with me." She stood up, a bit unsteadily, and he wrapped the shawl, still warm from the grate, around her shoulders. She stepped into her shoes, and he bent down to button them for her.

"But perhaps we should wait, here?" she said. "Who's to say that we will be harmed?"

"A nurse," he said, still fastening the shoes, "would not be—not if they have the slightest shred of decency. But a nurse with your peculiar affliction," he said, standing and looking into her emerald eyes, "might prove to be another matter. How should you explain it to them?" He did not even need to elaborate on the additional problems that a British officer, also so afflicted, might face, should he fall into the wrong hands. If there was one thing that he had learned from his time in the East, one thing that he knew could be relied upon, it was the boundless cruelty of one man to another.

He had also learned to trust no one; if you prized your life at so much as a farthing, it was critical to do your own reconnaissance and make your own decisions. Otherwise, you could find yourself in dire straits indeed ... riding, to take a wild example, straight down the barrels of a Russian gun battery ...

When he had wrapped her as warmly as he could, he climbed up onto the stool, saw that the two men had gone, then, getting down, went to the door. He pried it open a crack—the wind came howling in to greet him—and then enough to step outside.

Looking to either side, he saw no one—only low dark buildings, made not of wood but of tin or some other metal—squatting, at intervals, along a barren concourse. The sky had the same burnished glow he remembered from the deck of the *Coventry*, when the snowy albatross had sailed onto the yardarm and watched, impassively, as he and Eleanor were grappled in chains and hurled into the freezing sea.

Eleanor tentatively stepped out after him, lifting her face to the sun; she closed her eyes, and to Sinclair her skin looked as smooth and white and lifeless as marble. Her long brown hair blew loosely around her cheeks, and her lips parted to take in the frigid air as if she were about to taste some rare delicacy. In a way, that's just what it was—windblown air, as cold and unsullied as a glacier, coursing across their exposed skin. Cold as it was—so cold it made their faces burn and their fingers tingle—it was the taste, and the scent, and the feeling, of being alive. For years—centuries, perhaps—they had been immured in their frozen cell, unmoving and untouched. But this, even more than the breaking of the ice, or the warming air from the grate, brought back that painful bliss of living. Sinclair didn't have to say a word, nor did she; they simply stood there, at the top of the snowy ramp, savoring the physical world—even one as hostile and intemperate as this.

One of the dogs across the way looked up from licking his bowl and let out a low growl. Eleanor opened her eyes and took them in.

"Sinclair ..." she began, but he interrupted, saying, "There's a sled, too."

"But where will we go?" Her eyes traveled down the dreary alleyway and off at the distant mountains.

"The dogs will know. Surely they're employed to go somewhere."

He took her hand before she could offer it and started down the ramp. His boots were ill suited to the snow and ice and he found himself slipping several times. His scabbard clanged against the metal handrail, and he quickly looked about in alarm, but in the roar of the wind it was doubtful anyone had heard. They scurried across the passage, and into the glare of the shed, where they were separated from the dogs only by a wooden partition a few feet high.

As Eleanor leaned back against the wall—already she was exhausted, and her knees were shaking—Sinclair made straight for the clothing rack on the wall. He selected a long, billowy coat—it was as smooth as silk, but its fabric had no sheen—and forced Eleanor into it. It weighed much less than he thought it would, and was so big that she could virtually wrap it around herself twice. The bottom hung down onto the floor, and the hood, when he drew it up, fell around her face like a monk's cowl. But she had soon stopped her shivering.

"You put one on, too," she said.

Sinclair took a shorter coat from the pile—it was red with a white cross on its sleeves and another on its back, and hung down to his thigh. But he did not know how to fasten it at first; there was a long ribbon of tiny metal ribs that ran down its front, and he pushed them together, thinking they might bind somehow, but they did not. Fortunately, he also found some metal buttons, under a narrow placket, that he found would snap together when pressed.

The dogs were restive, and done with their food. Several of them stood, staring, at Eleanor and Sinclair. And when he went to the food sack, one of them barked, no doubt thinking he was about to receive a second ration. But Sinclair dipped into the bag, and came up with a handful of rounded pellets, the size of shot, and put them to his own nose. The smell was vaguely horsey. He put one in his mouth; the taste was gritty but acceptable. He swallowed one, then the whole handful. They were crunchy, but not nearly as hard as ship's biscuits.

"Here," he said, holding out another handful to Eleanor. "They're not much, but no worse than army rations."

But the smell seemed to upset her, and she turned away, shaking her head. Sinclair poured the pellets into one of the red coat's voluminous pockets. There wasn't time to argue about it now. He had too much to do.

He went to the chest at the rear of the pen and knelt beside it. The chains were gone, the hasp had been broken off, and the lid was barely attached. He raised it slowly, and inside found his sodden campaign coat, his stirrups, his helmet, a couple of his books— miraculously, still frozen solid and seemingly intact—and, finally, three unbroken bottles labeled, though illegibly, as Madeira from San Cristobal. He grabbed these first, wrapped them in the campaign coat, then carefully tucked the bundle into the shell of the sled. There were empty cargo bays, he discovered, running from the front of the sled to its rear stanchions, and he tossed everything else he could think of—his riding gear, his books—into them.

Finally, he dragged a sack of the food pellets toward the sled, and the dogs—now perhaps convinced that their provisions were being stolen—all stood up, on silent alert, at their neatly spaced stakes. That, or maybe it was just the odor he gave off. Sinclair had noticed that animals often became anxious in his presence...ever since Balaclava.

The lead dog—a massive creature with eyes like blue agate— barked furiously, and strained at his stake.

"Quiet down!" Sinclair urged, trying to keep his voice low but commanding. He prayed that the howling wind would keep anyone from hearing.

But as he lifted the bag into the sled, the dog leapt into the air, restrained only by the short chain running from its collar to the stake.

"Enough!" Sinclair declared. Eleanor was cowering against the wall, but Sinclair led her over to the sled and helped her to climb inside it.

"How will you ever harness them?" she asked, her voice nearly inaudible under the hood.

"The same way I've harnessed horses all my life." Though, truth be told, he was wondering himself. He had not expected a rebellion. And he needed to quell the noise, immediately, or his whole plan would be for naught.

He came around the wooden partition and lifted the front of the harness—not so different from what was used on a coach-and-four—and shook it out. The other dogs studied him intently, but the lead dog, again, would have none of it. Barking loudly, he jumped at the intruder, but was yanked back to the ground by the buried stake. Instantly, he scrambled to his feet, spittle flying from his jaws, and leapt again—only this time the stake bent, then burst up out of the ground. Even the dog seemed surprised by it, shooting past Sinclair and banging his snout against the wooden wall. Wheeling around, and dragging the chain and stake, the dog charged at Sinclair, who managed to step to the side and parry the attack with one arm. The loose stake got snared on another one, still rooted in the permafrost, and in the few seconds it took for the dog to shake itself free, Sinclair dodged behind the partition.

Eleanor shouted his name, but Sinclair warned her to stay in the sled. The dog started to come at him one way, but when he saw Sinclair retreat toward the rear of the pen, where the wooden stairs led to the loft, he changed his direction and ran around the other side. Sinclair was halfway up the steps when he felt the dog's fangs digging into his boot, ripping at the leather—oh, how he wished he had his spurs on now—and as he struggled up the last few steps, he had the dog hanging off his leg. With his bare fingertips, he clawed at the floorboards while kicking out at the dangling animal.

When the dog abruptly lost its grip and fell, Sinclair stumbled up and into the loft. The rest of the team was barking below, and as Sinclair turned around and braced himself, he could hear the loose dog's paws scraping for purchase on the narrow stairs; then he saw its huge head, eyes ablaze and jaws open, appearing at the top. He knew what he had to do, and as the dog hurled itself through the air at him, he drew his sword and met his enemy with the upturned blade. The dog yowled as its own weight and the force of its charge impaled it on the saber, pulling Sinclair's arm down with it. He fell beside the writhing animal, his wrist pinned below its neck. He pushed himself back, drawing the saber out as he went, but the weapon had already done its work. The dog, blood spurting from its wound and clotting the white fur, lay twitching on the straw-covered floor. He pushed himself farther away, out of reach of any last lunge, and waited for his own breath to return. There was a gurgling sound from the dog's throat, and now he could hear Eleanor's anxious cries.

"Sinclair! Are you all right? Sinclair!"

"Yes," he replied, trying to keep his own voice down. "I'm all right."

He looked at his torn boot, where the dog's spittle coated the leather, and he could feel his own blood seeping down his calf. The dog had bitten hard. He got to his feet and, stepping around the dying dog, went back down the stairs. The glaring white light, from some kind of globe he saw affixed to the ceiling, sent his own shadow lurching down before him. It was, most assuredly, a world of wonders—heat from smokeless grates, illumination from glass bowls, coats made of fabric he had never felt—but it was not altogether unrecognizable. No, he thought, as he wiped the scarlet stain from his hand, in its bloody essentials the world hadn't changed.

CHAPTER TWENTY-SIX

December 13, 7:30 p.m.

THE MOMENT MICHAEL RETURNED TO CAMP, he hurried back to his room, switched some of his camera gear, and went looking for Darryl. He was on his way to the marine lab when he bumped into Charlotte on the snow-covered walkway.

"Welcome back," she said. "Want to join me for dinner?"

"First things first," he said, lifting the camera slung around his neck. "It's been hours since I got a shot of the ice block."

"Then one more won't hurt," she said, slinging an arm through his and dragging him in the opposite direction. "Besides, Darryl's in the commons."

"You sure?" Michael said, digging in his heels.

"Positive," she assured him, "and you know he doesn't like anyone in his lab when he's not there."

Michael did know that Darryl was very territorial, but he would still have been willing to risk it—if Charlotte hadn't been clinging to his arm so insistently, and if he hadn't actually worked up quite such an enormous appetite on his journey to the whaling station. He told himself that he'd make it quick, then haul Darryl straight back to the lab with him.

On the short trip to the commons, Charlotte told him that she'd just finished attending to Lawson, who'd dropped some ski gear on his foot, but Michael was still having a hard time focusing. He had that itchy feeling that he sometimes got, the sense that he was missing out on something, and every time the camera thumped on his chest it only got worse.

"But I'll say this," Charlotte confided, as they mounted the ramp to the commons. "I don't have a single soul in the sick bay. If I can keep that up for the next six months, this won't be such a bad deal, after all."

In the commons, they ditched their coats and gear, then piled their plates high with beef stew, sticky rice, and sourdough rolls. In the Antarctic, salad just didn't cut it. Beakers and grunts were coming and going, and even Ackerley—a.k.a. Spook—who usually just grabbed a milk carton and some small cereal boxes and took them back to his botany lab, was sitting at one of the picnic-style tables with some of his cronies. Even though there were no hard-and-fast dining hours at the Point—no one would be able to keep them—the kitchen staff, headed by a grizzled old Navy cook who insisted on being called Uncle Barney, always seemed to keep things coming. No one, not even Murphy O'Connor, knew quite how the trick was pulled off.

Michael spotted Darryl before Charlotte did, nearly hidden behind a pile of rice and string beans, with his nose buried in some lab reports. He plopped his tray down across the table and Charlotte slid in next to him.

Darryl glanced up while dabbing at his mouth with a paper napkin. "Such a handsome couple," he said. Then he tapped the papers. "These are the readouts from the blood sample in the wine bottle." He said it as if that was what they had been waiting for.

"And this is what you bring to dinner?" Charlotte said as she snapped her napkin open.

"It's fascinating stuff," Darryl said, but when he started to elaborate on the sources of the putrefaction, Charlotte stuck a sourdough roll in his mouth.

"Didn't your mama tell you not to talk about certain things at the table?"

Michael laughed, and once the roll was removed from his mouth, so did Darryl. "But, really, you would not believe the blood-cell ratios," he said, starting up all over again, which Charlotte put a stop to by saying, "Michael, why don't you tell us about what *you* did today?"

Darryl gave up, broke open the warm bread and began to ladle in scoops of butter, while Michael regaled them with tales of the Norwegian station and piloting the dogsled back to camp.

"Danzig let you do that?" Darryl said.

Michael nodded, swallowing a particularly tough morsel of stew. "In fact, I thought I saw you coming back from the dive hut on a snowmobile."

Darryl admitted that he'd been there. "But nothing I brought up in the traps was worth keeping this time. I'll try again tomorrow."

They ate in silence for a few minutes—at pole, every meal was a sort of communion, a way to tell your body what time it was, a break in the unending day. There were many times when you had to stop and ask yourself whether it was lunch or dinner you were sitting down to, but Uncle Barney tried to make that easier for you by providing lots of sandwiches at lunch, and big hot entrees, like stew or spaghetti or chili con carne, for dinner. Betty and Tina had suggested candles be put out for the evening meal, but the grunts had overwhelmingly rejected that idea, in colorful language attached to the bulletin board outside Murphy's office.

Michael had tried to be patient, but before Darryl had quite finished with his hot peach cobbler, he said, "You are planning to go back to the lab tonight, aren't you?"

Darryl nodded, as he chased an errant slice of peach around his plate.

"Because I could always go on ahead of you," Michael said, "if you don't mind."

Darryl scooped up the peach, ate it, and said, "Gimme a break. I'm coming." He crumpled up his napkin and tossed it on the plate. "I want to see what's up just as much as you do."

Charlotte, sipping the last of her latte, said, "I'm in, too."

After donning their coats and goggles and gloves, they were all barely identifiable, even to each other. In the Antarctic, people tended to recognize other people based on something simple—a colorful scarf, a stocking hat, a way of walking—because apart from that, everyone looked like big fat bundles of down padding and rubber and wool.

The night was uncommonly still, and the sun was veiled by a thin scrim of wispy clouds—all betokening serious weather to come. Their boots crunched on the ice and snow as they walked by the glaciology lab—they could hear the buzzing of a drill from inside the core bin—and approached the sled shed. Off in the distance, the botany lab, where the grow lights were always on, beckoned. It all reminded Michael of Christmas nights as a kid, when his parents would take him to midnight mass, and there was such an air of anticipation hanging over everything. Back then, he knew that something wonderful was waiting for him in the morning, and now he knew that something amazing was waiting for him in that low dark module just around the bend.

Darryl trotted ahead of them and up the ramp. So as not to keep the door open any longer than he had to, he waited for them to catch up before opening it—no one ever locked a lab at Point Adélie; it was a safety point laid down as law by the Chief—and the three of them ducked inside all at once.

The first thing Michael noticed, even before he'd unzipped his coat, was the wet floor. The marine lab often had spills—that was why the floor was a slab of concrete, with drains at regular intervals—but it was a lot wetter than usual. His rubber boots made a sucking noise as he stepped around the lab counter, where the microscope and monitor sat, and followed Darryl over to the side of the central aquarium tank.

Water was still dripping over its sides, the PVC pipes were still operating, as far as he could tell, but apart from the seawater, the tank was otherwise empty. There was no block of ice, and certainly no floating bodies. Chunks of ice drifted around like tiny bergs on the gently moving water, and the whole lab had a strong, briny odor. But Michael was puzzled—and frankly, a little pissed. Was this Darryl's idea of a joke? Because if it was, he wasn't laughing. He, Michael, should have been consulted if the bodies were going to be relocated again.

"Okay—what gives?" he asked Darryl. "Did you tell someone to move them?" But from the stunned look he now saw on Darryl's face, he already knew the answer to that.

"Where are they?" Charlotte innocently asked, unwinding a long scarf from around her neck.

"I . . . don't . . . know," Darryl replied.

"What do you mean, you don't know?" she said. "You think Betty and Tina took 'em back?"

"I don't know," Darryl repeated.

The shock in his voice was apparent to her, too. She glanced over Darryl's head at Michael.

"Well, it's not like they got up and went anywhere on their own," she said.

But the silence hung heavy. Michael went around to the other side of the tank and turned off the PVC valves. He saw a stool, set up in front of one of the space heaters, and another one close to the door. Why, he wondered, would Darryl have moved the lab stools like that?

"I know you like your privacy, but has anyone else been working with you in here?" he asked.

"No," Darryl replied in a low voice, as if still unable to process the disaster. He hadn't moved from the lip of the tank.

"Murphy will know what's up," Charlotte said, in an upbeat tone. "He must have had the bodies transferred." She went to the intracamp phone mounted by the door, and even she looked puzzled for a second by the stool that stood in her way.

Michael, his thoughts reeling, used a mop to push some of the water toward the floor drains while Darryl looked into the tank as if staring long enough could make the bodies reappear. Charlotte talked on the phone, and Michael didn't have to pick up more than a few of her actual words—"not here," "are you sure?" "of course we did"—to know that Murphy O'Connor was as baffled by what he was hearing as anyone.

Darryl, his brow furrowed in thought, retreated to the lab counter, where he plopped down in front of the microscope. Michael used the mop to move the stool away from the heater and noticed that although the tank overflow hadn't really come up that far, there was a round puddle underneath where the stool had been. Almost as if something had been drying and dripping onto the floor there. He glanced over at the other misplaced stool, the one by the door, then leaned the mop up against the wall and walked over toward it.

Charlotte had just hung up the phone and announced that Murphy had no clue about what was going on. "He's contacting Lawson and Franklin. Maybe they'll know what's up."

Michael looked under the stool by the door, and although there wasn't any water there, he suddenly felt a cold sliver of air descending on his shoulders, and glanced up. A narrow, rectangular window, more of a vent really, ran along the roofline, and when he climbed up onto the stool, he found that the window had been cranked open. Flakes of snow and ice had already begun to congeal on the inside rim, and through it, he could see straight across the concourse and into the bright glare of the kennel and sled shed, where everything appeared quiet and undisturbed.

"Darryl," he asked, "did you ever crank this vent open?"

"What?" Darryl looked up at him, as he balanced precariously on the stool. "No. I doubt I could even reach it."

Michael cranked the window closed again, and got down. Somebody, he thought, had cranked it open—and recently—and they'd done it to get a glimpse of the outside.

"Want to hear something else?" Darryl said, resignedly.

"Is it good or bad?" Charlotte said.

"The wine bottle's gone."

"Was it on the lab counter?" Michael said, and Darryl nodded.

"It was right here," he said, "next to the microscope." He picked up a slide. "I've still got proof—this—that the damn thing existed. But no bottle, and no bodies, anymore."

But to Michael, it made perfect sense; whoever had come to make off with the bodies—but why, and what for?—had grabbed the wine bottle, too. The slide must have been overlooked. Was someone really going to try to destroy all the evidence and make it seem that the whole discovery had never happened? What would be the point of that? Or was it—and this made even less sense to him—somebody's idea of a moneymaking scheme? It was way too knuckleheaded for any of the beakers to try, but had a couple of the grunts found out what was going on and decided that they could spirit the frozen corpses back to civilization and make a fortune exhibiting them?

Or was it all just part of an immense, and not very funny, practical joke? If that's what it turned out to be, Michael knew that Murphy would have the heads of the perpetrators.

Michael realized that he was clutching at straws, that these ideas were crazy. He told himself to calm down. It had to be something simpler. Betty and Tina had probably reclaimed the ice block for further work, or something like that. And the mystery would be solved before they all went to bed.

"Weren't there some other bottles, in that chest that was brought up?" Charlotte said, and Darryl's eyes brightened.

"Yes, there were. Michael, where'd they put the chest?"

"Last I saw it, Danzig had unloaded it from the sled. It was in the back of the kennel."

"Then at least we might still have those!" he said.

"Why don't you and Charlotte look around the lab here—make sure nothing else is missing—and I'll go over to the kennel." Ever since he'd looked out of the vent, he'd wanted to check out everything across the way.

He zipped up his coat again, and as he descended the ramp, he looked carefully for any signs of a dolly's wheels, but the only markings were from bootheels. How the hell did whoever it was get the damn thing out? He marched across the snow to the kennel and found the chest at least right where Danzig had unloaded it. But despite the fact that a few odds and ends were still inside—a silver cup engraved with the initials SAC, a white cummerbund, yellow with age—the bottles were all gone.

"Hey, what the hell's going on?"

Michael turned around to see Danzig himself standing with his arms out in wonderment.

"I guess you just heard from Murphy."

"Heard what from Murphy?"

"Oh, about the missing bodies, from the ice block."

"The dogs, for Christ's sake—I'm talking about the dogs! There's one hell of a storm coming, and I came to make sure they were settled in for the night." He looked all around, like somehow he might have simply missed them. "Where the hell are they?"

Michael had been so set on retrieving the bottles that it hadn't occurred to him that something even more surprising was gone. But now he saw the dogs' stakes, still in the ground, and their empty food bowls, lying upturned on the straw.

"The sled's missing, too," Danzig said. "What the fuck is going on?"

Michael couldn't believe that anyone would dare to mess with the dogs, much less without Danzig's express permission—which would almost certainly not be granted.

"I was just checking to see if the chest had been looted," Michael said, feeling the need to explain his own presence. "It has been."

"I don't give a shit about that, or that pair of human popsicles. Where are my dogs?" Danzig boomed as he stomped around the kennel, his eyes fixed on the floor. "How long have you been here?"

"I got here just before you did."

"Goddammit!" He kicked one of the bowls clear across the kennel, then he stopped at the foot of the stairs, yanked off one of his gloves, and touched something on the steps. As Michael looked on, he raised it to his face, smelled it.

"It's blood," he said, lifting his eyes toward the loft. And then he was racing up the stairs as fast as his heavy boots and gear would let him.

Michael heard him cry, "Jesus, no!" and by the time Michael got up there, Danzig was down on the floor, cradling the bloody carcass of Kodiak in his burly arms.

"Who did this?" Danzig was muttering. "Who would do this?"

For Michael, too, it seemed unthinkable.

"I will kill the son of a bitch," Danzig said, and Michael believed him. "I will kill the son of a bitch who did this!"

Michael put a hand on Danzig's shoulder, not knowing what to say, when he saw the dog's eyes flicker, then open. "Wait, look..." he started to say, when the husky suddenly let out a low, angry growl. And before Danzig could even react, the dog had lunged up at his face. Danzig toppled backwards, and the dog was on him, snarling and tearing at his clothes and skin. His legs kicked out wildly, he was trying to stand, but the dog was too powerful and too insane with rage. Michael saw the short chain, with its stake still attached, dangling from its collar, and grabbed for it. It flew out of his hands, but he grabbed again, and finally got hold of it. He pulled back on it with all his might, and the dog's jaws, dripping with blood and foam, came away from Danzig's throat. It was still snapping, still trying to bite its master, when Michael yanked it away toward the stairs. Kodiak's paws scrabbled at the wooden floor, but only then did it turn its attention to Michael, whipping around, its cold blue eyes burning with fire, and leapt up. Like a matador, Michael stepped neatly to one side and the dog went flying down the open stairs; Michael heard a thump, a splintering sound, and a loud snap . . . and then silence.

When he looked down, he could see that the stake had wedged itself between two of the open steps, and the dog was now swinging by its broken neck from the short chain. The stairs creaked with the strain, and Danzig, clutching his throat on the floor, whispered "help" in a weak, burbling voice. The blood was pouring out between his fingers, and Michael ripped his own scarf off, wrapped it tightly around Danzig's neck, and said, "I'll be right back with Dr. Barnes." As he shot down the stairs, in shock, Kodiak's body swayed back and forth beside him, blood dripping from a puncture wound in its chest—how had *that* happened?—and matting the straw below.

CHAPTER TWENTY-SEVEN

December 13, 8 p.m.

SINCLAIR GUIDED THE SLED on a wide circle around the rear of the camp so as to avoid being seen, then across the snow and ice with the sea on one side and the distant mountain range on the other. Eleanor was battened down inside it, well protected by the voluminous coat they had stolen from the shed.

The dogs were running smoothly and seemed to know precisely where they were going. Sinclair had no idea where that was, but he was prepared to deal with any eventuality. At some point, he even detected tracks in the snow, and the dogs, he noted, were following them. He stood on the runners, gripping the reins, and though the air was frigid and the sun afforded no warmth at all, he held his face up and reveled in the cold wind scouring his skin and filling his lungs like a bellows. To feel! To move! To be alive again! No matter what happened next, he welcomed it, as nothing could prove more unendurable than his imprisonment in the ice. The red coat, with the white crosses on it, flapped around his legs. The gold braid on his uniform gleamed dully in the wintry air, but his blood felt hot in his veins and even the hair on his head seemed to tingle.

There were cries overhead, the restive cawing of a flock of birds—brown and black and gray—and though he might have hoped to see the snowy white bosom of an albatross silently keeping him company, he did not. These were scavenger birds—he could tell from their dirty color and their grating cry—and they followed the sled dogs in hopes of nothing more than a meal. He had seen such birds before, wheeling in circles in the hot blue sky of the Crimea. They'd come, Sergeant Hatch had told him, from as far away as Africa, drawn by the carrion feast that the British army had laid before them.

"Some of them," Hatch added, "are no doubt here for me."

For days, Sinclair had watched as the sergeant's skin went from a weather-beaten tan to a jaundiced yellow; even his eyes had a sickly tinge, and there were times he shook so violently in his saddle that Sinclair had taken the precaution of tying a rope from the man's shoulders to his pommel. "It's the malaria," Hatch had said, through chattering teeth. "It will pass."

The blades of the sled suddenly rose up on a hidden elevation, then dipped down again, as gracefully as a ballerina. Sinclair had never seen, or imagined, a contraption quite like it; for that matter, he could not even determine what exactly it was made of. The carriage, where Eleanor lay, was as slick and hard as steel, but lighter, much lighter, judging from the speed with which the dogs were able to drag it.

The birds kept pace overhead, skittering and darting across the sky. By comparison, the vultures in the Crimea had been more complacent, soaring in great lazy circles, and even occasionally roosting in the tops of the desiccated trees as the columns marched by. With their wings folded about their smudged brown bodies, and their beady black eyes, they watched and waited for the next soldier, mad from the heat, dying of thirst, to stumble out of formation and crumple in a heap by the wayside. Their wait was never long. Sinclair, plodding along on an emaciated Ajax, could only look on as the infantrymen first dropped their hats, then their coats, then their muskets and ammunition, as they struggled to keep up. The ones who had contracted cholera could be seen writhing in the dirt, clutching their stomachs, begging for water, begging for morphine, and sometimes simply begging for a bullet to end their agony. As soon as their suffering stopped, and they at last lay still, the vultures would flap their foul wings and plop onto the ground beside them. After a tentative peck or two, simply to make sure of things, the birds would set to with their hooked beaks and claws.

Once, unable to restrain himself, Sinclair had taken a shot at one—blowing it to pieces in a burst of bloody feathers—but Sergeant Hatch had immediately cantered up, listing in his own saddle, and warned him against doing that again.

"It's a waste of ammunition, and might even alert the enemy to our movements."

Sinclair had laughed. How could the enemy not be aware of their movements? There were sixty thousand men on the march, raising a cloud of dust into the sky, and ever since disembarking, they had been crawling slowly across the vast plains and the thorn and bramble-covered thickets of the Crimea. They had met the enemy at the banks of the River Alma, and the infantry had gallantly scaled mountains in the face of withering fire from the Russian batteries, capturing redoubts and sending the defenders fleeing.

But the cavalry—the 17th Lancers among them—had done nothing. By orders of Lord Raglan, the Commander in Chief, the cavalry was to be "kept in a bandbox"—those very words had circulated through the ranks—guarded and preserved so that they might protect the cannons and perhaps one day, if the army ever arrived there, help in the conquest of the Russian fortress of Sebastopol. For Sinclair, the entire campaign had so far been one long series of humiliations and delays. And at night, when they bivouacked in some mosquito-infested glade, he hardly had to speak to Rutherford or Frenchie; they all knew what the others were thinking, and they were usually too weary to do much more than swallow their rum, choke down their uncooked salt pork, and search desperately for some spring or pond where they could water their horses and fill their canteens.

In the morning, the men who had fallen sick in the night were loaded onto transport wagons, while the dead were quickly consigned to shallow mass graves. The stench of death traveled with the British army wherever it went, and Sinclair had despaired of ever scrubbing it off of his own skin.

"Sinclair," Eleanor said, her head turned toward him now from the sled, "I see something ahead. Do you see it?" She raised an arm and pointed feebly to the northwest.

He could see it, too, a clutter of black buildings, and a ship—a steamer, from the looks of it—beached on the shoreline. But was this place inhabited? And if so, by whom? Friend or foe?

He reined in the dogs and approached more slowly. But the closer he got, the more confident he became. There was no smoke from a chimney, no lanternlight shining in a window, no clatter of pots or pans. There was no sign of life whatsoever. The dogs, however, seemed well acquainted with the place and trotted into the labyrinth of frozen alleyways and dark, abandoned buildings with complete aplomb, bringing the sled to a halt in the middle of a wide and utterly desolate yard. The new lead dog—a gray beast with a broad white stripe, like a scarf, around his neck—turned and watched Sinclair for further instructions.

Sinclair dismounted, and seeing a clawed device between the runners, he stomped on it, hard, and felt its teeth dig into the ice and frozen soil. A bolt of pain shot up his leg, reminding him of the bite he'd received; the dog had torn right through his riding boot, leaving a flap of blood-tinged leather hanging loose.

Eleanor stirred in the sled, and said, in a voice as bleak as the surroundings, "Where have we come to?"

Sinclair looked around, at the warehouses and massive, abandoned machines—in one open shed, he could see huge iron vats, big enough to boil a team of oxen in, and a web of rusted chains and pulleys. There were train tracks, barely visible here and there, crisscrossing the yard, and iron wheelbarrows even more enormous than the ones he had once seen at the coal mines in Newcastle. Everything had been built with a purpose in mind—a plainly utilitarian one—and that purpose had been the making of money. The only way to do that, in a place so remote and forbidding, was by fishing or sealing or whaling. And on a grand scale. A black locomotive engine, covered with ice like a thin glaze of marzipan, sat at the end of a rusted track. There must have been twenty or thirty buildings scattered across the frozen plain, their windows cracked, their doors hanging off the hinges, and rising atop the hill at the rear Sinclair could see a spire, with a toppled cross.

For a second, it gave him pause...then it kindled a spark of defiance.

He stomped with his uninjured leg on the brake lever, and after a couple of tries he could feel it release.

"Onward!" he cried to the dogs, and at first they hesitated, but when he shouted again and shook the reins, they pulled at their harness and moved forward.

"Where are we going?" Eleanor asked.

"Up the hill."

"Why?" she asked, in an uncertain tone.

He knew what she was thinking. "Because it's the high ground," he offered, "and affords the best vantage point."

He knew that she suspected another reason.

The dogs threaded their way past what looked like a deserted blacksmith's shop—there were forges and anvils and lances almost as long as the one he had carried into battle—and a mess hall with long trestle tables, some with frozen candles still sitting on tin dishes. The candles, he thought, he might want to come back for.

As the dogs pulled the sled up the hill, their heads went down and their shoulders rose—these were powerful, well-trained beasts, and under other circumstances, he might have wished to compliment their owner. What Mr. Nolan had done with horses, someone had done with these dogs.

But when the sled approached the church, the dogs slowed down to navigate their way through a random collection of stones and worn wooden crosses, marking the gravesites of the camp's dead. There was no order to the graves, and the words that had been chiseled on some of the tombstones were so effaced by the constant wind that they were virtually obliterated. An angel with no wings stood atop one, a weeping lady with a missing arm atop another. All faced the frozen sea.

At the wooden steps leading up to the chapel, Sinclair applied the brake once again. He stepped off the runners and moved to Eleanor's side, but she was huddled down inside the sled and did not extend her hand to him.

"Let's go in," he said. "It seems the best shelter the camp affords."

And it would be needed soon. Dark clouds were filling the sky, and the wind was rising fast. He had seen such storms spring out of nowhere and batter the ship they had traveled on, driving them ever southward.

But Eleanor did not move, and her face, pale to begin with, looked positively ghostly now.

"Sinclair, you know why I—"

"I know perfectly well," he said, "and I don't want to hear a word of it."

"But there are so many other places," she said. "I saw a dining hall, on our right side as we—"

"A dining hall with no doors and a hole in its roof the size of St. Paul's."

His mention of the cathedral inadvertently reminded them both of a popular ditty they had once recited to each other, in happier days... about coconut palms as tall as St. Paul's, and sand as white as Dover. But Sinclair dismissed such thoughts from his mind and, putting a hand under her elbow, virtually lifted her out of the sled. "It's superstition and nonsense."

"It's not," she said. "You remember what happened... in Lisbon?"

It was not something he would soon forget. As they had stood before the altar in the Igreja de Santa Maria Maior—on what should have been a happy day for them—the hand of God himself had seemed to intercede. It was a lucky thing that Sinclair had been able to book passage on the brig *Coventry* for that very night.

"That was happenstance," Sinclair said, "and nothing to do with us. Why, that city has been struck by earthquakes countless times before."

He didn't want to indulge such fantasy. There were things to do, plans to make. As the dogs settled down among the gravestones, tucking their heads in and curling their tails around their hindquarters, he held Eleanor by one arm, and with his other hand on the hilt of his sword, ascended the snowy stairs. The birds that had been following them had alighted, lining the roof and spire like gargoyles. Eleanor's eyes went up and saw them, and when one cawed loudly, its beak extended and its wings flapping, she stopped in her tracks.

"It's a bloody bird," Sinclair said scornfully, dragging her up the remaining steps.

There was a pair of tall double doors at the top, though one was knocked off its hinges and simply frozen in place. The other one he was able to push, with considerable effort, until it opened enough to let them pass. A snowdrift had piled up just behind it, and once he had stepped over it, he took Eleanor's hand and helped her inside.

Their footsteps echoed hollowly on the stone floor. Rows of wooden pews faced the front, with moldering hymnals lying on some of the seats. Sinclair picked one of them up, but the few words that were still legible were not in English. Some Scandinavian tongue, if he had to guess. He dropped it on the floor, and Eleanor, instinctively, picked it up and put it back on the pew. The walls and roof, which had several holes of their own, were made of timbers that the relentless elements had polished to a fine flat sheen, every whorl and groove in the wood revealed as plainly as a wine stain on a linen tablecloth. The altar was a simple trestle table, with a rough-hewn cross hung from the rafters behind it. Eleanor, wrapped in the bulky coat, held herself back, her eyes averted, but Sinclair strode boldly up the nave. Stopping in front of the altar, he spread his arms and declared, as if presenting himself to a country squire who had invited him to come for a shooting party, "Well, here I am!"

His voice echoed around the walls, joined only by the wind whistling through the narrow windows where the glass had long since fallen away.

"Are we welcome here," he called out, tauntingly, "or are we not?"

A sudden gust blew the crest of the snowdrift up the aisle, the white flakes dusting the top of Eleanor's shoes. She quickly stepped into a row of pews.

Sinclair turned around and with his arms still out, said, "Do you see? Not a word of protest."

He knew that Eleanor feared him when he was in this mood—black and challenging and itching for a fight. But ever since the Crimea, this dark side had been brewing in him, as inescapable and ungovernable as a shadow.

"I can't imagine more suitable accommodations," he said. He looked all around, then spotted a door with great black hinges behind the altar. The rectory, he wondered? His black boots ringing on the stony pavement, he walked around the side of the altar—littered, he could see, with ancient rat feces—and pushed it open. Inside, he saw a small room, with one square window covered by a pair of shutters. It was furnished with a few sticks of furniture—

a table, a chair, a cot, whose blanket was rolled up in a ball at its foot . . . and a cast-iron stove. Dismal as it was, it was as if he had just stumbled into the drawing room at the Longchamps Club, and he could barely wait to show it to Eleanor.

"Come along!" he shouted. "We've got our suite for the night."

Eleanor clearly didn't like coming so close to the altar, but she also didn't want to cross Sinclair. She came to the door and peered in; he threw his arm around her shoulders and held her tight. "I'll get the things from the sled, and we'll see what we can make of this, eh?"

———————

Alone, Eleanor stepped to the window, parted the shutters, and looked out—a strong wind was blowing the snow across an icy plain, dotted with several more tombstones, most of them toppled and broken. On the far horizon, a ridge of mountains lay like the jagged spine of a reclining beast. There was nothing in any of it to greet the eye, or lift the spirit, or offer even a scintilla of hope; in short, there was nothing to persuade her that this was anything other than a panorama of damnation, lighted forever by a cold dead sun.

The wind rose even higher, whistling in the eaves of the church and rattling the very walls.

CHAPTER TWENTY-EIGHT

December 13, 9:30 p.m.

"JUST HOLD THE BANDAGE," Charlotte ordered. "Just hold it in place!"

Michael pressed it to Danzig's throat—blood was still seeping through—as she cut off the end of the sutures and dropped her scissors into the pan.

"And keep an eye on his blood pressure!"

Michael watched the monitor—the pressure was low, and dropping all the time.

From the moment she had rushed into the kennel, Charlotte's hands had never stopped moving with rapidity and assurance. She had bent over the gasping Danzig, and with her own fingers, closed the gaping hole in his throat. At the infirmary, she had inserted a breathing tube, anesthetized him, stitched the wound, and was now inserting an IV, to give him a transfusion.

"Is he going to make it?" Michael asked, not sure if he really wanted to know the answer.

"I don't know. He's lost a lot of blood—his jugular was

severed—and his windpipe's damaged, too." She hung the plasma bag on the rod and, after making sure it was working, readied a syringe. "I told Murphy to call for assistance. He needs a lot more help than we can give him here."

"What's the shot for? Rabies?" The bandage he held was damp and stained a deep pink.

"Tetanus," she said, holding it up to the light and tamping on the plunger. "We don't even have rabies vaccine down here. But then, there aren't supposed to be any dogs, either."

She administered the shot, but before she had even withdrawn the needle, there was a mad beeping from the BP and EKG monitors.

"Oh, shit," she said, tossing the used needle into the sink and ripping open a cabinet on the wall behind her. "He's crashing!"

An ominously steady tone filled the room.

She charged the defibrillator pads—something Michael had seen done on a dozen medical shows on TV—then applied them to the barrel of Danzig's hairy chest. His flannel shirt had been cut away, and the skin was orange from a coat of mercurochrome. One of the pads landed on a tattoo—the head of a husky—and Michael wondered if it was supposed to be Kodiak. Charlotte counted to three, yelled, "Clear!" then pressed the pads down while the sudden charge made the body jump. Danzig's head went back, and his body arched upward.

But the monitors kept up their steady drone.

Again she yelled, "Clear!" While Michael hovered a foot away, she hit Danzig with another charge. The body jerked again ... but the lines on the blue screens stayed flat. Several of the stitches had popped.

Breathing hard, her braids hanging down beside her face, she tried it one more time—there was the faint smell of barbecued meat in the room—but nothing changed. The body flattened out again, and lay perfectly still. Blood seeped slowly from his torn neck and Michael had nothing to sop it up with.

Charlotte mopped her brow with the back of her sleeve, glanced one more time at the monitors, then fell back onto the stool behind her, her shoulders slumped, her face wet with sweat. Michael waited—what were they supposed to do next? Surely this couldn't be it.

"Should I pump his heart?" he said, rising from his own stool and placing his hands above Danzig's chest.

But Charlotte simply shook her head.

"Shouldn't I at least try?" Michael said, pressing down with the heel of his hands, as he had seen done in CPR classes. "Should I give him artificial respiration?"

"He's gone, honey."

"Just tell me what I should do!"

"Nothing you *can* do," she said, looking up at the clock. "If you want to know, he was gone from the second that damned dog got at him."

Without looking behind her, she reached for and found a clipboard on the counter. She lifted the pen on its chain and recorded the time of death.

Danzig's eyes were still open, and Michael closed them.

Charlotte flicked off the machines, then picked Danzig's walrus-tooth necklace up off the floor, where she'd hastily thrown it.

"That was his good-luck charm," Michael said.

"Not good enough," she said, handing it to Michael.

They sat in silence, the corpse lying between them, until Murphy O'Connor put his head in the door.

"Bad news about the chopper," he said, then, taking in what had happened, mumbled, "Oh, sweet Mother of God."

Charlotte removed the transfusion line. "No rush," she said. "They can come anytime."

Murphy ran his hand back over his salt-and-pepper hair, and stared at the floor. "The storm," he said. "It's gonna get a lot worse before dawn. They said they'd have to wait for it to blow over."

Outside, Michael could hear a raging wind pummeling the walls of the infirmary like a hail of angry fists. He hadn't even noticed it till now.

"Christ almighty," Murphy muttered. He started to turn away, then said to Charlotte, "I'm sure you did everything possible. You're a good medical officer."

Charlotte looked unaffected by the praise.

"I'll send Franklin in, to help with the body." Then he looked at Michael. "Why don't you come down to my office? We need to talk."

Murphy walked away, and Michael wasn't sure what to do. He did not want to leave Charlotte alone—not with the body—at least not until Franklin, or somebody, got there.

"It's okay," she said, as if intuiting his problem. "You work the ER in Chi-town, you get used to dead people. Go."

Michael got up and slipped the walrus-tooth necklace into his pocket. Then he went to the sink, where he scrubbed his hands clean.

Franklin came in and, as Michael went out to the hall, Charlotte called after him, "And thanks, by the way. You make a good nurse."

In Murphy's office, he found Darryl warming his hands around a cardboard cup of coffee—it was clear that Murphy had just told him about Danzig's death—and the chief himself was sitting back, looking utterly depleted, in his desk chair. Michael leaned up against a dented file cabinet and for a minute or so no one said a word. They didn't have to.

"Any ideas?" the chief finally said, and another silence fell.

"If you're referring to Danzig and the dog," Darryl finally ventured, "no. But if you're referring to the missing bodies, then there's one thing that I think is pretty clear."

"What's that?"

"Somebody's gone off his rocker. Maybe it's a case of the Big Eye."

"I've been doing a check," Murphy replied, "and so far everybody's accounted for—even Spook. Nobody's in a daze—at least any more than usual—and nobody's gone off the reservation."

Darryl pondered this, then said, "Okay. Then whoever it is, they hid the bodies somewhere—it's cold enough out there that they'll just freeze solid again—then they hightailed it back to the base."

"And the dogs?"

Darryl had to think about that, but Michael knew that the dogs, unless they were restrained somehow, would have come back on their own.

"Can they survive in a storm like this?" Darryl asked, and Murphy snorted.

"For them, it's a day at the beach. They'll hunker down and sleep right through it. The bitch of it is, any tracks they left are already gone."

But Michael had a hunch where they might have gone. "Stromviken," he said. "That was their routine exercise run."

"Could be," Murphy said, mulling it over, "but if somebody drove them there—even if there was time, which looks pretty damn unlikely—how'd he get back to base without them? Nobody, not even I, could have walked back here alone, much less in this weather. Ain't nobody going nowhere in this soup."

"What if he was using a snowmobile?" Michael said. "Could he have towed it along behind the sled?"

Murphy assumed a quizzical expression. "I guess," he said. "But then he's got the dogs towing the snowmobile, plus the bodies in the ice block—"

"The ice block was very diminished," Darryl interjected. "It would have completely collapsed soon."

Murphy paused, then plowed ahead. "Whatever you say. But then, whoever this is, he's leaving the bodies and the dogs out there somewhere—the whaling station, the rookery, an ice cave that we don't know about—and racing back here on the snowmobile, a snowmobile that nobody noticed was missing—"

"And that nobody heard either coming or going," Michael threw in.

"Right," Murphy said, wearily rubbing his graying hair again, "that, too. You see how none of this is adding up?"

Michael saw his point, clearly. That was actually the first chance he'd had even to try putting the pieces of the puzzle together, but it was no surprise that Murphy already looked exhausted and utterly stumped.

On Darryl's face, Michael noted a look of just plain anger. His lab had been desecrated and his most prized specimen stolen. "I don't think anyone could have done it alone," he declared. "Getting those bodies out of the tank and into the sled, and in the very limited amount of time between the last time I'd been in the lab and when I found them missing?" He shook his head and said, "It had to be two people, at least, to carry this whole thing off."

"So," Murphy replied, "what are you saying? You got any candidates in mind?"

Darryl sipped the coffee, then said, "Betty and Tina? You sure you've accounted for them?"

"Why on earth would Betty and Tina do this?" Murphy asked.

"I don't know," Darryl said, in exasperation. "But maybe they wanted to do the work themselves. Maybe they thought I took it away from them. Maybe they have some other agenda altogether." He sounded not only as if he was grasping at straws, but as if he knew it himself. He threw up his hands in disgust, then let them flop back onto his lap.

"I'll follow up with them," Murphy said, in an unconvincing tone.

"In the meantime, I want a lock for my lab," Darryl insisted. "I've got my fish to look out for."

"You honestly think somebody's gonna come back for your fish, too?" Murphy replied. "Don't sweat it—I'll find you a lock."

CHAPTER TWENTY-NINE

December 13, 10:30 p.m.

WHILE SINCLAIR WENT BACK and forth fetching provisions from the sled, Eleanor tried to make herself useful in the rectory. She unrolled the woolen blanket at the foot of the cot—it was stiff as a washboard—and found an old broom in the corner with which she tried to sweep some of the rodent leavings from the floor. She opened the grate of the cast-iron furnace and found a petrified rat inside, lying on a bed of splinters and straw. She lifted it out by its tail, tossed it through the window, then battened the shutters tight again. On the table, next to the stump of a candle and a ring of rusty keys, she found a packet of lucifers, and to her own amazement she was able to get one to light. She touched it to the tinder, and after a few seconds she had a small fire glowing in the furnace.

She thought Sinclair would be pleased, but after he had set down some books and bottles from the sled, he looked askance at the blaze. "The smoke from the chimney," he said. "It will give us away."

To whom? she thought. Was there another living soul for miles? Her heart sank at the idea of extinguishing the tiny, cheerful fire.

"But this storm will dissipate it," he said, thinking aloud. "Go to it, my love."

He went back out again, and Eleanor slumped, suddenly bereft of all her strength, onto the edge of the cot. The exertions of the past few hours had been too much. She felt as if she were about to swoon, and lay back, still bundled in her coat, on top of the coarse, striped blanket. The room was swimming around her. She closed her eyes, with her hands clutching the sides of the cot, just as she had done on the awful voyage to Constantinople so many years ago. The ship, a steamer called the *Vectis,* had pitched and rolled in the heavy seas, and after leaving the port of Marseilles, it had lost its engines altogether for a time. Moira had been convinced that they were all about to die, that the ship was sure to break up in the storm and drown them all, and Eleanor had had to console her until the next morning, when the weather abruptly changed and the ship regained its power. Many of the nurses had been seasick or worse, and the sailors had to carry them up onto the stern deck where they could recover themselves in the fresh air and sunshine. Moira had dropped to her knees by the rail and offered up a volley of prayers.

Miss Florence Nightingale, herself a victim of the rough voyage, had passed right by them, simply inclining her head in their direction, as she leaned on the arm of her friend, Mrs. Selina Bracebridge. Selina was married and Florence was not (indeed, she was the most famous spinster in the British Isles), but it had been decided by the military board of governors that it would be unseemly for unmarried women to be employed overseas, attending to the wounded soldiers. So with the sole exception of their leader, all thirty-eight of the women in the nursing contingent, regardless of their actual marital status, were given the honorific title of "Mrs." They were also given uniforms expressly tailored to render the wearers as unappealing as possible and to obscure their figures completely. The dresses were gray and shapeless and hung like woolen sacks, and the bonnets were silly white contraptions that deliberately complimented no one's features. One of the nurses, in Eleanor's hearing, told Miss Nightingale that she could put up with all the other hardships of the job, but "there is caps, ma'am, that suits one face, and some that suits another's, and if I'd known, ma'am, about the caps, great as was my desire to come out to nurse at Scutari, I wouldn't have come, ma'am."

They were an unusual bunch, the nurses who had signed on to the mission, and Eleanor was well aware of the suspicion they engendered in many of the people back home. In some quarters of the British public and press, they were lauded as heroines, going off to do grim but honorable work under the most appalling conditions. But in others, they were written off as immodest and opportunistic fortune seekers, young women of working-class backgrounds hoping to romantically ensnare a wounded officer at his most susceptible moment. And though fourteen of the nurses had been recruited from public hospitals, as were Eleanor and Moira, Miss Nightingale had also selected six holy sisters from St. John's House, eight from Miss Sellons's Anglican sisterhood, and ten Roman Catholic nuns—five of them from the Norwood Orphanage and five from the Sisters of Mercy at Bermondsey. While many of the soldiers were themselves Roman Catholic, the idea that these nuns might be closely tending to wounded men who were not so inclined—men who followed the Protestant faith, for instance—was shocking to many back home. What if, under the guise of nursing, the sisters used this golden opportunity to proselytize in secret for the sinister Church of Rome?

As the *Vectis* approached the Dardanelles, Eleanor observed Miss Nightingale steady herself at the ship's rail and gaze off at the passing land. Her dark hair was neatly done, with a severe part down its center, and her long face, paler than usual, wore an uncommon expression of rapture. Eleanor looked off in the same direction, but all she saw were arid, yellow fields. The ocean breeze picked up some of Nightingale's words, and Eleanor heard her extolling to Mrs. Bracebridge "the fabled plains of Troy, where Achilles fought and Helen wept." She looked transported by the sight. Eleanor knew that Miss Nightingale was from a fine family, and had been educated at the finest schools, and she envied her for it. She herself had gone to London in hopes of improving herself, but the hard and unending work at the Harley Street hospital had left her little time, or money, to pursue such ends.

Sinclair had briefly changed that.

But how would he have reacted, had he known that she was

coming over to the theater of war? He would, she felt certain, have warned her not to do so. But the thought that a time might come when he would need her—and she would be thousands of miles away, unable to help—was too much to bear. When the word had gone out that volunteers were needed for the field hospitals, Eleanor had jumped at the chance, and Moira—whose attachment to Captain Rutherford was, perhaps, more practical than ardent—said, "Birds of a feather flock together," and blithely signed an application of her own.

What, she wondered, had become of Moira? Long gone now, of course.

Bustling into the room again, his arms filled with hymnals, Sinclair said, "These should do nicely." He bent down to the furnace, ripped several of the books into pieces, and fed the crumpled pages into the burgeoning fire. Eleanor said nothing though the sacrilegious act added to her discomfort.

When the fire was roaring, he closed the grate and announced that he had collected some other things, too. He went to the door and dragged in a canvas sack that he had left outside; from it, he produced candle stubs, tin plates and cups, bent spoons and knives, a cracked decanter. "Tomorrow, I'll make a more thorough reconnaissance, but for now we have everything we need." He was back in his military mode, scouting his surroundings, gathering provisions, planning strategies. Eleanor was relieved to see it, and hoped the mood held...for she had learned that something far darker could always, at any moment, supplant it.

Grabbing at the bag of food from the kennel, now propped against the table leg, he said, "Should we warm some up for dinner?" He made it sound as if he was asking if she would care to indulge in a chocolate soufflé. "Food," he said, before adding, as he placed one of the black wine bottles on the table, "and drink."

CHAPTER THIRTY

December 14

THE INFIRMARY AT POINT ADÉLIE did not actually have a proper morgue, but then it didn't really need one. The whole continent of Antarctica was a cold-storage unit, and Murphy decided to keep Danzig's body in the coldest and most protected spot of all—the glaciology vault built ten feet under the core bin. After the geologist's body had been recovered from the crevasse the year before, that was where they'd kept his body, too. Betty and Tina were less than thrilled, but they understood the gravity of the situation and were willing to make the accommodation.

"Just so long as you seal the body up tight," Betty said. "We can't have any risk of contamination to the core samples."

"And I don't want to feel the poor guy's eyes boring through the back of my skull," Tina added. "It's spooky enough already down there."

With that, Michael had to agree. He had volunteered to help Franklin with the removal of the corpse; he felt he owed at least that much to Danzig. After Charlotte had made some basic preparations, the body was zipped into a clear plastic body bag, then into a second bag of olive-green canvas. Michael and Franklin had used a gurney to transport it down the bumpy concourse to the glaciology lab; the wind was blowing so powerfully that the gurney was tipped over twice, and each time that Michael had to lift the body again, he felt a chill descend his spine. The corpse was already beginning to stiffen up, either from rigor mortis or the effects of the subzero temperatures. It felt to Michael like he was lifting a human statue.

The steps down into the ice vault had been cut out of the permafrost, and rather than try to negotiate the gurney down them, Franklin and Michael simply carried the body, by its shoulders and feet, underground. A single white light on a motion sensor went off as they entered and bathed them in a hollow glare. There was an earthen slab carved from one corner of the vault, and Franklin gestured at it with his chin. Michael hoisted up his end—the head and shoulders—and they swung the body onto the slab. It landed with a thump. On the other side of the vault, a cylindrical ice core rested on a long lab table, held by a vise. Several drills and bits and saws hung from a wall rack. In a continent of cold, this place struck Michael as the coldest spot of all—and the most frightening. A frozen tomb that called only for a millstone to be rolled across its entrance.

"Let's get the hell out of here," Franklin said, and Michael thought he saw him surreptitiously cross himself.

At the top of the stairs, huddled in the freezing wind with her arms around herself, was Betty. "I hope he's not going to have to be there long," she said to Franklin.

"Whenever the next plane can make it in," he said, already stomping off toward the rec hall. But Michael lingered. He had a generous slice of cold roast beef in his pocket for his pet skua, and when he pulled it out, Betty smiled. "Ollie will be beside himself."

Michael brushed away the snow that had once again piled up in front of the plasma crate, knelt and looked inside. There he was—bigger than ever—his gray bill poking up out of a nest of slender wood shavings. Seeing his benefactor, the bird shook himself all over and waddled to his feet. Michael held out the roast beef, and after regarding it for a second, Ollie lunged forward, grabbing it in one swoop and gulping it down. "Next time maybe I should bring some horseradish," Michael said. The bird looked up at him, perhaps waiting for more. "One day he's going to have to fly away," Michael said over his shoulder, and Betty chuckled.

"What, and give up a good thing?"

When Michael stood up again, she said, "Face it—that bird is tame and probably wouldn't survive a day in the wild. They don't serve roast beef there."

"But what happens when my time here is up?" Michael said. "I can't exactly take him back to Tacoma."

"Don't worry," Betty said. "Tina's already drawing up adoption papers. Ollie will be fine."

That put his mind to rest, at least on that one small point. It seemed so long since he'd been able to rectify anything in this world—much less save it—that he was grateful even for any little unforeseen break. Maybe the curse he'd felt ever since the Cascades disaster could be lifted, after all . . . one tiny bit at a time.

Trudging back toward the commons, he passed one of the search teams Murphy had sent out—one made up of Calloway, the divemaster, and another grunt whose hat, with a big brim and earflaps, was pulled so far down that Michael couldn't even identify him. "Evening, mate," Calloway called out, waving a flashlight, and Michael lifted a gloved hand in acknowledgment. "If you see any lost dogs," Calloway added, "you'll let me know, right?"

"You'll be my first call."

As he approached the marine biology lab, Michael saw that the lights were on, and even under the wind he could hear the strains of classical music playing inside. Detouring to the lab, he tried the door, but it stopped short, and he could see that a rope had been tied around the handle on the inside.

"Who's there?" he heard Darryl shout.

Michael shouted back, "It's me, Michael."

"Hold on."

Darryl came over to the door, slipped the rope off the handle, then let him in.

"That's some high-tech security system you've got there," Michael said, stamping the snow off his boots.

"It'll have to do until Murphy gets a real lock put in."

"But it only works when you're inside. What do you do when you're not here?"

"I'm posting a sign."

"That says what?"

"That says there are several amphibious specimens loose in here and that they're all poisonous."

Michael laughed. "And you think that will work?"

"No, not really," Darryl admitted, returning to his lab stool, "but then I think the thieves have already got the only thing they actually wanted."

On the counter in front of him, Darryl had a fish, about a foot long, splayed open from one end to the other, with pins holding its skin back. The whole thing was nearly transparent. Its gills were white, and its blood—if there was any—had no more color than water. Only its eye, fixed and dead, was golden. Michael was unpleasantly reminded of biology class in high school. The next victim was already lined up, sitting almost motionless at the bottom of a supercooled tank with frost coating its rim, on the other side of a row of glass jars, the size of shot glasses; all the jars were filled with solution, but two or three also contained small organs extracted and preserved for further study.

"Should he be watching this?" Michael said.

"That's why I've blocked his view with the jars."

"Looks sort of like a perch," Michael said, of the fish being dissected.

"You've got a good eye," Darryl said. "It's part of the perchlike suborder, *Notothenioidei.*"

"Come again?"

"Over the past fifty-five million years," Darryl began, clearly happy to hold forth on such topics, "the temperature of the Southern Ocean has steadily decreased, from about twenty degrees centigrade to its present-day extremes, roughly minus one point eight degrees centigrade. The Antarctic marine environment also became more and more isolated. The water got colder, migration got harder, and the shallow-water fish either had to adapt, or die. Most of them went extinct."

"But not these guys?"

"These guys," Darryl said, with evident fondness and satisfaction, "toughed it out. The notothenids hung out at the bottom of the sea, biding their time. They acclimated themselves by developing a lower metabolic demand and raising their individual oxygen solubility. They could store the oxygen and hold on to it longer in their tissues."

"Not in their blood?" Michael asked, remembering Darryl talking about some of this before their first dive. "They have no hemoglobin?"

"So you do pay attention," Darryl said. "I'm impressed. Since they have no red blood cells, their blood is clear, but it does carry a natural antifreeze, a glycoprotein that's made of repeating units of sugar and amino acids. The glycoprotein depresses the freezing point of water two hundred or three hundred times more than would normally be the case."

Michael could follow only the gist of the explanation. "So, they've got their own natural antifreeze, like you put in your car?"

"Not exactly," Darryl said, at the same time delicately extracting the fish's heart and plopping it with tweezers into one of the jars. Michael got a whiff of formaldehyde. "Unlike the ethylene glycol you put in your radiator, the molecules of fish antifreeze behave differently; yes, they do protect the fish from freezing, even in supercool water, but just so long as the fish is careful not to—"

There was a loud banging on the door, and when Michael turned he could see the improvised rope handle stretch.

"Now what?" Darryl complained.

"It's probably Calloway—they're doing a complete search of the base."

Darryl grudgingly got off his stool. "But why come here? To search the scene of the crime?"

"They're not looking for the bodies," Michael warned him. "Murphy's keeping all that as quiet as he can."

Darryl stopped and looked at Michael. "They think I've got the dog team in here?" Shaking his head, he unlooped the rope.

"Hey, mate, what you afraid of?" Calloway said as he barged in, with the grunt in the long-brimmed cap close behind.

They stood just inside the lab, pounding the snow off their coats and boots.

"I just prefer it when people call ahead."

"I'll do that," Calloway said, clapping him on the shoulder, "next time." He caught sight of the lab bench and its eviscerated subject.

"Icefish?" Calloway said. "You know, the bigger ones make some pretty fine filets." He moseyed over, and scanning the specimen jars said, "But I think I'll take a pass on what's left of this mess."

The grunt in the cap—Michael recognized him now, his name was Osmond and he worked with Uncle Barney in the kitchen— trailed along after, poking his nose into some cabinets and under some counters. What on earth, Michael wondered, could he possibly think he would find there?

"But this fish here, this fella's still fresh," Calloway said, sticking with his customary outback impression, and gazing down into the cooling tank. "Judging from those bony lips, I'd say this one is a Charcot's icefish."

"You would be correct," Darryl said, sounding mollified; he was always appreciative when anyone displayed some knowledge of marine life. "We just caught it in the last batch of traps."

Michael came around to the other side of the table to get a better look, and he saw a long fish with an armor-plated head and a flat nose, like a duck's bill. Its skin was so thin that he could see the complex pattern of plates and bones just inside. Darryl, too, came around, perhaps to point out some of its unusual features, but bumped into Osmond, who'd completed his rudimentary inspection of the premises and had decided to join the party.

"You can see right through it," Osmond said, slowly; Michael didn't think he had a lot going on upstairs. "It's like he's Casper the friendly fish."

There were smiles all around as Osmond bent his head over the tank to get a closer look, but then Darryl suddenly glanced at the brim of his hat, and shouted, "No! Get back!"

Darryl swiped at the cap, but it was already too late—a great blob of snow and ice, shimmering like a cascade of diamonds, slid down off the brim and splashed into the tank. The fish moved, surprised by the movement, and, possibly thinking that some food source had wandered by, raised its head toward the surface. The rain of ice crystals pattered on the surface, some bobbing a few inches down, and touching the fish on its nose and gills.

"Goddammit!" Darryl cried, and a second later Michael could see why—the quivering fish stopped moving, its body straightened out, and as Michael looked on with amazement, a fine latticework of ice swiftly rippled across its entire length in a chain reaction, turning it as stiff as a board and as dead as a doornail. Slowly it floated, staring and transparent, back to the surface of the tank.

Michael was confused. "But I thought you said these fish had antifreeze in their blood."

"They do," Darryl said mournfully, "and that's what keeps them alive in supercool water, at the lower depths. But ice floats, remember, and so it doesn't penetrate the benthic regions. If these fish actually come into contact with ice, the ice crystals act as a nucleus, a propagating agent, and overwhelm their defenses."

"Geez," Osmond said, holding his wet cap in his hands now. "I'm really sorry. I never knew something like that could happen." He looked around at the others to see if he was in serious trouble.

"It's all right, mate," Calloway said. "If it's no good to the beakers, it's still fine for the bouillabaisse."

"Not this one," Darryl said. "I can still thaw it out and drain the blood."

"The blood," Calloway said, dubiously. "That's what you want?"

"That blood, my friend, contains secrets the world will be very glad to have one day."

Calloway tapped Osmond on the sleeve, as if to say 'Let's leave the loonies to their crazy experiments,' and they skulked off toward the door. "I'm sure you're right about that, Doc," he said, then they ducked out into a blast of howling wind and whirling snow.

Darryl picked up a pair of tongs, lifted the icefish out by its tail, and laid it on the counter. It was so hard it actually wobbled in place.

"Now I can see why you don't exactly put out the welcome mat to the lab," Michael said.

"And why I wanted that lock," Darryl replied. But then, picking up a scalpel, he plunged right back into his work as if Michael wasn't even there. A minute or two later, Michael pulled on all his gear and went out into the teeth of the gathering storm.

CHAPTER THIRTY-ONE

December 15

THE GALE, rather than passing through, seemed to have settled down over the base, and Murphy's lockdown order, to Michael's frustration, was still in effect. No one was leaving the compound for any reason. "Wherever those bodies are, they're frozen stiff," Murphy told him, "and the dogs, well, they know how to survive."

Michael had to take his word on that.

Word of Danzig's death had of course cast a dismal pall over the base, and the memorial service, held in the rec hall, was crowded. The Ping-Pong table was folded up and pushed out into the corridor, and an assortment of desk chairs was wheeled in to join the sofas, but there still weren't enough for everyone to sit on. The rest of the grunts and beakers simply sat around on the threadbare wall-to-wall carpeting, their arms wrapped around their knees, as Murphy stood up in front of the blank plasma-screen TV. He was wearing, in acknowledgment of the occasion, a dark necktie over his denim shirt.

"I know a lot of you knew Erik a lot better than I did, so I want to leave time for all of you to say something."

Michael had almost forgotten that Danzig had a first name; in the fratlike atmosphere of the base, most everyone went by a last name, or a nickname.

"But personally, I never knew a guy who was more up for anything, anytime—except for maybe Lawson."

There was some low laughter, and Lawson, who was sitting against the wall with Michael and Charlotte and Darryl, smiled shyly.

"And those dogs—man, did he love those dogs." He lowered his head and shook it sadly. "Whatever went wrong there, whatever happened to make Kodiak go off like that—a brain tumor, a fever—the weird thing is, I know that, even now, Danzig—Erik— would have understood it. Those dogs loved him as much as he loved them." He ran a hand over his own head. "And that's why we are going to find the other dogs. I promise you—we're going to find them for him."

"When?" one of the grunts called out.

"Soon as it's safe," Murphy replied. "And when we know that the other dogs aren't affected in the same way."

The threat of contagion hadn't actually occurred to Michael. What if the other huskies had contracted something from Kodiak? What if they'd all become killers?

Murphy looked down at some notes he had in his hand. "I don't know how much a lot of you knew about Danzig's life out in the real world, but for the record he was married to a great woman— Maria—who's a county coroner." The immediate irony of that stopped him for a second. "She's living down in Florida."

Miami Beach, Michael remembered.

"I've spoken to her a couple of times now, and told her everything she needed to know, and she said she wanted me to give her blessing to everyone down here—especially Franklin, Calloway, and Uncle Barney, for all the grits and gravy—and thank you all for your friendship. She said he was never happier than when he was down here, on the back of the sled, with the temperature thirty below." He glanced nervously at the papers again. "And oh yeah, she wanted me to say a special thanks to Dr. Charlotte Barnes, for trying so hard to save his life—"

All eyes turned toward Charlotte, whose chin was resting atop her folded arms. She gave a small nod.

"—and Michael Wilde."

Michael was caught off guard.

"Seems he'd been telling her a lot about you, Michael, something about how you were gonna make him famous."

"I'll still do my best," Michael said, just loudly enough for all to hear.

"He told Maria there were going to be photographs of him and the dogs—the last dogs, I don't need to remind anyone, that you'll ever see down here—in that magazine of yours, *Eco-World*."

It was *Eco-Travel*, but Michael wasn't about to correct him. "There will be," Michael said, appropriating the editor's prerogative. In fact, he'd try to persuade Gillespie to put a shot of Danzig and the sled dogs on the cover sometime. It was the least he could do.

While Murphy offered up a few more details about Danzig's life—apparently, he'd worked a million different jobs, from bee-keeper to dog catcher to mortuary chauffeur ("that's how he met Maria")—Michael just kept his head down and thought his own thoughts. For one thing, he meant to get Maria's home address before he left the base; he still had Danzig's walrus-tooth necklace, and he wanted to mail it back to her as soon as he was back in civilization. Maybe with a print of a shot he'd taken of her husband, in all his glory, sledding through a snowstorm.

He also knew he should be calling the Nelsons' house back in Tacoma; he wanted to hear how the move had gone and whether Kristin had shown any sign at all of being aware that she was back in her old house. He pretty much knew what the answer would be— and he knew that it would be Karen who'd tell him—but still he felt that it was his duty to keep checking in. And he wondered how long that would continue; from what he knew of comas and vegetative states, Kristin could go on indefinitely.

Uncle Barney, sitting a few feet away, blew his nose loudly into a red handkerchief. Murphy was telling a story about some colossal meal Danzig had consumed.

Calloway stood up next and told a long, funny anecdote about once trying to cram Danzig into a regulation-size diving suit, and Betty and Tina talked about how helpful Danzig had been one day when they were trying to unload some ice cores in a driving storm.

Michael could hear the blizzard that was raging, whistling around the narrow windows and the corrugated steel walls of the module they were all sitting in. It could abate in an hour, or it could go on for another solid week. At pole, he had learned, all bets were off.

After everyone had spoken, Murphy haltingly led them in a recitation of the Lord's Prayer, and when a few moments of silence had passed, Franklin sat at the piano in the corner, and played a rousing version of the old Bob Seger hit, "Old Time Rock 'n' Roll." It was one of Danzig's favorite songs, and Franklin was able to give it a suitably gritty rendition. A lot of the others joined in on the lines, "Today's music ain't got the same soul, I like that old time rock 'n' roll!" And when the music died down, Uncle Barney announced that, in Danzig's honor, hot grits and gravy were being served in the commons.

On the way out, Murphy waved Michael and Lawson over to one side and said, "You guys see Ackerley anywhere?"

Even when Spook was in the room, it was easy to miss him; he was that quiet and self-effacing. But Michael had to say no.

"Probably talking to his plants," Lawson said, "and lost all track of time."

Murphy nodded in agreement, but said, "You mind going to see if he's okay? I just tried him on the intercom but he's not picking up."

Although Michael had hoped to join Charlotte and Darryl in the commons—he'd spent the whole day making notes in his room and had pretty much forgotten to eat—he could hardly say no.

"Don't worry," Murphy said, "I'll be sure to save you some grits." He turned to Lawson. "But how's your leg? You up to it?"

Lawson, who'd dropped the ski gear on his ankle, said, "It's fine—no problem at all. Use it or lose it."

To Michael, he always sounded a little like a coach on the sidelines of a big game.

"Might want to use some poles," Murphy said, and Lawson agreed. "Wind's gusting at eighty miles per hour."

They suited up and grabbed some ski poles from the equipment locker, and while the others poured into the brightly lighted commons, they turned the other way, up a long bleak concourse where the wind was whipping up little cyclones of ice and snow and sending them whirling, like tops, back and forth from one side to the other. Some gusts were so strong that Michael was blown back against a wall or half-buried fence, and had to wait to push off again until the wind had died down. Not that it ever stopped. There were times, in Antarctica, when you wished for nothing more than still-ness, a temporary truce with the elements, a chance to stand still and catch your breath and look up at the sky. The sky could be so beautiful—so blue and pristine it looked like the most perfect thing imaginable, an enameled bowl fired to a hard blue glaze—and at other times, like now, it was simply a smudged bucket, a dull broad glare that was impossible to distinguish from the endless continent of empty ice it glowered over.

The ski poles were a good idea; Michael doubted he could have stayed upright without them. Lawson, with his sore ankle, would surely have been toppled. In fact, Michael made it a point to stay a couple of yards behind Lawson, just in case he went over and started to roll. Once the wind caught you and knocked you down on an icy patch, you could roll like a bowling ball until you hit some kind of obstruction; Michael had seen a beaker named Penske, a meteorologist, rolling past the Administration module one morning until he collided with the flagpole and hung on to it for dear life.

Michael rubbed one mitten across his goggles to clear away some of the snow, and for a second he wondered if he could make his fortune by marketing goggles at the South Pole that had their own windshield wipers. He'd have liked to call out to Lawson, to ask him if the leg was really okay or if he wanted to turn back, but he knew that the wind would blow the words right back into his mouth—and the temperature was so low you could crack your teeth if you kept your mouth open too long.

They made their way past the glaciology lab—Michael glanced inside for Ollie, but if the bird had learned anything so far, it was to stay inside the crate on a night like this—and the marine biology lab, and the climatology lab, until Michael saw Lawson heading off to the left, toward a big, rusted-out trailer squatting on its cinder blocks like an old red rooster. Bright light shone out through its narrow window panels.

Lawson stopped to rub his ankle under the rough wooden trel-lis that framed the ramp, and motioned for Michael to go on ahead. The door was a steel plate—dented, scratched, and covered with the faded remnants of Phish decals—and Michael banged on it with his fist. Then, having given warning, he shoved it open and went inside.

His goggles immediately fogged up, and he had to slip them back on top of his head. He parted some thick plastic curtains, threw his hood back, and found himself standing in a sea of metal shelves and cabinets, all at least six feet high, and crammed with samples of indigenous moss and lichens. There were little white labels, inscribed in a spidery hand, on each shelf or drawer. Fluorescent lights flickered in the ceiling, and from somewhere among the impenetrable racks he heard the tinny sound of cheap speakers playing an endless jam.

And he also heard something else—a low, wet, snurfling sound. When Lawson came through the door, Michael instinctively motioned for him to keep silent. Lawson looked puzzled, but Michael gestured for him to stay where he was, by the door, and then, still carrying his ski poles, he started to thread his way through the maze of cabinets. Could it be another one of the dogs, Michael wondered? Or more than one? Should he back off and call the chief for reinforcements? But what if Ackerley was in big trouble and needed help right now?

The music was getting louder, but so was the strange lapping sound. Like somebody slurping soup. Or cereal. Was that all it was? Ackerley, deaf to the world, eating a bowl of cornflakes and rocking out? Michael found himself wedged between two towering cabinets, one marked GLACIAL MORAINE, SW QUADRANT, and the other reading SPECIMENS, STROMVIKEN SITE. But there was a chewing sound, too, so maybe it wasn't cereal. More like a stew maybe. Why would you eat some microwaved crap in a lab trailer when Uncle Barney was serving up hot grits at the memorial dinner?

He peered through some of the shelves and saw a long lab counter, not so different from Darryl's, with a couple of sinks, a microscope, some bottles of chemicals. But no one was sitting on the lab stool. And now that he looked again, he saw that a couple of potted plants were upended, and one of them had smashed onto the floor. An iPod was cradled on a shelf between its own tiny speakers. Michael stepped out of the shelves and closer to the lab table. The eating noises were coming from the other side, from down near the floor, and as he moved around the corner, he saw the tips of two rubber boots, their clasps undone, sticking out. He gripped the ski poles harder.

The eating sound became a rending sound, like flesh being torn, and when he got all the way around, he saw first the broad expanse of a flannel shirt, stretched across the shoulders of a big man, huddled over a body on the floor, and busy at work. If he hadn't known better, Michael would have thought, in that first instant, that it was Danzig.

Who was dead.

He raised one of the sharp-tipped ski poles and shouted, for want of anything better to say, "Hey! You! Stop what—"

But he got no further. The huddled man's head whipped around, startled, the beard so matted with blood it looked like it had been coated with a bright red paintbrush. His eyes were red-rimmed, too, and blinking furiously. Michael was so stunned he fell back, and the man leapt up at him, snarling. One of the poles went flying, clattering against a cabinet, and Lawson hollered, "What's going on?" and started crashing through the labyrinth.

The man clutched at Michael's collar, almost as if seeking something—*his help?*—and his breath reeked of blood and decay. But worst of all, it *was* Danzig—dead and frozen Danzig, with his throat torn out by the dog—whose fingers were ripping at the fabric of Michael's coat. Michael staggered back against another set of shelves, and the whole rack toppled over, taking him and Danzig down onto the floor amid a hail of dirt and seeds. Michael banged him in the face with the handle of the pole, wishing he could somehow get the sharp end into action. Danzig's face hovered above his own, his teeth stained with blood. His eyes were black with rage and—though Michael would only have time to think of it later—a bottomless grief, too.

Another pole suddenly flashed past Michael's head and gouged a hole in Danzig's shoulder. The man reared back, then jumped at Lawson. But his boots skidded on the loose seedpods, and he had to scramble to get up again. Michael quickly rolled over and stumbled to his own feet. Danzig had shoved Lawson, not all that steady to begin with, out of the way; he was sprawled on the floor, waving his ski poles wildly.

But instead of continuing his attack, Danzig stumbled away and went barging through the shelves with his arms swinging like an ape's, pulling one rack after another down onto the floor behind him. Sod and seeds and gravel flew everywhere, and by the time Michael had clambered over the detritus and made it through the plastic curtains and out to the door, the only thing he could see was a slick of blood on the ramp and a dark shape staggering blindly through the trellis and on into the maelstrom outside.

December 15, 10:30 p.m.

"What the *hell* are you talking about?" Murphy said, once Michael and Lawson had cornered him in the kitchen. Uncle Barney was just out of earshot, frying up one final skillet of grits. "Danzig is dead, for Christ's sake!"

"He's not," Michael repeated, keeping his head and his voice low. "That's what we're trying to tell you."

"You saw him, too?" Murphy said to Lawson, looking for confirmation of the impossible.

"I saw him, too." Lawson glanced at Michael, as if urging him to continue.

"And he's killed Ackerley," Michael said.

Murphy looked as if he was about to swallow his own tongue. The blood drained from his face.

"We found Ackerley in his lab," Michael said, "already dead, and Danzig was mauling the body. In fact, he's out there somewhere right now."

Murphy leaned back against a freezer, plainly unable to process what he was being told—and Michael couldn't blame him. If he hadn't seen it with his own eyes—if he hadn't been attacked himself—he wouldn't have believed it either.

"So, he's not in the body bag," Murphy said, thinking out loud, "and he's not in the core bin where we put him."

"No," Lawson said, "he's not."

"And Ackerley's dead, too," Murphy repeated, as if simply to let the terrible information sink in.

"That's right," Michael said. "We should go after him—now—before he gets too far."

"But if he's gone stark raving mad," Murphy said, as if clutching at a ray of hope, "he'll just freeze to death out there."

Michael didn't know what to say to that. It sounded perfectly reasonable—of course a crazy man, without even a hat on, would surely die either from exposure or from falling into a crevasse—but at the same time he wasn't sure of it at all. Nothing made sense anymore. He had been with Danzig in the infirmary; he'd watched as Charlotte recorded his time of death. Whatever was running around out there on the ice wasn't necessarily Danzig at all. Michael didn't know what to call it.

"What did you do with Ackerley's body?" Murphy asked, trying hard to collect himself.

"It's where we left it," Michael said. "Charlotte should examine it as soon as possible. And then we need to store it somewhere."

Uncle Barney said, "Excuse me, gents," opened the freezer to retrieve some butter, then limped back out of earshot.

"Not where we put the last one," Murphy said, keeping his voice low. "We'll use the old meat locker outside. If Dr. Barnes is wrong about this one too, I don't want it running amok like the other one." He suddenly caught himself, and said, "You know what I'm saying. I mean, Danzig was a great guy, and Ackerley was a nice enough fella, too, but this is all just so goddamn bad, so goddamn awful . . ." He trailed off, clearly flummoxed at everything he had to deal with.

But Michael didn't think Charlotte *had* been wrong. Impossible as it was to accept, Danzig *had* died, then somehow come back to life—though that was not an argument he was prepared to make just now.

Lawson bent down to nurse his bad ankle, made worse by the scuffle in the botany lab. And Murphy's hair suddenly looked a lot more salt than pepper.

"We could look for Sleeping Beauty at the same time," Michael said, eager to get the go-ahead from Murphy. "And her Prince Charming."

"Not to mention the sled dogs," Lawson said. "If the NSF finds out that the last team ever allowed down here—the dogs that poor Danzig had to get grandfathered in—are missing in action, it's going to be a bureaucratic nightmare."

"Danzig used to run them to Stromviken," Michael said, "and the forecast's good, for a change. This storm is passing."

"Not for very long," Murphy said. "Last report, a new front's due by early evening tomorrow."

"All the more reason to get on it," Michael said.

Lawson nodded his agreement.

"What about your ankle?" Murphy asked. "Looks like you're favoring it."

"Snowmobiling's no problem. And if we do find them—the dogs or the bodies—at least I know how to drive the sled back to camp."

"All right," Murphy said, as if he could no longer argue the point. "But not tonight. Get some solid rack time, then, first thing in the morning, if the weather allows, I'll log you in on a trip to the whaling station." Reaching for the walkie-talkie fastened to his belt, he added, "I'll tell Franklin to have a couple of snowmobiles at the flagpole, gassed up and ready to go, by nine a.m."

CHAPTER THIRTY-TWO

December 16, 9:30 a.m.

SINCLAIR HAD BEEN GONE FOR HOURS, and while Eleanor's greatest fear was that something would prevent him from returning at all, she also dreaded the state in which he might return. He had been in a black humor when he left, seething with rage at the endless storm and bristling at his confinement in the freezing church.

"Damn this place to Hell!" he'd shouted, his words echoing around the abandoned chapel and up to the worn beams in the roof. "Damn these stones and damn these timbers!" With one arm, he'd swept a candleholder off the altar and sent it spinning across the floor. Stomping down the nave, his bootheels ringing on the stone, he'd thrown open the creaking door to the graveyard outside and hurled his imprecations at the leaden sky. He'd been answered by a chorus of forlorn howls from the sled dogs, curled up in balls among the markers and tombstones.

She especially feared him when he was like that, when he chose to issue his challenges at the heavens. She was convinced that he'd already had his answer, in Lisbon, and she had no wish to hear that verdict again.

"Sinclair," she'd ventured, leaning for support against the door-jamb of the rectory, "shouldn't we bring the dogs into the church? They'll die if left outside, unprotected."

His head had whipped around, and in his eyes she could see that mad feverish gleam she had first seen at Scutari.

"I'll warm them up," he growled, and then, in his greatcoat, he'd stalked out into the storm, not even bothering to pull the door closed behind him; he seemed impervious to the hostile elements. A cloud of ice and snow had whirled into the church, and she had heard the barking of the dogs as Sinclair harnessed them to the sled.

Eleanor had gathered her coat around her, the one made from the miraculous fabric, and made her way to the open door. She had seen Sinclair standing at the back of the sled, swearing at the dogs as they ran down the snowy hillside. When they were out of sight, she put her weight against the rough wood and pushed it closed.

The exertion made her weak, and she slumped into the last pew. Afraid she was about to faint, she bent her head to the back of the pew in front of her and rested it there. The wood was cold but not entirely smooth, and she could see, very close up, some words—a name?—carved into it. But whatever it was, it wasn't English and the letters were nearly worn away. All that she could discern were some numbers, in the form of a date—25.12.1937. Christmas Day—1937. And she simply let her gaze remain there, while her mind turned this information over and over. It had been 1856 when she and Sinclair had embarked on their ill-fated voyage aboard the *Coventry*. And if this inscription, these numbers, were indeed a date, then they had been carved eighty-one years after she had been cast into the sea.

Eighty-one years. Time enough for everyone she knew—and everyone who knew her—to be dead.

Then her thoughts leapt forward again, because the place had so clearly been deserted for years, probably decades, and how many more years did that suggest? How long was it, she wondered, that she had slept in the ice at the bottom of the ocean? Had centuries passed? What world was it that she now, however unhappily, inhabited?

She removed her glove and ran her fingers over the letters in the wood, as if to feel the truth of them. At first, even this sensation was unnerving, its tactile nature so overwhelming; she still wasn't yet used to feeling anything physical at all. After so long in the ice, her skin was new, almost foreign, even to her. Between Sinclair and herself, there had been little communion. Of course, there was always the question of propriety—their secret, and aborted, union in the Portuguese church counted for naught in her mind. And there was, in the frigid and awful place where she found herself now, nothing to kindle ardor of any kind...or nurture so much as a warm thought.

But in her heart, Eleanor knew that there was also something more than that standing in the way, something that would always be there, serving as a constant reminder and an ever-present reproach, and while it was the one thing that bound her to Sinclair, possibly for eternity, it was also the one thing that held them apart. Each could see, in the other's pallor and in the other's desperate eyes, a more urgent need and imperative desire. Tellingly, their lips were cold, their fingers like icicles, and their hearts as guarded as swords in their sheaths.

In that respect, little had changed since the Crimea. Deprivation was all she knew.

No sooner had the Nightingale nurses arrived at the Barrack Hospital in Scutari—so named because it had originally been the Selimiye Kislasi barracks of the Turkish army—than they discovered there was not enough of anything, whether it was bandages or blankets, medicines or stump pillows (to support what remained of amputated legs or arms). Eleanor had never seen, or even imagined, such squalor as she encountered there, and even some of the ladies who had served in workhouses and prisons declared that they, too, were shocked at the way the British wounded were treated. Men who had had limbs sawn off on the battlefield were left unattended and without medication of any kind, unable to move or even feed themselves. Soldiers who had succumbed to dysentery, uncontrollable diarrhea, or the mysterious "Crimea fever" that had raged through the ranks lay in the crowded corridors, on thin, blood-soaked pallets, begging in vain for a cup of water. The stench from the open sewers that ran below the barracks was unbearable, but the cold from the broken windows was so great that the men had taken to stuffing the holes with straw, which further intensified the miasma in the wards. Several of the more delicate ladies immediately fell ill themselves, and so became more burden than help from the very start.

Eleanor and Moira, like most of the others, were first put to work darning sheets and washing linen—not what they had come all that way to do. They had come to nurse the wounded men, to assist the doctors and medical staff with their surgical operations, but there was such hostility and suspicion on the part of the doctors that the nurses were refused admission to many of the wards and given no cooperation when they did gain entry.

"You'd think we was trying to steal their cuff links," Moira said in disgust at having been turned away from one of the sickrooms filled with casualties. "I can hear the poor beggars lyin' on their rags, pleadin' for a bucket, or a drop of morphine, and here I am, not more than ten steps away, doing what? Mending a hole in a sock!"

At first, Eleanor, too, had been puzzled that Miss Nightingale did not fight harder on behalf of her charges, but she soon came to see the wisdom of it. The British army had its own ways, and they had been set in stone for hundreds of years; by limiting the challenge her nursing corps presented, and avoiding confrontation whenever possible, Miss Nightingale had been able to gradually and unalarmingly expand the duties and responsibilities of her staff. Once the military command had come to see the benefits of clean linen and fresh bandages, they also began to appreciate the advantages of the hot tea and cereal, beef broth and jelly that the nurses prepared in their makeshift kitchen. And the men—mutilated, suffering, many times breathing their last on a threadbare blanket, far from home—came to bless the nurses, in their shapeless smocks and their silly caps.

But it was Florence Nightingale, in particular, who had won their hearts and admiration forever. She had fearlessly entered even the fever wards, where the doctors themselves refused to go (their attitude being that the wretched souls inside would either struggle through it somehow, or else they would succumb, and that whatever the outcome, there was no point in their exposing themselves to the contagion). And although, for time immemorial, the officers had received the best available help and succor, while the privates and infantrymen were left to suffer the most horrible agonies with scarcely any attention paid to them at all, Miss Nightingale ministered to all the soldiers equally, whether they were aristocrats or common conscripts. By breaking with such established protocols, she had proved herself a traitor to her own class, winning few friends among the officers, but an undying devotion among the troops—and from Eleanor, too.

On their fourth night in Scutari, Miss Nightingale had come upon Eleanor refilling her water jug from the trickling fountain in the hospital—the water was a cloudy yellow, and barely potable at all—and asked her to accompany her on her nightly rounds. She was wearing a long gray dress, with a white kerchief gathered around her dark hair, and holding a Turkish lantern by the curved handle on its flat, brass base. "And please bring the jug with you."

Eleanor, who was seldom spoken to directly by Miss Nightingale, filled it to the brim, tucked a roll of bandages under her arm, and followed obediently a few steps behind. Eleanor was exhausted—it had been another grueling day—and although she knew that she would now be on her feet for hours, still she would not have given up this chance for anything. The Barrack Hospital was vast, and a tour of all its wards, which Miss Nightingale conducted nightly, was a journey of four miles. Wherever they went in the hospital, even the most antagonistic surgeons and impudent orderlies stood aside in Miss Nightingale's presence, and the two women were greeted instead by murmurs of thanks and signals of respect from the suffering soldiers. A boy who could not have been more than seventeen lay weeping in a cot, both of his legs gone below the knee, and Miss Nightingale stopped to comfort him and kiss his brow. Another soldier, missing an arm and an eye, she offered a cup of water, which he held in a shaking left hand, and for a moment Eleanor had to wonder if he was shaking from physical infirmity, or from the shock of having such a well-bred lady tending to the likes of him.

Most of the wards were dark, save for the moonlight slanting through the broken windows and loose shutters, and Eleanor had to watch her feet lest she step on a sleeping, or dead, body. Miss Nightingale, a slight woman of erect carriage, seemed to move unerringly among the cots and patients, the glow of her lamp falling like a benediction on the dirty, bruised, and bloodied faces. More than once, Eleanor saw a soldier lean forward on the stump of a missing limb and bend his own lips to the air after she had passed. *Why, they are kissing her shadow,* she thought.

Several times, Miss Nightingale stopped to offer a thirsty soldier a drink from the jug, or to replace a filthy bandage with a fresh one, but given the immensity of the hospital, and the bottomless well of need, she could only offer a smile, or a word, to most of those she passed. But it was clear to Eleanor that this visit was a kind of covenant, a holy pact between Miss Nightingale and the soldiers, and she felt privileged to witness it.

At the same time, her heart was forever in her throat. At each ward they entered, and in every bed they passed, she was looking for Lieutenant Sinclair Copley—desperate to see him again, terrified of what she might find once she did. Each morning she checked the rolls, but she knew that they were fragmentary and sloppy at best, and Sinclair could be suffering and speechless, unconscious from a blow or delirious with fever, just a ward away. She had made what inquiries she could, and she had learned that his brigade, the 17th Lancers, had been dispatched under Lords Lucan and Cardigan to aid in the siege of Sebastopol. But news traveled slowly from the front, and even when it did come it was no more dependable than the hospital rolls.

They had nearly completed their circuit and were passing through the last of the wards, when Eleanor thought she heard someone mutter her name. She stopped, and so did Miss Nightingale, who obligingly lifted the lamp up to cast a wider glow. On iron bedsteads, a dozen soldiers raised their heads or turned their eyes, but none of them spoke. The voice came again, and now Eleanor could see, in the farthest reach of the ward, below a window whose empty panes were stuffed with rags, a figure lying under a soiled sheet, his face turned toward them.

"Miss Ames?"

His face was so filthy she would not have recognized him, but the voice she knew.

"Lieutenant Le Maitre?" she said, moving closer.

The figure chuckled, then coughed. "Frenchie will do."

"This is an acquaintance of yours?" Miss Nightingale said, following Eleanor to his bedside.

"Yes, ma'am, it is. He is one of the Seventeenth Lancers."

"Then I will leave you to visit," she said, in a gentle voice. "We are nearly done, anyway." Taking a candle stub from the windowsill, she lit it with the flame from the lamp and left it with Eleanor. "Good night, Lieutenant."

"Good night, Miss Nightingale. And God bless you."

Miss Nightingale modestly inclined her head, then turned away, her long skirt rustling as she navigated past the other cots and patients.

Eleanor put the candle on the window ledge and knelt by the narrow bed. Frenchie, who had always been so smartly groomed, was wearing a torn white shirt crawling with lice; his hair was long and unwashed, and hung down over his fevered brow. He was unshaven, and his damp skin, even in the feeble candlelight, displayed a greenish pallor.

Eleanor had seen hundreds of men in such condition, and she knew it did not bode well. Quickly, she dipped a clean bandage in the remaining water and used it to begin mopping the sweat from his forehead. She only wished that she had a clean shirt with her, so that she could rip the lice-ridden one from his limbs. The sheet clung wetly to his lower body.

"Is it a fever," she asked, "or have you been wounded?"

Laying his head on the pallet, he drew the sheet away from his legs. The right one was scarred and bloody, but the left was worse—a yellowed bone protruded through the skin, and red striations ran up and down the shin. "You were shot?" she said, in horror...and in shame that her thoughts had immediately gone to Sinclair. Had he been in the same battle?

"I was shot *at*," he said. "But my horse plunged into a ravine and rolled over on my legs."

She dipped the rag into the water again, and as she did so, he answered the question he knew she wanted to ask.

"Sinclair was not there. The last I saw of him, he was riding with Rutherford, and the rest of the company, toward a place called Balaclava." He pulled the sheet back over his ruined legs and licked his lips. "My canteen," he said, "it's under the bed."

She rummaged around—something with many tiny legs scuttled over her hand—before she found it and unscrewed the cap for him. She could smell that it was gin inside. She held it to his lips and he took a swig, and then another. His eyes closed. "I should have guessed that you would be one of the nurses," he whispered.

"What would you like me to do for you?" she said. "I'm afraid I don't have most of my supplies with me right now..."

He shook his head feebly. "You have already done it," he said.

"Tomorrow, I'll come back on my rounds, and I'll bring you a fresh shirt, and a clean sheet, and a good razor..."

He raised one hand an inch from the mattress to stop her. "What I would like," he said, "is to write a letter to my family."

It was a common request, and Eleanor said, "I will bring a pen and paper."

"Come as soon as you can," he said, and she knew why he was in such haste.

"Rest now," she said, touching his shoulder and rising from the bedside. "I'll see you in the morning."

He sighed, his head still flat against the mattress, and blowing out the candle, she slipped quietly out of the ward.

CHAPTER THIRTY-THREE

December 16, 10 a.m.

MICHAEL AND LAWSON WERE BARRELING across the ice at full throttle, but there had been no sign at all of Danzig, or the missing dogs. Michael knew he ought to slow down; new crevasses could appear at any time, anywhere. But motion—and speed—had always been his remedy of choice. Whenever anything threatened to overwhelm him, he went into action—physical action. So long as he was moving, and caught up in the split-second decision-making of rock climbing, or kayaking through rapids, or snorkeling through a coral canyon, he could leave the dark thoughts that haunted him behind. He was smart enough to know that he couldn't actually outrun them—how many times had he tried?—but the temporary reprieve was generally enough to let him breathe again.

Right now, for instance, he tried to anchor himself in the moment, focusing first on the bow of the snowmobile coursing across the barren landscape, then, as he approached the shoreline, the languid soaring of a large white albatross overhead. It had been accompanying him for a while, dipping and rising in lazy circles that kept perfect pace with the progress of the two machines. Lawson had fanned out to his left and was making a more direct approach to the whaling station, while Michael hewed more closely to the shore, passing between the beach, strewn with bleached bones, and the ramshackle factory buildings. The two snowmobiles came together again in the wide-open flensing yard, and when the engines were turned off, the silence fell like a blanket. It took a few seconds for the ears to adjust, then Michael could hear the wind blowing snow across the frozen ground and the distant cry of the albatross. As he looked up, the bird circled again on its wide, outstretched wings, but showed no sign yet of alighting.

Lawson slipped his goggles onto his forehead and said, "If the dogs were here, they'd have heard us coming—"

"And we'd have heard them by now," Michael agreed. "But we've got some time before the storm comes in, so why don't you look around down here while I go up the hill?"

Lawson nodded, and taking hold of some ski poles for balance—Michael noticed that he was definitely limping—said, "I'll catch up with you in an hour."

Michael checked his watch, then climbed back on his snowmobile and revved the engine. He shot down the bleak alleyway that ran between what were once the boiling rooms, then up toward the church, with its crooked bell tower. Rather than try to navigate through the tombstones surrounding the church, he stopped the machine halfway up the hill and marched the rest of the way to the steps. Putting his shoulder against the heavy wooden door, he shoved it open, stepping into a humble, stone-floored church, with worn wooden pews; at the end of the center aisle, a trestle table had been set up as the altar. A crudely carved crucifix hung on the wall behind it. He'd been in such a hurry to leave the base that he hadn't bothered to bring all his camera equipment, but he ran off a few quick shots with his trusty Canon, nonetheless; knowing he still had a couple of weeks left on his pass, he planned to come back again and do it right—especially as, even then, perhaps a century or more since the church had been built, the place retained a strange air of expectancy. Somehow he would want to capture that, the feeling that at any moment the pews might once again be filled with weary whalers and the pulpit with a preacher reciting Scripture by the light of an oil lamp.

Under a pew, Michael saw the torn covers of a prayer book, but when he tried to retrieve them, he found they were frozen in place. He took a shot of that—too arty? he wondered—then slipped the camera back under his parka and, pulling his gloves back on, walked toward the altar. He thought he heard a scratching sound—could there still be rats?—and stopped. So did the noise. An old leather volume, its title obliterated by time, rested on the trestle table. He took another step, and the sound became clearer. It was coming from behind the altar, where he saw a door, with a black iron bolt thrown across it. Perhaps, he thought, that was where the preacher had once lived. Or maybe it had been a storage space for whatever valuable objects—chalices, candlesticks, Bibles—the church had once contained.

He rounded the trestle table, and suddenly he heard a sound that stopped him dead in his tracks.

He went closer, and it came again, more distinctly. It was a voice—a woman's voice!

"Open the door! Please, I can't stand it! Open the door, Sinclair!"

Sinclair? Michael pulled off a glove again so that he could manipulate the lock and bolt, and through the wood he could hear the woman, breathing heavily, nearly sobbing.

"I can't be alone! Don't leave me here!"

He threw the rusty bolt and pried open the creaking door.

What he saw left him dumbfounded. A woman—a young woman, loosely wrapped in a long orange down coat—staggered backwards, her face white with fear. She had long brown hair that fell around her face, and green eyes that, even in this dim light, offered a penetrating gaze. She backed up between a wooden table, with a bottle of wine on it, and a cast-iron stove that gave off a dull glow. Shredded prayer books and jagged pieces of wood were heaped in a corner.

They stood speechless, staring at each other. Michael's mind was reeling—he knew this woman. He knew her! He had first seen those eyes at the bottom of the sea. He had first seen that ivory clasp, now peeking up on her breast, beneath a slab of milky ice. Sleeping Beauty.

But she wasn't sleeping, and she wasn't dead.

She was alive—breathing hard, and haltingly.

Michael's mind went into a kind of shock. The woman was there, right before him, cowering only a few feet away, but he could not accept the evidence of his own eyes. That woman, who'd been frozen stiff, was moving and sensate. His thoughts went off in a dozen directions, searching for some reasonable explanation, but came rushing right back again empty-handed. What explanation could there possibly be—suspended animation? a vivid hallucination that he would awaken from at any second? Nothing he could think of could possibly account for the terrified young woman now standing, feebly, a few feet away.

Raising his bare hand to calm her, he noticed a tiny tremor in his own fingers. "I'm not going to hurt you."

She appeared unconvinced, cringing against the wall, beside the window.

Slowly, without taking his eyes away from her, he pulled his glove back onto his already numb hand. What else should he say? What should he do? "My name is Michael . . . Michael Wilde."

The sound of his own voice was oddly reassuring to him.

But not, it appeared, to her. She didn't answer, her eyes flitting around the room as if assessing any chance of escape.

"I've come from Point Adélie." This, he surmised, probably meant nothing to her. "The research station." Would that make any sense, either? "The place where you were. Before . . . this place." Though he knew she spoke English—and with an English accent, no less—he wasn't sure if his words were making any impression at all. "Can you tell me . . . who you are?"

She licked her lips, and nervously brushed a strand of hair away from her face. "Eleanor," she said, in a soft but agitated tone. "Eleanor Ames."

Eleanor Ames. He said the name to himself several times, as if trying to anchor it in reality that way.

"And you're from . . . England?" he ventured.

"Yes."

Placing a hand on his chest, he said, "I'm from America." The whole thing was becoming so absurd he could almost laugh—he felt like he was reading from a bad sci-fi script. Next he should pull out a ray gun, or she should demand to be taken to his leader. He wondered for a second if he was on the brink of losing his wits.

"Well, it's nice to meet you, Eleanor Ames," he said, again nearly laughing at the sheer absurdity of it all.

And damned if she didn't gently subside, in a quick curtsy.

Quickly, he let his eyes sweep the room. The iron bedstead was covered with a dirty old blanket, and there were a couple of the bottles, the ones from the sunken chest, nestled underneath it.

"Where is your friend?"

She didn't answer. But he could see a fast calculation going on behind her eyes.

"I believe you called him Sinclair?"

"He's gone," she said. "He's . . . abandoned me."

Michael didn't believe that for a minute; he could tell that she was, for whatever reason, covering for him. Whoever, and whatever, this woman would truly turn out to be, her expression and voice betrayed all the palpably human emotions; nothing too mysterious was going on there. And as for the mystery surrounding the whereabouts of this Sinclair person, it paled in comparison to all the other questions thick in the air. How had she become imprisoned in a glacier? And when? How had she escaped from the block of ice in the lab? Or found her way here, to Stromviken?

Or—and this was the biggest, most inconceivable, question of all, the one that rendered all the others incidental—how had she actually come back to life?

If there was a polite way of asking any of them, Michael sure as hell didn't know what it was.

A bag of dog kibble was propped against the wall. He'd start simple, with an easy one. "So this Sinclair," he said, "he's got the sled dogs with him?"

Again, another quick calculation, before she must have realized there was nothing to gain from further lies. Her shoulders slumped. "Yes."

There was an awkward pause. He could see now that her eyes were red-rimmed, and her lips were cracked. She licked them. His eyes went to the open bottle on the table. He knew what was in it.

But did she know that he knew?

When he looked at her again, he could see that she did. Her eyes were downcast, as if in shame, and a hectic flush rose into her cheeks.

"You can't stay here," he said. "A storm is coming. It will be here soon."

He could see that she was lost, and confused. What *was* her relationship to Sinclair? He had, after all, locked her in this room and gone off God knows where. Was he her lover? Her husband? Was he the only person in the living world that she knew? Was he the only person in the world that she *could* know? Michael wasn't even sure what questions to ponder. All he did know was that he couldn't leave her there, in the freezing church. He had to find a way to get her to leave with him, right away.

"We can come back for Sinclair later," Michael suggested. "We won't abandon him. But why don't you come with us now?"

At the mention of the word "us," he saw her eyes grow wide and glance through the open doorway into the empty church. Who else, she was clearly wondering, was about to intrude upon her?

"I have a friend with me," Michael explained. "We can take you back to the station."

"I can't," she said.

Michael could guess what she was thinking—or at least some of it. "But we can take care of you there."

"No, I won't leave," she said, though her voice faltered and even her expression seemed to change. It was as if the protest alone had drained the last of her energy. She moved away from the window and sat on the edge of the bed, her hands supporting her on either side. A rising wind rattled the shutters, and a draft made the fire in the grate glow brighter.

"I give you my word," he reassured her, "no one will harm you."

"You won't mean to," she said, "but you will."

Michael wasn't sure what she was getting at, but he heard in the distance the buzzing of Lawson's snowmobile as it climbed the hill. Eleanor looked up in alarm. What, Michael wondered, would she make of that noise? Would it have any significance?

What world—what time—had she come from?

"We have to go," Michael said. Eleanor sat, clearly trying to concentrate her thoughts, as still as a statue, as still as he had seen her in the ice.

As still as Kristin had been, in her hospital bed.

The snowmobile was coming closer, the roar of its engine penetrating the empty church. And then it stopped outside.

Eleanor Ames looked fixedly at Michael, as if trying to think through a confoundingly difficult puzzle—just as he was doing. He could only imagine all the questions in her mind, all the factors she was trying to balance out. The lives—not only her own—that she was trying to save, or protect.

"Hello?" Lawson called out. "Anybody home?" His footsteps echoed on the stone floor.

Eleanor's fingers worried the ratty blanket.

Michael, for fear of saying the wrong thing, said nothing more.

"Hey, Michael, I know you're in here somewhere!" Lawson called out, strolling toward the altar. "We've got to get rolling."

Eleanor's expression was filled with anguish ... and an exhaustion Michael had seen only once before, on the face of a man who had spent the entire night single-handedly trying to save his house from a wildfire in the Cascades. To no avail.

She coughed, but she was too weary to lift a hand to cover her mouth.

"Can you tell me something?" she said, in a voice filled with defeat and resignation.

"Of course. Anything."

Lawson was close enough that Michael could hear the squelching of his boots just outside the door.

"What *year* is this?"

CHAPTER THIRTY-FOUR

December 16, 11:30 a.m.

THE WIND, when Sinclair left, had been low, but it was coming up fast. He had guided the dogs down through the ramshackle buildings of the whaling station—past the blacksmith's shop, where dozens of harpoons, some as long as the lance he had carried into battle, were still mounted in racks against the wall—and toward the northwest, where he could see a low ridge of ice, obscuring anything beyond. He doubted he would find anything on the other side, but what choice did he have? Surrender himself, and Eleanor, to the ministrations of those from whom they had narrowly made their escape? Sinclair trusted no one . . . and never would again.

Even, sad to say, his own beloved. He'd locked Eleanor in the rectory before leaving because, in her present weakened state, he did not know what she would do; he feared that when she awoke, she might succumb to some sudden impulse and attempt to do away with herself. How precisely that could be done, he wasn't sure. He knew that their corruption, despite its awful price, afforded them protection from maladies that would kill anyone else—cholera, dysentery, the mysterious Crimea fever... even a hundred years, or however long it had been, imprisoned at the bottom of the sea. But whatever devilish mechanism fueled their endless life could not, he suspected, withstand corporeal destruction. He glanced down at the back of his torn boot, where the dog had ripped at his calf. The wound beneath had stopped bleeding, it had even healed over, but in some indefinable way it was not living flesh. It was a patch, a scab, a plaster—something helping to hold together a walking, talking, breathing skeleton. He could break, it seemed, but he could not wither.

Not at all in keeping with the brigade's motto, he reflected wryly. It was neither death, nor was it glory. Instead, it was a sort of way station, reminding him of the idle days the Light Brigade had been forced to endure in the Crimea.

For weeks, they had done nothing but wait about, observing the infantry actions from their standing mounts, held in reserve, constantly, for a decisive moment that never seemed to come. Under the direction of Lords Lucan and Cardigan—two men, brothers-in-law, who despised each other thoroughly—the 17th Lancers had been shifted from one remote outpost to another, always held in check lest they be spent too soon. Sinclair, like many of the others, had begun to feel that they were becoming an object of derision among the other troops—the fancy horse soldiers, in their plumes and pelisses, their gold braid and their bright cherry trousers, munching on hard-boiled eggs and biscuits—while their compatriots did the dirty work of storming the redoubts. When, at one critical juncture, the Russian cavalry had been allowed to escape in total disarray without being pursued and annihilated, Sergeant Hatch, barely recovered from his bout with the malaria, had broken his pipe in disgust and thrown the pieces into the dirt.

"Is it a gilded invitation they're waiting for?" he snarled, while reining in his impatient horse and throwing a dark look up at the heights, where the Commander in Chief, the elderly, one-armed Lord Raglan, could be seen with his telescope, surrounded by aides. "They won't get a better one than that."

Even Captain Rutherford, known as much for his imperturbable nature as his bushy muttonchops, appeared impatient, and after taking a long sip from his flask—filled with rum and water—leaned across his saddle and offered it to Sinclair. "It may be another long day," he said.

Sinclair had taken it and drunk deeply. Ever since the 17th Lancers had set sail, the war had been a vast, costly anticlimax—a violent journey across pitching seas that had killed off countless horses, followed by endless marches through narrow gorges and empty plains, all the while leaving bodies in their wake, food for vultures and vermin . . . and the strange, scuttling creatures that they glimpsed only at night, lurking just beyond the pickets at their posts. Sinclair had asked one of the Turkish scouts what they were, and, after superstitiously spitting over his own left shoulder, the man had muttered, "Kara-kondjiolos."

"But what does it mean?"

"Bloodsuckers," the scout replied, with disgust. "They bite the dead."

"Like jackals?"

"Worse," he said, searching for the right word. "Like . . . the cursed."

Whenever one had been spotted—never as anything more than a hunched-over shape clinging to the shadows or crawling close to the ground—Sinclair had noted that the Catholic recruits ostentatiously crossed themselves and everyone, regardless of faith, sidled closer to the campfires.

It was a far cry, the foreign land he was traveling through, from his home. And though he had seen nothing so stirring ever since, he remembered well the flags and bunting, the brass bands and fluttering handkerchiefs, when the army had first boarded the ships in England. Even the town of Balaclava, once an idyllic little seaport, had been rendered unrecognizable. Before the British troops had arrived, the town had been a favorite retreat of the residents of Sebastopol, its pretty little villas famous for their green-tiled roofs and neatly cultivated gardens. From all reports, every cottage and fence post had been adorned with roses, clematis, and honeysuckle, and light green Muscatel grapes, ripe for the picking, hung in great clumps from the vines. Orchards carpeted the hillsides, and the pristine waters of the bay sparkled like crystal.

And then the *Agamemnon,* the British navy's most powerful man-of-war, had steamed into the harbor, and the army—twenty-five thousand strong at that landing point alone—had made the town its base of operations. The villas were overrun, the gardens churned to mud, the vines trampled underfoot. With many of the soldiers sick or dying from diarrhea, the tiny landlocked harbor had become an immense and reeking latrine, foul with waste and refuse. Lord Cardigan, no fool, had elected to stay several miles away, on board his private yacht, the *Dryad*. There, his meals were prepared by his French chef, while a flock of orderlies and aides rode their weary horses up and down the steep hills to the harbor, carrying his dispatches. Among the troops, when out of earshot of an officer, he had come to be called "The Noble Yachtsman."

"Any word of Frenchie?" Rutherford had asked, but Sinclair shook his head. No letters had reached the front for weeks, nor any word from the field hospitals. Sinclair had seen his friend's leg after the horse had fallen over on it, and he knew that even if he did see him alive again, Frenchie would not be the man he once was.

Would any of them be?

It was a beautiful day, clear and bright, and Ajax pawed the ground, eager to move. Sinclair stroked his long, chestnut neck, and tugged gently on the black mane. "One day, my boy, one day . . ." he said, reconciling himself to many more hours of listening to the sounds of a skirmish somewhere off in the distance, or the faraway boom of Russian cannons. For so much of the campaign he had felt like someone stranded just outside a theater, hearing the tumult and voices inside, but unable to get in the door. He wondered what Eleanor was doing, and whether she was safe, and if his own letters had ever made it back to her in London.

Rutherford grunted and pointed his chin to Sinclair's right. An aide-de-camp had just left the commander's side, and was riding pell-mell down the almost vertical hillside. The track was barely there, and many times the horse nearly lost its footing, but the rider was always able at the last second to regain control and continue his mad descent.

"Only one man that I know of can ride like that," Sergeant Hatch observed from his own mount.

"And who might that be?" Rutherford asked.

"Captain Nolan, of course," Sinclair put in. The same Captain Nolan whose equitation techniques were sweeping the Continent.

The rider came on, rocks and gravel and dust kicking up behind his horse's hooves, and once he had reached the plain below, he spurred his horse on ever faster. Lord Lucan, in his white-plumed hat, trotted toward the approaching figure and reined in his horse not more than ten yards in front of Sinclair, between the tight formations of the Light and the Heavy Brigades which he commanded.

Nolan galloped up, sweat streaming from his horse's flanks, and pulled a communiqué from his sabretache, slapping it into Lord Lucan's hand. Though Sinclair was well aware of Nolan's low regard for Lord Lucan (shared by most of the cavalry), still he was surprised at the peremptory manner in which he had delivered the message. Lucan had a famously bad temper, and any such misstep could lead to arrest for insubordination.

Lucan, glowering, read the orders, then looked up at Nolan, whose horse was still pacing anxiously about, and challenged him in some way. Sinclair could not make out all the words, but he heard something to the effect of "Attack what? Attack what guns, sir?"

Sinclair traded a look with Rutherford. Was Lord Lucan— "Lord Look-On" to his idled troops—once again going to keep his men from entering the fray?

Nolan urgently repeated something, his dark curls shaking about his head, and gestured at the paper in Lord Lucan's hand. And then, with his arm thrown out toward the Russian batteries at the far end of the North Valley, and in a voice that even Sinclair could clearly hear, Nolan shouted, "There, my lord, is your enemy. There are your guns!"

Sinclair expected to see Lord Lucan go into a rage at this further impertinence and order Captain Nolan to be arrested on the spot, but instead he simply shrugged, turned his horse away, and trotted off to consult with his archenemy, Lord Cardigan. Whatever had been written in that communiqué, it was sufficiently important that he did not wish to ignore it or to take some unilateral action.

After several minutes of intense deliberation, Lord Cardigan saluted, not once but twice, and galloped back toward Sinclair and his fellow Lancers. Quickly, he ordered the brigade to form up in two lines, with the first line composed of the 17th Lancers, the 13th Light Dragoons, and the 11th Hussars; the second line was made up of the 4th Light Dragoons and most of the 8th Hussars. The Heavy

Brigade, meanwhile, was being drawn up to their rear. The Horse Artillery, which might have been expected to follow under normal circumstances, was not ordered up—perhaps, Sinclair concluded, because the valley before them was partly plowed and consequently hard to traverse.

If he'd had to guess, Sinclair would have said that the North Valley, into which the brigade was entering, was about a mile and a quarter long, and not even a mile wide. It was a flat plain, offering no sort of cover, and on all three sides it was under the control of the Russian forces. On the Fedioukine Hills to the north, Sinclair could make out at least a dozen gun emplacements, along with several battalions of infantry. To the south, the Causeway Heights were even more fearsome, with as many as thirty guns and a field battery that had captured the redoubts earlier in the day. But it was at the end of the valley that the greatest danger of all lay. If the Light Brigade was to attack that point, it would not only have to pass through a gauntlet of fire the entire way, it would then have to ride straight up into the muzzles of a dozen cannons, backed by several lines of densely packed Russian cavalry.

For the first time in his life, Sinclair had a distinct premonition of death. It came not as a shiver, or even as an urge to flee, but as a cold, stark fact. Up until then, even as others had fallen by the wayside with cholera or fever, or been picked off by snipers in the hills, he had never truly considered his own vulnerability. He had felt impervious. But no one, staring down the bore of the North Valley, could continue in such an illusion.

Sinclair was riding in the first line with Rutherford on his left, and a young chap named Owens on his right. Sergeant Hatch had been conscripted into the second line.

"Five quid," Sinclair said to Rutherford, "that I reach the gun battery first."

"You're on," Rutherford said. "But have you got five quid?"

Sinclair laughed, and Owens managed a weak smile at overhearing the exchange. He had a receding chin and a thin face, and his skin had gone as white as whey. His hand trembled on the upright lance.

A trumpet sounded, and Sinclair fell silent, as did all of those around him. Lord Cardigan had ridden several lengths in front of the entire company, and all alone he drew his sword and raised it. In a calm voice that nonetheless carried to the men behind him, he said, "The Brigade will advance. Walk, march, trot."

The sound of the trumpet had died away, and it was only as the cavalry advanced, lances held high, that Sinclair noted the strange, almost unnatural hush that seemed to have fallen over the entire valley. No rifles were fired from the heights, no cannons boomed, no breeze rustled the short grass. All he could hear were the creaking of the leather saddles and the jingling of spurs. It was as if the whole world was holding its breath, waiting to see how this spectacle would unfold.

Sinclair held his reins loosely in his hands, knowing that the time would soon come when he would have to tighten his grip and urge Ajax on into a maelstrom of fire. The horse lifted its head, snorting at the fresh air, happy to trot at last on level, hard-packed ground. Sinclair tried to keep his gaze fixed firmly ahead, on the trim figure of Lord Cardigan, sitting erect in his saddle, his gold-laced pelisse not dangling from his shoulder, as was the custom, but worn as a coat. Cardigan never once turned around to observe his troops, for to do so, as any cavalryman knew, was to signal uncertainty, and Lord Cardigan was nothing but certain of himself. Whatever Sinclair and the other men thought of him in general, much as they might mock him for his luxurious ways and petty insistence on protocol, on that day he was an inspiring figure.

And then Sinclair saw, at the far end of the valley, a puff of smoke, as delicate and round as a dandelion head, then another. The boom of the cannon fire arrived only a second or two later, and a fountain of dirt and grass erupted into the air. The shots had fallen short, but Sinclair knew that the Russian gunners were simply finding their range. The front line had advanced no more than fifty or sixty yards, when to Sinclair's astonishment Captain Nolan broke from the ranks and raced, in a gross breach of all military etiquette, directly across Lord Cardigan's path, waving his sword; he had wheeled in his saddle and was shouting something at Cardigan that was impossible for anyone to hear over the rising thunder of the guns. For a moment, Sinclair thought that Nolan had lost his head entirely, and was trying to take over the charge. But before Cardigan could even react to this shocking display, a Russian cannonball exploded in the dirt, and a shell fragment ripped across Captain

Nolan's chest with such savagery that Sinclair could see the man's beating heart. Then he heard a scream, like none he had ever heard before, as Nolan's bloody body, still somehow erect in the saddle, was carried back through the lines by the panic-stricken horse. The sword had dropped from Nolan's hand, but his arm remained inexplicably outstretched, as if he were still attempting to direct the attack. The scream continued, too, until the horse had bolted into the 4th Light Dragoons, where the body, finally silent, toppled from the saddle.

"Good God," Sinclair heard Rutherford mutter. "What was the man trying to do?"

Sinclair had no idea, but to see Captain Nolan, the most capable rider in the whole British cavalry, slain so soon, did not bode well. The pace of the brigade increased, but only slightly. Lord Cardigan, who had still not so much as turned in his saddle to ascertain Nolan's fate, was leading the troops in close formation and at a measured pace, for all the world as if they were simply performing a drill on a parade ground, rather than marching into a mounting cascade of fire.

"Close in!" Sinclair heard Sergeant Hatch call out behind him, ordering the riders to move up and fill in the gaps left by fallen men and horses. "Close in to the center!"

The pace picked up, and Ajax lowered his chestnut muzzle, with its blaze of white, and carried Sinclair forward, his sword and sabretache slapping at his side, his helmet lowered to shield his eyes from the bright sun. The shaft of the lance grew unwieldy in his hand, and he longed for the order to lower it and cradle it beneath his arm. And he prayed that he would survive long enough to use it.

Halfway down the valley, the brigade had come within the withering cross fire of the cannons and infantry rifles on both the Causeway Heights and the Fedioukine Hills. Musket balls and cannon shells, grapeshot and round, whizzed and blazed through the ranks, tearing into the horses' flanks, or knocking the riders clear out of their saddles. The troopers could no longer restrain their terrified horses, or for that matter restrain themselves, and the ranks became increasingly disarrayed as horses and men galloped forward, desperate to escape the deadly hail. Sinclair heard cheers and prayers, mingled with the agonized shrieks of wounded horses and the screams of dying men.

"Come on, Seventeenth Lancers!" he heard Sergeant Hatch shout, as his horse drew along Sinclair's right side. "Don't let the 13th get there before us!"

Where was young Owens, Sinclair wondered, or his horse? He had not even seen the man killed.

A bugle sounded, and Sinclair at last lowered his lance, and touched his spurs to Ajax's heaving sides. The battlefield was so clouded with smoke and dust and debris that Sinclair could barely make out the gun battery ahead. He could see flashes of flame, and hear the cannonballs crashing through the lines, taking out a dozen men at once as if they were ninepins. The noise was deafening, so loud and harsh that he could hear nothing but a ringing din. His eyes burned from the smoke and fire, and his blood was pounding in his veins. Horsemen who had charged ahead of him were scattered on the ground, blown to pieces, their steeds struggling to rise on shattered or missing legs. Ajax leapt over a standard-bearer, draped across his headless mount, and confident in his master, galloped bravely into the maelstrom. The ground hurtled past as Sinclair struggled to hold the lance straight and true. Not more than fifty yards away, he could glimpse the gray uniforms and low-brimmed caps of the Russian gunners, as they frantically loaded another shell into the cannon. He was riding straight for its barrel as they rammed the cannonball home, but he could not get out of its way. Sergeant Hatch was close on one side, and Rutherford's horse, keening with fright, was keeping him company on the other; the empty stirrups clanked, but there wasn't any sign of its rider. Sinclair would have no choice but to vault over the gun before it could be fired. He heard cries in Russian, saw a sputtering orange torch being touched to a fuse, and with his head down and his lance extended toward the man who held the flame, he charged the gun. Ajax leapt into the air just as the cannon went off, and the last thing Sinclair remembered was flying blind through a red-hot stew of blood and smoke, guts and gunpowder . . . and then nothing.

CHAPTER THIRTY-FIVE

December 16, 11:45 a.m.

JUST WHEN CHARLOTTE HAD STARTED to think this might not be such a bad gig, after all—terrible weather and camp fever, true, but no big medical crises to deal with—all hell had started breaking loose.

First, Danzig had been attacked and killed by his own husky and now—*now* Murphy was trying to tell her that the mutilated body lying before her on the floor of the botany lab was the dead Danzig's handiwork.

"That's not possible," she said, for the hundredth time. "I pronounced Danzig dead myself. I stitched his throat closed with my own two hands, I hit him twice—no, three times—with the defib paddles, and I saw him flatline." She knelt and put a hand to the side of Ackerley's cold neck. "And I saw him zipped into the body bag."

"Well, somehow he got out," Murphy insisted. "That's all I can tell you. Wilde and Lawson both swear to it."

If she didn't know better, she'd have asked if they were drunk at the time, or flying high on something even more potent. But she knew Michael and she knew Lawson and she knew they would never make up anything so awful. And this was indeed about as awful as it could get. The throat and shoulders had been savagely torn, and the gushing blood had saturated his shirt and pants. Somehow his glasses, though spattered with gore, had managed to stay on throughout the attack. Whoever, or whatever, had done this, was something far worse than anything she had encountered even on the worst night in the Chicago ER.

"I know you'll want to do a more thorough exam," Murphy said, nervously pacing behind her, "but in view of what's happened to Danzig, I'm not taking any chances." She had already noticed the telltale bulge of a gun and holster under his coat.

"What's that mean?"

"I'll show you."

What it meant, Charlotte discovered, was that the body was to be packed up and then loaded, by the two of them, onto a toboggan, which they then dragged, as inconspicuously as they could, around the back of the out buildings and to a seldom-used storage shed and meat locker. The old meat locker turned out to be a cavernous, dilapidated shed. In it, there were crates of Coke and beer and culinary supplies. Murphy went all the way to the back, then with one arm swept a couple of cans and utensils off a long crate about three feet high. A thick metal pipe, with flaking red paint, ran along the wall just above it.

"Let's lay him down here," he said. Murphy took the shoulders, and Charlotte the feet, and they put the body down as gently and respectfully as they could. As Charlotte straightened up, she saw that the crate was stamped, in black letters, MIXED CONDIMENTS: HEINZ.

"And why is this better than taking him to the infirmary for the autopsy?" Charlotte said.

"Because we can keep it quiet," Murphy replied, "at least for a while. And it's safer here."

"Safer from what?" Whatever that Danzig situation turned out to be, did the chief really think that this mutilated corpse was going to make a comeback?

Murphy didn't answer that, but she certainly didn't like the look in his eye, or the pair of handcuffs—handcuffs?—that she now saw dangling from his back pocket. "Give me a minute alone, will you?" he said. "I'll be right out."

Charlotte went outside and stood on the ramp. The wind had really kicked up—a storm was blowing in. What in the world was going on here? Two dead in a matter of days? And though she felt terrible even thinking about it that way, on a personal note she did have to wonder—was this going to look bad on her record as resident medical officer of Point Adélie?

"All squared away," Murphy said, coming up behind her and securing the door with a padlock and chain, wrapped in a tight plastic sleeve to keep the moisture out. "Needless to say, I've told Uncle Barney that this unit is off-limits till further notice."

Charlotte vowed, just to be on the safe side, never again to use a Heinz condiment of any kind.

"And I don't need to tell you, I want all of this kept on the q.t. At least until we've got a better grip on things—Danzig in particular."

December 16, 2 p.m.

Eleanor was only vaguely aware of what was going on. She remembered being helped, nearly carried, to the door of the church, then being placed atop a cumbersome machine, on a sort of saddle. She had been encouraged to put her arms around the man sitting in front of her—Michael Wilde, he'd said his name was; she wondered if he was Irish—but that would have been far too forward and with her remaining strength she had resisted.

The other man had then tied a rope around her, made of some thin but sturdy fiber, and fastened the hood of her coat down tightly around her head. The machine had roared off across the snow like a stallion, but the wind, and icy spray, was so strong that, like it or not, she had had to lean her head down and rest her cheek against Michael's back. And before long, just to keep her stability, lift her arms around him.

If not for the hood, the noise might have been deafening, and as they rumbled across the barren landscape, she felt herself oddly lulled. All day, she had been growing weaker, and fighting to resist the allure of the black bottles Sinclair had left in the rectory, and now she felt the last of her energy ebbing away. Her eyes closed, and her limbs relaxed. She felt powerless, but not unpleasantly so. The rattling of the machine reminded her of the thrumming of the engines on the ship she had taken to the Crimea...under the ever-watchful eye of Miss Nightingale. But oh, what would her employer make of a scene such as this? She knew perfectly well that Miss Nightingale disapproved of her nurses fraternizing with the soldiers or breaking with most of the social conventions. Scandal was to be avoided at all costs, and for all of her natural ease with the troops, Miss Nightingale often seemed humorless and inflexible with her female staff.

On the morning after finding Frenchie among the wounded, for instance, Eleanor had known enough to rise an hour early and creep, as quietly as she could, out of the staff quarters. The stairs were still dark, and she nearly tripped twice as she made her way down out of the tower and back to the ward where Lieutenant Le Maitre lay. But in addition to a clean shirt, she had in the pocket of her smock a sheet of folded paper and the stub of a pencil.

Although some of the men were still asleep, many others lay rocking in their beds, sick with fever or racked with pain, their eyes glazed and lips parched. Two or three of them reached out to her as she hurried by, but she had to neglect their entreaties and keep to her mission. She would have to be back at her regular post in less than an hour.

As she approached the ward, she passed one of the surgical carts being set up for the day's bloody business. Two orderlies—one with jug ears and a cowlick standing straight up—said, "Morning, Missus. You're up bright and early." The other, a burly fellow with a badly pitted face, said, "Care to join us for a cup of tea?" He lifted a battered kettle from the cart. "Still hot."

Eleanor declined, then swiftly crossed to the far corner, where she found Le Maitre wide-awake and staring up through the broken window at the early dawn. She crouched down beside his bed, and it was only when she said, "I've come back," that he seemed to take any notice of her. "And look what I've got," she said, displaying the paper and pencil.

He licked his lips, and nodded at her. "And this, too," she said, holding up the clean shirt. "We'll get that old one off of you, and this new one on, just as soon as I've found some water for a wash." He looked at her as if he barely understood what language she was speaking. The night, she realized, had taken its toll on him.

"Frenchie," she said, in a low voice, "I'm ashamed to admit that I don't even know your true first name."

And for the first time, he smiled. "Few do."

She was so glad to see even this spark of life in him.

"It's Alphonse." He coughed, dryly, then added, "Now you know why."

She perched on the side of his bed, careful not to touch his damaged legs, and flattened the paper on her lap. "Is this letter to your family?"

He nodded, and recited an address in West Sussex. She took it down and waited.

"Chers Père et Mère, Je vous écris depuis l'hôpital en Turquie. Je dois vous dire que j'ai eu un accident—une chute de cheval—qui m'a blessé plutôt gravement."

Eleanor's pencil hung in the air. It had never crossed her mind that Le Maitre's family might actually speak in French. "Oh, dear," she said, "I cannot write in French." She looked up and saw that he had closed his eyes to focus his thoughts better. "Can you say it in English?"

There was a rattling of wheels at the door of the ward, and several voices engaged in discussion. The hospital was waking up.

"Of course." His voice was barely a croak. "How silly of me. It's just that, at home..." He stopped talking, then started again. "My dear mother and father, I am sending you these words from the hospital in Turkey. A friend is writing them down."

The rattling got louder.

"I'm afraid I was injured... in a fall from my horse."

Eleanor, scrawling the words down, looked up to see the jug-eared orderly pushing the surgery cart like a flower wagon toward their corner. The other one was carrying a white screen, furled like a sail, under his arm. There was no mistaking their intentions.

"Oh, can't you wait just a little while?" Eleanor said, rising to her feet.

"Doctor's orders," the first one said, as the second dropped the base of the screen onto the floor and quickly spread it out to shield the bed from view. Until Miss Nightingale's arrival, all amputations had been done in clear view of the other patients. But Miss Nightingale, not only to ensure some measure of privacy for the amputee but to spare the others the full grisly spectacle of what might await them next, had insisted upon the use of these screens.

"The lieutenant has just begun dictating a letter to his family—surely you can attend to someone else first?"

"Eleanor?" Frenchie said, clutching at her sleeve. "Eleanor!"

She turned back to him, and saw that he had drawn a silver cigarette case out from under his mattress.

"Take this!"

It was the same case she had once seen at the Longchamps Club, after the day at the races. It bore the regiment's grim insignia—a Death's Head—and its motto, "Or Glory."

"See that my family gets it—please!"

"But one day you'll be able to give it to them yourself," she said, as he pressed it into her hand.

"Missus, we have our work to do," the burly orderly said.

She let the cigarette case fall into the pocket of her smock, as the white-haired surgeon strode toward the cot. "What's the obstruction here?" he bellowed, throwing a murderous glance at Eleanor. "We haven't got all day." He whipped the sheet away from Frenchie's mangled leg, inspected the damage for no more than a few seconds, then said, "Taylor, place the block."

The jug-eared orderly took a wooden chopping block, encrusted with dried blood, and began to wedge it under the leg to be amputated. Frenchie howled in agony.

"Smith, bind his arms."

"As for you," the surgeon said to Eleanor, "I do not recall giving permission for Miss Nightingale's protégées to interfere on my wards."

"But doctor, I was only—"

"You'll address me as the Reverend Dr. Gaines, if you must address me at all."

A cleric *and* a physician? Even in the short time Eleanor had served at the Barrack Hospital, she had come to dread the devoutly Christian doctors more than any others. While chloroform was, undeniably, in short supply, there was usually some to be found for the amputations, but the more pious surgeons were often opposed to its use. For them, anesthesia of any kind was a novelty, a recent invention that only served to lessen the noble and purifying pain that the Lord had ordained. She turned to look at Frenchie, whose face, now that his leg had been raised, was flushed with blood. His arms had been bound to his sides by ropes passed under the iron bedstead.

Taylor was holding a glass of whiskey to his lips, but most of it was dribbling down Frenchie's quivering chin.

"Give him the mouth guard," the doctor ordered, as he tied the strings of his white apron behind him, and Taylor took a worn chunk of leather and stuck it between Frenchie's teeth. "Mind you bite down on that," Taylor advised, "or you could lose your tongue." He patted him on the shoulder in an amiable way, then left his hands there, one on each side, as he stood at the head of the bed.

"All right, Smith," the doctor said, pressing a hand to the raised knee, "hold the other leg, please."

Smith leaned his weight on the right leg, with one hand on the thigh and one on the shin, while the left leg, like a turkey's neck, was stretched across the chopping block. Eleanor was standing at the foot of the bed, speechless with horror, as Dr. Gaines took a bone saw with a wooden handle from the cart. Glancing over at Eleanor, he said, "Stay if you like—you can clean up after."

But Eleanor had already decided that she could not leave. Frenchie was staring at her as if his very life hung in the balance and she could not have abandoned him at such a time. Dr. Gaines roughly adjusted the leg, making sure that a spot a few inches above the knee was positioned in the center of the block, and while he held the leg in place with one large hand, he laid the jagged blade of the saw against the green and empurpled skin—Eleanor thought, disconcertingly, of a bow being placed to the strings of a violin—then, taking a deep breath, drove the saw across and down.

A fountain of blood erupted into the air and Frenchie screamed, the mouth guard flying. His body buckled, but the doctor bore down, and before the first scream had even ended, he had drawn the blade back across, bearing down hard, and the bone had cracked, then splintered. Frenchie tried to scream again, but his agony was so great no sound came out. The leg was nearly severed from his trunk, only a few shreds of flesh and bone still connecting it, but Dr. Gaines made quick work of those, too. He ran the saw back and forth—it made a wet whistling sound—and the leg suddenly tumbled against his blood-spattered apron and onto his shoes. He paid no attention to it, but simply dropped the saw on the bed, and grabbing a tourniquet from the cart, tied it tightly around the geysering stump. Frenchie had passed out. The doctor tore away the ragged ends of skin with his fingers, then took a threaded needle from the pocket of his apron, and proceeded to sew the wound closed with coarse black stitches. When that was done, he poured a liberal dose of grain alcohol over the madly twitching stump and said to Eleanor, "I see you're still standing."

Her legs were trembling, but yes, she had remained upright— if only to deny him the satisfaction of seeing her faint.

"We'll leave him then to your ministrations," he said, wiping his hands down the front of his apron. "And get rid of that," he said, nudging the severed leg with the toe of his boot. He turned and left the ward. It had all taken no more than ten minutes.

Taylor and Smith remained to gather the utensils and fold up the screen, then, touching a finger to their foreheads in farewell, the caravan moved on. "Next one's a hand," she overheard Taylor say, and Smith replied, "Short work that'll be."

The bed was soaked in blood, the floor was slick with it, but Eleanor's first order of business was to dispose of the limb. She pulled the sheet, which was already halfway off the bed, completely free, then used it to wrap the leg. Then she dropped the whole bundle in a refuse bin, fetched a bucket of water and a mop, and came back to clean the floor. The sun was up now, and the light coming through the window was a buttery yellow; it would be a fine day. When that was done, she remembered the clean shirt she had brought, and though she didn't want to wake him for anything in the world, she wanted desperately to remove the lice-covered shirt, wash him, and put on the clean linen. He should not wake up from his terrible ordeal in such filth. As gently as she could, she lifted his shoulders from the mattress. His head lolled back listlessly, and his skin was cold. His lips were a pale blue.

"Excuse me, Missus?" a soldier in a nearby bed said.

She looked up, while still holding Frenchie.

"I do believe the man is dead."

She laid him down again, and put a hand to his heart. She felt nothing. She put her ear to his chest, and heard no sound. She fell back against the wall. A bird alighted on the windowsill behind her head, singing gaily. The tower bell rang the hour, and she knew Miss Nightingale would soon be looking for her.

CHAPTER THIRTY-SIX

December 16, 5 p.m.

MICHAEL KNEW that if Charlotte's door was closed at that hour, the poor woman was probably trying to grab a much-needed nap, but he really didn't have a choice.

He knocked, and when there was no immediate answer, he knocked again, louder.

"Hang on, hang on," he heard, as her slippers shuffled toward the door. She opened it, wearing her reindeer sweater and a baggy pair of purple Northwestern University sweatpants. When she saw it was Michael, she said, "I've got to warn you—I just took a Xanax."

From her drowsy look, he believed it. "We need you to look at someone."

"Who?"

How could he say this, without her thinking he was playing some stupid prank? "You know that woman? The one who was frozen in the ice?"

"Yes," Charlotte said, stifling a yawn. "You find her again?"

"We did," Michael said. "And well, the thing is, we've brought her back."

"To the base?"

"To life."

Charlotte just stood there, idly scratching the side of her face with the back of her fingernails. "What'd you just say?"

"She's alive. Sleeping Beauty is awake, and she's alive."

From the look on her face, Michael guessed that she did think it was a joke, and a bad one, to boot.

"You woke me up for this?" she said. "Because I've just had a very rough day and—"

"—I'm telling you the truth. It's for real." He stared her straight in the eye, so that she could see not only that he was sincere, but that he also wasn't suffering from the Big Eye. That this was the real deal.

"I don't know what you're up to," Charlotte said, dropping her resistance, "but you've got me up now. Where is this phenomenon?"

"Next door—in the infirmary."

Michael got out of her way as she went next door, rolling from side to side, still a bit groggy. Lawson, standing around in the waiting area like an expectant father in a maternity ward, said nothing as Charlotte entered the examining room with Michael close behind.

Eleanor was laid out on the table, like a body on a bier, her hands folded across her bosom. The orange down coat was thrown on a chair. She was wearing a long, old-fashioned gown, dark blue, with a white brooch fastened on her breast. Her eyes were closed, but she wasn't asleep. She was breathing weakly through her open mouth.

And Michael could see that Charlotte was—quite suddenly—waking up.

———————

Get a grip, was the first thing Charlotte told herself.

This young woman—whoever she was—sure as hell did look like that woman Charlotte had been allowed to glimpse in the ice.

"She collapsed an hour ago," Michael was saying, "when we tried to get her to leave the old church at the whaling station."

The whaling station? The old, abandoned whaling station?

This girl—what was she, maybe nineteen or twenty years old?—lying here in the antique clothes? None of it was making any sense at all. Charlotte swore to think twice before ever taking Xanax again. She took the woman's wrist and felt for a pulse. It was steady but feeble, though her fingers felt like frozen fish sticks.

"Her name, by the way, is Eleanor Ames."

Charlotte looked down at her face—a beautiful face that reminded her of nineteenth-century portraits she'd seen hanging in the Art Institute of Chicago. The features were delicate and refined, the eyebrows thin and arched, but the overall effect was oddly ethereal and unreal, as if she was in fact looking at a portrait, or a lovingly created waxwork. Something that wasn't quite real.

Focus, Charlotte thought. *Just focus on doing your job. Don't get distracted by all the other stuff you can't make sense of yet.* It was a lesson she'd learned, over and over again, in the ER.

"Eleanor," she said, leaning close, "can you hear me?"

The eyelids fluttered.

"I'm Dr. Barnes. Charlotte Barnes." She glanced over at Michael. "She speaks English?"

Michael nodded vigorously. "She *is* English."

Charlotte took a second to absorb this, too. "Can you open your eyes for me?"

Eleanor's head turned slightly on the headrest, and her eyes opened. She looked up at Charlotte with a confused expression, her gaze fluttering to the reindeer prancing across the sweater, then back to her broad face.

"That's good," Charlotte said, encouragingly. "That's very good." She patted Eleanor on the back of her hand. *But if she isn't the woman from the ice, if she isn't Sleeping Beauty, who else could she be? And how else could she have gotten here—to the South Pole?* Charlotte chased the thoughts away. *Focus.* "We're going to get your body temperature up, and you'll be feeling a whole lot better in no time."

Charlotte used her stethoscope to listen to her heart and lungs. The woman's dress, done in a Victorian style, gave off a briny, icy odor. *Almost as if she's been underwater.* Charlotte asked Michael to go to the commons and get "something nice and hot, maybe hot chocolate," while she completed the cursory examination. She proceeded with caution, so as not to do anything that might shock a patient with an antique sensibility. Whoever she really was, and wherever she'd come from, she obviously lived, even if it was only in her own head, in another century. Charlotte had once seen a patient who thought he was the Pope, and she had always been careful to address him as Your Holiness. As might have been expected, Eleanor appeared mystified by the blood-pressure cuff, and the penlight, used to peer into her eyes, also occasioned astonishment. The whole time, she was watching Charlotte with a gradually increasing awareness, shaded with perplexity. What, Charlotte wondered, would she be making of her—a big, black woman in a boldly patterned sweater, purple pants, and braided, streaked hair piled up in a messy knot on top of her head?

"You are . . . a nurse?" she finally whispered.

Oh well, it could have been worse, Charlotte thought. "No, I'm a doctor." She did have an English accent.

"I too am a nurse," she said, one pale hand lifting toward her bosom.

"Is that right?" Charlotte said, glad to hear her talking, as she readied a syringe for a blood sample.

"With Miss Nightingale."

"How about that?" Charlotte said, before the words had really sunk in. Eleanor had said them as if she hoped they might make an impression. And of course they did. Holding the needle up to the light, Charlotte paused and said, "Wait—as in what? Are you talking about Florence Nightingale?"

"Yes," Eleanor replied, apparently happy to hear that this name was still familiar. "In the Harley Street Hospital . . . and then the Crimea."

Florence Nightingale? The lady with the lamp? From . . . when? History had never been Charlotte's favorite subject. It had to have been, what, a couple of hundred years ago? More or less?

Concentrate, Charlotte reminded herself yet again. *Concentrate.* And don't do anything to alarm the patient, or—in a case like hers—upset a belief system that might be crucial to her mental stability.

"Well, then, Miss Ames, you've come one very long way to get to a place like this." Charlotte rolled up a sleeve of the dress—the fabric was coarse and stiff, and felt like a stage costume. "Even today, it's not easy getting here." She swabbed a spot with alcohol.

"Now you just hold real still—you're going to feel a little prick—and it'll be over in a few seconds."

Eleanor's eyes went down to the needle and watched the blood being drawn, as if she had never seen the procedure before. Had she, Charlotte wondered? *Could* she have? Out of curiosity alone, Charlotte planned to look up Florence Nightingale as soon as the exam was over. Purely, she told herself, for academic reasons.

Just as she was removing the needle, Michael came in, carrying a tray on which he'd placed not only a cup of cocoa, but a blueberry muffin and some scrambled eggs under tight plastic wrap. While he looked for a place to put it down, Charlotte opened the minifridge, where the perishable meds and the red plasma bags were kept, and deposited the blood sample inside for safekeeping. Eleanor, she noticed, was still following her every move. For someone who claimed to be well into her hundreds, she was certainly looking more alive by the minute.

But frozen, in an iceberg, for centuries? Hard as that was for Charlotte to believe, there was only one thing even harder—and that was coming up with some other explanation—any explanation—for who she was or how she came to Point Adélie, one of the most remote and inaccessible spots on the face of the earth.

"Are you hungry?" Michael said, finally finding a place for the food on a standing instrument tray. He rolled it over toward the examining table, and asked, "Can you sit up?"

With Charlotte's help, he was able to put his arm around Eleanor's frail shoulders and lift her into a sitting position, her back cushioned by the pillows. She regarded the food with a kind of polite disinterest, as if it were something she had seen once before but couldn't quite place.

"Try the cocoa," he said. "It's hot."

As she lifted the mug to her pale lips, Michael said to Charlotte, "Murphy's outside—he wants to talk to you."

"Good, 'cause I'd like to talk to him, too."

Charlotte took her clipboard, on which she'd been recording the results of the exam, and left the mysterious Eleanor Ames to Michael. Truth be told, she was glad to leave. She'd been feeling a chill ever since entering the infirmary, and she didn't think it was just a reaction to the patient's cold, clammy skin or her frosty clothes. It was as if, for all her years of training, she'd finally been presented with something utterly beyond her experience and beyond her scope.

———————————

Apart from the wind whistling outside the window, it was silent in the infirmary. Eleanor took the mug away—a bit of white foam still on her lips—and with her eyes still downcast, said to Michael, "I'm sorry if I hurt you in the church."

He smiled. "I've taken worse hits."

When he and that other man—Lawson?—had tried to escort her out of the little back room, she had refused to go, and even remembered pummeling Michael on his chest and arms with a flurry of blows that wouldn't have injured a sparrow. A second later, after having expended her last ounce of strength in the attack, she had crumpled to the floor, weeping. Michael and Lawson had carried her, protesting but unable to offer further resistance, outside, and placed her on the seat of Michael's machine. Then they had set off back toward the camp with the storm coming on fast.

"I know that you were only trying to help."

"That's all I'm still trying to do."

She nodded almost imperceptibly and lifted her eyes to meet his. How could he ever know, or even imagine, what she had been through? She broke off a piece of the muffin, then glanced around the room.

"Where am I?"

"The infirmary. At the American research station I told you about."

"Yes, yes . . ." she murmured, finally eating the tiny piece of the muffin. "But then, is this a part of America?"

"Not really. This—Point Adélie—is a part of the South Pole."

The South Pole. She might have guessed as much. Apparently, the *Coventry* had been blown so far off course that they had indeed reached the Pole itself. The most unexplored place on earth. She wondered if the ship had survived the voyage, and if any of the men aboard had ever lived to tell the tale. And if they had, would they have been bold enough to tell *all* of it? Would they, for instance, have regaled their friends at the tavern with their story of binding the heroic soldier and the invalid nurse in a length of iron chain and hurling them into the ocean?

"The eggs have some melted cheese in them," Michael said. "That's how Uncle Barney—that's our cook—likes to make them."

He was trying to be kind. And he had been. But there was so much that he could never know, and she could never say, to anyone. How could they even believe what little she had told them so far? Had she not lived it herself, she would have thought it too fantastical to be true. She picked up the fork, and tried the eggs. They were good, salty and still warm. This Michael Wilde was watching with approval as she ate. He was tall, with an unshaven face and black hair that looked as wild and unruly as her younger brother's used to be when he'd return from flying his kite in the downs.

Her younger brother who had been in his own grave for well over a hundred years already.

Gone. They were all gone. It was as if a death knell were clanging in her head. It didn't bear thinking of. She took another bite of the eggs.

———————

Even though he was still brimming with questions, Michael did not want to interrupt her meal. Who knew how long it had been since she'd last eaten hot food? Years? Decades? More? Everything about her, from her clothing to her manner, suggested someone from another era altogether.

How would he ever be able to wrap his mind around such a concept?

In fact, it was Eleanor who broke the silence by asking, "And what do the people do here, at this encampment?"

"Study the flora, the fauna, the climate changes." Global warming? He'd let that wait. Something told him she'd already had enough bad news in her life. "Personally, I'm a photographer." Would even that make sense? "I do daguerreotypes, sort of. And I write, for a magazine. In Tacoma—that's a city in the northwest United States. Near Seattle. People in Seattle like to make jokes about it."

He felt like he was babbling. But as long as he was talking, she was eating, and that made him happy. She wasn't exactly digging in, more just going through the motions . . . as if dining were a skill she was trying to remember.

"And the negress? She is a doctor?" she said, with a note of incredulity.

Okay, Michael thought, wherever and whenever Eleanor was from, there was bound to be a learning curve. "Yes. Dr. Barnes—Charlotte Barnes—is a very respected physician."

"Miss Nightingale does not believe that women should be doctors."

"Which Miss Nightingale is that?"

"Miss Florence Nightingale, of course." She'd said it as if she were pulling out her calling card, the reference that would legitimize her somehow.

Michael wanted to laugh. It all just kept getting stranger by the minute. He wondered if she'd run this professional reference by Charlotte.

"She is quite ardent in our defense as nurses, but she also believes, as do I, that there are distinct roles in which the two sexes should serve."

A *long* learning curve.

Michael let her nibble at her food, and they talked, though with many hesitations, about other things—the weather, the mounting storm, the work done at the station—and he had to mentally shake himself from time to time, just to remember that he was talking to a woman who claimed—with little evidence so far to contradict her—to have been born sometime in the nineteenth century. Someone who had clearly drowned—how else did you wind up frozen in an underwater glacier? He'd have liked to ask her directly about all that, but they'd just met, as it were, and the words weren't easy to come by, even for a journalist trained to ask tough questions.

And he feared the reaction she might have. Could it trigger some sort of breakdown?

Eleanor sipped her cocoa.

"We were thinking that you could stay here, in the infirmary, for now," Michael did say. "You'll have complete privacy, and Dr. Barnes, if you need her, is right next door."

"That's very thoughtful," she replied, dabbing her lips with the paper napkin, then glancing with curiosity at the floral motif that ran along its border.

"We can even try to rustle up some extra clothes," he said, "though I can't say they're gonna fit all that well." Eleanor was slim and slight, and anything he borrowed from Betty or Tina or Charlotte was going to look like a tent on her.

"What I have on will do," she said, "though I would like the opportunity to launder them...and," she said, blushing, "perhaps to bathe?"

It was precisely such considerations that had persuaded Michael and Murphy and Lawson to house Eleanor in the infirmary, under close wraps—not only for her own health and safety, but because she was bound to be an object of the most intense scrutiny if the other grunts and beakers got wind of her. She'd be the Miley Cyrus of Antarctica. And her life going forward, Michael knew, was going to be like no one else's had ever been. Once a supply plane carried her back out again, back to the world—to *Dateline NBC* and *People* magazine and her interviews with Larry King and Barbara Walters—she was not going to know what had hit her. And all Michael could do now was try to protect her as long as he could.

Even when he'd carried Kristin down off the mountain, it had made the local news. That was enough. He wouldn't wish the media glare on anyone.

Eleanor finished the cocoa and neatly folded up the paper napkin again, clearly intending to preserve it. Charlotte returned, carrying a fresh pair of hospital pajamas and a terry-cloth robe; she glanced at Michael, as if to convey that Murphy had filled her in on the game plan and she could take it from here.

"Okay then, I'll see you both tomorrow," Michael said, lifting the tray away. Eleanor looked just a little alarmed at his departure—not surprising, he thought, given that he had become her first friend in this world—but Michael smiled and said, "Fresh muffins again tomorrow. I promise."

From the bereft expression on her face, it appeared to be small consolation.

CHAPTER THIRTY-SEVEN

October 26, 1854, past midnight

HOW LONG HE HAD LAIN THERE on the battlefield, Sinclair never knew. Nor was he sure what had awakened him. He only knew that the moon was out, and full, and the sky was filled with stars. A cold wind was blowing, making the torn pennants flutter and carrying the low moans of soldiers and their steeds, still unwilling, or unable, to die.

He was one of them.

His lance was still in his hand, and when he raised his head a few inches from the ground, he could see that its shaft was broken in two, though not, apparently, before it had skewered the Russian gunner. He had to put his head back down, to catch his breath—even with the wind, the air stank of smoke and decay. His jacket and trousers were stiff with blood, but he sensed that it wasn't his.

When he could lift his head again, he saw his horse, Ajax, lying dead some feet away. The white blaze on his muzzle was stained with blood and dirt, and for some reason Sinclair felt it vitally important that he wipe it clean. The horse had served him well, and he had loved the beast. It wasn't right that he should be left in such an ignoble state.

But he did not get up, nor could he. He lay there, listening to the night and wondering what had happened. And how it had all ended. And whether or not, if he called out, a friend would come to help him, or an enemy appear to finish him off. His eyes burned and his throat was parched, and he groped at his belt in the hopes of finding a canteen there. Then he searched in the dirt around him, and found a spur, then the boot to which it was attached. He rolled onto his side, and saw that it was a corpse. Using the leg as an anchor, he pulled himself up the length of the body. His bones ached, and he could barely move, but he felt inside the jacket—a British jacket—and discovered a flask. He managed to open it, then took a long swig. Of gin.

Sergeant Hatch's favorite libation.

He rubbed the back of his hand across his eyes and leaned up to study the corpse's face, but the features were all gone, taken off by the blast of the cannon. He groped around the neck, and found a chain, and though the moonlight was not bright enough to read by, he knew that the medal dangling from it would commemorate the Punjab Campaign. He let go of the medal, drained the flask, and lay back again.

He wondered how many of the brigade had survived the charge.

A cold mist was coming up, spreading itself across the ground. In the distance he could occasionally hear the crack of a pistol shot. Perhaps it was only the farriers, putting the mutilated horses out of their misery. Or wounded soldiers, doing the same for themselves. An uncontrollable shudder ran down his frame, but despite the coldness of the ground, his skin was warm and clammy beneath his uniform.

Before he heard any sound of the thing's approach, he felt a tiny vibration in the earth and forced himself to lie still. It was all he could do to keep his limbs from shivering. But whatever it was, it was coming toward him stealthily, moving under cover of the clinging mist. He had the impression that it was on all fours, head close to the ground...sniffing. Was it a wild dog? A wolf? He took a shallow breath and held it. Or could it be one of those unseen creatures that had haunted the campfires in the dead of night? The Turks had a word for them—Kara-kondjiolos. Bloodsuckers.

It was lingering now over the carcass of Ajax, but all he could make out without raising his head was a pair of sharp shoulder blades hovering over the already rotting flesh. His saber was tangled at his side, still in its scabbard, and he knew he could never draw it out, much less wield it successfully, from the ground. He touched his holster, but it was empty; the pistol must have been thrown free in his fall. He reached out instead toward Hatch's corpse, felt for the leather of his riding belt, then traced his fingers along it until he found the sergeant's holster. The pistol, blessedly, was still in it. As silently as he could, Sinclair withdrew it.

The creature made a low gabbling sound, something strangely between the cry of a vulture and a human utterance.

Sinclair cocked the pistol, and the creature stopped. Sinclair glimpsed a sleek skull, with shiny dark eyes, rising from the mist.

It crawled, carefully, over the dead horse . . . and stopped to inspect Sergeant Hatch's missing features.

Then it came on, and Sinclair felt a hand—or was it a paw?—something with sharp nails in it, anyway, touching his leg. He lay still, as if dead, and felt an eager mouth lapping at the blood that covered his clothes. He knew that he might be able to get off only one shot, and he had to be sure that it counted. The beast followed the trail of blood onto his chest, and now he could smell its breath, like dead fish, and see its pointed ears. A hot tongue scoured the cloth—and even that he could endure—but when the teeth suddenly nibbled at his flesh, drawing his own blood, and the wet mouth suckled at the wound, he flinched.

The creature's head sprang back, and for the first time he could see its face, though he could never have adequately described it. His first thought was that it was human—the eyes were intelligent, the mouth was bowed, the forehead was rounded—but the shape of the skull was oddly elongated, the leathery skin stretched tight over a gaunt, grimacing mask.

He aimed the pistol, his hand wavering, and fired.

The thing screeched and a hand flew up to its torn ear in shock. It looked down on him indignantly, but scuttled backwards. Sinclair struggled to sit up. The creature was still in retreat, moving in a slow crouch, but Sinclair could have sworn that it had draped a fur pelisse around its shoulders, just as a cavalryman would do.

What *was* this thing?

He rolled onto his side and tried to shout, but his cries were barely audible. The mist swirled around the vanishing marauder, leaving only an empty pocket in the night. Sinclair held tight to the pistol grip and fired another round after it.

And he heard footsteps warily approaching from another direction. "Who's firing there?" a Cockney voice asked.

A lantern swung close to the ground.

"Are you an Englishman?"

And then the yellow light of the lamp fell on his face and he was able to mumble, through his ragged and bloody lips, "Lieutenant Copley. Of the Seventeenth Lancers."

December 16, 6 p.m.

If he had survived all that—the doomed charge of the Light Brigade, the night on the battlefield—Sinclair now reflected, then what could he not survive? Especially with Eleanor at his side.

Driving the sled, he relied entirely upon the dogs' unerring sense of direction to find his way back to the whaling station. It was all he could do to crouch on the runners, his face buried in his hood and his gloved hands clinging to the bars. The dogs twice made a wide turn around newly opened crevasses that Sinclair doubted he would have spotted on his own, but that the dogs seemed to sense. He would reward them with generous slabs of blubber and meat from the dead seal stored in the sled.

He had gone as far north as he thought safe and wise, searching for any sign of further habitation, but he feared that they had truly been transported to the end of the earth. He remembered that the *Coventry,* long ago, had been sailing south, driven by the punishing winds, accompanied only by the lonely albatross circling above its yardarms, and from everything he had been able to glean of their present surroundings, he and Eleanor had arrived at a place so remote, so frozen, and so barren that it could only be the Pole itself... that most dreaded destination of all.

But the seal might help. He had seen Eleanor failing, and he knew that what the bottles contained was old, and foul, and not nearly so potent as it had once been. He was surprised, given its origins, that it had any efficacy at all; on their journeys through Europe, he had been reduced to siphoning the blood from the dead he came across on battlefields and charnel houses. He had gone in search of fresh meat, fresh blood, even if it was only animal, and he had found it down among the bleached skeletons and wind-blasted rocks along the shoreline. There, the seals liked to bask in the cold glare of the sun, sprawled among the millions of broken bones, like so many bathers at Brighton Beach. He had avoided the larger ones, no doubt the bulls, one of whom had waddled toward him, trumpeting, and instead picked what was probably a female, with sleek brown fur and long black whiskers. She was off by herself, lying under the vast arc of a whale's backbone, and as he approached her, she showed no fear. Indeed, she showed little reaction at all, watching impassively as he shook his sword free of its scabbard. He stood above her, planting his boots to either side. She looked up at him with bulging, liquid eyes as he tried to judge where her heart might lie. He wanted the wound to be as small and precise as possible, so that the blood would remain inside the carcass rather than pooling across the ground. He touched the point of the blade to the spot he'd chosen—and only then did the seal look down at it, slightly curious—before he put all his weight into it and pressed down. The blade entered smoothly, and the animal buckled from both ends as the sword went clean through and struck the permafrost below. He did not withdraw it, but let it stand in order to stanch the flow, and within a minute, the seal had ended its contortions and lay still.

While the other seals had looked on, still unalarmed—indeed unconcerned, about what had just befallen their compatriot—he wiped his sword clean on the snow, then dragged his prize back to the sled. There would be provisions for some time to come... though what he and Eleanor would do in the longer term was as dire a prospect as it had ever been.

Sinclair was no sailor, but as someone who had been on the run for well over two years after Balaclava, he had learned to read the weather signs as well as anyone. He could tell that the temperature, brutal to begin with, was falling even more, and the sky on the far horizon was growing darker and more ominous by the minute. Under normal circumstances, Sinclair had a fine sense of direction— more than once he had advised his fellow cavalry officers on the proper course to follow—but in this accursed place it was well-nigh impossible. There was no night, so there were no stars, and there was no day—not day as one would commonly know it; how could one gauge the movement of a constant sun, or track shadows that barely changed? And as for landmarks, at times he could make out—though inland, and too distant to be reached—a black ridge of mountains, snaking through the otherwise flat expanse, like a jagged scar on a smooth white cheek. But that was about all.

Once he had gotten under way again, the weather changed even more rapidly, the wind buffeting the sled, the dogs often having to pull straight into it. He was fortunate to be wearing, atop his own uniform coat, the new red coat, with the white crosses on the back and sleeves, that he had salvaged from the shed—and to huddle behind the windbreak provided by the sled itself. His knees ached from crouching there, but to stand up was to risk being blown clear of the sled altogether. He worried, too, about Eleanor and what condition he would find her in. He had not liked to lock her in the rectory, but he feared for what she might do. Whether she was in possession of her wits, or temporarily out of them, he could not be sure.

From experience, he knew that the fever could come and go, like the bouts of malaria that Sergeant Hatch had endured, but he also knew that the terrible craving never went away. It was always there, sometimes running like an underground stream, at other times bursting forth and demanding gratification, and he wondered how Eleanor—slim as a reed at the best of times, and so young—continued to survive its relentless pull. Their affliction was at once their salvation, preserving them from a hundred mortal frailties, and the curse that held them forever in its own dark power. Liberator and jailer, simultaneously. There were times when he doubted Eleanor's will, and even her desire, to go on under such circumstances. But the force of his own will, he felt sure, was strong enough for them both. Whether she wished it so or not, she needed what he was bringing to her—and, above all, she needed him. He shouted at the dogs, urging them on, but the wind seemed to gather his words and fling them back into his chattering teeth.

CHAPTER THIRTY-EIGHT

December 16, 8:15 p.m.

MICHAEL LEFT THE INFIRMARY with his thoughts teeming. It was all too unbelievable, too astonishing, too impossible to comprehend. Had he really just been talking to someone who'd been frozen in the ice for over a hundred years before he'd even been born?

He had to calm down, he told himself. Take things logically. Go one step at a time. And just then, those first steps, as he clung fast to the guide ropes strung between the modules, took him past the glaciology lab. He knew that Danzig was out there somewhere, but why not make sure he wasn't just hiding out in the lair where his body had been deposited? Murphy had no doubt checked on it already, but Michael needed to confirm it with his own eyes. At least that would be one thing he could nail down, beyond any doubt, and if there was anything he needed at that moment, it was certainty. Of something. Anything.

With reality threatening to slip its moorings completely, he was more determined than ever to tie it to the dock.

Betty and Tina, to his relief, were nowhere in evidence. Warily, he clambered down the icy steps into the vault where Danzig's body had been laid. The plastic body bags had been ripped apart and lay in shreds on the frozen slab. The tableau reminded him, unavoidably, of some terrible version of the resurrection. Jesus rising from his tomb and leaving only the shroud behind.

Once he climbed back to the top of the stairs, there was more bad news. When he stopped at the plasma crate to check on Ollie, he found the box empty. The wood shavings in back were still shaped like a nest, but apart from a loose gray feather or two, there was no sign of the bird at all. He took some fried grits from his pocket—he'd snagged them when he fetched the food for Eleanor—and dropped them in the box, in case the bird returned. It was only a skua, considered no more than Antarctic riffraff, but he was going to miss the little guy.

Then, with his head down, he made his way back, past the rec hall, where he could hear some raucous voices and piano playing. Normally, he might have gone in and joined them, but not right now. At the moment, all he wanted was time to think, alone, and let his thoughts settle.

Fortunately, Darryl was not in their room. He drew the curtains across the horizontal windowpane and turned on the desk lamp, with a rare incandescent bulb that he had "liberated" from a tiny lounge area at the end of the hall. Then he kicked off his shoes and sweaty socks and dug his toes into the shag carpet. Work. He just needed to focus for a while on his work; he'd been letting it slide. He took the bottle of Scotch from the shelf in the closet and poured himself three fingers' worth. With his laptop on the table, he started downloading the dozens of photographs he'd taken since first arriving at Point Adélie. There were shots of the Weddell seals, which had been whelping on the ice floes for the first few days there, and others of the birds—the snowy petrels and assorted scavengers—who frequented the base. His fingers hovered over the keyboard for a second as he wondered anew what had become of Ollie.

There were shots of the dive hut, and a couple of Darryl inside it, looking like one of Santa's elves, in his full dry suit and his red hair wet and shining; in one, he was holding a speargun like a javelin over his shoulder. There were a bunch of pictures of Danzig and the dogs, some posed, and some that Michael had taken on the fly when the team was being exercised. And there was one with

Kodiak licking the ice crystals from Danzig's beard. Selecting a few of the best shots, he moved them to a separate file. Then he downloaded another batch and found himself looking straight into the face of Sleeping Beauty.

Or Eleanor Ames, as he now knew.

Her eyes were open, and she was gazing out through a thick film of the ice. He enlarged the photo, and her green eyes came into even greater relief. It was as if they were looking right at him, and he felt as if he were looking right back. As if he were looking across a chasm of time, and the gulf between life and death. He took another sip of the Scotch. Was that indeed what he'd been doing?

The wind came up another notch and battered the sides of the module. The curtains stirred; the window would have to be closed more tightly.

Michael sat back, staring at the photo and wondering what Eleanor was doing now. Was she sleeping? Or was she awake and terrified by her new captivity?

And then he thought he heard something—a lot like a human cry—mingled with the howling wind. Rising from his chair, he parted the curtains, hooded his eyes, and looked outside, but in the swirling snow he couldn't see a thing. For that much, he was grateful. What could he have done, he wondered, if it had been Danzig...

He gave the window crank another turn.

But then he thought he heard the cry again, and this time he could have sworn it was a deep voice, wailing words that were indecipherable. But even after turning off the lamp, hooding his eyes and staring out again, he could see nothing.

Whoa, he thought, drawing the curtains firmly closed, *that Scotch must be higher proof than I thought.*

He plopped back into the chair, and after one more look at the photo of Eleanor, flicked open some shots he'd taken of the abandoned whaling station. The rusted hulk of the *Albatros* gaped on the beach, piles of bleached bones lay scattered among the rocks, gravestones leaned at crazy angles in the churchyard. The curtains stirred again, but he knew it wasn't because of the window. The door at the end of the hallway must have been opened, and that always sent a draft blowing straight down the hall, all the way to the communal bathroom and sauna. It was probably Darryl, and Michael was already preparing what he would say—or not say, in respect to the discovery of Eleanor—as he listened to the sound of wet footsteps trudging down the hall. He closed the file on the computer just as they stopped outside. He waited to hear Darryl's key enter the lock—locked dorm rooms had become the rule, according to Murphy—but instead he simply saw the doorknob turn. Just a little bit, before the lock kicked in.

He could see a shadow under the door, and he could hear breathing outside—labored breathing. The hair on the back of his neck suddenly prickled, and he got up, slowly, and tiptoed barefoot to the door. He took hold of the door handle, just as it was jiggled again; he held it firm, and put his ear to the door. It was thin plywood, and never in his life did he wish harder for a slab of solid oak. A trickle of icy water ran under the door and touched his toes.

The handle was tried again, the other way, but it still didn't give. Michael tried not to breathe.

He heard a full exhalation, and the sound of rustling, frost-covered clothes. Michael pressed his ear tighter against the door and leaned his shoulder against it, too.

"Give . . ." the voice mumbled " . . . it . . . back."

Michael's blood froze in his veins, and he waited, ready to do anything to blockade the door, when he heard some laughing at the other end of the module—the bathroom end—and the snapping of a towel.

"Grow up!" someone shouted.

The jiggling abruptly stopped, and the shadow under the door disappeared. There was a rapid, squelching sound—wet boots on dry carpet—and a few seconds after Michael heard the outer door slam at the far end of the module, the bedroom door started to open. He was still holding the knob, and he heard Darryl mutter, "Fuck this key . . ."

Michael let go, and the knob turned. Darryl came in, in his bathrobe and flip-flops, with a towel wrapped around his neck. He looked startled to see Michael standing there behind the door.

"What are you, the doorman now?"

Michael ducked around him and stuck his head into the hall. "Did you see anybody out here?"

"What?" Darryl said, vigorously toweling his head. "Oh, yeah, I think somebody was just going out." He tossed his key onto the dresser. "Why?"

Michael closed the door and locked it. The icy trickle had already begun to dry on the carpet.

Noticing the open laptop, Darryl said, "You were working?"

"Yeah," Michael said, turning it off now. "I was."

"Turn up anything interesting at Stromviken?"

"No, nothing new," Michael said, turning away to conceal any expression that might betray him.

Spotting the glass of Scotch, Darryl said, "I'll have a shot of that."

While Michael poured some of the Scotch into a glass, Darryl tossed his towel toward their dresser. It fell off, carrying a hairbrush and some other stuff with it. "Sorry," he said, "my three-point shot was always weak." He bent down and picked a few things up off the carpet, but the last item he weighed thoughtfully in his hand.

When Michael handed him the glass, Darryl offered him the item he'd just retrieved—a walrus-tooth necklace that unspooled into Michael's palm like a snake.

"When you get back to the world," Darryl said, "I guess you could always mail it back to his widow. She'd probably like to have it."

December 16, 8:20 p.m.

Once Michael had left the infirmary—and Eleanor was sorry to see him go—the doctor ushered her into the bathroom, showed her how the hot shower worked, and left her everything else she'd need. There was a slender cylinder, for example, soft to the touch, that emitted a paste for scrubbing the teeth—the taste reminded her of lime—and a brush, too, with very fine, clear bristles. Eleanor wondered for a moment what animal the bristles could possibly have come from.

"You need anything else, I'm right next door," the doctor said.

And then Eleanor was alone—alone in a lavatory that resembled nothing she'd ever seen, with fresh apparel to put on, for the first time in over 150 years, and with no idea what would happen to her next. Or to Sinclair, wherever he might be. Was he still reconnoitering? Or hunting? Had he been caught, too far from the church, in the midst of the storm, and was he stranded in the alien landscape?

Or had he come back, only to find the bolt on the door thrown back and the room empty? He would know that someone must have intruded on her. She felt a sharp pang, the pang she knew she'd have felt if their positions had been reversed . . . if she'd had reason to believe that Sinclair had been taken from her, God knew where. Ever since the day he had been brought back from the battlefield, and she had seen his name on the roster of the newly admitted, they had been united in a way that she could never have explained to anyone.

How could anyone else have ever understood?

She had found him in one of the larger fever wards. Stained muslin curtains hung from sagging rods, and since few of the doctors, or even the orderlies, cared to risk the chance of contagion, there was no one to ask about exactly where he had been billeted. Ignoring the piteous cries for water or help, from men dying of thirst or lost in some terrible fever dream, she had stumbled through the ward, looking everywhere . . . until she spied a fair-haired head lying on a straw bolster on the floor.

"Sinclair!" she'd exclaimed, running to his side.

He looked up at her, but said nothing—and then he had smiled. But it was a dreamy smile, a smile that told her he did not believe she was really there. It was the smile of a man consciously enjoying what he knew to be a reverie.

"Sinclair, it's me," she said, falling to her knees beside his flimsy pallet and taking hold of his limp hand. "I'm here. Truly."

The smile faltered, as if her touch was eroding, rather than reinforcing, his fragile dream.

She pressed her cheek to the back of his hand. "I'm here, and you're alive, and that's all that matters."

He withdrew the hand—peeved—at this further intrusion.

Tears welled up in her eyes, but she searched the ward until she found a pitcher of stagnant water—the only water available at all— and returned to mop his brow and face. There were flakes of blood in his moustache, and she wiped those away, too.

The soldier lying on the floor behind her, a Highlander judging from what was left of his uniform, clutched at the hem of her skirt and begged for a drop of the water. She turned and poured some of the water over his cracked lips. He was an older man, somewhere past thirty, with broken teeth and skin the color of chalk. He would not, she knew, be long for this world.

"Thank'ee, Missus," he murmured. "But mind you, steer clear of him." He meant Sinclair. "He's a bad 'un." He turned his pallid face away, suddenly overcome by a barking cough.

Delirium, she thought, before turning back to Sinclair. But it was as if, in those few seconds, his mind had cleared somewhat; he was looking at her now with comprehension. "My God," escaped his lips. "It *is* you."

Her tears burst forth, and she bent to embrace him. She could feel his skin and bones through the thin nightshirt he had been issued, and wondered how quickly she could fetch some hot porridge from the kitchens. Or find him a proper bed.

He was weak and frail but able to speak a few words at a time, and Eleanor filled in the rest. She didn't want to exhaust him—and she knew that she had duties to fulfill—but he seemed to be gaining strength from her very presence and she dreaded leaving him, even for a few hours. When, finally, she had to do so, promising to return at her first opportunity, he followed her with his eyes until she was obscured by the muslin curtains billowing like shrouds.

Even as she looked at herself now in the spotless lavatory mirror, she could perfectly remember the look on his face, and see it as clearly as her own. She turned the shower handles as the doctor had shown her—and after piling the last of her clothes atop a wicker hamper, stepped gingerly into the hot spray. The water poured from a circular device, and seemed to pulsate as it rained down on her. A bar of soap—green, of all things—lay in a shallow niche on the tiled wall. And just as the paste she had used on her teeth had a taste of citrus, the soap had a fragrance, of evergreen trees. Did everything in this strange new world bear a foreign flavor or aroma? Eleanor let the hot torrent fall over her arms, then her shoulders. Unsure how long the miraculous cascade might last, she put her face up to the spray. Everything was so alien, and so unexpected, it was as if she had landed in the Crimea all over again.

The water felt like a thousand tiny raindrops drumming on her eyelids, coursing down her neck and breasts. Slowly, she inched forward, until the water was rushing over the crown of her head, draping her long brown hair down either side of her face. It was one of the most delicious sensations she had ever experienced, and she stood there for many minutes, leaning forward with her palms flat against the white tiles, steeping, she thought, like tea leaves, as the water made a shallow pool around her feet. For the first time in ages, her skin felt warm, all over, and she wondered, if she stood there long enough and the water did not run out, if its heat could finally penetrate as far as her heart and assuage the unremitting ache that had been her companion for so long.

CHAPTER THIRTY-NINE

December 17, Midnight

THE BELL IN THE STEEPLE was ringing when Sinclair finally returned to the church, but it was only the wind banging the clapper. Still, the sound had helped him and the dogs to find their way through the storm. He staggered in, the dead seal draped around his shoulders, and the dogs, released from their harness, yapping wildly around his feet. In an instant he saw that the rectory door was ajar. Throwing the seal upon the altar, he crossed to the open door and looked inside.

The fire was dead in the grate, and Eleanor was gone.

He stood there, his arms extended to either side of the doorframe, breathing hard. It was possible, though unlikely, that she had found some way to unfasten the lock and escape. But where?

And why?

"Eleanor!" He shouted her name again and again, setting off a reciprocal chorus among the dogs roaming the aisles. He thundered up the stairs to the belfry and peered into the cyclone of snow and ice, but he could barely see the warehouses and sheds below. Even if he ventured out into the storm on foot, the blizzard was so intense he would not be able to orient himself or move in any consistent direction. If Eleanor had gone into it, he would never be able to find her . . . or his own way back.

There was nothing to do, he knew, but wait. He must bide his time until the storm abated. Though he hated to concede it, it *was* conceivable that she had done something rash and unforgivable . . . that she had chosen, of her own free will, not to go on. He was well aware of her despair, being no stranger to it himself . . . but in his heart he could not accept that she had done that. He scoured their humble quarters for a telltale sign of farewell, or a message of any kind, torn from letters in the hymnals perhaps. But there was nothing, and he knew that Eleanor, no matter how possessed by grief she might have been, would not have left him that way. She would not have left him without a word. He knew her too well ever to believe such a thing.

Which left only one alternative . . . that Eleanor had been taken. Against her will.

Had men from the camp come in his absence and made off with her? Any tracks they might have left in the snow would have already been obliterated, and with the wet dogs in the church, it was impossible to see any footprints the intruders might have left there, either. But who else could it have been? And where else but their camp could she have been taken?

Finally—and that was where all his thoughts were tending—how could he best effect her rescue?

The obstacles to that were immense, especially because he could not see what the endgame would be. Even if he were successful at finding and freeing her, where could they flee on this icebound continent? He felt as if he were staring down a narrow defile to certain doom, just as he had done on that brisk October morning in Balaclava. But somehow, he reminded himself, he had survived that apocalypse, and even worse. Regardless of how black the page, he had always managed to turn it and move on to a new chapter in his life.

And he did have certain advantages, he reflected grimly. A cup of fresh seal blood rested like a chalice at his elbow, next to a book of poetry that had traveled with him all the way from England to the Crimea, and now to this dreadful outpost. He opened it, and let the pages fall where they would. His eyes dropped to the yellowed paper, stiff as parchment, and there he read . . .

Alone, alone, all, all alone,
Alone on a wide, wide sea!
And never a saint took pity on
My soul in agony.

The many men, so beautiful!
And they all dead did lie:
And a thousand thousand slimy things
Lived on; and so did I.

Though there was precious little balm in the words for most men, for him they provided comfort. Only the poet seemed to guess the awful truth of his situation. The dogs howled, and Sinclair sawed off another slab of blubber from the dead seal lying on the table and tossed the pieces into the nave below. The dogs scrambled to get them, their claws scraping on the stone floor, their barks echoing up to the rafters.

From his tall stool behind the desecrated altar, Sinclair surveyed his empty realm. He could envision the faces of the whalers who had once occupied the pews, their faces smeared with grease and soot, their grimy clothes encrusted with dried blood. They had gazed up at that very altar, hats in hand, listening to the minister extol the virtues of the life beyond, the bounteous treasures they had laid up in Heaven to compensate them for the torments they endured day after day. They had sat there, in the desolate church— even the crucifix was rough-hewn and plain—in a frozen waste, surrounded by flensing yards and boiling cauldrons, piles of entrails and mountains of bones, and they had listened to stories of white clouds and golden sunlight, of boundless happiness and eternal life. Of a world that was not a reeking slaughterhouse . . . and oh, Sinclair reflected, oh, how they had been duped.

As he had once been duped by tales of glory and valor. Lying on his pallet in the Barrack Hospital, consumed with the mounting and inexplicable desire, he had been driven to a deed he had long regretted but could never undo. The bloodlust engendered by that unholy creature on the battlefield at Balaclava had proven too strong to resist, and he had preyed upon a helpless Highlander too weak to fend him off.

The Turks would have numbered him among the cursed. And he would not have disputed it.

Still, the next night, when Eleanor had come to his side, he had felt distinctly stronger. Revived. He felt that he could truly breathe again and see more clearly. Even his faculties seemed to have been restored.

Was that how it felt to be one of the damned?

But in Eleanor's face, he had detected something troubling; he had seen what he thought was the first glimmering of the mysterious Crimean fever, and he knew the signs well; he had noted them countless times in many others. His fears were confirmed when she swayed on her feet, spilling the soup, and the orderlies had escorted her from the ward. The following evening, when it was Moira, and not Eleanor, who came to assist him, he knew the worst.

"Where is Eleanor?" he had demanded, lifting himself on one elbow from the floor. Even that was painful; he suspected he had fractured a rib or two in the fall from his horse, but there was nothing to be done for a broken rib, and anything the surgeons might attempt would no doubt kill him.

"Eleanor's resting today," Moira said, trying not to meet his eye as she set down the bowl of soup, still warm, and a mug of brackish water.

"The truth," he said, clutching her sleeve.

"Miss Nightingale wishes her to gather her strength."

"She's ill, isn't she?"

He could see the furtive look in her eye as she wiped a spoon on her apron pocket and put it into the soup bowl.

"Is it the fever? How far has it gone?"

Moira stifled a sob and quickly glanced away. "Eat your soup, while it's still hot."

"Damn the soup. How far has it gone?" His heart seized up in his chest at the very thought of the worst. "Tell me that she's still alive."

Moira nodded as she dabbed at her tears with a wretched excuse for a handkerchief.

"Where is she? I need to go to her."

Moira's head shook, and she said, "That's impossible. She's in the nurses' quarters, and can't be moved."

"Then I'll have to go there."

"Seeing her like this... she don't want it. And there's nothing you can do to help her."

"I'll be the judge of that."

He threw back the ratty blanket and staggered to his feet. The world spun around him, the dirty walls, the muslin curtains speckled with flies, the wretched bodies lying in disorderly rows all across the floor. Moira threw her arms around his waist and steadied him.

"You can't go there!" she protested. "You can't!"

But Sinclair knew that he could, and that Moira would help him to do so. He groped around the straw he'd fashioned into a pillow and pulled out the jacket of his uniform, wrinkled and soiled though it was. With Moira's reluctant help, he finished getting dressed, then lurched toward the door. It opened out onto two endless corridors, equally dim and cluttered, but leading in opposite directions. "Which way?"

Moira took his arm firmly and led him to the left. They passed room after room filled with the sick and the dying—most of them silent, a few softly muttering to themselves. The ones who were in such agony or delirium that they could not be kept quiet were given a blessed dose of the opium, and it was simply hoped that they would not awaken again. Occasionally, they passed orderlies or medical officers who gave them a curious glance, but by and large the hospital was so vast, and everyone working in it so overwhelmed by their own duties and responsibilities, no one could spare any further concern.

Since the hospital had originally served as a barracks, it was built as an enormous square, with a central courtyard sufficient for mustering thousands of troops, and towers at each of the four corners. The nurses' quarters were in the northwest tower, and Sinclair had to lean heavily upon Moira's ample arm and shoulder as they mounted the narrow, winding stairs. When they came to the first landing, they saw the glow of a lantern descending toward them, and Moira had to usher Sinclair quickly into a shallow recess. As the light came closer, Moira stepped forward and said, "Evening, mum," and from the shadows Sinclair saw that it was Miss Nightingale herself, lamp in hand, a black lace handkerchief draped over her white cap, whom she had greeted.

"Good evening, Mrs. Mulcahy," she replied. The white collar and cuffs and apron she wore stood out in the lantern glow. "I expect you are returning to your friend's side."

"That I am, mum."

"How is she? Has her fever abated at all?"

"Not so's you'd notice, mum."

"I'm sorry to hear that. I shall look in on her when I have finished my rounds."

"Thank you, mum. I know she would appreciate that."

As Miss Nightingale trimmed her lamp, Sinclair held his breath in the dark corner.

"As I recall, the two of you enlisted in this mission together, did you not?"

"We did, mum."

"And you shall return from it together, too," she said. "Just be sure that the bonds of friendship, however strong, do not divert you from our more general purpose here. As you know, we are—all of us—forever under a magnifying glass."

"Yes, mum. Indeed, mum."

"Good night, Mrs. Mulcahy."

And then, in a rustle of black silk, Miss Nightingale continued down the steps, and when the light from her lamp was gone, Sinclair stepped out of the shadows. Moira said nothing, but beckoned him on. At the next landing, he heard the voices of several nurses, wearily exchanging the news of the day—one was describing a pompous officer who had demanded that she stop dressing an infantryman's wound in order that she might fetch him a cup of tea—while others were washing up. Moira put a finger to her lips and led him up yet another flight, to the very top of the tower, where he found a tiny alcove with a tall window overlooking the dark blue waters of the Bosporus.

Moira, lifting her skirts from the floor, hurried to the side of the bed and whispered, "Look who I've brought you, Ellie."

Before Eleanor could even turn her head on the pillow, Sinclair had knelt by the bedside and taken hold of her hand. It was limp and hot, damp to the touch.

Her gaze was unfocused, and she seemed strangely annoyed at

the interruption; he doubted that she had actually registered his presence. The fever, as he well knew, could blur the line between fancy and reality.

"If the instrument is out of key," she said, "then it ought not to be played."

Moira met his eye, as if to confirm that Eleanor went in and out of sensibility.

"And put the music back in the bench. That's how it gets lost."

She was back in England—perhaps at her family home, or more probably at the parsonage, where she had told him she once used to go to practice the piano. He pressed the back of her hand to his lips, but she pulled it away and whisked it above her blanket, as if trying to scatter a horde of flies. They were everywhere in the hospital wards, but here, he noticed, so high up in the tower and facing the sea, there were none.

How, he wondered, could he get rid of Moira? To do what he needed to do—what *had* to be done to save Eleanor's life—he would need to be alone and unobserved. Moira was wringing a cloth in a bucket of water, then dabbing at Eleanor's face with it.

"Moira, can you get some port wine, do you think?"

"More easily said than done," she replied, "but I'll try." Moira, no fool, handed him the cloth, then tactfully withdrew.

Sinclair studied Eleanor's face in the moonlight. Her skin had a hectic flush, and her green eyes glittered with a mad delight. She was not aware of her own suffering; for all intents and purposes, she wasn't even there. Her spirit had left her body and was traveling in the Yorkshire countryside. But her body, he feared, would soon go, too. He had seen a hundred soldiers rant and rave, mutter and laugh, just like this, before suddenly turning their heads to the wall and dying with a single breath.

"Can you play me something," he said, "on the pianoforte?"

Eleanor sighed and smiled. "What would you like to hear?"

He gently drew the blanket away from her shoulders, the heat from her fevered body welling up from beneath the wool.

"You choose."

"I am fond of the traditional songs. I can play you 'Barbara Allen,' if you like."

"I would like that very much," he said, slipping the chemise from her shoulder. She shivered in the breeze from the open window. He bent his head above her.

Eleanor's fingers twitched, as if they were caressing a keyboard, and under her ragged breath she hummed the opening bars of the song.

Although her skin was still hot to the touch, gooseflesh had already begun to form. He placed his hand above her breast to protect her from the night air. Even then, beneath the scent of camphor and wool, she smelled as sweet to him as a meadow on a summer morn. And when his lips grazed her skin, she tasted like milk fresh from the pail.

She was singing, very softly, "Oh mother, mother, make my bed..."

What he was about to do, he feared could never be undone.

"O make it saft and narrow..."

But what choice was there?

"My love has died for me today..."

By daybreak she would be gone. He put his arms around her, the breath choking in his own throat.

"I'll die for him to-morrow..."

And when he bestowed it—his mouth closing on her skin, her blood mingling with his own corrupted spittle—she flinched, as if from the sting of a bee, and her singing abruptly stopped. Her body became rigid.

Moments later, when he lifted his head again, his lips wet from the dreadful embrace, her limbs relaxed and she looked at him dreamily, saying, "But that is such a sad song." She stroked his tear-stained cheek with her fingertips. "Shall I play you something gay now?"

PART IV
THE VOYAGE BACK

"I looked to heaven, and tried to pray;
But or ever a prayer had gushed,
A wicked whisper came, and made
My heart as dry as dust.

I closed my lids, and kept them close,
And the balls like pulses beat,
For the sky and the sea, and the sea and the sky
Lay like a load on my weary eye,
And the dead were at my feet."

The Rime of the Ancient Mariner,
Samuel Taylor Coleridge, 1798

CHAPTER FORTY

December 18, 9 a.m.

JUST AS MICHAEL SHOWED UP at the infirmary, stomping the snow off his boots, Charlotte came out the door with a finger to her lips. She put her arm through his and guided him back toward the outer door. "Not now."

"She okay?"

She tilted one hand back and forth while pulling on her gloves. "She's still having a rough time and running a low fever. I've got her on some sedatives and a glucose drip. Best to let her rest."

Michael found he was even more disappointed than he'd have imagined. Ever since rescuing Eleanor from the whaling station, he'd been haunted by her face, the sound of her voice, the chance to uncover the rest of her story.

"And Murphy stopped by to remind me to keep quiet about her being here."

"Yeah, I got that memo, too," Michael said.

"Come on," Charlotte added, throwing the hood over her

head. "What I need right now is a mug of Uncle Barney's industrial-strength coffee."

Holding on to each other in the gusting wind, they inched their way down the ramp and over to the commons. A fake Christmas tree, strung with tinsel and a few battered ornaments, had been set up overnight and stood forlornly in a corner of the room.

Darryl was already in possession of a table in back, where he was plowing through a plate piled high with fried tofu (Uncle Barney said he'd radio for more on the next supply flight) and mixed veggies. Charlotte slid onto the bench next to him, and Michael sat down with his tray on the other side. With her braids all pulled together onto the top of her head, she looked like she was wearing a pineapple.

The first thing she did was to pour a lot of sugar into her coffee mug, and take a good long drink.

"Just getting up?" Darryl asked. " 'Cause if you don't mind my saying so, you look like you should have stayed in bed."

"Thanks for the kind words," she said, putting her mug down. "How does your wife not shoot you?"

Darryl shrugged. "Our marriage is built on honesty," he said, and Michael had to laugh.

"The weird thing is," she said, "when I was in Chicago, and I had car alarms going off in the middle of the night, and neighbors having parties till four in the morning, I slept like a baby. Here, where the place is as silent as a grave and the nearest car is parked about a thousand miles away, I'm awake half the night."

"You pulling your bed curtains closed?" Darryl asked.

"Not on your life," she said, dipping some dry toast in a runny egg. "Too much like a coffin."

"How about the blackout curtains on the window?"

She paused, chewing slowly. "Yeah, I got up to fiddle with those last night."

"The idea," Darryl admonished her, "is to close them *before* you get in bed."

"I did, but I could have sworn..." She stopped, then went on. "I could have sworn I heard something outside, in the storm."

Michael waited. Something in her voice told him what was coming.

"Heard what?" Darryl asked.

"A voice. Shouting."

"Maybe it was the banshee," Darryl said, burrowing into his plate.

"What was it shouting?" Michael asked, as casually as he could.

"Best I could make out—and the wind was pretty high—it was something like 'Give it back.' " She shook her head and went back to her toast and eggs. "I'm starting to miss those car alarms."

Michael could barely swallow his food, but he decided to keep his own counsel for a while.

"Which reminds me," she said, fishing in the pocket of her overcoat and removing a blood sample in a plastic vial. "I need a full blood assay done on this."

Darryl didn't look thrilled. "Why am I so honored?"

"Because you've got all that fancy equipment in your lab."

"Whose is it?" he asked.

"Just one of the grunts," she said, offhandedly. "No big deal."

"Well," he said, dabbing at his mouth with the napkin, "as it so happens, I do have some big news of my own."

Michael wasn't sure if he was kidding or not.

"You are sitting, my friends, in the company of greatness. In that last set of traps, I captured a heretofore undiscovered species of fish."

Both Michael and Charlotte suddenly gave him their full attention.

"This is for real?" Michael asked.

Darryl nodded, grinning. "Although it is closely related to the *Cryothenia amphitreta*, which remained undiscovered until 2006, this specimen is as yet unrecorded."

"How can you be sure?" Charlotte asked.

"I've consulted the definitive sourcebook, a little tome called *Fishes of the Southern Ocean*, and it's not there. Its head morphology alone is like nothing I've ever seen. It's got a bifurcated ridge above its eyes, and a purple crest."

"That's fantastic," Michael said. "What are you going to call it?"

"For the time being, I'm calling it *Cryothenia*—which means, 'from the cold'—*hirschii*."

"That's modest," Charlotte said with a laugh.

"What?" Darryl replied. "Scientists name things after themselves all the time—and it will truly piss off a guy named Dr. Edgar Montgomery back at Woods Hole."

"Then I say go for it," Michael said.

"Now, what I'd really like to do," Darryl said, "is catch a few more of them fast; there might be a whole school in the vicinity. The one I've got I'll need to dissect, but it'd be great to have a few spares that I could keep intact."

"Maybe you'll get lucky," Michael said.

"Murphy's ordered everyone to stay on base until the storm clears, but if I can get permission to go just as far as the dive hut, I'm going to drop some more nets and traps. You're welcome to come along—both of you. You could tell your grandchildren that you were there while history was being made."

Charlotte blotted up some more yolk, and said, "Much as I'd like to freeze my butt off fishing, I think I'll take a nice long nap instead."

But Michael, jumping at the opportunity to get off the base any way he could—especially since Eleanor was off-limits—said, "I'm game. When do you want to go?"

One hour later, they were cruising across the ice on a snowmobile, with Michael driving and Darryl hanging on in back. Michael had been riding snowmobiles for years, and normally he'd found the experience exhilarating, but snowmobiling in Antarctica was something else. The air was so blisteringly cold that any inch of skin that was exposed could burn like fire, then go totally numb, in a matter of seconds. He had to keep his head down over the handlebars, with his ski mask covering his face, his goggles over his eyes, and his fur hood gathered tight around his head.

It was a blissfully short ride to the dive hut, squatting out there on its cinder-block legs, and Michael let the vehicle glide to a slow stop at the foot of the ramp leading up to the door. The moment the sound of the motor died away, the roar of the wind took over. It whipped around them, nearly knocking Darryl over. Michael grabbed him by the shoulder to steady him, then helped carry the gear inside. Just getting the door closed again was a fight in itself, the gusting wind threatening to tear it right off its hinges.

"Jesus," Michael said, collapsing onto the wooden bench and brushing his hood back with his mitten. The hut, with its gaping hole in the middle of the floor, was not much warmer than it was outside, but at least they were protected from the wind. Darryl flicked on the heaters, and they both simply sat, shivering, for a minute or two before trying to do anything at all. As the heaters worked, a fine mist rose up off the water below and hung like a pall over the diving hole.

"Got a lot of ice clogging up the hole," Michael observed. "We're gonna have to break that up before we try to lower anything."

"Why do you think I invited you along?" Darryl said as he tried, without removing his thick gloves, to fasten his nets and traps to the long lines.

"I should have known." Michael looked around at the racks of tools and equipment fixed to the wall or lying on the floorboards. Ice saws, steel cables, spearguns. The most likely candidate was a sharp-tipped spade, but he found it impossible to hold without taking off his mittens; reluctantly, he did so. He still had glove liners on underneath, but at least they were slim enough that he could slip his fingers through the handle.

The water, covered with a thin film of fresh ice, lay a couple of feet below, and it was awkward work to plunge the tip of the spade down, crack the ice, then pull the spade back again for another strike. It reminded Michael, inevitably, of shoveling the driveway after a big storm when he was a kid. His dad was always telling him to get out there and do it now—"it won't get any easier when it's had time to freeze over"—and Michael remembered well the peculiar pain, the one that would travel right up his arms, when he drove the tip of his shovel into what looked like loose snow but turned out to be hard-packed ice. The shudder would course down the length of his entire spine and even his teeth would ache. He was getting to relive that sensation, only over and over, and the shoulder he had dislocated in the Cascades began to complain bitterly.

Eventually, he had reduced the ice at the bottom of the hole to a slushy mush, though he knew the ice would quickly start to knit itself together again.

"You about ready?" Michael asked, feeling a rivulet of sweat running down the small of his back.

"Almost...there," Darryl said, testing the clamp on a trap shaped like an hourglass. The line was like a giant charm bracelet, looped and coiled around the baseboards of the hut, with nets and lures tied to it at various spots. Darryl crawled toward the hole on his knees, and at its very rim he leaned over to drop the weighted end of the cable into the water.

"Clear away?" he asked, and Michael used the spade to spread the slush to one side. Darryl fed the line into the hole, and the lead weight at its end pulled it straight down. The winch, to which it was attached, hummed as the line dropped, carrying several of Darryl's devices into the depths of the polar sea.

Michael used the spade to keep the ice shards away, until it was suddenly jerked, mysteriously, from his grasp, and rattled down the ice hole like a log shooting down a flume.

"What the hell?"

Darryl laughed and, looking up, said, "Murphy's going to charge you for that."

Michael started to laugh, too, but then Darryl plunged forward, too, headfirst, into the hole. Michael thought he must have been snagged by the cable somehow, and instinctively he stamped his foot on it to keep it from playing out, but the line simply burned beneath his rubber boot and kept on unspooling.

And it wasn't the cable, anyway.

A big beefy hand, cobalt blue, was reaching out from under the floorboards of the hut and wrestling with the collar of Darryl's parka. Darryl's feet were kicking wildly, and he had one arm in the water and one flailing at his attacker.

Michael grabbed at his boots and struggled to pull him up.

A head, too, appeared now, from the space between the floorboards and the ice. A big head, with a frozen beard, and crazed white eyeballs.

Danzig.

His eyes locked on Michael, and like a lion distracted by more appealing prey, he loosened his grip on Darryl and started to haul himself up into the hut.

Michael kicked him in the chin—it was like kicking granite—and pulled again on Darryl, who had managed to push himself up from the funnel. Ice crystals sprayed around the hut, and Darryl was screaming for help.

Michael couldn't offer any. Danzig, covered with a silver sheen of ice, had propped both of his arms on the floorboards and was lifting himself like Poseidon rising from the deep.

"Give ... it ... back," he snarled, through what remained of his ravaged throat, and Michael kicked out at him again. Danzig grabbed at his boot, but it was wet, and it slipped right through his fingers.

Darryl had backed up out of the hole and rolled under a bench, where he was scrubbing the frozen water from his head in a panic. He still looked like he didn't know what had hit him or what was happening.

But Michael did, and Danzig was on his knees now, lumbering to his feet, icy water streaming off his soaking flannel shirt and jeans. Michael whirled around, scanning the walls, and his eye fell on the speargun normally used in defense against the leopard seals. He leapt over the wooden bench and yanked it from the wall. Danzig stumbled over the cable line and nearly fell, and Michael just had time to prime the gun and point it at the hulking creature coming at him. There was barely enough room to extend it between them before he pulled the trigger and the triple-pronged barb exploded into Danzig's heaving chest. The force of the thrust sent him reeling, backpedaling on the wet floor, until he managed to stop himself at the very edge of the gaping hole, his fingers clutching at the spear embedded in his flesh. His mouth opened wide, then, as he looked up in shock, Michael put out a boot and sent him tumbling backwards into the icy funnel. There was a loud splash, and a gurgle, a crackling of ice ... and then, apart from the hum of the heaters, silence.

Darryl was moaning and shaking the frigid water from his head, as Michael dropped to the rim of the hole, still holding the speargun, and looked down.

There was nothing to see but the taut, steel-reinforced cable holding Darryl's traps, and a shimmering tracery of blue-white ice, already weaving itself together again above Danzig's watery grave.

CHAPTER FORTY-ONE

December 18, 1 p.m.

SINCLAIR STOOD IN THE OPEN DOORS of the church, and stared out into a blinding white snowstorm so thick he could not see as far as the bottom of the stairs. Even the dogs would not be able to navigate in those conditions.

Putting his shoulder to the doors, he pushed them closed again and turned around to take in his kingdom . . . a bleak chapel, where the sled dogs lay sprawled on the stone floors or curled up into tight balls between the ancient pews. Where the relentless wind battered the walls and whistled through the cracks in the timbers and window frames. A massive cage, that's all it was . . . and he was the beast imprisoned inside it.

His thoughts wandered to a day—a Sunday afternoon—when he had taken Eleanor to the London Zoo. He had hoped to amuse her, but it had not gone as well as he had expected. Each animal in its cage seemed only to make her more forlorn, and though he had never looked at them in that way, he began to see the captive creatures through her eyes. So many were alone, confined to small spaces with no natural elements—no bushes or trees, no rocks or sand or cooling mud—to afford them a sense of what they knew, or instinctively desired. Eleanor had clutched his arm and they had wandered down the winding path, past the rows of thick iron bars, until they had come to the most popular exhibit of all.

The Bengal tiger.

Its coat a sleek tapestry of black and orange and white stripes, the tiger had padded back and forth and back and forth in a space barely wide enough for it to turn around in. A crowd of onlookers gawked from only a few feet away, and several children pulled faces whenever the beast leveled its baleful glare in their direction. One of them whipped an acorn through the bars, and the nut bounced off the tiger's snout. The tiger roared, and they laughed and clapped each other on the shoulder with glee.

"Stop that, right now!" Eleanor said, stepping forward to smack the hand of the boy about to launch another nut. The boy turned, stunned, and his scruffy friends rallied around him until Sinclair, too, stepped forward.

"Get out of here," he said, in a low but stern voice, "or I'll try tossing you into the cage."

The boy looked torn between impressing his friends and pre-serving his hide and when Sinclair reached out to grab his sleeve, he chose the latter course and scampered out of reach. But once he was a safe distance away, he stopped to hurl another acorn at Sin-clair and shout a few defiant words.

Sinclair turned back to Eleanor, who was staring fixedly at the tiger, which had stopped its endless rounds and was staring back at her. He dared not say a word—it was as if Eleanor and the tiger were silently communing. For as much as a minute, they held each other's gaze—an elderly spectator with white whiskers was heard to say, "Why, the lady's been Mesmerized"—but when she slipped her arm back through Sinclair's to walk away, there was a tear in her eye.

———————

Michael felt like he'd played the scene too many times before, trying to convince Murphy that the impossible was possible, that the un-thinkable had occurred—a woman had been found frozen in the ice, that Danzig had been killed by one of his dogs, or that, after

murdering Ackerley, he had returned once more to attack Darryl in
the dive hut. The only advantage was that Murphy had by then become so accustomed to these strange conferences that he had
stopped questioning Michael's veracity, or his sanity. Sitting behind
his desk now, he simply combed his fingers through his thick salt-
and-pepper hair—more salt, Michael thought, by the day—and
asked his questions in a resigned, almost perfunctory manner.

"But you're sure you got him this time, with the speargun?" he
asked Michael.

"Yes," Michael said. "He's gone, for good." But was he really as
sure as he'd just sounded?

"Either way," Murphy said, "nobody goes to the dive hut until
further notice. Make sure Mr. Hirsch gets that message loud and
clear."

There was a burst of static from the radio behind his chair.
"Wind speed, one hundred twenty, north, northeast," a faint voice
reported. "Temperatures ranging from forty to sixty below, Fahrenheit, anticipated to rise to..." There was further interference, then
the voice returned, saying, "...high-pressure front, moving southwest, from Chilean peninsula toward Ross Sea."

"Sounds like we might get a break tomorrow," he said, swiveling in his chair and flicking it off. "About fucking time." Then he
turned back toward Michael with a printout in his hand. "Dr.
Barnes's report," he said, slipping on a pair of glasses to read aloud.
" 'The patient, Ms. Eleanor Ames, by her own declaration an English citizen, of approximately twenty years of age' "— he stopped,
glancing at Michael over the rim of his glasses—" 'is in stable condition, with all vital signs now holding steady. There are still signs of
recurring hypotension and heart arrhythmias, coupled with extreme anemia, which we will aggressively address once the blood
work is complete.' " He lowered the paper and asked, "Got any idea
when Hirsch will be done with that?"

"Nope."

"Don't be too obvious, but give him a nudge."

"Wouldn't it be better coming from you?"

"I don't want to arouse his suspicions any more than they might
be already," Murphy said. "For all he knows, he's just got another
ordinary blood sample—let's keep it that way. And in case you

hadn't noticed, he doesn't do well with authority figures." He sat back, still brandishing the paper. "So this paper is the first official document, date- and time-stamped, confirming the existence of Sleeping Beauty."

"Eleanor Ames," Michael corrected him.

"Yeah, you're right. She's real enough now." He conspicuously slipped the sheet into a blue plastic folder. "And as a result, every-thing from now on either has to go by the book," he said, "or else it has to be left temporarily undocumented—and absolutely uncircu-lated. No paper trail, in other words, or loose lips. You do catch my drift?"

Michael nodded.

"The last thing we need here—the last thing in the whole fuck-ing world—is any more scrutiny than we're already going to get, from the NSF and just about every other agency we deal with. I've got two years until I qualify for a full pension. I don't want to spend them filling out forms and giving depositions." He gestured at a teetering stack of official-looking papers and forms in a desk tray. "See that? That's just the routine shit. Imagine if the latest headlines get out."

Michael could well imagine. Already he was wondering what he would say—or not say—to Gillespie the next time they talked.

"So that's why I'm going to ask you, for the time being, to keep whatever you can under your hat. And while you're at it, do me one more favor."

"I'll do whatever I can."

"I want you to be the liaison, or whatever you want to call it, to Ms. Ames. Help Charlotte out, and keep me informed of what's up—how the patient's doing, what she's doing, what you think we need to address. I don't need to tell you, nothing that looks like this has ever happened before—anyplace or anytime—and I don't par-ticularly want to broadcast that she's here to anybody who doesn't already know about it. I want to take that nice and slow."

"But do you plan to keep her completely confined to the infir-mary?" Michael asked. "Because she could go stir-crazy in there. I know I would."

"We'll figure that out as we go, and as we get the info back from Darryl and Charlotte."

"And what about her companion," Michael pressed, "the man

she calls Sinclair? If the forecast's right, can we go back to Stromviken to find him?"

"Tomorrow, if the weather does improve. Maybe then we can do a search party." He sounded as if he'd just as soon not; Michael suspected he was hoping that this Sinclair—just another huge problem, from Murphy's point of view—would simply disappear.

"I mean, one thing at a time," Murphy resumed. "Assuming that she is who she says she is, and what she says she is—"

"I'd be hard-pressed," Michael interjected, "to come up with another explanation for all this. And believe me, I've tried."

"Yeah, well, keep trying," the chief replied. "But granting, simply for argument's sake, that you're right, what if she was to catch something from somebody here, something that she has no immunity against?"

Michael hadn't thought of that and let out a "huh."

"See?" Murphy said, throwing up his hands. "That's the kind of stuff I've got to consider. I mean, I'm no doctor. Hell, if I were, I might know what to do about Ackerley."

Michael had been wondering about that, too. No announcement of his death had been made, and it was only a matter of time before somebody noticed that even the notoriously elusive Spook hadn't been seen in a while.

"What did you do with his body?" Michael asked.

"Cold storage," Murphy replied. "I've notified his mother—he lives with her, back in Wilmington—but frankly, she didn't seem all there. I haven't put in the official report yet, because the second I do—coming so close on the heels of what happened to Danzig—I'll be lucky not to have a goddamned FBI delegation sent down here to investigate." A sudden gust of wind shook the whole module on its cinder blocks. "And I asked Lawson to go in and clean up the botany lab, maybe try to preserve whatever he was working on."

That seemed like a good, and laudable, decision, but Michael wondered if anyone would know how to keep all the plants alive, especially the orchids on their long and delicate stems. Everything in the Antarctic seemed to conspire against survival, against life, and as he got up to go, he thought of the one thing, the one person, that the eternal cold had actually protected and taken to its bosom.

"And don't forget what I said about the Ames woman," Murphy called out. "Treat her with kid gloves, all the way."

On the chance that she might be awake and alert, Michael stopped off at the infirmary. He didn't want to look like the importunate suitor, but at the same time he was desperately eager to begin getting her story. In his backpack, he was carrying his reporter's pads, his pens, and a palm-sized tape recorder; he'd debated bringing his camera, but there was something too intrusive about it. He was afraid of discomfiting her. The pictures, he decided, could wait.

But he sensed his timing wasn't great. He knocked on the closed door—the infirmary was generally left wide open—and he could hear Charlotte bustling about inside. "Yes?" she said. "Who's there?"

He identified himself, and the door opened enough for him to slip in. Charlotte, in her green hospital scrubs, looked harried, and Eleanor was out of sight, inside the sick bay.

"She awake?"

Charlotte sighed but nodded.

"Everything all right?"

Charlotte cocked her head to one side and said in a low voice, "We're having what you might call some technical difficulties."

"Meaning?"

"Psychological. Emotional. Adjustment problems."

He heard a sob from the sick bay.

"I mean, it's not exactly a shock," Charlotte said, "given the circumstances. I've just given her another mild sedative. It should help."

"You think it's okay for me to go in and talk to her before it takes effect?" Michael whispered.

Charlotte shrugged. "Who knows—maybe the distraction will help." But as he started for the sick bay, she warned, "As long as you don't say anything to upset her."

How, Michael wondered, could you talk to Eleanor Ames *without* saying something that might upset her?

When he entered the sick bay, he found Eleanor standing in a fluffy white robe and staring out through the narrow panel window; much of its glass was covered with blowing snow and only admitted the palest simulacrum of sunlight. Her head turned quickly when he came in—scared, skittish, and plainly a bit ashamed at being seen in such bedroom attire. She hastily pulled the lapels of the robe closed, then went back to gazing out the window.

"Not much to see today," Michael said.

"He's out there."

Michael did not have to ask whom she was talking about.

"He's out there, and he's all alone."

A largely untouched meal sat on a tray on the bedside table.

"And he doesn't even know that I left him unwillingly." Eleanor paced back and forth in a pair of white slippers, her tearful eyes still riveted on the window. The transformation was strange; when Michael had first seen her, in the ice and later on in the church, she had looked so alien, so out of time and so out of place. It was never in doubt that he was talking to someone from whom he was un-questionably separated by an immeasurable gap of time and expe-rience.

But now, with the collar of the white robe gathered up about her face, her freshly washed hair hanging down, and the slip-ons scuffing along the linoleum floor, she looked like any other beautiful young woman newly emerged from the treatment room at a posh spa.

"He's survived so much," Michael said, choosing his words carefully. "I'm sure he can survive this storm, too."

"That was before."

"Before what?"

"Before I abandoned him." She had a clump of tissues wadded in her hand, and she used them to dry her tears.

"You had no choice," Michael said. "How long could you have gone on like that? Eating dog food and burning prayer books to keep warm?"

Had he spoken too precipitously? He was trying to comfort her, but her green eyes flashed in warning.

"We have been through worse than that together. Worse things than you could ever know. Worse than you could ever imagine." She turned away, her frail shoulders heaving beneath the terry-cloth robe.

Michael put his backpack on the floor and sat down on the plas-tic chair in the corner. Part of him said that the sensible thing was simply to leave and come back later when she was calmer, but some-thing else—was it wishful thinking?—told him that, despite her grief and confusion, she did not really want him to go...that she could still derive some solace from his being there. In the artificial environment in which she had been placed, he might actually provide a note of familiarity.

"The doctor tells me I'm not to leave here," Eleanor said, in a more tranquil tone.

"Certainly not to go out into that storm," Michael joshed.

"This room."

Michael knew that that was what she'd meant. "Only for the time being," he assured her. "We don't want to expose you to anything—germs, bacteria—that you might not have any natural defenses against."

Eleanor gave a bitter laugh. "I have nursed soldiers through malaria, dysentery, cholera, and the Crimean fever, which I myself contracted." She breathed deeply. "As you can see, I have survived them all." Then she turned toward him, and said, more brightly, "But Miss Nightingale, of course, has been making great strides in that realm. We have begun to air the hospital wards, even at night, in order to dissipate the miasma that forms. With improvements in hygiene and nutrition, I believe that countless lives can be saved. It is just a matter of persuading the proper authorities."

It was the longest speech he had ever heard her make, and she must have been surprised at her own volubility, too, because she suddenly stopped herself, and a faint flush came into her cheek. It was clear to Michael, though he would have guessed as much, that she had taken her duties as a nurse quite seriously.

"What am I saying?" she mumbled. "Miss Nightingale is long dead. And everything I have just said has no doubt sounded foolish. The world has gone on, and here I am telling you things that you must know have been proven right, or utterly wrong, years ago. I'm sorry—I forget myself."

"Florence Nightingale was right," Michael said, "and so are you." He paused. "And you will not be confined to these quarters for long. I'll see what we can do."

She'd already been exposed to him, and whatever germs he might carry, so what harm, Michael figured, could further contact cause? And as for her being encountered by others on the base—grunts and beakers alike—well, there were probably plenty of ways to get around without too much interaction. Point Adélie was not exactly Grand Central Station.

Eleanor sat down on the edge of the bed, facing Michael. The sedative must have started working, for she had stopped crying and was no longer wringing her hands. "It was after the battle," she said. "That was when I caught the fever."

Michael ached to take out his tape recorder, but he didn't want to do anything that might puzzle her or disturb the fragile mood.

"Sinclair—Lieutenant Sinclair Copley, of the Seventeenth Lancers—was wounded in a cavalry charge. It was while nursing him that I succumbed myself."

There was a kind of faraway look in her eye, and Michael realized that even the mildest tranquilizer might have an inordinate effect on someone who had never had one before.

"But he was fortunate, really. Nearly all his fellows, including his dear friend Captain Rutherford, were killed." She sighed, her eyes dropping. "From what I was told, the Light Brigade was utterly destroyed."

Michael nearly fell out of his chair. The Light Brigade? Was she talking about the famous Charge of the Light Brigade, the one immortalized in the poem by Alfred, Lord Tennyson? And was she talking about it from firsthand experience, yet?

Was she suggesting that her frozen companion—this Lieutenant Copley—was a survivor of that charge? Whatever all this was—a sustained fantasy, or an historical account of unimaginable, firsthand authenticity—he had to get it down.

Slipping a hand into his backpack, he deftly removed his small tape recorder. "If you don't mind," he said, "I'm going to use this device to keep a record of our conversation." He pressed the ON button.

She looked at it pensively, the little red light glowing to indicate that it was running, but she seemed otherwise unconcerned. He wasn't sure she'd grasped what he'd said, or what the machine actually did. He had the sense that so much was new to her—from black, female doctors to electric lights—that she chose only certain things, one at a time, to process and engage.

"They were told to attack the Russian guns," she said, "and they were annihilated. There were artillery pieces on the hills, on every side of the valley. The casualties were overwhelming. I was working night and day—so was my friend Moira, and all the other nurses—but we could not keep up. There were too many battles, and too many wounded and dying men. We could not do enough."

She was back there now, reliving it; he could see it in her eyes.

"I'm sure you did everything in your power to help."

A rueful cast came over her face. "I did things that were beyond my power," she said, bluntly. Her eyes clouded over at the recollections of events that manifestly haunted her still. "We were forced, all of us, to do things we could never have prepared for."

And then Michael could see she was swept away on that tide of memory.

It was the night after she had found Sinclair—she remembered it well—and she had secretly appropriated several items, including a vial of morphine. The latter was more valuable than gold, and Miss Nightingale accordingly kept a sharp eye on the supply. It was after her rounds, when Eleanor was supposed to be in the nurses' quarters, fast asleep, but instead she crept down the winding stairs with a Turkish lamp in her hand, and made her way back to the fever wards. Several soldiers, mistaking her for Miss Nightingale herself, whispered blessings in her wake.

"This was after what battle?" Michael gently prompted her, his voice startling her from her reverie.

"Balaclava."

"What year was that?"

"Eighteen fifty-four. It was late October. And the Barrack Hospital was so crowded, the men were lying on straw, shoulder to shoulder."

The Highlander, she recalled—the one who had warned her, in his delirium, that Sinclair was a bad one—had been stowed close beside him. If he, too, was suffering too much, she had resolved to share out the contents of the vial between the two of them. But when she got to the ward, it was clearly unnecessary. Two orderlies with kerchiefs over their faces were bending over the Highlander's body, tossing the two sides of his filthy woolen blanket over him... but not before Eleanor caught a glimpse of his face. It was white as a whitewashed fence, and the skin looked like a piece of dried fruit from which all the juice and pulp had been sucked.

"Evening, Missus," one of them said. "It's me, Taylor." She recognized his protruding ears, from the day of Frenchie's fatal amputation. "And Smith there, too," he said, indicating the burly fellow hastily stitching the two sides of the blanket together. The filthy covering, she knew, would serve as both the dead man's shroud and casket, and his body would be heaped into one of the communal graves dug in the nearby hills.

On three, they lifted the body from the floor, and Taylor laughed under his kerchief. "This 'un's light as a feather." They shuffled out of the ward, the blanketed body swaying between them, and she had knelt in the newly cleared space, to tend to Sinclair, who looked, to her relief, unexpectedly improved.

"And you, and the other nurses under Miss Nightingale—how many of you were there?" Michael prompted her.

"Not many—a couple of dozen at most," she said, wearily. "Many fell ill and left. But Moira and I stayed. I had found a fresh shirt, and a razor, for Sinclair. I used the razor to cut his hair—the lice were running wild in it—then I was able to help him shave his face."

"He must have been very grateful."

"In my pocket, I had the vial of morphine."

"Did you give him that, too?"

A doubtful look came over her. "I did not. I thought he looked so much recovered that I should save it . . . for fear he might have a relapse and need it more then." She raised her eyes to Michael. "It was very hard to procure."

"It still is," Michael said. "That's one thing that hasn't changed. But obviously he recovered," Michael said. "You must have been very glad of that . . . and proud, too."

"Proud?" Proud of what? Eleanor would never have used that word. Once she knew his dreadful needs—and once she had actually helped him to satisfy them—she had never in her life felt pride again.

And after she had come to share those needs, she had felt nothing but an all-abiding disgrace.

"What did you do once he was well, and the war was over? Did you both return to England?"

"No," she said, her thoughts drifting away for a few moments. "We did not go home, ever again."

"Why was that?"

How could they, given who—and what—they had become? For as Sinclair had recovered, she had declined. The fever ward had done its work, and by the next morning Eleanor had felt the initial symptoms. A slight dizziness, a sticky warmth to her skin. She did her best to dissemble, because she knew that once she was relieved of her duties, she would not be able to see Sinclair, but when she went to his side, carrying a bowl of barley soup, she had tripped over her own feet, spilling the soup and nearly collapsing on top of him. Sinclair had clutched her in his arms and called for help.

A kerchiefed orderly had eventually shambled over, the stub of a cigar wedged behind one ear, but when he saw that it was Eleanor, and not just another dying soldier, who needed help, he'd picked up his pace.

Sinclair had looked stricken, and she had tried, even in her own extremis, to assure him that she would be all right. She was escorted back to the nurses' quarters in the tower, and Moira had immediately pressed a glass of port to her lips—where she was always able to find such things remained a mystery—and put her to bed. Over the next week, Eleanor would remember little of what transpired... apart from Moira's worried face, hovering over her... and, on one unforgettable night, Sinclair's.

There was a low hissing sound from the machine that she only became aware of when she stopped talking. She had almost been unaware that she *was* talking.

"Why," Michael asked again, "did you never go back to England?"

"We would not have been welcome there," she finally said, leaning back on her hands. "Not then... not as we were. We became... what do you call them?" She was starting to feel hazy, confused; whatever substance the doctor had given her was clearly having its intended purpose. "People who have been banished from their own country?"

"Exiles?"

"Yes," she murmured. "I believe that's the word. Exiles."

She heard a little click, and looked down to see the red light stop flashing on Michael's hissing little box. "Ah. Your beacon has gone out."

"We'll put it back on another time," Michael said, gently lifting her feet off the floor and resting her legs on the bed. "Right now, I think you should just sleep for a while."

"But I have rounds to make..." she said, even as she struggled, unsuccessfully, to keep her head from falling back onto the pillow. She felt an increasing sense of urgency. Why was she lying down when she should be visiting the wards? Why was she babbling on when soldiers were dying?

She felt the slippers being taken off her feet.

"And I am so far behind in my duties..."

———————

Once her eyes had closed, Michael threw a blanket over her. She was fast asleep again. He put his tape recorder and notepad away, then pulled down the blackout shade and turned off the light.

Then he simply stood there, like a sentinel, watching over her in what little light still penetrated the room. He had been on vigils like this before, he reflected. The blanket barely moved as she breathed, and her head lay turned on the pillow. Where was she now? And what strange concatenation of events had led to her terrible demise? To being wrapped in a chain and consigned to the sea? That was a question he would never know how, or when, to ask. But time, he knew, was already running short; his NSF pass had less than two weeks left to run. Still, who knew what reaction she might have to reliving such a trauma? The silken strands of her hair lay across one cheek, and though he had a momentary impulse to brush them away, he knew better than to touch her. She was somewhere far away... an exile, in a place and time that no longer even existed.

CHAPTER FORTY-TWO

December 19, 2:30 p.m.

UNTIL HE'D GOTTEN SIDETRACKED by that blood sample Charlotte gave him, Darryl thought, things had been going great.

He'd been hard at work on the blood and tissue samples from the *Cryothenia hirschii*—the discovery on which he was going to make his scientific reputation—and the preliminary results were remarkable: The blood from the fish was not only entirely hemoglobin-free, but also mysteriously low in the antifreeze glycoproteins he had been studying. In other words, this species could thrive in the frigid waters of the Antarctic Sea, but only so long as it remained extremely careful. It had even less protection against the ice than all the other species he had studied—a mere touch of actual ice could propagate across its body like lightning and flash-freeze it on the spot. Perhaps that was why he had discovered the first one—and the two others now swimming in the aquarium tank—relatively close to shore, and hovering near the warm current from one of the camp's outflow pipes. Or maybe they had just liked the shafts of sunlight, dim as they were, that had been admitted to the depths by the dive hut holes. Whatever the reason, he was grateful to have them.

He was reveling in all the new data, which made his find increasingly distinctive and newsworthy, when he remembered the favor he had promised Charlotte. He fished the sample out of the fridge and noticed then that the label had only initials on it—E.A.—and no name. He quickly ran through the beakers in his mind, but none of them had those initials. So it had to be from one of the grunts; he wasn't familiar with a few of them, and a couple just went by nicknames like Moose or T-bone. The other thing Charlotte hadn't given him was any specific instructions on what he should be testing for, and that was more than a little irritating. Didn't she know he had his own work to do?

Fortunately, the marine biology lab was provided with everything a hematologist could ask for, from state-of-the-art autocrits to a high-volume analyzer that could incorporate monoclonal assays, fluorescent staining, and advanced optical platelet readings in pretty much one fell swoop. He ran the whole battery of tests, from alanine aminotransferase to triglycerides and everything in between, and while he'd expected to simply shoot the results back to Charlotte, he had to stop when he read through the printouts. Nothing in them was making any sense, and in some respects he could just as well have been looking at the results from one of his marine samples. While a normal cubic millimeter of human blood contained an average of 5 million red blood cells and seven thousand white, this sample was nearly reversed. If the results were right, Charlotte's patient made his newly discovered fish look positively red-blooded and vital.

That convinced him that the results *couldn't* be right, or that he had somehow inadvertently mixed up the samples. *Jeez*, he thought, *maybe you're getting the Big Eye and don't even know it.* He'd have to ask Michael for a reality check. But just to see if the equipment was functioning properly, he ran a sample of his own blood, and it came back fine. (His cholesterol, he was happy to see, was even lower than usual.) With what was left of the E.A. sample, he ran the tests again . . . and got back the same results as before.

If this was human blood, the toxicity levels alone should have killed the patient off in a heartbeat.

Maybe, he considered, he had to get out of the laboratory for a while and clear his head. Ever since his last visit to the dive hut—where Danzig had nearly drowned him—he'd been holed up in his room or the lab. His scalp and ears still itched from frost nip, and as a precaution he'd been taking blood thinner and a course of antibiotics. At the South Pole, inattention to the slightest thing—a blue spot on your toes, a burning sensation at the tips of your fingers—could wind up costing you a limb . . . or even your life. Nor had the relentlessly bad weather made outdoor activities any easier; he wondered, as he stuffed the lab printouts into the pockets of his parka, how the Point Adélie personnel who "winter-overed," as it was called, managed to survive. Six months of foul weather was bad enough, but six months of foul weather with no sun was hardly conceivable.

Outside, the wind was so strong that he could lean completely into it and still remain upright. He put his head down and plowed slowly ahead, clinging to the guide ropes that had been strung along all the concourses between the labs and the communal modules. Off to his left, the lights were burning bright in Ackerley's botany lab. He hadn't seen Ackerley lately, it occurred to him, and he thought it might be nice to drop in and say hello. Maybe even snag a fresh strawberry or two.

When he got to the wooden trellis in front of the door, he had to hang on until a particularly powerful gust of wind had passed, then he swung himself up the ramp and into the lab. Ackerley had rigged up a double sheet of thick plastic to stop the drafts from the door, and once Darryl had parted the curtains, he found himself in the familiar heat, humidity, and bright light of the lab. *I should come here more often,* he thought—*it's like a vacation to the South Seas.*

"Hey, Ackerley," he called, while stomping his feet on the rubber mats. "I need some salad fixings!"

But the voice that answered him wasn't Ackerley's—it was Lawson's—and it came from behind some metal partitions. Darryl shrugged off his parka and hat and gloves and goggles, draping them on a rickety coatrack fashioned from a whale's bone, and went in search of Lawson.

He found him on a stepstool, tending to a cluster of ripe red strawberries hanging from a latticework of misting pipes. All around his head there were other clumps of gleaming wet fruit, and on tables there were clear containers holding a veritable jungle of other plants—tomatoes, radishes, Bibb lettuce, roses, and, most wonderful of all, orchids. The orchids came in a dozen different colors, from white to fuchsia to golden yellow. They rose up on strangely tilting stalks that looked like the legs of cranes.

"What are you doing here?" Darryl asked. "Isn't that Ackerley's job?"

"Just helping out," Lawson said, noncommittally.

"It's like Hawaii in here," Darryl said, putting his face up to the bright, warming lights that were mounted in the ceiling above the pipes. "No wonder Ackerley hates to leave." Darryl eyed a particularly succulent-looking strawberry and said, "You think he'd mind if I tried one?"

Lawson glanced down from the stool. "No. Go ahead."

Darryl reached up and plucked the lowest of the hanging berries, then popped it into his mouth. Uncle Barney turned out a lot of good food from the commons galley, but there was nothing to beat the flavor of a strawberry fresh from the vine.

"Where is he, by the way?"

Lawson shrugged. "Ask Murphy."

That seemed odd to Darryl. Why would Murphy know? And it was also odd that anyone else was there when Ackerley wasn't; he was a lot like Darryl in that way—he didn't like strangers roaming around his lab when he wasn't there.

Come to think of it, the place didn't look right, either. Usually it was spic-and-span. But off to one side, Darryl could see a clumsy path where a couple of cabinets had been overturned, spilling dirt and lichens and moss samples onto the floor. A broom and dustpan leaned up against one of the racks, along with a black plastic garbage bag that appeared to be full of refuse. *What's going on? Has Lawson been appointed the new assistant gardener?*

Darryl tried a couple more conversational gambits, but he got the distinct impression that Lawson wanted him out of the lab. Normally, the guy was pretty friendly—even, at times, positively gregarious—but not today. Maybe he wasn't happy about his new duty and just wanted to get it over with as quickly as possible.

Darryl thanked him for the strawberry and put all his gear back on. Sometimes it felt like he spent half his time at pole just taking off and putting on the same layers of clothing.

Leaving the botany lab, he slogged toward the main quadrant, holding tight again to the guide ropes. The snow was so thick in the air it was hard to see more than a few yards ahead, but when he approached the administration module, he saw Murphy and Michael, their own heads down, forging their way across the concourse and toward some of the storage buildings. He'd have called out to them, but he knew his voice would be obliterated by the wind. Instead, he just followed in their path. They were heading for one of the ramshackle sheds, where they unfastened the padlock on the corrugated steel doors, then slipped inside.

Darryl's curiosity was aroused. Never, he thought, present a scientist with a mystery that you don't then expect him to try to solve.

Darryl sidled into the shed, and after whipping off his snowy goggles, looked around. He was in a kind of anteroom, but even it was filled with crates of kitchen and camp supplies. There was another pair of steel doors just beyond, and they were open, too—leading into what Darryl guessed had once served as a huge meat locker and storeroom.

He stepped inside, then stopped dead when he saw Murphy whirl around on him, with a gun extended. Michael was armed, too, with a speargun.

"Mother of God, what the *fuck* are you doing here?" Murphy said in an urgent whisper.

Darryl was still too shocked by the weaponry to reply.

Michael lowered the spear, and said, "Okay, what's done is done. Just stay back and be quiet."

"Why?"

"You'll know in a minute."

With Murphy cautiously leading the way, they moved down an aisle stacked ten feet high with boxes and crates until they rounded a corner and Darryl saw a long wooden crate marked MIXED CONDIMENTS: HEINZ and, above it, inexplicably hanging from a thick pipe, a bloody handcuff.

"Shit," Murphy muttered. "Shit, shit, shit."

What the hell were they looking for, Darryl wondered? What had they been expecting to find? For a second, he wondered if Danzig had returned. *Hadn't the speargun through the chest sent him safely to the bottom of the sea?*

"Ackerley," Murphy said, in a slightly raised voice. "You in here?"

Ackerley? That was who they were looking for? In there, of all places? If so, what the hell were they so afraid of? The man was as harmless as one of his cabbages.

There was a scratching sound, like a pen on paper, and they crept toward the next aisle. It, too, was empty, but the scratching sound grew louder. Murphy, the gun out in front, moved to the next aisle, and there they saw Ackerley—or a close facsimile of him. He was gaunter than ever, his ponytail loose and hanging down like a dead squirrel on the back of his neck. Draped around his shoulders, he wore a shredded plastic garbage bag. He was sitting on a crate of Coca-Cola, and all around his feet there were empty soda cans and various papers—printed invoices, ripped from the boxes—that he had been scrawling on. With a clipboard on his lap, he was scribbling on the back of another one even then, working with the concentration of a physicist straightening out an especially complex equation.

"Ackerley," Murphy said, and Ackerley, his little round spectacles creeping down his nose, said, "Not now," without looking up.

Murphy and Michael exchanged a look, as if to say *What next?* while Darryl simply looked on, aghast. What had happened to Ackerley? His throat, partially revealed under the plastic bag, looked ravaged, and the wrist of his left hand, which limply supported the clipboard, appeared broken and bruised. Flakes of blood crusted the skin.

"What are you doing?" Michael asked, in a deliberately innocent voice.

"Making notes."

"About what?"

Ackerley kept writing.

"What are you writing about?" Murphy repeated.

"About dying."

"You don't look dead to me," Darryl said, though it wasn't entirely true.

Ackerley finished a sentence, then slowly raised his eyes. They were red-rimmed, and even the whites were tinged a pale pink.

"Oh, I am," he said. "It just hasn't taken yet." His voice carried a low, gurgling sound. He took a swig from an open can, then just let it drop from his hand.

Murphy had allowed the barrel of the gun to drift toward the floor, and Ackerley gestured at it.

"I wouldn't do that if I were you."

Murphy quickly raised it again, and Ackerley let the last paper waft to the floor to join all the others.

"I've numbered them," he said, "so you'll be able to follow along."

"Follow what?" Michael said.

"What happens," Ackerley replied, "afterwards."

There was silence, and then Ackerley dragged the plastic bag away from his throat; the skin was so mangled that Darryl was surprised that he had been able to speak at all. The vocal cords could be seen pulsating.

"Now," Ackerley said, nodding at the gun, "you'd better use that."

"What are you talking about?" Murphy said. "I'm not gonna shoot you now. We'll figure something out."

"That's right," Michael interjected. "We'll talk to Dr. Barnes. There must be a way to help you."

"Use it," Ackerley said, in a ghastly rasping voice, "and afterwards, just to be on the safe side, cremate my remains." Slowly rising to his feet, he took a faltering step in their direction. "Otherwise, you might wind up like me." All three fell back. "It apparently passes from one host to another quite easily."

"What does?" Darryl said, bumping up against a shelf of pots and pans that clanged in their boxes.

"The infection. Either through blood or saliva. Like HIV, it seems to be present, to some degree, in all the bodily fluids." Staggering closer and focusing on the gun, he muttered, "Do it, or I *will* kill you. I'm not sure I have much choice in the matter." His eyes, behind his glasses, blinked slowly. His foot knocked one of the empty cans toward them, and it spun in a lazy circle on the concrete.

Michael tried to prod him back with the tip of the speargun, but Ackerley brushed it aside.

"Use the handgun," he said. "Do it right."

He kept on coming, and there was less and less room to retreat. Darryl stepped back, past the kitchen equipment aisle, but at close range he could see the demented, though utterly determined, look in Ackerley's eye. He meant what he said.

"Shoot!" Ackerley cried, a bubble of blood popping from his open throat. "Shoot me!" and with his hands extended he deliberately lunged at Murphy's arm.

The gun went off with a blast, echoing for several seconds in the cold confines of the locker. Ackerley's head snapped back, his glasses flying off, and he dropped to the concrete floor.

But his eyes were still open, and he was mouthing the word "shoot" one more time before he suddenly grew still, and the last bloody bubble rose, then burst, on his throat.

Murphy's arm was shaking, and he lowered it to his side.

Darryl started to kneel by the body, but Michael said, "Hold on."

Darryl held back.

"Yeah," Murphy said, his voice quavering, "give him some room."

"I think," Michael said, solemnly, "we just need to wait a while."

And so they sat, on the wooden crates, their heads down but their eyes on the corpse, huddled around it in a ragged circle. How long they waited, Darryl wasn't sure. But it was Michael who eventually knelt down to feel for a pulse and listen for a heartbeat. He shook his head to indicate there were none.

"But I'm still not going to take any chances," Murphy said, and Darryl knew enough to leave it at that. Murphy would do what Murphy wanted to do, and it was best not to inquire too deeply.

CHAPTER FORTY-THREE

December 20, 11 p.m.

MICHAEL HAD BEEN PREPARING for the call for months, but when it came, it was still a shock. "It was a blessing," Karen was saying, for at least the third time. "We both know Krissy, and she wouldn't have wanted to go on like that."

The vigil was over. He sat hunched over, as if protecting himself from a punch in the stomach—because that was still how it felt—in the cramped communications bay. The last occupant of the chair had left a partially completed crossword puzzle on the SAT-phone desk.

"When exactly did it happen?"

"Around midnight, on Thursday. I waited till now to call because, as you can imagine, it's been kind of crazy around here."

He tried to cast his mind back to Thursday night, but even such a short time was hard to fix. Everything was so fluid in the Antarctic, it was tricky to remember the day of the week, much less anything from the days before. Where was he, what had he been doing, at precisely that time? Practical and hardheaded as he was, he still felt that he should have known, that he should have had some weird psychic inkling that Kristin was leaving. That she was gone for good.

"Of course, now my mother secretly blames my father; she thinks if he'd left Krissy in the hospital, she'd still be alive, if you want to call it that."

"I would never have called it that."

Karen sighed. "And neither would Krissy."

"What about the funeral?"

"Tomorrow. Very small. I, uh, took the liberty of ordering some sunflowers in your name."

That was a good choice. Sunflowers—with their bold, bright yellow faces—were Kristin's favorite. "They're not namby-pamby flowers," she'd once told him, as they'd hiked through a field of them in Idaho. "They say, hey, look at me, I'm big, I'm yellow, get used to it!"

"Thanks," Michael said. "I owe you."

"They were $9.95. We can let it go."

"You know I meant for everything else . . . including this call."

"Yes, well, when you get back to Tacoma, you can buy me the Blue Plate special at that Greek diner you like."

"The Olympic."

There was a pause, filled with the low crackle of static on the line.

"So," Karen said, "when *are* you coming back?"

"I've got till the end of the month on my NSF pass."

"Then what? They just chuck you out at the South Pole?"

"Then they stick me on the next supply plane flying out."

"Are you getting what you need? A good story?"

If Michael had been in the mood to laugh, he'd have laughed then. How could he even begin to explain what had been happening?

"Yeah," he said, "let's just say I don't think I'm going to be short of material."

When they hung up, he simply sat there, staring down at the open crossword puzzle. His eye happened to fall on a clue that read "Kinky female photog." Five letters. He picked up the blue pencil the previous guy had left and filled in "Arbus." Then he just continued to sit there, twirling the pencil, lost in thought. Letting the news sink in.

"Say, you done with the phone?" one of the grunts asked, leaning in the doorway.

"Yeah," Michael said, tossing the pencil back on the desk, "all done."

He went back to his room but Darryl had already turned in, and there was no way in the world Michael was going to be able to fall asleep—not without a couple of sleeping pills, and he was trying to cut back on those, anyway, in preparation for his reentry to the real world. He packed up his laptop and a bunch of his papers and, slinging his backpack over his shoulders, braved the last of the storm to head over to the rec room and set up shop. Murphy had said that the weather report indicated a brief but temperate window the next day, which might allow them time to go back to Stromviken in search of the elusive Lieutenant Copley.

Having heard so much about him from Eleanor, Michael was especially curious to make his acquaintance.

He got a cup of coffee from the standing machine and turned off the TV, which was playing a DVD of *Notting Hill*; Betty and Tina must have been the last ones in there. But the place was blissfully empty. The wall clock indicated it was just past midnight. Michael turned on the CD player instead, and a blast of Beethoven—even he recognized the opening of the Fifth Symphony—came on. It was a compilation CD, and no doubt belonged to one of the beakers. He lowered the volume, plunked himself down at a card table in the back, and spread out his work.

Don't think about Kristin, he told himself, when he realized he'd been sitting there for at least one full movement of the symphony thinking of nothing but. *Think about something else.* His eyes fell on the work he'd brought—most notably the loose pages Ackerley had been scribbling on in the old meat locker—and he almost laughed. When it came to pleasant distractions, the South Pole was noticeably lacking.

Ackerley's handwriting was a spidery scrawl, reminding Michael of the labels the man had carefully affixed to every drawer of moss and lichen samples in his botany lab. But these pages were especially hard to read, smudged as they were with blood and written on the back of billing invoices and inventory sheets.

The first page or two—carefully numbered, as Ackerley had promised, in the upper-right-hand corner—recounted the attack, how he had turned to see Danzig lumbering down the aisle toward his lab counter. "I remember being thrown to the floor—destroying a meticulously cultivated orchid (genus *Cymbidium*) in the fall—and being set upon with great force and no provocation. The assault, though apparently random and senseless, did ultimately reveal itself to be deliberate in its intent."

Michael sat back, stunned. He really had to hand it to him; even after being savagely mauled—and rising from the dead, as it were—Ackerley had managed to retain his scientific composure and prose style. The notes, written in a meat locker under what might only be called extreme duress, read like an article being submitted to a scholarly journal for peer review.

"Upon consideration, Mr. Danzig's efforts,"—*Mr. Danzig?*—"however wild and distracted, were all directed toward the breaking of the skin and accessing the blood supply. What the reasons for that might have been, or the particular components of the blood that were most sought after, was unclear at the time of the event, and remain so. I am, however, inevitably reminded of the *Nepenthes ventricosa* and its own hematophagous needs."

His sangfroid was beyond belief.

"Death—in any previously understood construction of the term—occurred no more than a minute or so into the event. The interval between that time and what I shall hereinafter refer to as the Revival is unknown to me, though as I have ascertained no material decay it can't have been excessive. (Must consult morbidity and decomposition graphs.) Quick refrigeration of my remains appears to have helped considerably."

The next few lines were hopelessly smudged, and Michael had to go looking for the next sequentially numbered page. They were scattered all over the tabletop in front of him, like pieces of a jigsaw puzzle.

"The Revival was gradual," Ackerley continued, in the margins of a purchase order, "much like awakening from a deep, possibly hypnagogic state. The line between the dream state and the real was imperceptibly crossed, though it was immediately followed by a sense of panic and disorientation. I was in total darkness, confined somehow, and the fear of premature burial was, of course, paramount in my mind; to be blunt, I screamed and fought against the constraints, and was greatly relieved to establish that I was encased only in plastic sheets, which were permeable and easily shredded."

My God, Michael thought. Ackerley's ordeal was like something out of Edgar Allan Poe—and the fact that he had had a hand in it gave him a sharp and guilty pang.

"But my left wrist had been inexplicably handcuffed to a pipe. That would lead me to believe that someone—Mr. O'Connor?—had reason to believe that (a) a third party might try to make off with my body (for what purpose?) or (b) something like the Revival might have been expected to happen. It was the work of several hours—including the abrasion of much skin and, I believe, the dislocation of three fingers—to free myself.

"My liberty obtained, I must record that the strongest sensation—quite overpowering in its way—was one of thirst. Attempts to assuage it with beverages found in the locker were useless. It was accompanied by a visual disturbance. I am a scientist—or, more accurately, *was* a scientist, as I remain convinced that my present, and quite unnatural, state will soon come to an end—and I feel it's incumbent on me, while I can recall it, to describe to the best of my abilities the sensations I underwent."

Michael had to search for the next page, which he found under his coffee mug. This one was written on the back of an advertising flyer for Samuel Adams Lager.

"There was a washed-out look to everything in my visual field. I can only compare it to the illumination from a bank of feeble fluorescent lights. Slightly dim. But blinking, as I did repeatedly, seemed to refresh the image. Then it would fade again. I am doing it even now, to continue writing. It is possible that this ocular disturbance is a sign of the Revival ebbing. I'll try to write faster, just in case. Note: Please forward my love and effects to my mother, Mrs. Grace Ackerley, at 505 French Street in Wilmington, DE."

Michael had to pause at that. *Jesus.* Then, reaching for his coffee mug, he read on.

"A certain shortness of breath has also been introduced. It is as if I am insufficiently oxygenated, leading to dizziness, though my lungs and airways do not in any way feel obstructed."

Michael was aware of being watched before he actually saw anyone. He raised his eyes above the rim of the coffee mug and saw a slim figure, bundled in an orange coat, lurking just inside the wide, arched entryway.

And even with the hood pulled forward, and the coat hanging almost to the floor, he knew it was Eleanor.

He put the cup down and said, "Why aren't you in bed?" But what he really wondered was, *Why are you out of the infirmary? You're supposed to be in virtual quarantine, and definitely out of sight.*

"I can't sleep."

"Dr. Barnes could give you something to help."

"I've slept enough." But he saw the hood swivel, as she turned her head, perplexed, around the room. She looked at the piano, and its empty bench, then back around the rec hall. "I heard the music."

"Yes," he said. "Beethoven. But maybe you know that."

"I know some of Herr Beethoven's compositions, yes. But . . ."

"It's a CD," he said, gesturing at the player on the shelf. "It plays music." He got up from his chair, went to the CD player, hit stop, then start. The opening notes of the *Moonlight Sonata* began to play.

Eleanor, mystified, drifted into the room and pushed the hood back off her head. She went straight to the machine and stood a few feet in front of the speakers, almost as if she were afraid to get any closer. When Michael, just to surprise her, hit FORWARD and it skipped ahead to the *Emperor* Concerto—and the lush sounds of a full orchestra again—her eyes opened wide in even greater amazement, and she looked over at him . . . with a smile on her lips. The first such smile, of sheer amazement, he had ever seen there. Her eyes sparkled and she nearly laughed.

"How does it do that? It's like Covent Garden!"

Michael wasn't really up to giving a lecture on the history of audio electronics—not that he'd have known where to start. But he was enthralled at her obvious delight. "It's complicated," he simply said. "But it's easy to use, and I can show you how."

"I would like that, very much."

So would I, he thought. The aroma from the coffee machine was strong, and he asked her if she'd like some.

"Yes, thank you," she said, "I have had Turkish coffee before. In Varna and Scutari."

"Yes, well, this is what we call Folger's. It's in the same family."

He was keeping his eye on the door the whole time he filled the mug. It wasn't likely that anyone else would be popping in at that hour, but he didn't know how he could explain her away if anyone did. New faces didn't just turn up out of nowhere at Point Adélie.

"Sugar?" he asked.

"If you have it, please."

He shook a packet of sugar, then tore it open and poured it in for her. Even that she watched with interest, and he had to remind himself, yet again, that every single thing in his world—in the present day—was likely to be strange, foreign, and sometimes even alarming to someone who wasn't born into it.

"I'd offer you milk, but it looks like we're all out."

"I would imagine it's very difficult indeed to get milk in a place as remote as this. Surely you don't keep cows?"

"No, we don't," Michael said. "You're right about that." He handed her the mug and asked if she'd like to sit down.

"Not yet, thank you." With her coffee mug in hand, she moved slowly around the perimeter of the rec hall, taking in everything from the Ping-Pong table—where she stopped to bounce a ball once or twice—to the plasma-screen TV—which she studied, without asking what in the world it was; thank God it wasn't turned on. There was no way Michael was going to get into all that just now. There were framed posters on the wall—provided, no doubt, by some governmental agency—since every one of them commemorated a national triumph. One was the United States Olympic hockey team celebrating in 1980, another was Chuck Yeager standing, helmet in his hand, next to the X-1 research plane, and the last, before which Eleanor lingered, showed Neil Armstrong in a space suit planting the American flag on the moon. *Please no*, Michael thought. *She'll never believe me.*

"He is in the desert," she inquired, "at night?"

"Sort of. Sure."

"He's dressed almost the way we do here." She put the cup down on top of the TV, then took her down coat off, and laid it on the worn-out Naugahyde sofa. She was wearing her own clothes again, freshly cleaned and laundered, and looked to Michael like a figure from a painting. The dress was a dark blue, with white cuffs and collar, and billowy sleeves; on her breast, she wore the white ivory brooch. Her shoes were black leather, buttoned up well above her ankle, and her hair was drawn back from her face and fastened behind with an amber comb he'd never noticed before.

She glanced over at the table where he'd been sitting, and asked, "Have I interrupted your work?"

"No, no problem." The pages from Ackerley were the last things he'd ever want her to see, and he quickly went back and gathered them into a neat stack, with the Sam Adams Lager ad showing on top.

"You're anxious," she said.

"I am?"

"You keep looking toward the door. Are you really so afraid that I'll be discovered?"

She didn't miss a thing, he thought. "It's not for my sake," he said. "It's for yours."

"People are always doing things for my sake," she said, ruminatively. "And strangely enough, I'm the one who suffers for it."

She went to the piano and ran her fingertips lightly across the keys.

"You can play it if you like."

"Not while the orchestra..." she said, indicating the ambient music with a wave of the hand. Her voice was sweet, and with the English accent she sounded to Michael like someone from one of those Jane Austen movies.

He flicked off the CD player—she looked at him as if he were a magician who had suddenly waved his wand—and pulled out the piano bench for her.

"Be my guest," he said, and he could tell, even though she held back, that she was eager to play. "In for a penny, in for a pound." That was one expression he felt she'd recognize.

She smiled, and blinked. Slowly. More like the shutter of an old-fashioned camera opening and closing. Michael stood stock-still. Had everything, as Ackerley had put it, suddenly assumed a "washed-out" appearance to her? And was she now "refreshing the image"?

Impulsively, she swept her skirt up behind her and slid onto the piano bench. Her fingers, slender and pale, extended over the keys but without touching them. Michael glanced toward the door again, then heard the first notes of a traditional old song, "Barbara

Allen"; he remembered it from an old black-and-white version of *A Christmas Carol*. He looked down at Eleanor, whose head was tilted toward the keyboard, but whose eyes were closed again. Once or twice she hit wrong notes, stopped, and picked up again where she had left off. She looked...transported. As if, after a very long time, she was finally going somewhere she'd dreamt of.

He stood behind her, one eye on the door, until, finally, he stopped doing duty as a sentinel and simply listened to the music. She played well, despite the occasional missed note. There was a wealth of feeling and expression, and he could well imagine how long, and how tightly, it had all been bottled up inside her.

After the piece was ended, she sat very still, eyes closed. And when she opened them again—and how green and alive they were, Michael thought—she said, "I'm afraid I'm a bit out of practice."

"You've got a good excuse."

She nodded and smiled, pensively. "Do you play?" she asked.

"Just Chopsticks."

"What's that?"

"It's a very difficult piece, reserved for concert pianists only."

"Truly? I'd like to hear it," she said, starting to rise.

"Stay put," he said. "This will only take a second." He sat down beside her on the bench, and as she scooted over, he put his index fingers on the keyboard and banged out the tune. That close to her, she smelled of Irish Spring soap, and when he'd finished and looked at her to see if she was amused, he realized that he'd made a terrible mistake. A blush as fierce as fire was in her cheek, and her eyes were downcast. His shoulder was brushing hers, his foot was touching her boot, and she looked shocked by the sudden, physical contact. Shocked, but so loath to offend him that she hadn't jumped up and moved away, but simply sat and waited for it to be over.

"I'm sorry," Michael said, getting up. "I didn't mean to offend you. I forgot..." *Forgot what? That over 150 years ago, what I just did was probably considered pretty forward?* "It's just that, today, it's not a big deal to—"

"No, I'm not offended," she said, her voice strained. "That was...a very interesting piece." She smoothed her skirt. "Thank you for playing it for me."

"There you are!" came from the door, and Michael saw Charlotte, her coat flapping open over sweatpants and rubber boots, breathing a huge sigh of relief. "I did a bed check, and when you were gone, I imagined all kinds of disasters."

"I'm quite well," Eleanor said.

"I don't know if I'd go that far," Charlotte replied, "but you're definitely on the upswing. I can see that now."

"You are aware, I hope, that I can't be confined forever."

Charlotte looked like she didn't want to get into all that. "You didn't steal her, did you?" she asked Michael.

Michael raised his palms in a gesture of innocence, and Eleanor came to his defense—"No, he did not"—and then to her own. "I've been deprived of many things, including my liberty, for quite a long time, but there is one thing I still retain."

Michael and Charlotte waited for her to finish.

"I do still have a will of my own."

And Michael had just caught a welcome glimpse of it.

CHAPTER FORTY-FOUR

December 21, 3:15 p.m.

"VAMPIRES."

The word hung in the air of Murphy's crowded office like a piece of rotten fruit, and no one wanted to be the first to taste it. Darryl had tossed it out, but Michael and Charlotte and Lawson just sat there, stunned, waiting for someone else to take the bait. It finally fell to the chief to break the impasse.

"Vampires," he repeated. "That's what you're saying we have on our hands?"

"Only in a manner of speaking," Darryl said. "I took some samples from Ackerley, analyzed them, and they show the same remarkable properties I saw in the samples from Danzig." Turning to Charlotte, he said, "And, by the way, they were the same properties as I saw in that sample you asked me to analyze. The one marked E.A."

"Eleanor Ames," Charlotte said, and when Murphy threw her a look like *that's supposed to be a secret,* she retorted, "As long as we keep operating in the dark, we're not going to get anywhere. Can't we all just get on the same page?"

And Michael had to agree. "Eleanor Ames is the name of the woman from the ice," he explained to Darryl.

"Sleeping Beauty?"

"We found her at Stromviken."

"How'd she get there?"

"By dogsled."

"Yeah, but who took her there? And why?"

"She went on her own. With Sinclair, the man who was frozen with her."

"You're missing my point. Who drove the sled?"

"They're alive," Michael said. "They went there on their own. That's what I'm trying to tell you."

Darryl laughed, and even slapped his knee lightly. "Right, yeah, okay. I thought we were having a serious meeting here."

"We are," Michael said, and when Darryl looked around, from Lawson to Charlotte to Murphy, and saw that no one else was laughing, the smile left his own face.

"Holy moly," he said, solemnly.

"Holy moly's about right," Murphy seconded.

"And she's been quarantined in the sick bay ever since," Michael added. He saw no reason to mention her little excursion to the rec hall.

Darryl looked around at them all one more time, just to make sure they weren't pulling his leg, but the sober expressions they still wore told him they were not. His next reaction was indignation. "And you didn't tell me? You all knew, and nobody thought I should be told, too? Especially since I was the guy who had to do all the donkey work back in the lab?"

"It was my call," Murphy said. "I didn't want word getting out. This place has been enough of a circus already."

Darryl was still fuming, but after he'd sputtered out a few more words of protest, and they'd managed to apologize and calm him down, he went on with his disquisition. "Well, their blood—that's including your Miss Ames, who I'd really like to meet sometime, now that I've finally been voted into the inner circle—isn't like any human blood I've ever seen."

"In what way?" Charlotte asked. To Michael, it sounded as if she was the one holding something back. How could they ever solve this puzzle if everyone had separate and secret pieces?

"It's not just depleted of the red cells," Darryl said. "It's actively consuming them. It's as if this blood were from cold-blooded creatures trying to become warm-blooded, as if reptiles, or some of those fish I've been dredging up from the bottom, were trying to emulate mammals by ingesting hemoglobin—but failing at it over and over again, and having to then replenish their supply."

"Which they can only get from other human beings?" Michael suggested.

"I'm not so sure about that. The species barrier should make that the case, but this is such a strange disease that I can't actually confirm it. Someone suffering from it would probably make no such distinctions. The anemia would become so great, they would try to rectify it with anything available, like a drug addict scrambling for any kind of a fix."

"But how can they keep going at all," Charlotte asked, perched on the edge of her folding chair, "without red corpuscles to carry the oxygen through the bloodstream? Their organs would stop functioning, and their muscles and other tissues would decay. Wouldn't they just run out of steam?"

"That's close to what Ackerley described in the notes he wrote in the meat locker," Michael interjected.

It was Charlotte's turn to look puzzled—what notes?—but Michael just gave her a wave to indicate he'd fill her in on all that later. There were *way* too many secrets still.

"He said he had the sensation of being oxygen-deprived," Michael went on, "as if his lungs weren't filling, no matter how deeply he breathed. And he said he needed to blink a lot, to clear his vision."

"Yes, that would make sense," Darryl said. "The ocular mechanism would be compromised, too. But I'll say one thing in favor of this blood—it is amazingly, stupendously recuperative. Per milliliter, it's loaded with more phagocytes than—"

"English, please," Murphy interrupted, and Lawson nodded in agreement.

"Cells that consume foreign or hostile particles," Darryl explained. "Like a little cleanup squad. So if you couple that feature with its ability to extract whatever it needs from any outside source, you've got a very neat and self-regenerating system. Theoretically speaking, as long as its raw supply is periodically replenished with new blood—"

"Its host can go on forever," Charlotte concluded.

Darryl simply shrugged in acknowledgment, and Michael felt as if a cold hand had reached inside his shirt to brush his chest. They were talking about these "hosts" as if they were the anonymous subjects in some medical experiment, but in fact they were talking about Erik Danzig and Neil Ackerley and, most important of all, Eleanor Ames. They were talking about the woman he had discovered in the ice, and brought back to life—a woman he had played the piano with, and interviewed on tape—as if she were some creature from a horror flick.

Another silence fell, as the revelation and its ramifications made themselves felt in the room. Michael himself experienced an odd twinge of vindication. If anyone had still been harboring any doubt about the validity of Eleanor's story, if they were still questioning how she might have survived for so many years, frozen beneath the sea...

But it did leave another question—what, if anything, could be done to remedy the disease?—unresolved. Michael knew it was what they were all thinking.

Finally, the mood was broken by Murphy, who leaned forward, his fingers steepled on his desk, and said, "What's wrong with having her go cold turkey? What if she were confined and medicated and tranquilized—you guys have more drugs than you know what to do with—until the need just went away?"

Darryl pursed his lips and tilted his head skeptically to one side. "If you'll forgive the analogy, that would be like denying insulin to a diabetic. The need wouldn't go away. The patient would simply go into shock, a coma, and die."

"Then how are we supposed to keep her adequately supplied?" Lawson asked, voicing the question they were all pondering. "Start a blood drive?"

Murphy snorted and said, "I can tell you now, it'd be a hard sell with the grunts."

"But transfusions, from our present blood supply, could address the problem on a temporary basis," Darryl suggested. He looked around at all of their faces. "Until we can figure out a cure—

assuming one exists—I don't see how we can avoid doing something like that."

"I think she may have a head start," Charlotte said, and Michael guessed that this was what she'd been holding back. "A plasma bag has gone missing. I thought I'd misplaced it, even though I couldn't imagine how. But now, well, I guess I know what happened to it."

Michael could hardly credit what he knew, in his heart, was probably true.

"That's just great," Murphy said in exasperation. "Just great."

Michael knew what was going through the chief's head—the endless reports he would have to write and the internal investigations he would have to conduct in order to account for all of this to his overlords. And how could he, really? They'd be carting him off to Bellevue in no time.

"And let's not forget that there's still another one out there," Murphy added. "And he's still on the loose."

The young lieutenant, Michael thought. *Sinclair Copley.*

"It's awfully dangerous out there," Lawson commented. "Unless he made it back to the whaling station, he's probably at the bottom of some crevasse by now."

"From your lips to God's ear," Murphy said.

But Michael wasn't prepared to give up so easily, nor did he feel it would be right. Given all that this man had already survived, who was to say he had succumbed to the storm, or the polar extremes? Glancing out the window at the clear skies and the low, drifting snow, he said, "We've got a break in the weather. We could use it to mount a search. If we know anything at all about the guy, it's that he's got a powerful will to live."

"And there's something else, too," Charlotte put in. "We've got the most important thing in the world to him. Someone he'll want to get back—no matter what."

The cold hand that had brushed across Michael's chest earlier suddenly brushed him again, and to his own surprise clamped down like a vise.

"Charlotte's right," Darryl said. "When it comes to bait, we have the best."

CHAPTER FORTY-FIVE

December 21, 11 p.m.

ELEANOR FELT LIKE A PRISONER who had been returned to her cell. Dr. Barnes had left her yet another of the blue pills and a glass of water, but she did not want to take it. She did not want to sleep anymore, and she did not want to hide in the infirmary any longer ... especially because the temptation in the white metal box was too great. (What, she pressed herself, had they called it? A fridge? Was that it?)

Regardless, she'd seen the bags inside—clear like a haggis casing, but brimming with blood. And she could feel the need coming upon her, again. The very walls around her seemed drained of color, and she often had to close her eyes, then reopen them, simply to restore everything to its natural state. Her breath, too, was growing short and shallow. Dr. Barnes, she believed, had noted the change in her respiration, but Eleanor could hardly explain to her the cause—much less the remedy.

And here she was, alone again, or, as Sinclair had often recited from his book of poetry, "All, all, all alone, alone on a wide, wide sea!" *Where is Sinclair right now? In the church, sheltered from the storm? Or lost in the snow and ice, searching for me?*

She paced the room like a tiger she had seen in the London Zoo, back and forth, over and over again; even then she had felt for the poor beast's isolation and confinement. She struggled to keep her gaze from the "fridge" and her thoughts from straying into the same dismal channels. But how could they not? Her past life had been taken from her completely—her family, her friends, her very country—and her present life was reduced to a sick bay at the Southern Pole . . . and a ravening need that it appalled her even to think of.

On that fateful night in the Barrack Hospital, after Sinclair had come to her, she had indeed rallied. By the next day her fever was nearly gone. Moira had exulted over her, and Miss Nightingale herself had brought her cereal and tea and drawn a chair up to her bedside.

"We have missed you on the wards," Miss Nightingale said. "The soldiers will be glad to see you back."

"I will be glad to see them, too."

"One soldier, I should think, in particular," Miss Nightingale said, and Eleanor had blushed.

"Isn't he the man who once barged into our hospital in London," Miss Nightingale went on, while holding up a spoonful of cereal, "and required stitching up?"

"Yes, mum, he is."

Miss Nightingale nodded, and when Eleanor had eaten the cereal, said, "And an attachment has formed between you since?"

"It has," Eleanor admitted.

"My greatest fear, when recruiting my nurses, was that they would become too attached to certain soldiers in their care. It would reflect badly on the nurse herself, and more importantly, it would put our entire mission into question. You know, of course, that we have many detractors, both here and at home?"

"I do."

"Narrow-minded people who believe our nurses are nothing more than opportunists and worse?"

Miss Nightingale offered another spoonful of the cereal, and though Eleanor had not yet regained her appetite, she was not about to refuse it. "That is why I must ask you to do nothing—and I cannot emphasize this strongly enough—that would bring your service here, or ours, into disrepute."

Eleanor signaled her assent with a mute tilt of the head.

"Good," Miss Nightingale said. "Then I think we understand each other." She got up, carefully placing the cereal bowl on the seat of the wooden chair. "I trust in your judgment and take you at your word." With a rustle of her skirt, she went to the door, where Moira was waiting. "I'm afraid there has been more bloodshed near the Woronzoff Road. I will need you both to report for duty tomorrow at first light."

Then she was gone. Eleanor's head fell back on the pillow and stayed there until the night came . . . and with it, again, Sinclair.

He had studied her face in the candlelight as if he were looking for clues, but seemed happy with what he saw. "You're better," he said, putting his hand to her brow. "The fever's gone."

"It is," she said, resting her cheek against his palm.

"Tomorrow, we can leave this accursed place."

Eleanor didn't know what he was talking about. "Leave?" Sinclair was in the army, and she was to report for duty in the morning.

"We can't very well stay here, can we? Not now."

Eleanor was confused. Why not? What had changed, apart from the fact that they had both recovered?

"I'll manage to find some horses," he went on, "though we might have to make do with just one."

"Sinclair," Eleanor said, worried that his own fever might have returned after all, "what are you saying? Where would we go?" Was he delusional?

"Anywhere. The whole damn country is a battlefield. Wherever we go, we shouldn't have any trouble finding what we need."

"What we need?"

That was when he had met her gaze most steadily, cupping her face between his hands, before speaking. He had knelt by the bed and, in a low voice, told her a story, a story so terrible she had not believed him—not a word of it. A tale of creatures that haunted the Crimean night, and preyed upon the dying. ("I see it in my dreams every night," he said, "and still I could not tell you what it was.") Of a curse, or a blessing, that defied death itself. Of a need that never stopped . . . and to which she was now, like him, a slave. She couldn't believe it, and she wouldn't believe it!

But she *could* feel the wound just above her breast—it had left a telltale scar—which Sinclair said was the proof.

He kissed it now, contritely, and she felt the hot tears burning in her eyes. She turned her face to the wall, gasping for breath. The room, which had a tall window opening onto the sea, suddenly felt unbearably close and stifling.

Sinclair clutched her hand, but she withdrew that, too. What had he done to her? What had he done to them both? If he was lying, then he was mad. If he was telling the truth, then they were both doomed to a fate worse than death. Eleanor had been raised in the Church of England, but she had never been particularly devout; she left that to her mother and her sisters. But what Sinclair was telling her was even to her mind a sacrilege of such magnitude that she could barely contemplate it . . . or dwell on the life that it would necessitate.

"It was the only way I could save you," Sinclair was saying. "Forgive me. Eleanor. Please say that you can forgive me."

But at that moment, she could not. At that moment it was all she could do to breathe the damp air of the Bosporus, and consider what she might do . . .

Even now, it was a dilemma that offered no easy way out.

As she paced the floor of the infirmary, it was a struggle to keep her thoughts from the white metal box—with the blood inside it— that stood before her. All she had to do was reach out, open it, and take what she needed. There it was, beckoning to her.

She forced herself to look away and went to the window.

The constant sun imparted a dull glare that reminded her of the light in the sky on their ill-fated voyage aboard the *Coventry*. By the clock, it was getting on toward midnight, but she knew that there would be no proper night. Here, it was all a seamless unraveling of time, and she knew that she'd already taken, in the eyes of God, far more days than could ever have been her allotted share.

Michael. Michael Wilde. The moment he came into her mind, she did feel her thoughts lift. He had been so kind, and then, when he had taken the liberty of joining her on the piano bench, so mortified at his transgression. Importunate as his conduct had seemed, Eleanor did understand she was in a new world, where customs differed. There was so much she would have to learn. Symphony orchestras that played from little black boxes! Lights that came on and burned steadily with the flick of a switch. Women—and African women, to boot—serving as doctors!

Then she remembered how shocked her mother had been at the idea of her traveling to London—a single, unaccompanied young woman—to become a nurse. Perhaps everything that was once shocking eventually became routine. Perhaps the terrible toll of the Crimean War had startled the conscience of humanity and put an end to such mindless slaughter. Perhaps this world was a more enlightened one. A world where even ordinary things were made to smell sweet and nations settled their differences with raised voices but never raised swords.

She allowed herself to feel an unfamiliar ray of hope.

It had felt so good—so *normal*—to be seated at the piano again. Her fingers had so enjoyed touching the keys. It had brought back all of her lessons from the parson's wife, playing in the front parlor with the casement windows flung open and the family's cocker spaniel chasing rabbits across the wide green lawn. Mrs. Musgrove had a standing order with a music shop in Sheffield, and twice a year they sent her a selection of popular compositions. That was how Eleanor had come to fall in love with so many of the old, traditional ballads and songs, like "The Banks of the River Tweed" and "Barbara Allen."

Michael had seemed to enjoy the song, too. He had a sensitive face, but there was something haunted about it, too. He had borne his own tragedy, of some kind, and perhaps that was why he had elected to come to such a lonely place. Who would choose such a destination if it had not, in some way, been chosen for him? She wondered what it was that had befallen him . . . or from what memory he might be fleeing. She did not recall seeing a ring on his finger, and in their time together he had certainly never mentioned a wife. Though she couldn't have said why, he struck her as a bachelor.

Oh, how she longed for sunlight—*true* sunlight, not an empty imitation. Sunlight as warm and golden as syrup, pouring over her. She had lived an eternity in the shadows, fleeing with Sinclair from one town to another lest they linger too long in one place and their secret be discovered. They had made their way from Scutari through the Carpathians, then on to Italy, where Eleanor had held her face out the carriage window just to catch every ray she could of the warm Mediterranean sun. Often, she had suggested they stop and stay somewhere, but as soon as Sinclair felt any of the local inhabitants taking too much of an interest in who exactly this mysterious young English couple was, he insisted they leave again. He lived in dread of his desertion being discovered, and often said that he hoped his father would hear only that he had been lost on the battlefield at Balaclava.

As for Eleanor, she didn't know which she feared more—never seeing her family again or seeing them and knowing that they could sense she had changed in some ineffable way.

In Marseilles, Sinclair had spotted an old friend of his family strolling along the quay, and dragged her into an artisan's shop to escape detection. When the shopkeeper asked what he could show them, Sinclair answered, in perfect French so far as Eleanor could tell, that he was interested in the first thing his eye happened to fall on—an ivory brooch, with a gold rim, lying on a worktable.

The shopkeeper had lifted the brooch into the light from a window, and Eleanor had marveled at its execution. It was a cameo of a classical figure—Venus rising from the waves.

"What more perfect theme could we have chosen," Sinclair declared, pinning it to her bodice, "than the goddess of love."

"It's lovely," she said, in a low voice, "but shouldn't we save what money we have left?"

"Combien d'argent?" Sinclair asked the shopkeeper, and settled the bill without question. Eleanor never knew where their funds came from, but somehow there was always enough to transport them to the next spot. She suspected that Sinclair, posing as someone he was not, managed to borrow funds from Englishmen they encountered abroad, and parlayed those loans into even greater sums at the gaming tables.

In Lisbon, they had taken a room at the top of a small hotel, overlooking the crenellated façade of Santa Maria Maior. The ringing bells of the cathedral were like a constant reproof, and one morning, Sinclair, perhaps intuiting her thoughts, said, "Shall we marry there?"

Eleanor did not know how to answer. Already she felt damned in so many ways, and much as she would have liked to be properly wed, the very thought of entering a church, and taking holy vows in her present state, was too daunting. But Sinclair prevailed upon her, saying, "At least let's go and look. From all accounts, it's a very beautiful church."

"But we cannot enlist a priest, not with all the lies we would have to tell."

"Who said anything about a priest?" Sinclair scoffed. "They speak Portuguese, anyway. We can stand there, if you like, and make our own vows. God can hear them without the help of some Papist intermediary . . . provided, of course, that there's a god to hear them at all." He made it sound like a very dubious proposition.

And so she had put on her finest dress, and Sinclair his uniform, and arm in arm they had crossed the square to the cathedral. They had made a handsome couple, and she could see the impression they made in the eyes of passersby. The church itself had been built in the twelfth century, and though badly damaged by the earthquakes of 1344 and 1755, it had been repaired and rebuilt where necessary; its twin bell towers rose like a white fortress on either side of the high, nobly arched entranceway. Between the arches was a rounded window, through whose colored panes the sunlight lent a golden hue to the antique gilding and massive columns of the interior. Marble tombs, each with its coat of arms, were ensconced in private chapels behind iron gates. On one tomb, Eleanor saw the figure of a recumbent nobleman in armor, holding his sword and guarded by his dog; on another, a woman in classical dress, reading a Book of Hours. The cathedral was vast, and though there were worshippers in the pews, and visitors in the aisles, a hush prevailed over everything, and all Eleanor could really hear was the sound of their own footsteps echoing up the nave.

An elderly priest in a black robe, a white rope belted around his waist, was consulting with several well-dressed men and ladies at one end of the transept, and Eleanor instinctively moved in the other direction. Sinclair felt the tug on his arm and smiled.

"Are you afraid he's picked up our scent?"

"Don't make such jests."

"Do you think he'll chase us out?"

But she didn't answer him at all this time.

"We don't have to go through with it," he said. "I was only doing it for you."

"That's not a very becoming sentiment," she replied, pulling away, wondering what had possessed her to do this in the first place.

Sinclair came after her, clutching her sleeve. "I'm sorry. You know I didn't mean that."

Eleanor felt several people observing them—they were creating a scene, the last thing in the world she wanted to do—and she ducked behind the column closest to the altar itself, raising a handkerchief to conceal her face.

"I would marry you anywhere," he said, in a low but urgent voice. "You must know that. In Westminster Abbey, or in the middle of the forest with no one there to witness it but the birds in the trees."

Eleanor did know it, but it wasn't enough. Sinclair had lost his faith in everything, and he had profoundly shaken hers. What *were* they doing there? What had she hoped would come of it? It was a terrible mistake, and she'd known it the moment she crossed the threshold of the cathedral.

"Come," he said earnestly, slipping a hand into the crook of her elbow. "Let's stand in the open."

She tried to resist, but he pulled her out of the shadows, and afraid of causing any more commotion, she let him prevail.

"We have nothing to hide," he said.

He drew her first into the center aisle, then out in front of the ornate and glittering altar itself. The stained-glass window, in brilliant blues and reds and yellows, glowed like a kaleidoscope that Eleanor had once seen in a London optical shop, and it was so beautiful she could hardly take her eyes away.

Sinclair clasped both of her hands in his, and in a soft voice said, "I, Sinclair Archibald Copley, do take thee, Eleanor—" He stopped. "Isn't that odd? I don't know your middle name—do you have one?"

"Jane."

"Do take thee, Eleanor Jane Ames," he continued, "to be my lawfully wedded wife. To have and to hold, for richer or for poorer, in sickness and in health, until death do us part."

Eleanor felt that they were being far too conspicuous, and she tried to lower her hands.

But Sinclair hung on. "I hope I remembered that correctly. If there's anything I missed, please tell me."

"No, I believe you had it right."

"Good, then once you recite the vows yourself, we can go and have a toast at that noisy cantina on the square."

"Sinclair," she pleaded, "I can't."

"You can't?" he inquired, a brittle edge entering his voice. "Or you won't?"

Eleanor was sure that the priest had taken notice of them. He had a long white beard and sharp dark eyes under bushy brows. "Sinclair, I think we should leave now."

"No," he said. "Not until we have asked the assembled congregation—"

"What congregation?" The *other* Sinclair, the one she dreaded, was coming to the fore.

"Not until we have asked the congregation if any of them knows of any just impediment to our being wed."

"That's meant to come before the vow," she said. "Don't make any more of a mockery of this than we already have."

She knew that they had to go. She could see, out of the corner of her eye, the priest disengaging himself from the Portuguese aristocrats.

"We are making a spectacle of ourselves," she whispered, "and it isn't safe. You know that better than anyone."

He fixed her with a dull glare, as if wondering how much further to go. She'd seen that look in his eye before; he could be tipped over—from mirth to fury, from kindness to callousness—in an instant.

He had just opened his mouth to speak when she heard a rumbling in the stone slabs beneath her feet, and from the wall behind the altar—a wall that had stood for centuries—she saw the heavy crucifix tilt, then sway. The priest, who'd been striding toward them, stopped and looked up in horror as cracks rippled through the plaster. All around her, people screamed, or threw themselves to the floor with their hands clasped in prayer.

As Sinclair and Eleanor stepped back, the cross broke free, ripping bricks from the wall and throwing up a cloud of white dust.

Sinclair dragged her behind a column and they huddled there, expecting the earthquake to level the entire church around them. The great stained-glass window fractured like sheer ice on a pond, then crumbled into a thousand shining shards of glass. Dust and debris billowed out into the nave. Eleanor clutched her handkerchief over her mouth and nose, and Sinclair raised the sleeve of his uniform over his own. Through the cloud, Eleanor could discern the priest, crossing himself, but pressing forward . . . toward them.

"Sinclair," she said, coughing. "The priest, he's coming."

Sinclair turned around and saw the man waving the plaster dust out of his path.

"This way," he said, leading Eleanor toward one of the side chapels. But a couple of men—the ones wearing fine velvet tailcoats—were standing there, aghast but stubbornly unmoving, and he had to suddenly change course. By the time he did, the priest had intercepted them, and was clutching at the gold braid on Sinclair's doublet and shouting angry words that they could not understand. His arms waved, as if indicating that the chaos had been brought on by some terrible sacrilege Sinclair had been performing.

Had it? Eleanor wondered.

Sinclair batted the man's hands away, and finally, when that didn't stop him, he drew back his fist and punched him hard in the belly. The old priest fell to his knees, then, gasping for air, toppled over into the dust. Clutching Eleanor's hand, Sinclair hurried down the nave and out a side door near the chapel of the knight in armor. The bright sunlight blinded them for a moment, and the earth gave another jolt. People were still fleeing from their shops and houses; dogs were barking and pigs were squealing in the street. They turned down a flight of winding steps and into a cobblestoned alley. Loose red tiles skittered off a roof and shattered in their path. A few minutes later, they had lost themselves in the mayhem of a panicked marketplace.

It was not the wedding day that Eleanor, as a young girl lying in a meadow in Yorkshire, might have imagined.

And now? Now she was standing in front of the squat white box—the fridge—her breath shallow, and the room in the infirmary fading to white before her eyes. She put out a hand to steady herself, but her knees were weak. She let herself sink and came to rest with her head against the cool surface of its door. Inside it, she knew, was what she needed, and without really willing it, her fingers found the handle. She opened the box, and took out one of the bags, with the blood sloshing inside. It said "O Negative" on it. She wondered what that meant, but not for long. With her teeth, she tore it open, and there on the floor, her soft white robe spread out around her, she suckled at the bag like a newborn babe.

CHAPTER FORTY-SIX

December 22, 10 a.m.

SINCLAIR WASN'T SURE what had awakened him. He was slumped forward on a high stool, his head lying on the altar, the book of poetry under one hand and his other hand resting on a nearly empty chalice. A sputtering candle sent a thin trail of smoke into the air.

A dog, sitting on his haunches in the aisle, let out a hungry cry.

He'd been dreaming of Eleanor—what else did he ever dream of?—but it was not a happy dream. It was hardly a dream at all. He was remembering a quarrel that they had had, just before he'd gone off hunting. From the belfry, he had done some reconnoitering and determined that the coast bellied out to the northwest, promising perhaps some escape route. "We may not be so marooned, after all."

"Sinclair," she'd replied, softly and with great deliberation, "we are marooned as no two people have ever been before."

"None of that," he replied, tearing another hymnal into pieces and tossing it into the fire. "We've as much right to the world as anyone else."

"But we're not like anyone else. I don't know what we are, or what the Lord intended for us to be, but this . . . this cannot be His plan."

"Well, then, it's mine," he barked, "and for the time being, that will have to serve." He could feel the shortness of breath, the dimming of his vision, as he stared into the blazing grate. "I've seen God's plan, and I'll tell you this much—the Devil could have done no worse. The world's a slaughterhouse, and I've played my own damned part in making it so. If I've learned anything at all, it's that we must make up our own fate, from scratch, every day." He ripped another hymnal in two and added it to the fire. "If we hope to survive at all, we must fight for every breath we take, every bite we eat, and every drop we drink." Looking around for the nearest bottle, he'd concluded, "God helps no one."

Raising his eyes to the dog now baying in the aisle, he saw no sign of God there, either . . . unless it was in the strange silence outside. The storm had passed. The wind had died to just a whisper. Perhaps it was the cessation of the constant battering that had awakened him . . . awakened him to the chance, at last, of going in search of Eleanor.

God helps no one, but if he could find the strength to harness the dogs and provision the sled, he could help himself. He could take matters into his own hands. He lifted the chalice and drained its last drops.

Michael, not surprisingly, was the first to arrive at the flagpole, the rendezvous spot for the search party. Standing by his snowmobile, he stomped his feet on the ground to keep the blood flowing. Someone had wrapped a long chain of red-and-green tinsel around and around the flagpole; it had become pretty much soldered to the metal, and Michael doubted anyone would ever be able to get it off. It would forever be Christmas at Point Adélie.

He glanced up at the sky; even through his sunglasses, it was a hard, blazing blue, the color of Easter eggs he'd painted as a kid. A bird shot across his field of vision—a dirty gray bird—and wheeled in the sky, then returned to swoop down at his head. He ducked fast, and heard it squawking as it came back for another pass. He held his gloved hand up above his head, remembering that the birds always dived for the highest point of their target, but it was only when it swooped by again that he realized there was no nest anywhere near here—at least none that he could see—and no carrion that the bird could have been claiming for itself. He quickly wiped the ice crystals from his glasses to get a better look at the whirring bird. Could it, by any chance, be Ollie?

It was flitting in a wide circle around the top of the flagpole, where Old Glory flapped listlessly in the cold breeze, then landed atop the administration module. Michael dug into his pocket, and found a rock-hard granola bar. Skuas, he knew, weren't too particular. With his gloved fingers, he fumbled to remove the wrapper, as the bird watched him intently. He held it up for inspection, then tossed it onto the ground a few feet away. These birds were scavengers and they knew enough not to miss a chance; in a second, it was zooming off the roof and plopping down with its beak already open. With a couple of quick pecks, it had broken the bar into several pieces, and one or two had already gone down the hatch. Michael studied him, hoping to see anything that might tell him if it was Ollie or not. The bird gulped down the last of the granola bar, and Michael crouched to get a better look.

"Ollie?" he said. "Is that you?"

The bird's beady black eyes regarded him impassively, but he didn't fly away. When Michael put out his gloved hand—not, he knew, the smartest thing to do with omnivorous skuas—the bird took one hopping step closer, pecked gently at his palm, then waited there.

"I'll be damned," Michael said. And though he would have been hard put to say why, he felt a lump form in his throat. Maybe it had something to do with the fact that the little runt had managed to survive, after all . . . or that it was one of the few things Michael had touched that had. He flashed, oddly enough, on Kristin lying in her hospital bed . . . and then on the funeral he had not been able to attend. In his mind's eye, he saw a bunch of sunflowers—big and yellow—surrounding a coffin. The bird pecked at his hand again, and he wished he had something else in his pockets to give it.

"All out," he said, standing up again with his empty hands extended.

The skua strutted around the immediate ground, then gave up the hunt and shot back into the air like a rocket. Michael watched it skim the quad, then disappear in the direction of the dive hut. Several other birds gathered in the sky to join it, and Michael felt, stupidly, like a parent whose kid had just been accepted on the playground by his classmates.

There was an increasing roar from the concourse behind the administration module, followed by the sight of Murphy, Lawson, and Franklin, all riding their own machines. They reminded Michael of a posse, especially when he noticed that they were armed. Murphy had his gun in its holster, and the barrel of Franklin's rifle stuck out of the cargo compartment.

"I thought this was a search party," Michael said, "not a SWAT team."

The chief gave him a look that said, *Grow up.* "Weren't you ever in the Boy Scouts? Be prepared." He pulled out a speargun from his own cargo bay and tossed it to him. Lawson, Michael noticed, was carrying one, too. "When we get to Stromviken," Murphy announced over the idling engines, "Franklin and I will sweep in from the ocean side, you and Bill here will head straight into the yards." Then, before lowering the visor on his helmet, he said, "And watch where you're going. I lost one beaker in a crevasse last year and I don't feel like losing anybody else." The visor dropped, and a second later he took off across the ice with a deafening roar.

Franklin sat down on his own Arctic Cat and said, "Best if you follow in a single file. That way you can be sure the ground ahead is solid."

Lawson followed. The snowmobiles were powerful machines, well over five hundred pounds each, with raised mountain-style handlebars. Michael snapped down the hood of his helmet, with its oversized eye port and antifog screen, and settled himself on the seat. He twisted the throttle, harder than he should have, and the four-stroke engine growled. The tracks bit into the snow and the front skis lifted, and he shot forward in Lawson's wake. The machine he rode was nothing like the snowmobile he'd owned when he was growing up—one of the early Ski-Doos. On the Cat he could feel the massive horsepower rumbling under him. Not to mention the heavy-duty suspension; he was used to feeling every bump in the ice and every rough patch of rugged ground, but on this it was as if he were flying across the snowfield on a magic carpet.

That, he knew, was the danger of it. Already he could see Murphy and Franklin and Lawson peeling in a straight line across the vast white field, but a crevasse could still appear out of nowhere, at any moment, and swallow any one of them whole. In snow school, right after he'd arrived at Point Adélie, Michael had gotten the full rundown from Lawson, and though he didn't necessarily remember the exact differences between a marginal crevasse, a longitudinal crevasse, and a bergschrund, he did remember that they were often camouflaged by the previous year's snowfall. A fragile white bridge was formed across the top—a bridge that could hold for one man and suddenly give way under the next, revealing a jagged, blue-walled canyon of ice a hundred feet deep. At the bottom, where the air was supercooled to forty degrees below, lay a bed of frozen salt water. Very few people who fell into a crevasse ever emerged alive . . . or, for that matter, at all.

Michael tried to follow in the tracks laid down by the others, but it wasn't always easy to see them. There was a steady glare off the snow, and an occasional sharp stab of light off a slab of wind-polished ice. He hunkered down on the seat in order to let the windshield cut the blast of frigid air coming at him. The helmet helped, too; padded at the cheek and chin, it had a wraparound neck roll that muffled the engine noise, along with vents that sucked the heat and moisture out of the face shield. It reminded Michael of the deep-sea diving gear he'd worn when freeing Eleanor from the glacier.

Eleanor . . . Sleeping Beauty . . . who'd metamorphosed, in his companions' minds, into the Bride of Dracula. How long her living presence could be kept a secret at Point Adélie was an open question . . . and how long she could be kept there at all was an even more daunting one. Michael's NSF pass had only nine days left to run, and he knew that as soon as the next supply plane landed—it was scheduled for New Year's Eve—he was going to have to go back on it. But what would happen to Eleanor then? Who would look out for her? Who would she tell her story to? Who, above all, would she trust? Michael had every confidence in Charlotte, but Charlotte had a job to do—she was the medical officer for the whole base, and she couldn't be expected to be a nursemaid. And Darryl—well, Darryl wasn't exactly the kind of guy who would dote on her, especially if there were fish to be dissected and hematology studies to be done. And what if Sinclair Copley never turned up? Lawson had made it sound pretty unlikely. More and more, Michael thought, Eleanor would again be abandoned, isolated and lonely in a prison not much bigger than that block of ice.

Unless...

The snowmobile hit a mogul, soaring above the ground, then thumping back, its rear briefly fishtailing.

Concentrate, he told himself, *or you'll break your neck and all bets will be off.* He shook his helmet to loosen some snow from the visor and gripped the handlebars more tightly. But his thoughts went right back where they'd been...to the coming day, not far off, when he would have to leave the Point...and Eleanor.

But what if—and he marveled that he hadn't considered the idea before (or had he?)—what if she were to go back with him? What if she, too, were to board that supply plane? The thought was so crazy he could barely believe he was entertaining it. But Murphy, if it came to that, would be nothing but relieved to see her go— and, as chief of operations, he could use his considerable leverage over the few others on the base who knew about her at all to buy their silence; he could make their life there as easy, or as difficult, as he liked. Still...how could Michael engineer such a thing? How could he get someone like Eleanor—and had there ever *been* anyone else like Eleanor?—all the way back to the States? Someone who had never seen an airplane, or an automobile, or for that matter a CD player? Who had no citizenship—unless Queen Victoria was around to confirm it—and certainly no passport to prove it?

And apart from all the obvious difficulties that the journey alone presented, how could he care for someone in her unheard-of condition? How far, he wondered, was the nearest blood bank in Tacoma?

A half a mile or so ahead, Michael could see the black clutter of smokestacks, warehouses, and sheds and, high on the hill in the distance, the steeple of the church. He was glad to see Murphy and Franklin, as planned, steer their snowmobiles off to the right, toward the beach of bleached bones and the wreck of the *Albatros.* If Sinclair was here at the whaling station—and what would they do with him if they did find him alive? Would they shutter him away in the infirmary as well?—there was a good chance he was barricaded in the church, in the room behind the altar, and Michael wanted to be the one to find him first. To calm his fears and reason with him. If he was alive, he would be wary, suspicious, even hostile; from his perspective, he had every reason to be.

That was why Michael would need to be alone with him if and when he was found.

Once Lawson had pulled to a stop in the flensing yard, where the iron tracks for the skip wagons threatened to destroy the snowmobile's treads, Michael pulled up alongside and cut his own engine. The sudden silence was awesome. Michael raised the visor on his helmet, and the cold air felt like a slap in the face.

"What now?" Lawson said, and Michael, just to be free of him, said, "Why don't you start looking around these yards and outbuildings? I'll start from the top of the hill and work my way down."

Lawson, toting his speargun, nodded. He hung his helmet on the handlebar of his snowmobile and trudged off. Michael stowed his own helmet and set off for the church. From here, he could see the teetering tombstones and, soon, the doors—both of which were now closed. An interesting sign, since one of them had been propped open by a snowbank before. Somebody might be home.

As he mounted the steps, his shadow, cut short by the solstice sun directly overhead, fell straight onto the wood between his feet, and he heard from within a scrambling, then a bark. He put his shoulder against the creaking frame, pushed the door open, and was greeted by a mad rush of sled dogs. He knelt and let them lick his face and gloves and dance in wild circles all around him, while his eyes swept the empty chamber. There was a pile of supplies and gear gathered by the door, as if someone had been planning to leave shortly.

On the altar, he could see a candlestick and a black wine bottle.

He didn't know if he should shout to announce his presence or creep in quietly and hope to surprise his quarry.

But then, was he there to rescue Sinclair . . . or capture him?

He moved cautiously up the aisle, past the ancient pews, then around the altar to the room beyond. The door was ajar, and when he pushed it open the rest of the way, he saw that the bed had been slept in but the fire in the grate had gone out. There was a smell of cold ashes and damp wool, but through the open window—flung wide, the shutters banging—he glimpsed a furtive figure scrambling through the gravestones, picking its way around the back of the church.

And it wasn't anyone from the search party.

He was wearing a red down coat, open, with a white cross on the back—Michael recognized it as one of the many coats that hung on the kennel clothes rack—and his head was bare. He had dark blond hair, and a moustache of the same color.

So this was Sinclair . . . Eleanor's beloved. Alive, after all.

Michael felt a strange pang, gone almost before he'd noticed it.

He ran back out of the room, his boots clomping and sliding on the stone floor, the dogs leaping and gamboling in his way.

"Not now!" he cried, pushing their furry heads aside.

By the time he got to the doors, Sinclair was well down the slope, sometimes running, sometimes sliding with his arms outspread. Under the open down coat, Michael saw the glint of gold braid on a uniform jacket and a scabbard clattering at the man's side; he was making for the factory floors, where the evisceration and rendering of the whales was once done. Then he disappeared into a narrow alleyway that ran between two of the vast ramshackle buildings, but Michael, trying to run with a speargun in hand, had to make his way more carefully down the frozen hillside. He was also trying to think where Sinclair might be heading. He might have heard the approach of the snowmobiles, or he might have been caught off guard. The gear stacked at the door suggested he'd been planning a mission of his own. But if he'd simply wanted to hide, why hadn't he done so? There must be something in the yards and warehouses that he wanted.

And the only thing that Michael could think of was weaponry.

There was a flash of red far ahead, darting between two sheds, and Michael followed it. Lawson, fortunately, was nowhere to be seen—the last thing Michael wanted was any interference—and he could hear the distant rumbling of Murphy's and Franklin's snowmobiles down along the waterfront. If he could catch him, Michael would have Sinclair all to himself, at least for a while.

Then he remembered the rack of rusty harpoons in what had probably once been the blacksmith's shop. But where was it?

Michael stopped for a second to catch his breath and get his bearings. He had seen the place when he'd been here before. It was far
ahead, and somewhere on his left, but he felt sure he could find it
again; an enormous rusted anchor had leaned beside the door.

Michael trotted along with the speargun down at his side, afraid
that if he tripped and fell, the damn thing would go off. He passed
one vacant building after another, giving each a quick glance inside—
he saw hanging chains and frozen pulleys, long, scarred worktables,
hacksaws, and enormous cauldrons squatting on stubby iron legs.
He began to understand that, as random and scattered as the buildings appeared, there was an underlying plan to the way they were
laid out. You could see it in the crisscrossing of the railroad ties that
the skip-wagons ran on; everything was organized like a primitive
assembly line—or *disassembly* line, to be more precise—to carve up and
process the carcass of the whale, from skin to gristle. Their bones
and teeth, even petrified eyes the size of medicine balls, still lay scattered here and there, blown into haphazard piles against the walls.

He came to an intersection, with footpaths or alleys leading off
in many directions, and he had to re-create his first entry into the
town. He had come in from the southwest, which meant he probably had traveled along the windswept concourse veering off to his
right. He followed along it, until, to his relief, he saw the anchor
next to a low and darkened doorway.

He slowed down as he approached, but there was absolutely no
sight, or sound, of life within. Perhaps his guess had been mistaken.
Lowering his head to duck inside, he had just looked up again—
there was another open doorway at the rear, partly blocked by a
bunch of hooped barrels—when something whizzed past his cheek
and pierced the wall a foot away. The harpoon stuck fast in the
wood, the shaft still thrumming beside his ear.

"Don't take another step," Michael heard, though in the dim
confines of the cluttered shop, he still couldn't see his adversary.

"And drop your weapon."

Michael let the speargun clatter to the brick floor.

There was a huge, freestanding chimneystack made of red
bricks—no doubt the forge—and a black iron anvil just in front of
it. A figure emerged from behind the chimney. He had doffed the
overcoat, and was wearing only a scarlet cavalry uniform, with the

sword hanging down at his side and another harpoon already in his hand.

"Who are you?"

"My name is Michael. Michael Wilde."

"What are you doing here?"

"I've come to find you."

There was an uneasy pause, filled only by the moaning of the wind that had found its way down the chimney and into the cold forge. There was a faint scent of old, dead coals.

"You must be Lieutenant Copley," Michael said.

The man looked taken aback but quickly recovered.

"If you know that, then you must have Eleanor."

"Yes. We do. And she's safe," Michael assured him. "We're taking good care of her."

An angry spark lighted in Sinclair's eye, and Michael immediately regretted his choice of words. Surely Sinclair thought no one but he should be charged with that duty.

"She's at the camp," Michael went on, "at Point Adélie."

"That's what you call it?"

Sinclair looked, and certainly sounded, like a British aristocrat—someone Michael might have seen in a movie—but there was also a patently mad and unpredictable gleam in his eye. Not that it should have come as such a surprise. Michael just wished he could figure out what he could say that would get him to put down the harpoon.

"We haven't come here to do you any harm," Michael said. "Far from it. We can help you, in fact." He wondered if he should keep on talking, or simply shut up.

"How many of you are there?" Sinclair's ragged breath fogged in the air. For the first time, Michael could see what this exertion had cost him; the man was defiant but weak on his feet.

"Four. Just four of us."

The tip of the harpoon wavered. His eyelids slowly shuttered, then sprang back open again in alarm.

Had he just "refreshed the image," in Ackerley's words? Michael was reminded, not that he needed to be, of what a dangerous foe he might be facing.

"We're working here at the South Pole," Michael volunteered. "We're Americans."

The harpoon declined farther, and Michael could swear he saw the tiniest glint of a smile cross the lieutenant's lips.

"I had a fancy, a long time ago, to see America," Sinclair said, coughing once or twice. "It seemed ideal. I knew no one there, and no one knew me."

Out of the corner of his eye, Michael saw movement in the rear doorway, and Sinclair must have followed his glance. He whirled around, the harpoon raised, and before Michael could do anything more than shout "Stop!" Franklin had barged through the barrels, rifle at the ready.

Sinclair hesitated for just a second, but when the muzzle of the gun came up, he let the harpoon fly. Simultaneously there was a deafening blast from the gun, and chunks of the redbrick chimney exploded in all directions. One of them stung Michael's cheek like a hornet and a smaller bit flew into his eye. He dropped his head to wipe the grit away, and when he looked up again, blearily, the harpoon was quivering in the side of a barrel. Franklin was still holding the rifle up, but he was staring down at Sinclair, who was slumped over the anvil, his arms hanging loose and his fingers twitching.

Murphy was just charging in with his own pistol raised, too.

"What did you do?" Michael exclaimed. "What did you do?"

"He threw a harpoon at me!" But even Franklin looked shaken. "I didn't hit him, anyway. I hit the chimney."

Michael knelt by Sinclair and saw blood seeping from his scalp and matting the blond hair at the back of his head. "What's this then?"

"A ricochet. I was using rubber bullets. It must have ricocheted."

Murphy crouched on the other side of the anvil, and together they gently lowered Sinclair to the floor, then turned him over onto his back. His eyes were receding into his skull, and his lips were blue. All Michael could think of was how this would affect Eleanor.

"Let's get him back to camp," Michael said. "We'll need Charlotte to take a look at him, fast."

Murphy nodded and stood up. "We'll have to tie him up first—"

"He's out cold," Michael interjected.

"For now," Murphy shot back. "What if he comes to?" He glanced over at Franklin. "Then we'll load him onto the back of my snowmobile. At the Point, he goes straight into quarantine. Send up a flare so Lawson knows we're here and ready to go."

As Franklin went outside to shoot off the flare, Michael remembered Ackerley in his own quarantine, laid out on a crate in the meat locker . . . and how well that had turned out.

"You know the drill," Murphy said to Michael. "Until further notice, nobody but us needs to know he's there. Got it?"

"I got it."

"And that goes double for Sleeping Beauty."

Michael was perfectly willing to keep the secret. What was one more? He was getting to be an old hand at keeping secrets. But he wondered how long it could really be kept. Even if the others at the camp didn't find out about Sinclair, Eleanor might well be another story. For all Michael knew, there was some sort of psychic connection between them. A connection so strong that he would not have been surprised if she was already aware that Sinclair had been found . . . that he had been injured . . . and that he was on his way back to her.

CHAPTER FORTY-SEVEN

December 22, 7:30 p.m.

AS DARRYL TRANSPORTED THE FISH to the aquarium tank, it wriggled so hard in his hands that he nearly lost it.

"Hang on," he muttered, "hang on," then he plopped it back into the section of the tank carefully reserved for his previous specimens of *Cryothenia hirschii*. It swam a bit, nosing around, then settled slowly toward the bottom of the tank, to lie there—virtually motionless and all but transparent—like its companions. If the fish did prove to be an undiscovered species—and Darryl was all but sure that they would—it wouldn't be the most exciting find to a civilian observer. They weren't much to look at. But in the scientific community—where it counted—the discovery would make his name.

Quite apart from their general morphology, their blood alone would launch a thousand lab tests. The antifreeze glycoproteins the blood carried, slightly different from those in the other Antarctic fish he had studied, could one day be used for myriad purposes already under consideration, from deicing airplane wings to insulating deep-sea probes...and who knew what else.

But Darryl's present experiments had an even more bizarre focus. The moment Charlotte Barnes had mentioned that a plasma bag had gone missing from the infirmary, neither of them had doubted for an instant what happened to it. Eleanor Ames had gotten to it. But if she were ever to leave the shelter of Point Adélie to take up residence again in the outside world, she would first have to overcome her dreadful addiction. Darryl was no fool—he knew the kind of media storm she would be the center of, and there would be no way to satisfy, much less keep secret, such an insatiable need.

He had taken additional samples of Eleanor's blood and immediately begun to run assays, screens, and other tests, working on a hunch that was as outlandish as the problem. Her blood, like Ackerley's, had a phagocytic index that was virtually off the charts, but instead of eliminating only the bacteria, foreign particles, and cell debris in the bloodstream, her phagocytes devoured the red blood cells, too—first their own, then whatever they could ingest from outside sources. But what if, Darryl thought, he was able to find a way to leave the normally toxic index level alone—clearly, it helped to sustain life under the most adverse conditions—while introducing an element that might obviate the need for foreign erythrocytes? What if, in short, Eleanor was able to borrow a trick or two from the cold-blooded, hemoglobin-free fish that filled Darryl's aquarium and holding tanks?

He'd made up a dozen different blood combinations, all of which were kept in carefully marked test tubes, under a steady temperature in the same minifridge where he kept his soft drinks, and he regularly checked them to see what had developed. He was just about to do so again when there was a loud banging on the lab door.

When he opened it, Michael clomped in, his wet boots squelching on the rubber mat.

"Want a cold drink?"

"Very funny," Michael replied, throwing his snowy hood back.

"I wasn't joking." Darryl went to the minifridge, popped the top of a root beer, and perched on top of his lab stool. "Where have you been?"

"Stromviken."

Darryl knew there was only one reason to have gone there. "Did you find him?"

Michael hesitated, but that was enough to tell Darryl what he needed to know.

"Was he alive?"

Michael balked again, as he unzipped his parka and plopped down on a neighboring stool.

"Forget whatever Murphy told you," Darryl said. "You know I'm going to have to be told eventually, anyway. Who else knows how to do a blood assay around here?"

"Yes," Michael finally replied. "But he didn't come easy. He got hurt, and Charlotte's taking care of him right now."

"How badly did he get hurt?"

"Charlotte thinks it's just a mild concussion and a scalp wound."

"So he's in the infirmary?" Darryl said, ready to race over and collect some fresh blood samples.

"No, the meat locker."

"That again?"

"Murphy doesn't want to put the whole base at risk."

However reluctantly, Darryl had to concede the chief's point. After all, he had seen Ackerley in action—and who could tell what might come of reuniting Eleanor with this other lost soul, presumably afflicted in the same way she was. It could create an unholy alliance.

"So," Michael said, a little too casually, "how's it coming?"

"How's what coming?"

"The cure. You find any way to help Eleanor out?"

"If you're asking me whether or not I've managed to solve one of the most puzzling hematological puzzles in history in the space of, oh, say a few days, the answer is no. Pasteur took his time, too."

"Sorry," Michael said, and Darryl regretted being short with him.

"But I am making some progress," he said. "I have some ideas."

"That's good," Michael said, visibly perking up. "That's great. I have faith in you. I think I will have that soda."

"Help yourself."

Michael went to the fridge, opened a bottle, then stood sipping it by the aquarium tank with the *Cryothenia hirschii* in it.

"Because I had this wacky idea of my own," he finally said, without turning around to face Darryl.

"I'm open to all suggestions," Darryl replied, capping another vial and labeling it, "though I was not aware that this was your field."

"It's not," Michael said. "My idea was, Eleanor should go back on the supply plane with me."

"What?"

"If you could find a cure, or at least a way to stabilize her condition," Michael said, turning around now, "I could shepherd her back to civilization."

"She doesn't belong on an airplane," Darryl said, "she belongs in quarantine. Or at the CDC. She's still got a blood disease with—what should we call them to be kind?—serious side effects?" But there was a look in Michael's eye that he didn't like. "This woman is off-limits, in a big way. You do get that, right?"

"Jesus, of course I do," Michael said, as if taking offense at the very suggestion.

"And now, in case you've already forgotten, we've got a second patient with the same problem. Were you planning to take him back with you, too?"

"If we had a solution," Michael said, though with a touch less enthusiasm, "yes, I would." He took a long drink from the soda bottle. "I would have to."

"That's insane," Darryl said. "The plane is due in what, nine days? I sincerely doubt that anyone but you will be going back on it."

Michael looked deflated, but accepting, as if he knew he'd been floating a very leaky trial balloon.

"What you can do," Darryl said, to buck him up, "is ask Charlotte to get me some blood samples from—what was his name again?"

"Sinclair Copley."

"From Mr. Copley, as soon as possible. And now, instead of distracting me with any more of your lame ideas, you should go back to the dorm and crash. Maybe you'll wake up tomorrow with some more great ideas."

"Thanks. I just might."

"Can't wait," Darryl said, already returning to his work.

———————

But Michael had one more stop to make before sleeping; he'd been avoiding it for days, and Joe Gillespie had left three increasingly urgent messages for him. For a host of reasons, he'd been postponing the conversation. What was he going to tell him? That the bodies discovered in the ice had been successfully thawed out—and they'd then absconded? That they were now alive, in fact, and under lockdown? Oh yeah, that would be an easy sell. Or should he go into what had happened to Danzig, and then Ackerley—tell him how dead men had come back to life, insane with some unknown disease that turned them into a polar version of the living dead? How far would he get with any of that, he wondered, before Gillespie started to speculate on just how crazy his reporter had become? And what would Gillespie do then? Would he notify the NSF headquarters in Washington that an immediate evacuation of his hallucinating staffer was required? Or, would he simply try to contact the base commander himself, none other than Murphy O'Connor? The same Murphy O'Connor whose last pronouncement on this subject had been, "What happens at Point Adélie, stays at Point Adélie."

Michael called Gillespie at home, on the SAT phone, hoping he'd get a machine, but Gillespie picked up on the first ring.

"Hope I'm not waking you," Michael said, over the low crackle of static.

"Michael?" Gillespie nearly shouted. "You're a very hard man to reach!"

"Yeah, well, it's kind of a topsy-turvy place down here."

"Wait a second—let me turn the stereo down."

Michael stared down at a notepad on the counter; somebody had been doodling a sleigh with Santa on top and it really wasn't bad. Michael flashed on Christmas the year before—Kristin had given him a pup tent, and he'd given her an acoustic guitar . . . that she'd never had time to learn how to play.

"So tell me," Gillespie said, back on the line, "where are we on this story? I want to get the art department started on the cover and the layout as soon as possible, and anytime you have a rough draft of the text—and I don't care how rough it is—I want to see it." His words were coming so fast they were tumbling over themselves. "So what's the latest with the bodies in the ice? Have you thawed 'em out? Or figured out anything about who they were?"

What, Michael wondered, could he say? That he not only knew

who they were, but knew their actual names? Because they had told him?

"The girl's the one I'm particularly interested in," Gillespie confessed. "What's she look like? Is she completely decayed, or would she be something we could feature in a full-page shot without scaring our younger readers?"

Michael was at a total loss. He didn't want to start laying down a bunch of lies, but he was definitely not about to divulge the truth. The thought of describing Eleanor to him, of *pitching* her, as the subject of some photo opportunity . . .

"I hope she's going to be well enough preserved to go on display somewhere," Gillespie rattled on. "The NSF, I'm sure, is going to want to show her off, and I wouldn't be surprised if they set up some kind of show around her at the Smithsonian."

Michael's heart sank even lower in his chest. He regretted the haste with which he had informed Gillespie of the find in the first place, and he wished, more than anything, that he could simply roll back time and start all over. That he could take it all back. Maybe now, it dawned on him, he could start. "You know," he said, "it looks like I was a bit quick on the draw there."

"Quick on the draw," Gillespie repeated, slowly for a change. "What do you mean?"

What *did* he mean? He could picture the fuzz on Gillespie's head getting fuzzier by the second. "The bodies, well, they didn't turn out to be what I thought they were."

"What the hell are you getting at? They're either bodies, or they're not. Don't do this to me, Michael. Are you saying that—"

While he talked, Michael shook the phone, and when he went back on a few seconds later, he said, "Sorry, you were breaking up. Could you repeat that last bit, Joe?"

"I was saying, is this story for real or not? Because if you were just jerking my chain, I'm not amused in the slightest."

"I was not jerking you around," Michael replied, holding the phone at arm's length for maximum effect. "I guess I was fooled myself. It looks like, well, it looks like maybe it wasn't an actual woman at all. Just a carved wooden figurehead."

"A . . . carved . . . wooden . . . figurehead?"

"Attached to a bowsprit." Michael was momentarily impressed

at his own ingenuity. "Quite old, and very beautiful, but not a woman. Or a man, either—he just turned out to be some more wood—though nicely painted—in the ice behind her. They must have been part of some shipwreck." He could embellish it further, but he didn't want Gillespie to get too excited about shots of the figurehead, because then he'd have to find a way to manufacture some. "I just can't tell you, Joe, how embarrassed I am."

"Embarrassed?" Michael heard, faintly. "That's all? You're embarrassed? I was planning to make you the poster boy for *Eco-Travel Magazine.* I was planning to shell out real money to hire a PR firm, just to plaster your face all over the media."

Michael knew that with every syllable he'd just uttered, his chances of making news—winning awards, getting famous, maybe even getting rich—had withered, and vanished into the thinnest of air. "But I've got some other great stuff—an abandoned whaling station, the last dogsled team in the Antarctic, a big storm rounding the Horn. Tons of material."

"That's great, Michael, just great. We'll talk more as soon as you get back here, after the first of the year. You can show me what you've got then."

"You bet," Michael said, still silently assessing what he had done to his career. He had taken what could have been a career-making moment, and torched it.

"And you're feeling okay?"

"Absolutely," Michael replied.

"And the situation with Kristin? Has that changed at all?"

He could see what was going through Gillespie's mind—he thought that Michael had begun to come a little unhinged over the lingering tragedy. And, much as he hated to exploit something like that, Michael did see an opportunity.

"Kristin passed away," he said.

"Oh jeez. You should have said something sooner."

"So between that, and the weird conditions down here, maybe yeah, I have been a little out of whack." He made sure his tone implied that that was definitely the case.

"Listen, I'm really sorry about Kristin."

"Thanks."

"But at least her ordeal is over. And yours, too."

"I guess."

"Just take it easy—don't overextend yourself—and we'll talk again, maybe in a day or two."

"Sure."

"And Michael—in the meantime, why don't you check in with the doctor on the base? Have him make sure—"

"Her. It's a woman."

"Okay—have *her* look you over. Can't hurt."

"Will do." Michael waved the phone in the air, then rubbed his sleeve against it to create some more static. Whatever bromides Gillespie was offering next, he didn't hear. Michael mumbled a good-bye into the receiver, hung up, then sat with his hands hanging down between his knees. He still wasn't sure, but he suspected that he'd just done the dumbest thing in his life. He'd always operated on instinct—picking which route to take up a cliff face, which fork in the rapids to run, which cave to explore—and just now he'd gone with his instincts again. And he wasn't even sure why. All he did know was that something inside him had rebelled—recoiled, even—at the thought of delivering Eleanor. To Joe Gillespie. To the world. Sure, what he'd done was a lie, but anything else would have felt like a betrayal.

Michael, he said to himself, *you have well and truly fucked yourself.*

He trudged alone to the commons, where he grabbed a sandwich and a couple of beers. Sam Adams Lagers, which only served to remind him of the flyers that Ackerley had written his last notes on. Uncle Barney had laid out a tray of Christmas cookies—gingerbread men decorated with pink icing—and Michael had a couple of those, too. But the Christmas spirit, which ought to have been easy to come by in a snowy landscape like the Pole, wasn't anywhere around. Yeah, they'd all sung Danzig's favorite songs at his memorial service, but he hadn't heard a lot of singing since. A kind of pall still hung over everything and everyone at the Point.

He thought about stopping off at the infirmary on the way back to his dorm, but kept on going instead; he had no heart to face Eleanor just then, much less to lie to her about Sinclair, as he had been enjoined to do. He had some serious soul-searching to do—especially since he had derailed things with Gillespie. He just needed to be alone with his thoughts.

That was getting to be a constant refrain for him.

What had started as a fleeting question, in the back of his mind, was becoming something more than that, something that his mind kept returning to. What *was* going to happen to Eleanor? She couldn't stay at Point Adélie forever, that was for certain. But how, and under what circumstances, could she leave? Did Murphy have some secret plan of his own? As far as Michael could see, she was going to require a friend, no matter what—someone she knew and trusted, to usher her into the modern-day world. And he also realized that, without any conscious deliberation, he had cast himself in that role.

In the communal bathroom, he took a long look at his own weary face in the mirror, and decided to shave. Why not shave before bed? At the South Pole, everything else was upside down.

But it wasn't just Eleanor—there was Sinclair to consider. The two of them would want to be together. And what role would he serve then? He'd wind up as a kind of chaperone, shepherding the two lovers back into a brave, new, and bewildering world.

His beard was so rough the razor kept snagging, and drops of blood appeared on his cheek and chin.

If he was honest with himself, what other scenario had he been imagining? Brewing inside him, he knew, were feelings that did not bear close scrutiny. He was a photojournalist, for Christ's sake, there on an assignment—that was it, and that was what he needed to focus on. The rest was just noise in his head.

He wiped some steam away from the mirror. His gaze was wide but dull—was he skirting the edge of the Big Eye?—and he needed a barber, too. His black hair was thick and unruly and curling over his ears. A couple of guys were yakking in the sauna behind him—from their voices he thought it might be Lawson and Franklin. He splashed some cold water on the spots where he'd cut himself, then took a quick shower and went back to his room.

Once there, he pulled the blinds down tight—he never thought he could hate the sun, but he did at that moment—and got into a fresh T-shirt and boxer shorts. He hoisted himself into his bunk and tried to straighten out the bedclothes; Darryl, he had noted, made his bed every day, but Michael saw no reason to do something at Point Adélie that he never bothered to do at home. He tugged the sheet up to keep the scratchy blanket off his legs, then yanked the bed curtains closed on all sides. Lying back in the narrow confines of the bunk, with the foam-rubber pillow wedged under his head, he stared up into the blackness.

His hair was still wet in back, and he lifted his head for a second to rub it dry. His eyes closed, and he took a long breath to relax himself. Then he took another, slow and deliberate. But his thoughts were still teeming. He pictured Sinclair on the cot set up in the old meat locker—the condiments box had been moved to make way—with a battery of space heaters running and Charlotte tending to his wound. She had needed to put in six stitches. Franklin and Lawson were assigned to keep watch in eight-hour shifts. Michael had volunteered to share the job, but Murphy had said, "Technically, you're still a civilian. Let's try to keep it that way."

His mattress sagged in the middle, and Michael inched over toward the wall. Regardless of what Murphy thought, someone would eventually have to tell Eleanor about Sinclair. But how would she react? It should have been a simple question, but Michael wasn't so sure that it was. She'd be relieved, of course. Delighted? Probably. Passionate? Would she insist on going to him at once? Michael didn't know if it was wishful thinking, or some deeper insight, but he suspected that there was something in Eleanor that feared Sinclair. From what she had told him of their story—as fantastical a tale as any that he'd ever heard—Sinclair had taken her on a wild and dangerous odyssey . . . an odyssey that was still unfolding.

But as much as she might love him, was she still as dedicated to that journey as she had been at the start?

He pictured the brooch she wore. Venus, rising from the sea foam. It was appropriate, wasn't it? Eleanor had risen from the sea. And she was beautiful. Immediately, he felt disloyal even to have entertained such a thought—Kristin was barely in the ground.

But there it was. He couldn't deny it any more than he could stop it.

Eleanor's face haunted him. The emerald eyes under their long dark lashes. The rich brown hair. Even the ghostly pallor. She seemed as if she came from another world—perhaps because she had—and he feared for her entry into his. He wanted to protect her, to guide her, to save her.

The bunk itself was as silent and black as any grave.

He remembered his first sight of her, entombed in the ice.

And then coming upon her, frightened and alone, in the abandoned church. But she had not cowered. There was a spirit in her that had never been extinguished, despite everything she had endured.

What was it she played on the piano in the rec hall? Oh, yes, that sad old ballad—"Barbara Allen." The plaintive notes tumbled through his head.

The curtains at the foot of the bed stirred.

He remembered the blush in her cheek when he had sat down beside her on the bench. The rustle of her dress, with its billowing sleeves. The tapered toes of her black shoes, touching the pedals.

The mattress sagged...as if it were accepting some other burden.

He thought of her scent, soapy but delicate...and the aroma seemed to envelop him now.

He thought of her voice...soft, refined, accented...

And then, out of the pitch black, he heard it.

"Michael..."

Had he just imagined that? The wind wailed outside.

But then he felt a warm breath on his cheek, and a hand touched his chest, as gently as a bird alighting on a branch.

"I can't bear it anymore," she said.

He didn't move a muscle.

"I can't bear being so alone."

She was lying on top of the blanket, but he could feel the shape of her body, pressing against his. How on earth had she...

"Michael...say my name."

He wet his lips, and whispered, "Eleanor."

"Again."

He said it again, and he heard her sob. The sound nearly broke his own heart.

He turned toward her, and lifted his hand to her face in the darkness. He found a trickle of tears...and he kissed them. Her skin was cold, but the tears were hot.

She burrowed closer, and he could feel her breath—shallow and hurried—on his neck.

"You did want me to come to you...didn't you?"

"Yes," he murmured, "yes, I did..."

And then he found her lips. They were soft and pliant...

but cold. He longed to warm them. He kissed her harder, and held her close. But the blanket was so coarse, and it came between them.

He shoved it down, and his hands groped in the dark for her body. She was slim as a sapling and wearing only a slip of some kind... something as sheer as a sheet, and as easily dispensed with.

God, how good it felt to touch her. He ran his hand up her naked side, and she shivered. She was still so cold, but her skin was so smooth. He felt the knob of her hip, the flat plain of her stomach—the flesh quivering at his touch—then the soft swell of her breast. The nipple hardened like a button under his fingers.

"Michael..." She sighed, her lips against his throat.

"Eleanor..."

He felt her teeth nibble at his skin.

"Forgive me," she whispered.

Before he could ask why, he felt the teeth sink into his throat like ice-cold pincers. A hot wet stream—his blood?—coursed down his neck, and he tried to cry out. But he strangled on the sound of his own scream, and he kicked out hard, to free himself from the bed-clothes. His hands pushed at her, and kept pushing...

The bed curtains screeched back.

He could see her, rearing back, naked, with his blood on her lips, her eyes blazing...

Bright light shone in his face.

He pushed again, to throw her from the bunk...

And a voice was crying, "Michael! For God's sake, Michael... wake up! Wake up."

His hands were still pushing, but someone had grabbed hold of them.

"It's me! It's Darryl!"

He stared out from his upper berth.

The lights were on. Darryl was hanging on to his hands.

"You're having a nightmare."

Michael's heart was hammering in his chest, but his hands stopped flailing.

"The mother of all fucking nightmares, I'd say," Darryl added, as Michael started to subside.

Michael's breath slowed. He glanced down. The sheet and blanket were twisted around his legs. The pillow was on the floor.

He felt the side of his neck. It was damp, but when he looked at his fingertips, they were only covered with sweat.

"You're lucky I came back," Darryl said. "You might have given yourself a heart attack."

"Bad dream," Michael said, his voice hoarse. "Guess I was having a bad dream."

"No kidding." Darryl blew out a heavy breath, then turned to take off his wristwatch and laid it on the nightstand. "What the hell was it about?"

"I don't remember," Michael replied, though he could recall every detail.

"You forgot it already?"

Michael dropped his head back onto the pillow and stared numbly at the ceiling. "Yeah."

"For the record, I thought I heard you say Eleanor."

"Huh."

"But I'll never tell." Darryl grabbed his towel off the hook on the door, and said, "Back in five. No matter what, do not go back to sleep."

Michael lay there, alone again, waiting for his heart to slow down and the last of the panic to pass . . . and seeing, in his mind's eye, Eleanor's long brown hair tumbling down over her pale white breasts, and her wet red lips, still open and wanting more . . .

CHAPTER FORTY-EIGHT

December 23, 10:30 p.m.

"I'M THIRSTY," Sinclair said loudly, and Franklin got up off the crate he was sitting on, picked up the paper cup with the straw, and held it out to him.

Sinclair, whose hands were cuffed, sucked through the straw, greedily. His throat was parched, but no amount of water, he knew, would ever quench it. He was sitting up on the edge of the cot. Ranged around him in the storeroom were mechanical devices the size of blacking boxes, capable of sporadically emitting waves of heat, even though they were supplied with no coal or gas source that he could detect.

It was truly an age of wonders.

There was a nagging pain in the back of his head, where the bullet fragment had grazed his skull, but he was otherwise intact. Around his left ankle he wore an improvised shackle, a chain looped through a pipe on the wall and clamped with a padlock. The room was stacked with boxes, and on the floor off to one side he noted a broad russet stain, which could only have been caused by blood.

Was this where prisoners were normally taken for interrogation, or worse?

He had tried to engage his guard in conversation, but beyond learning his name—Franklin—it had proved hopeless; he wore something in his ears, connected by a string, and buried his face in a gazette with a half-naked girl on its cover. Sinclair had the impression that Franklin was afraid of his prisoner—justifiably so, if it came to that—and that he had been ordered not to exchange any information. But if the opportunity ever presented itself, Sinclair would very much like to repay him for that wound on the back of his head.

The time crawled. His own clothes had been removed—he could see them neatly piled on a crate belonging to a "Dr Pepper," whoever that was—and replaced with an embarrassing pair of flannel pajamas and a pile of woolen blankets. He longed to get up off the cot, reclaim his clothes, and go in search of Eleanor. She was somewhere at this encampment, and he meant to find her.

And then...what? It was like running smack into the proverbial brick wall. What were their prospects, marooned as they were at the end of the earth? Where could they run? And for how long?

There had been boats, he remembered, at the whaling station— a big one, the *Albatros*, that he would never be able to launch on his own. And smaller, wooden whaling boats that might, with some repair, prove seaworthy, but Sinclair was no sailor. And they were surrounded by the most perilous of oceans. His only chance would be to embark in decent weather, and hope to be rescued by the first passing ship they encountered. Apparently, there was some commerce, and if he and Eleanor could acquire modern clothing, and come up with some plausible explanation, they might be able to board another ship and be transported back to civilization again. To lose themselves among people who did not know, nor would ever learn, their terrible secret. Once that much was done, Sinclair could rely on his native wits to carry them along. He had become, of necessity, a great improviser.

The outer door opened with the scraping of metal on ice and a burst of frigid air, refreshing after the stifling heat generated by the little heaters. Once all the coats and gloves and goggles had come off, Sinclair recognized him as the man—Michael Wilde—whom he had first encountered in the blacksmith's shop. There, he had seemed a fairly reasonable chap, though Sinclair remained determined to trust no one.

He was carrying a book bound in black leather, with a gilded binding, in his hand.

"I thought you might want this back," Michael said, extending the book, but Franklin was up like a shot to intervene.

"The chief said not to give him anything. You don't know what he could use, or how he could use it."

"It's just a book," Michael said, letting it be inspected. "Of poetry."

That made Franklin frown. "Looks pretty old," he said, riffling through the pages.

"Probably a first edition," Michael observed, with a glance at Sinclair, to whom he handed it.

"It's by a man named Samuel Taylor Coleridge," Sinclair said, accepting it awkwardly between his cuffed hands. "And so far as I know, it's never hurt a soul."

Michael recognized the need for all the precautions but was embarrassed by it, nonetheless.

"So I saw," Michael said, before reciting the few lines he remembered from school: " 'In Xanadu did Kubla Kahn, a stately pleasure dome decree: Where Alph, the Sacred River, Ran, Through caverns measureless to man, Down to a sunless sea.' I'm afraid that's about all the poetry that ever stuck," he said, but Sinclair looked nonplussed all the same.

"You know his work? Even now?"

"Oh yes," Michael was pleased to inform him. "The Romantic poets are taught in high school and college. Wordsworth, Coleridge, Keats. But I still don't know what the title of this book—*Sibylline Leaves*—means."

Sinclair was smoothing the cover of the book as if he were stroking the top of a dog's sleek head. "The Greek sibyls—seers?— wrote their prophecies on palm leaves."

Michael nodded. He'd been impressed that this should be the book Sinclair held closest to his heart; it had been packed in his gear by the door of the church. "And I saw that *The Rime of the Ancient*

Mariner is in it," he said. "That's still a very famous poem. It shows up on a lot of required reading lists."

Sinclair gazed down at the book, and without opening it, intoned, " 'Like one that on a lonesome road, Doth walk in fear and dread, And having once turned around walks on, And turns no more his head.' "

Franklin was looking utterly stumped.

" 'Because he knows, a frightful fiend,' " Sinclair concluded the passage, " 'Doth close behind him tread.' "

The words seemed to silence the chamber...and chilled Michael to the bone. Was that, he wondered, how Sinclair perceived his own flight? A lonesome journey, dogged by demons every step of the way? The haunted look on his face, the hollows around his eyes, the cracked lips, the blond hair matted to his head as if he'd been drowned—they all testified that it did.

Franklin, apparently afraid that the poetry recital might go on, said to Michael, "You mind if I take a break?"

"Go ahead," Michael replied, and Franklin, tossing his magazine onto the crate, left.

When he was gone, Sinclair put the book aside and leaned back against the wall, while Michael removed the well-thumbed copy of *Maxim* from Franklin's perch and sat down.

"You haven't got anything to smoke, do you?" Sinclair asked, for all the world like one gentleman, lounging in a club, idly asking another.

"Afraid not."

Sinclair sighed, and said, "The guard didn't either. Am I to be deprived of tobacco for a reason, or do men no longer smoke?"

Michael had to smile. "Murphy probably left orders not to give you anything like a cigarette or a cigar. He might have thought you'd try to burn this place down."

"With myself inside it?"

"Granted," Michael said, "it wouldn't be smart. But men do smoke—just not as much anymore. It turns out it causes cancer."

Sinclair looked at him as if he'd just seriously suggested that the moon was made of green cheese. "Well, then," he said, "do they drink?"

"Definitely. Especially here."

Sinclair waited, expectantly, while Michael debated what to do. He knew it would be a gross breach of Murphy's express orders to provide Sinclair with a drink, and Charlotte would probably tell him it was a bad idea, too. Hell, for that matter he knew it was inadvisable. But the man seemed so calm and so rational, and would there be any better way to gain his confidence and get him talking about the long and eventful journey he'd made? Michael still could not imagine how Sinclair and Eleanor had wound up wrapped in chains at the bottom of the sea.

"At the club, we always kept a decanter of very fine port on hand for our guests."

"I can tell you now, we don't have that. Beer is more likely."

Sinclair shrugged amiably. "Beer would not be unwelcome."

Michael looked around the locker. Most of the boxes contained canned goods, or crockery, but somewhere there had to be some Sam Adams crates.

"Don't go anywhere," Michael said, getting up and going into the next aisle, where Ackerley's blood had left a stain on the concrete floor. Stepping around it—and trying not to think about it—he found a Sam Adams box and broke it open. He took out two bottles, and used his Swiss Army knife to pop the caps. Then he went back and handed one to Sinclair. He clinked his own against it, then moved back to his seat.

Sinclair took a long drink, his head back, before studying the dark bottle with its bewigged man on the label. "There was once a great scandal, you know, over a bottle rather like this."

"A scandal?"

"It was a Moselle, served in a black bottle about this size, and set at Lord Cardigan's banquet table."

"Why was that such a problem?"

"Lord Cardigan," Sinclair said, giving the nobleman's name an especially orotund delivery, "was very punctilious about such matters, and he had expressly ordered that only champagne be served."

"When was this?"

"Eighteen forty, if memory serves. At a regimental dinner."

Michael found the conversation increasingly surreal. While Sinclair recounted the rest of the tale—"this is all, you understand, from the popular account, as I was still at Eton at the time"—

Michael kept reminding himself that Sinclair and Eleanor had lived in an era, and a world, that was long gone. What was history to Michael was simply the news of the day to Sinclair.

Sinclair took another drink, with his eyes closed, and then, slowly—very slowly—he opened them again.

Had he just adjusted his vision?

"Thin beer," he said.

"Is it?" Michael replied. "I guess the draft beer you were used to was heavier."

Sinclair didn't answer. He was looking fixedly at Michael. Pondering. He drained the bottle, and put it on the floor beside his shackled ankle.

"Thank you," he said, "all the same."

"No problem." Michael was considering how to steer the conversation in the direction he wanted, when Sinclair took the wheel instead.

"So," he said, "what have you done with Eleanor?"

This was definitely not where Michael would have wanted it to go. But he answered that she was well, and resting, which all seemed innocuous enough.

"That's not what I asked."

The lieutenant's tone had abruptly changed.

"Where is she?" he said. "I want to see her."

And Michael's eyes flicked, involuntarily, to the chain holding him to the pipe on the wall.

"Why won't you let us see each other?"

"That's just the way the Chief of Operations wants it for now."

Sinclair snorted. "You sound like some conscript, reduced to following orders." He took a deep breath, then loudly exhaled. "And I've witnessed what comes of that."

"I'll see what I can do," Michael replied.

"We're just a humble man and wife," Sinclair said, trying another tack, and in a more conciliatory tone, "who have come a very long way together. What possible harm could there be in our seeing each other?"

Man and wife? Michael hadn't known that, and he was sure he would have remembered it if Eleanor had said they were a married couple. Sinclair blinked again, slowly, and Michael noted that he seemed short of breath.

"Does that surprise you," Sinclair said, "that we are husband and wife? Or hadn't she mentioned it?"

"I don't think it came up."

"Didn't come up?" He coughed, shaking his head in disbelief. "Or you didn't want to know?"

"What are you talking about?"

"I'm no fool, so please don't take me for one."

"I'm not taking—"

"I'm an officer in Her Majesty's service, Seventeenth Lancers," he said, a steely resolve in his voice. Lifting his cuffed hands and rattling the chain secured to the wall, he added, "And if I were not at such a disadvantage, you'd soon regret trifling with me."

Michael stood up, surprised again at Sinclair's sudden change of tone. Was it the beer? Did alcohol have some unforeseen effect on him, because of his condition? Or were these mercurial moods a part of his everyday nature? Despite the chain, Michael backed a few more feet away.

"Do you want to call back the guard?" Sinclair taunted him.

"I think it's the doctor you should see," Michael said.

"What?" he said. "The blackamoor again?"

"Dr. Barnes."

"That bitch has already tapped me like a barkeep taps a keg."

What had happened here? What had gone wrong? Sinclair had gone from calm to crazy in a matter of minutes. And there was an unwholesome gleam in his bloodshot eyes.

Franklin ambled back in, his bushy moustache covered with frost. "You two still reading poems to each other?" he said.

Then he saw Michael standing back, and the look on his face, and knew that something was off. "Everything all right?" he asked Michael, and when he didn't get an immediate reply, he said, "What do you want me to do?"

"I think you should get Charlotte. Maybe Murphy and Lawson, too."

Franklin gave Sinclair a wary glance, then went right back out.

Michael had never taken his eyes off Sinclair, who sat on the edge of the cot, staring back with red-rimmed eyes.

And then, returning to the same measured voice he had used to recite the earlier lines, Sinclair intoned, " 'An orphan's curse would drag to hell, A spirit from on high; but oh, more horrible than that,

Is the curse in a dead man's eye!' " The look in his own eye was nothing short of murderous. "Do you know the lines?" he asked.

"No. I don't."

Sinclair rapped his knuckles on the cover of the old book. "You do now," he said, chuckling grimly. "Don't say you weren't warned."

CHAPTER FORTY-NINE

December 24, 8:15 p.m.

EVEN THOUGH SHE HAD TAKEN great care to hide the dreadful evidence, Eleanor soon knew that her secret had been discovered. No one had said anything to her, but all the other bags of blood had been removed from the infirmary. And there had been a wary look in Dr. Barnes's eye.

Eleanor was ashamed—mortified, truth be told, by her dreadful need—but she was also scared. What was she to do when the urge, the terrible thirst, came upon her again? And it would—she knew that it would. Sometimes she could go days, even perhaps a week, without it . . . but the longer she waited, the more urgent it became, and the more she was driven, even against her own will, to slake it.

How could she ever confess to such a desire? In whom could she confide?

She stared out the window of her tiny room, at the frozen square with the flagpole at its center. A tall man in a bulky coat and hood was standing there, looking up at the pewter sky, with something in his gloved hand, something that looked like several strips of bacon.

And although it was hard to recognize anyone, under all the coats and hats and boots, she knew instinctively that this was Michael.

Under the whining of the constant wind, she heard him whistle, loudly, still looking up, and after several seconds, a bird appeared. Perhaps it had been roosting atop the infirmary. It was a dirty gray, with a hooked beak, and it shot almost directly at his head. Michael ducked, and the bird skimmed the top of his hood. She heard him laugh, and it was only then that she realized how long it had been since she had heard anyone laugh like that. It was at once the most foreign, and agreeable, sound she had heard in ages. And she longed to run outside, into the snow and ice, and join it. To laugh, too, at the marauding bird, and to put her face up to the sun—what sun there was—and feel its rays beating on her eyelids.

As she looked on, Michael straightened up again and waved the bacon in the air. Then, as the bird doubled back, he threw the bacon high into the air—the strands separating—and the bird swooped down, catching one in its beak and flying off. The other strips landed on the hard-packed snow, and Michael simply waited—wisely, it seemed—for the bird to come back. It plunked itself down, rather inelegantly, and waddled from one to the next, gobbling them up. Another bird, bigger and brown, dropped down to investigate, but the first one ran at it, squawking, and Michael even tossed a chunk of snow to chase it off. Ah, Eleanor thought, the dusky bird is his favorite. His pet.

He crouched, extending one gloved hand, and the bird came toward him. It pecked at his glove—and although she couldn't see it, she guessed he had some bits of bacon left—and the two of them remained there, like a couple of old friends catching up. The wind ruffled the feathers of the bird and made the sleeves of Michael's coat ripple like tiny waves, but still they sat, and Eleanor felt so suddenly overwhelmed that she couldn't watch any longer.

Her whole life felt like a prison, and she slumped back on the edge of her bed as if she were condemned.

When the knock came on her door, her heart filled with dread. Was it Dr. Barnes, come to confront her about her crime? She didn't answer, but when the knock came again, she said, "You may come in."

The door opened only halfway, and Michael, his hood thrown back, put his head in. "Permission to visit?" he said, and Eleanor replied, "Permission granted, sir." She felt like she'd been given a reprieve. "But I'm afraid there's little I can offer you," she said, "besides a chair."

"I'll take it," Michael said, turning the chair around and straddling it. His cumbersome down coat hung down on either side, and given the size of the room, he was only a few feet away from her—so close, in fact, that she could feel the bracingly cold air radiating from his coat and boots. Oh, how she longed to be free.

———

Michael took a few seconds to unzip his coat and collect his own thoughts. It was always awkward enough, talking to someone under such bizarre circumstances as these, but it was even stranger in light of that harrowingly erotic dream he'd had about her. Even now, it was a little difficult to look her in the eye; the nightmare had seemed all too real.

He was also afraid that their close proximity—the sick bay was so small—was making her self-conscious.

Above the stiff collar of her blue dress, he could see the vein pulsing in her neck. She was looking down at her hands, crossed in her lap; he discreetly glanced at her fingers, but there was no wedding band.

"I saw you outside," she said, "with the bird."

"That's Ollie," he said. "Named after another orphan, Oliver Twist."

"You are familiar with the books of Mr. Dickens?" she asked in amazement.

"To tell you the truth, I've never read it," Michael confessed. "But I've seen the movie."

Now she looked blank again. And why not, he thought... *the movie?*

"My father was quite radical in his ideas," she continued. "He allowed me to attend school as often as possible, and even frequent the parsonage, where there was a library."

Her eyes, he thought, were as green and glistening as spruce needles after a rainfall.

"They must have had two hundred books there," she boasted.

What, he wondered, would she make of a Barnes and Noble?

"I so wanted to join you out there," she said, with a touch of sadness.

"Where?"

"When you were feeding Ollie."

He was about to ask her why she hadn't when he remembered that she was being kept a virtual prisoner. Her nervous pallor showed it. He surveyed the room, but there wasn't so much as a book or magazine here.

"Maybe tonight, late, we can sneak you into the rec hall," he said, "for another piano recital."

"I would like that," she said, but with less enthusiasm than he expected.

"What else would you like?" he said. "For one thing, I can definitely round up some decent reading material for you."

She hesitated, but then, leaning an inch or two forward, she said, "Shall I tell you what I would really like? What I would give anything for?"

He waited . . . afraid, to his own surprise, that it might have to do with Sinclair. How long could he keep that a secret?

"I should like to walk outside—no matter how cold it is—and hold my face up to the sun. I had only a taste of it on my visit to the whaling station. More than anything, I want to see the sun, and feel it on my face again."

"Sun we've got," Michael admitted, "but it isn't exactly warm."

"I know," she said. "And isn't that strange? We've come to a place where the sun never sets, but it offers so little in the way of warmth."

Michael sat very still, considering what she had said, and rolling over in his mind an outlandish idea that had just occurred to him. The consequences, if he got caught, would be bad; Murphy would skin him alive. But the thought of it so thrilled him—what, he wondered, would Eleanor make of it?—that he couldn't resist.

"If I said I could give you what you're asking for," he said, cautiously, "would you agree to follow my instructions to the letter?"

Eleanor looked puzzled. "You can smuggle me outside?"

"That part's easy."

"And make the sun shine hot, even in a place like this?"

Michael nodded. "You know what? I can." He'd been wondering what kind of Christmas present he could give her the next day . . . now he knew.

———————

"So?" Charlotte said, looking into the aquarium tank, where several dead fish floated in various compartments. "You've got some dead fish."

"No, no, not those," Darryl said. "Those were the failures. Look at the *Cryothenia hirschii* and the other antifreeze fish—the ones that are languishing quite comfortably at the bottom of the tank."

Charlotte craned her neck forward, and she could see the pale, almost translucent, fish, some nearly three feet long, their gills beating slowly in the salt water. "Okay, I see them," she said, still unimpressed. "So what?"

"Those fish may be Eleanor Ames's salvation."

Now Charlotte was interested.

"I've mixed their blood with samples of hers, and some of them in the tank are carrying the hybridized blood in their veins right now." He grinned at Charlotte, his spiky red hair electric with discovery. "And as you can see, they're doing fine."

"But Eleanor's not a fish," Charlotte said.

"I'm aware of that. But what's sauce for the goose . . ." he said, beckoning Charlotte over to the lab table, where the microscope was set up and a slide had already been inserted. The video monitor displayed another highly magnified picture of platelets and blood cells, the kind of thing that transported Charlotte back to her med-school classes.

"You're looking at a droplet of concentrated, hemoglobin-rich plasma," he said, snapping on a pair of latex gloves. "My own, in fact."

Charlotte could see the red blood cells, pale pink in color, with little white spots in the center of each circle.

"Now, watch what happens."

Darryl bent low over the microscope and opened the slide tray.

The video monitor went blank. With a syringe he deposited a tiny drop onto the slide, gently wiped it, and replaced it on the stage. "Normally, I'd fix it properly, but we haven't got time." He adjusted the view, and the image on the monitor returned.

And apart from the introduction of more leukocytes—the white cells responsible for defending an organism against disease and infection, along with some companion phagocytes—everything appeared the same. The white cells, larger and more lopsided, actively roamed around, as they were supposed to do, in search of bacteria and foreign agents.

"Okay," Charlotte said, "now we've got a more even mix. What did you just add?"

"A drop of Eleanor's first blood sample. Watch what happens."

For a few seconds, nothing did. And then all hell broke loose. The white cells, with no bacteria to destroy, began to surround and attack the red, oxygen-bearing cells instead, gobbling them up until none were left. It was a wholesale slaughter. And no warm-blooded organism, Charlotte knew, could survive very long with the kind of blood supply that was left.

Charlotte looked over at Darryl in shock, who simply said, "I know. But watch this."

Again, he swiveled the slide tray, and used another syringe to take a sample from one of the many glass vials on the counter—the masking tape on that one, Charlotte noted, was labeled AFGP-5—and then altered the original slide again.

The picture on the video, which had been reduced to a wildly heaving mass of white cells and phagocytes scavenging for further prey, gradually calmed down, like a sea after the storm had passed. Another element had intruded, and those particles moved like ships sailing on the now becalmed waters.

Unattacked.

"Those are the glycoproteins," Darryl said, without waiting for Charlotte to ask, "from the *Cryothenia* specimens. Antifreeze glycoproteins—AFGP, for short. They're the natural proteins that bind to any ice crystals in the bloodstream, immediately arresting their growth. In the fish, they circulate like the oxygen does, within the plasma itself. It's a very neat evolutionary trick, and one that might save Eleanor's life."

"How?"

"If she could tolerate its periodic ingestion—and her blood counts look like she could tolerate anything short of strychnine— she could live a fairly normal life."

"Where?" Charlotte said. "At the bottom of the ocean?"

"No," Darryl said, patiently, "right here. Anywhere. She wouldn't need red cells and hemoglobin any more than the fish do. But there *would* be a couple of caveats," he added, with a helpless shrug. "For one, she'd essentially be a cold-blooded creature, only able to warm herself from external sources—the way, say, that a snake does, by lying in the sun."

Charlotte shuddered at the thought.

"And the second poses a more immediate threat."

"It's worse?"

"You be the judge." Darryl picked up a clean slide, rubbed it vigorously against the dry skin on the back of Charlotte's hand, then put it under the microscope. The living and dead cells appeared on the video monitor. Then, he added a drop of the AFGP-5. Nothing happened; it was a picture of peaceful coexistence.

"This is a good sign?" Charlotte asked, glancing over at Darryl.

He was holding an ice cube between two gloved fingers, his pinkie delicately extended. Gently touching the ice to the surface of the slide, he said, "Keep your eye on the magic monitor."

On the screen, even the tiniest corner of the ice cube was like a glacier, instantly blotting out half the field. Darryl promptly removed it, but the damage had been done. Like a wind blowing across a pond, a million tiny fissures rippled across the surface of the slide, touching each skin cell and radiating outward in all directions until, finally, all activity had stopped. What had been moving and circulating only seconds before was completely still. Frozen. Dead.

"As you can see, once you let ice come into direct contact with tissue, all bets are off."

"I thought the AFGP-5 would prevent that."

"It can prevent ice crystals from propagating in the bloodstream, but not from binding to the skin cells," Darryl said. "That's why antifreeze fish stay well below the ice cap."

"Eleanor should have no problem with that," Charlotte said.

"But can she make sure—absolutely sure—that she never touches ice in any form? That she never takes a cold drink and lets an ice cube graze her lips? That she never slips on a sidewalk and puts her bare hand down on an icy patch of ground? That she never reaches into a freezer, absentmindedly, to remove a bag of frozen vegetables?"

"And if she did?"

"She'd freeze so hard, she'd shatter like glass."

CHAPTER FIFTY

MICHAEL HAD BUNDLED ELEANOR up in so many layers, even her own mother would not have known her. She was just a bundle of clothes, moving slowly across the frozen concourse. Michael kept a lookout in all directions, but there was no one around. That was the thing about going for a walk in Antarctica—you weren't likely to bump into many other pedestrians, even on Christmas Day. As they passed the old meat locker, he hurried her along, then, when they got near Betty and Tina's glaciology lab, he did so again; in the core yard, he could hear a buzz saw going. Eleanor gave him a curious glance, but he shook his head and pulled her along. At the kennel, a couple of the dogs stood up, their tails wagging, hoping to be taken for a run, but fortunately they didn't bark. The lights were on in the marine biology lab, which was a good sign. Michael hoped that Darryl was hard at work, perfecting some solution to Eleanor and Sinclair's problem.

Off in the distance, apart from most of the other modules, he saw his destination, and guided Eleanor toward it. They passed under the wooden trellis, then up the ramp. Even under all the clothes she was shivering.

Michael opened the door, parted the plastic curtains just inside, and ushered her into the botany lab proper. Hot, humid air suddenly engulfed them, and Eleanor gasped in surprise. He drew her farther inside and helped her to unzip her coat and pull off her hat and gloves. Her hair fell loose around her shoulders, but there was a welcome spot of color in her cheeks. And her green eyes shone.

Shrugging off his own outer gear, he said, "They study all kinds of plants in here—the local variety, to the extent that there are any, and foreign. Antarctica's still the cleanest environment on earth for lab work." He brushed away the long hair that was plastered to his forehead. "But the way things are going, it may not be for long."

Eleanor had already wandered away, drawn by the fragrant aroma of fat strawberries, ripening on the vines that hung from the hydroponic pipes that crisscrossed the ceiling. Their green leaves, with the serrated edges, were studded with white flowers and yellow buds, and the berries, wet from the misting tubes, glistened in the artificial light. Ackerley had rigged up the whole lab himself, so it was a mixture of high-tech equipment and jerry-built contraptions, aluminum tubes and rubber hoses, plastic buckets and high-intensity discharge lamps. At the moment, the lamps were on low, but as Eleanor, with her eyes closed, buried her face in the flowering vines, Michael flicked the lamps to high.

Instantly, the whole area was flooded with light, magnified by rows of reflectors that Ackerley had fashioned from coat hangers and tinfoil. The strawberries glowed like rubies, the white petals gleamed, the droplets of water clinging to the green leaves sparkled like diamonds. Eleanor's eyes sprang open, then she shielded them with her hand, laughing.

Michael hadn't heard her so happy since he'd introduced her to the miracle of Beethoven on the stereo.

"Didn't I tell you?" he said.

And she bobbed her head, still smiling, and said, "You did, sir, you did—though I still don't understand how it's been done." She quickly surveyed the glowing lamps and the silver reflectors, before once again protecting her eyes.

"Try a strawberry," Michael suggested. "The cook here uses them to make strawberry shortcake."

"Truly?" she said. "It's all right?"

Michael reached up and plucked a juicy one from the vine and held it toward her lips. She hesitated, a hot flush rising into her cheeks, then bent her head to the berry and neatly bit it in half.

The hot lights played across her hair as she savored it, and the golden rim of her brooch gleamed.

"Finish it," he said, still holding out the remaining half.

She paused, her lips moist from the berry, and their eyes met. His heart was overwhelmed by such a confusion of feelings—tenderness, uncertainty, desire—that he could barely hold her gaze.

But she held his, as she leaned forward and took the rest of the fruit into her mouth. Her teeth grazed the tips of his fingers before she withdrew, delicately plucking the green crown of the strawberry from her lips. He stood, transfixed.

And she said, "Thank you, Michael."

Was this the first time she'd used his name—for real and not just in a dream?

"That was a great treat."

"It's a Christmas present."

"It is?" she said, surprised. "Is this Christmas Day?"

He nodded, his shoulders positively aching from wanting to reach out and embrace her. But he didn't dare. That was not why he'd brought her to the lab. That was not in the game plan. There was no future in that.

So why did he have to keep reminding himself?

"At Christmas, we would decorate the house with mistletoe and ivy and evergreens," she said, meditatively. "My mother would make a pudding, stick a sprig of holly in the top, and douse it with brandy. When my father touched a match to it, the whole room would blaze like a bonfire."

After a few seconds, she turned around and stepped out of the glow from the lamps. "The light is very hot."

She moved down one of the aisles, the long blue dress with its billowing sleeves and high white collar emphasizing her slender frame; her fingers trailed across the rows of tomato plants on trusses, the lettuces and onions and radishes all being grown on tabletops and in shallow bowls of clear liquid.

"There is no soil," she said, over her shoulder. "How does anything grow?"

"It's called hydroponics," he said, following her up the aisle. "All the minerals and nutrients that the plants need are mixed into the water supply. Add light and air and you're done."

"It's miraculous," she said, "and rather like the hothouse at the Great Exhibition. My father took me there, with my sister Abigail."

"When was that?"

"Eighteen fifty-one," she said, as if it were generally known, "at the Crystal Palace in Hyde Park."

The shock never entirely wore off.

There was another bank of lights off to the rear, illuminating a tiny garden of roses and lilies and Ackerley's prized orchids.

"Oh, how beautiful," Eleanor said, stepping into the narrow aisle surrounded by the brilliant red roses and the multicolored orchids, on their long, crooked stems. Even without the soil, there was the hot, humid scent of a jungle. Eleanor unfastened the top button on her collar, but no more, and breathed deeply.

"I could not have imagined a place like this," she said, taking in the riot of color and scent, "in a country so remote and cold. Who takes care of all these plants? Is it you?"

"Oh, no," Michael said, "they'd be dead in a week if I were in charge." But how could he possibly explain, to her of all people, what had happened to Ackerley? And what would she say if he did? Would she then confess to him her own undeniable, but secret, need?

If there was one thing he knew, it was that he never wanted to hear words to that effect pass her lips.

"We all pitch in," he said, to provide some sort of answer. "But most of it's programmed by computers and timers."

He realized that none of this would make any sense to her. "It's mechanical," he added, simply, and she seemed content...but reflective, too. Even as she pressed her face to the roses to inhale their aroma, he could tell her thoughts had entered a darker channel. Her brow was furrowed, and her head held still.

"Michael," she finally said, without finishing her thought.

"Yes?"

After another moment of deliberation, she plunged ahead. "I can't help but feel that there's something you're not telling me."

She has *that* right, Michael thought, but there were so many things he wasn't telling her that he wouldn't have known where to start.

"Does it have to do with Lieutenant Copley?"

Michael hesitated; he didn't want to lie, but he was forbidden to tell her the truth. "We've been looking for him."

"You know that he will come looking for me. If he hasn't already, he soon will."

"I'd expect that," he said, "from your husband."

She looked at him intently, as if her suspicions—or at least some of them—had been confirmed. "Why would you say that?"

"Sorry, I just assumed—"

"In Sinclair's eyes, that may be so. But in the eyes of God, we are most assuredly not. For reasons I can't explain, it could never happen."

Why her peremptory tone should have pleased him so, he did not wish to dwell on. But since the topic had been introduced, he felt he couldn't let the opportunity go.

"But wouldn't you want to be reunited . . . assuming, of course, that he's alive and well?"

She studied one of the yellow orchids intently, rubbing her fingers on the waxy leaves.

He was surprised that she wavered at all.

"Sinclair was, and always shall be, the great love of my life."

Her fingers caressed the golden yellow petals themselves.

"But the life we are forced to lead together cannot be sustained . . . nor should it be."

Michael knew of course what she was referring to, but kept silent.

"And over the years, I fear that he has fallen in love with something else—something that holds him in its sway more powerfully than I can ever do."

The misters suddenly went off, sending a fine spray of cool water into the air above their heads, but Eleanor didn't move.

"What?" Michael asked.

And she replied, "Death."

The misters stopped again, and she turned to one side, as if ashamed by what she'd just admitted.

"He has been steeped in it so long that he has learned to live with it. He keeps it by him at all times, like a loyal hound. He wasn't always like that," she quickly added, as if regretting her betrayal. "Not when we met, in London. He was kind and attentive and always so eager to find ways to amuse me." That last caused her to smile.

"Why are you smiling?"

"Oh, just remembering. A day at Ascot, a dinner at his club in London. Poor Sinclair—I think he was often just one step ahead of his creditors."

"But didn't you tell me once that he came from a family of aristocrats?"

"His father was an earl—and Sinclair would have been one, too, one day—but he had called upon the family fortune on too many occasions already. His father, I believe, was sorely disappointed in him."

The mist had settled like a fine veil atop her hair.

"And his prospects . . . they were altered in the Crimea. Everyone who went there was changed by it, everyone who survived was damaged. It was impossible not to be."

She brushed the mist from her hair with the back of one hand.

"You cannot bathe in blood every night," she said, "and emerge the next morning unstained."

Michael couldn't help but think of all the wars that had passed since her time, and all the soldiers who had struggled, with that same futility, to put the horrors behind them. Some things never changed.

Without looking at him, she abruptly said, "How long do you think I'm to be kept here?"

To dodge the question he said, "Where would you want to go?"

"Oh, that's simple enough. I want to go home, to Yorkshire. I know that no one in my family will be there, and that many, many things will have changed . . . but still, it can't all be gone, can it? The hills must still be there, and the trees and the streams. The old shops in the village will be gone, but new ones will have taken their place. The town square, the church, the train station, with its tearoom and the smell of hot scones and butter . . ."

Michael wondered, as she spoke, if any of it was left, if the hills hadn't been leveled for an apartment complex and the train station hadn't been shuttered for years.

"I just don't want to die in a place like this. I don't want to die in the ice." Her head lowered, and her shoulders shivered at the thought.

Michael put out a hand and turned her gently toward him. "That won't happen," he said. "I promise you."

Tears were welling in her eyes. She looked up at him, desperate to believe.

"But how can you make such a promise?"

"I can," he said, "and I will. I promise I won't leave here without you."

"You're going?" she said, a note of alarm in her voice. "Where are you going?"

"Back home, to the United States."

"When?"

He knew what she was afraid of—not just dying in the ice, but of succumbing to her need before she could see her old home again. Even now, he thought, she's probably resisting, with every ounce of her strength, a nearly irresistible urge.

"Soon," he said, "soon," and he gathered her into his arms. Beads of moisture still clung to her hair.

She came willingly, pressing her cheek against his chest. "You don't understand," she said, softly, "and if you did, you would never make so rash a promise."

But Michael knew that he would.

He was reminded of another promise he had made, on a mountainside in the Cascades. And just like that one, he meant to keep it, come hell or high water. "I won't leave you behind," he swore.

CHAPTER FIFTY-ONE

December 26, 9:30 a.m.

SINCLAIR HAD MADE a studied assessment of his two jailers, trying to decide which one it would be wiser to move against.

While the fellow named Franklin was plainly the less intelligent of the two, he was also the more wary. Like a private in the army, he took his orders seriously and didn't like to think about them very much. He'd been told to stay clear of the prisoner, and he did. He even refused to engage in conversation, keeping his nose buried in one of those scandalous gazettes for the duration of each of his shifts.

The one named Lawson, on the other hand, was more intelligent, more sociable, and in general more curious. He was fascinated, Sinclair could see, by an unexpected visitor from another time and, despite the fact that he'd no doubt been given the same orders Franklin had, he thought nothing of defying them. When he came in to conduct his watch, Franklin couldn't leave fast enough, and Lawson positively settled in, stretching out his legs and leaning back against a crate for a nice long talk. Sinclair had noted that his boots looked very sturdy, with thick soles and heavy laces, and were in far better condition than his own riding boots, one of which had been torn by the sled dog.

Today, Lawson had brought with him a large book with many colored pictures in it. Sinclair could not see what it was, but he knew he would find out in good time. Lawson could not resist talking. After a few minutes, during which Sinclair silently waited him out, Lawson finally said, "Everything okay with you?"

Sinclair gave him a puzzled, but utterly benign, look.

"Oh, sorry. That just means: Is everything all right? You need me to call the doctor or anything?"

The doctor? Surely that would be the last request Sinclair would ever make. "No, no—not at all." Sinclair gave him a forlorn smile. "It's the enforced idleness, that's all. Our friend Franklin provides little in the way of company."

Why not flatter this fool?

"Oh, Franklin's a pretty good guy," Lawson said. "He's just following orders."

Sinclair chuckled. "If there's a swifter route to damnation than that, I'd like to know what it is." He knew that such pronouncements only served to pique Lawson's interest. His fingers, he noted, drummed on the cover of the big book.

With a weary pro forma air, Sinclair asked about Eleanor and her welfare—no one ever told him anything of substance, but he asked, nonetheless—and received the usual vague reply; on this subject, even Lawson apparently knew enough to keep mum. But just what *were* they keeping from him? Sinclair wondered. Was she truly well? How could she be? How could she be satisfying the peculiar need that neither of them could ever confess to anyone? Sinclair did not know how much longer he could last himself. And he'd recently had the benefit of the slaughtered seal.

But Lawson eventually turned the topic, as Sinclair knew he would, to his own interests. His fascination with Sinclair's odyssey had become evident over their past few sessions together, and the purpose of that big book became clear, too. It was an atlas, and there were little colored pieces of paper attached to the edge of certain pages. It was to these pages that Lawson threw the book open in his lap.

"I've been trying to map out your journey," he said, like some schoolboy swotting for an examination, "from Balaclava to Lisbon, and I think I've got most of it."

The man was a born cartographer.

"But I got a little lost around Genoa. When you and Eleanor left, did you sail across the Ligurian Sea to Marseilles or take the overland route?"

Sinclair remembered every step of the journey quite well, even after all this time, but he pretended to be confused. In fact, they had traveled by coach—he recalled stopping at a public house in San Remo, not far from Genoa, where he had won a large sum at the game of telesina, a local variation on poker. Another player had accused him of cheating, and Sinclair had of course demanded satisfaction. The man had assumed he meant a duel, and though that was accomplished the same night—Sinclair ran him through with his cavalry saber—true satisfaction took a bit longer. When Sinclair had finished with him, he washed the blood from his face in a fragrant grove of lemon trees, before returning to Eleanor at the inn where they were staying.

"I'm not sure I recall the name of the town," Sinclair said now, as if struggling, "but it was in Italy—it might have been San Remo. Can you find it there?"

He saw Lawson bend his head closer to the map and try to trace some route with his finger; he had one of those silly kerchiefs on his head, like some common seaman. It would only be a matter of time before Sinclair was able to persuade him to come closer and show him the map itself.

Then . . . he would shake off his chains and reclaim his stolen bride.

———————

"Tomorrow," Murphy repeated, leaning on the back of his desk chair. "The supply plane's coming tomorrow, at eight in the morning," and he ran one hand nervously through his hair again. The other hand clutched a red marker, with which he had just circled the next day's date on the whiteboard mounted on the wall behind his desk. "And you're going back on it," he said to Michael.

"What are you talking about?" Michael protested. "My NSF pass is good until the end of the month."

"We've got another massive low-pressure system moving in,

and by the time it's passed, the crevassing will be even worse out there than it is already. The plane won't be able to land."

"Then I'll take the next one out."

"Where the hell do you think you are?" Murphy said. "There's not gonna be a next plane out, not till maybe February."

Michael's mind was reeling. How could he possibly leave the next day? He'd made a promise to Eleanor, and he was not about to break it. He looked over at Darryl, sitting beside him, but all Darryl could do was return a sympathetic glance.

"What are you planning to do with Eleanor—and now Sinclair?" Michael said. "I'm the one who found them in the first place."

"And don't I wish you hadn't. Don't I wish I was rid of them both."

"No one has their confidence the way I do."

"Oh really?" Murphy replied. "Last time you visited Sinclair, I seem to recall you calling for reinforcements. What happened? Your trust break down?"

Michael still regretted that, but as Darryl jumped in to explain about some promising blood work he'd been doing in his lab, his thoughts kept racing ahead. Was this the time to broach his idea? When would he have another chance? Interrupting Darryl's monologue, he blurted out, "Then they should both go back with me."

Darryl stopped talking and turned toward him, while Murphy shook his head in exasperation. "And how do you suggest we arrange that?" he said, throwing up his hands. "This ain't the bus station in Paducah. The plane doesn't land—at pole, for Christ's sake—and pick up three passengers when the manifest calls for just one."

"I know that," Michael said, "but bear with me." He was fitting the pieces of the plan together even as he sat there. "Danzig's wife knows he died, but she doesn't know when to expect the body to be returned. Right?"

"Right. Somehow I never got around to calling her back to tell her that he'd turned into a zombie and was floating around somewhere under the polar ice cap. Kind of a hard call to make, don't you think?"

"And what about Ackerley?" Michael persisted. "Does his

mother know when his body is supposed to be returned to the States?"

"I'm not sure she knows it will be," Murphy said, starting to sound intrigued. "I told you, she was pretty out of it."

"Let me think," Michael said, putting his head down and concentrating with all his might. "Let me think." It was outlandish, but it was all coming together in his head. And it could, conceivably, work. "Danzig's wife—"

"Maria," Murphy supplied. "Maria Ramirez."

"She works for the county coroner's office in Miami Beach."

"Yeah, that's where she met Erik. He was driving a hearse in those days. In fact, he once told me—"

"Tell Maria that I'm accompanying her husband's body, and Ackerley's, to Miami Beach."

"But you're not," Darryl said, perplexed. "Danzig's never going to turn up again, except maybe in my nightmares."

"And frankly, she didn't want him to," Michael replied. "Remember, she said that he was never happier than when he was down here? And that, if he'd had his way, that's where he'd have wanted to be buried?"

"Yeah, but I told her Antarctic burials are prohibited by law," Murphy said.

"But what about Ackerley? You're going to dispose of his remains right here, aren't you?" Michael persisted. "Or were you planning to send back a corpse with a bullet in its head?" Murphy squirmed in his chair, and that's when Michael knew he had him. "A bullet from your gun, no less?"

Darryl frowned quizzically at that, and asked Murphy, "Now that it's come up, what *did* you do with Ackerley's remains? I know he asked to be cremated, but that would have been a contravention of the Antarctic protocols."

"That's right, it would have been," Murphy said, staring Darryl straight in the eye and holding it. "Officially, Ackerley went down a crevasse while doing his fieldwork."

Michael was relieved to hear it. "That's perfect."

"I'm still not following," Murphy said.

"Don't you see? If we want to, we can put two body bags on that plane, both of them fully accounted for. But the bodies inside don't have to be the same ones as the names on the tags."

Michael could see that the light had gone on in Murphy's head. He just had to press ahead convincingly with his case.

"Eleanor and Sinclair may not be able to leave the Point as *passengers* on that plane, but they can leave as *cargo*. Just use some of that bureaucratic pull you've got to book me—and them—back to Santiago, and from there on to Florida."

There was a silence in the room, punctuated only by the ticking of the clock. Finally, Murphy broke it by saying, "But it's a nine-hour flight just from Santiago to Miami. They'll die in transit."

"Why would they?" Michael said. "They've suffered far worse. Try a century of suspended animation. If they could live through that, this would be a piece of cake."

"It's different now," Murphy countered. "They're alive and kicking, and they've got a big problem that you seem to be conveniently forgetting."

"That's what I was trying to address," Darryl said, "before I was so rudely interrupted."

Michael slumped in his chair, more than happy to have someone else carry the ball a few yards downfield. But he quickly realized that Darryl wasn't looking for a first down; he was heading straight for the end zone. After proudly describing some of his laboratory breakthroughs with the *Cryothenia hirschii*, he strongly hinted that he might have found a cure—"or at least as close as we're going to come to one"—for the disease afflicting both Eleanor and Sinclair. If Michael understood him correctly, he was suggesting that he could extract the antifreeze glycoproteins from his fish specimens and transfuse them into the humans' bloodstream. Doing so apparently allowed the blood to carry oxygen and nutrients without constantly needing to be replenished by foreign supplies of hemoglobin. It seemed irrational, it seemed insane, it even seemed impossible—but it was also the first, and only, slender thread on which Michael could hang any hope. Michael would take it.

"It all sounds pretty cockamamie to me," Murphy said, "but I'm not the scientist here. How do you know it would work?"

"I don't," Darryl replied. "So far, the recombinant blood has been tolerated by the fish. But as for Eleanor and Sinclair, that's another question."

And there wasn't time, Michael reflected, to do any trial runs.

"But you've got to remember," Darryl reiterated, in portentous tones, "they're going to wind up in the same predicament my fish are. If their tissue touches ice, they're goners."

For the next half hour, the three of them debated and discussed how all the elements of the scheme might work. Murphy, by his own admission, had not been dutifully recording all the events of the day in the NSF logbooks—"I just couldn't find the right way to explain how corpses were coming back to life"—and he was particularly worried about what Michael had already told his editor. Michael assured him that he had already unwound that knot—"though it means I may never be trusted with another decent assignment for the rest of my days"—and they called a halt only when a conference call about the oncoming storm came in from McMurdo Station. Murphy waved them out of his office as he recited the barometric pressure readings recorded at Point Adélie in the past twenty-four hours.

In the hall outside, Michael and Darryl stopped to take a breath and contemplate everything that had just been said. Michael was so on edge he felt like he had electric current running through his veins.

"So, this transfusion," he said. "How soon can you try it?"

"I just need another hour or two in the lab. Then I'll have the serum ready."

"But we're surrounded by ice," Michael said, still fearful.

"Which they're never going to touch. They're going straight from the infirmary and the meat locker into the body bags. What's the alternative? You plan to oversee the procedure on your own, in Miami?"

That, Michael knew, would never work.

"If they're going to have a bad reaction," Darryl went on, "we'd better know it now, before they're zipped into the bags and shipped out."

"Eleanor first?"

"Sure," Darryl said. "From what I know of Sinclair, he may need more in the way of persuading."

Darryl was already turning away, when Michael took his elbow to stop him. "You think it will work?" he said. "You think Eleanor will be cured?"

Darryl hesitated, as if weighing his words carefully, then said, "If all goes well, I think that Eleanor—and Sinclair—will be able to live reasonably normal lives." He held Michael's gaze, as Murphy had earlier held his, and added, "But that's only if you consider living like a snake, who has to warm itself by lying in the sun, to be normal. With the help of an occasional booster shot, Eleanor will no longer feel the need she does now. But she will carry this contagion to the end of her days."

The words weighed like stones on Michael's heart.

"But so will Sinclair," Darryl added, as if that made things better. "They'll pose no danger to each other."

Michael mutely nodded, as if he, too, saw the wisdom and symmetry in that. But it didn't make the stones any less heavy.

CHAPTER FIFTY-TWO

December 26, 11:20 a.m.

"UNDER ASSUMED NAMES," Sinclair was saying. "We always traveled under assumed names, and changed them with some regularity. It became a game of sorts, choosing who we would be called in San Remo, or in Marseilles, or wherever it was we stayed after that."

Lawson was transfixed, and Sinclair had taken some pains to relate the more dramatic episodes from their journey—the midnight rides through mountain gorges, the narrow escapes from suspicious authorities, the high-stakes card play that had generally paid for their travels. But he had carefully skirted the more appalling aspects—most notably the constant quest for a fresh supply of blood. Certainly no need to go into that. And time was running short, anyway. In a couple of hours, the watch would change, and the more-wary Franklin would come back on duty. If Sinclair was to make his move, and gain the maximum amount of time before anyone had discovered his escape, he had to act now.

"From Marseilles, we continued west. In Seville, Eleanor fell ill, and I thought the sea air might revive her, so we traveled to a small town on the Gulf of Cadiz. Its name escapes me, but if I heard it again . . ."

"Was it Ayamonte?" Lawson said, consulting the atlas.

"No, that wasn't it," Sinclair said. "It was something longer. And it was on the way up the coast, toward Lisbon."

"Isla Cristina?"

"No," Sinclair said, tilting his head to one side, as if straining to remember. "But I do believe that if I saw it there . . ."

Holding the book open to the correct page, Lawson got up from the crate and came toward Sinclair—who readied himself.

He laid the book across Sinclair's lap, and before he was able to stand back again, Sinclair said, in his most innocent tone, "Where exactly are we on this map?"

"Right here," Lawson said, pointing to a yellow line that he had traced across the page, and while his eyes were trained on the book, Sinclair lifted the beer bottle he had been concealing and cracked him smartly across the back of the skull.

Lawson went down onto his knees, but if Sinclair was hoping for him to be knocked out cold, he was disappointed. That damned kerchief must have interfered. He cracked him again, and the bottle smashed, leaving a bloody gash, but Lawson was still conscious and trying to crawl away. Sinclair had to act quickly; his chain was fastened to the pipe on the wall and he had only a few feet of slack. Looping his cuffed hands over Lawson's head, he dragged him backwards toward the cot; fortunately, the man was sufficiently dazed by the blow that he could not put up much of a fight. Sinclair tightened the cuffs around his windpipe and pulled up. Lawson's hands went to the metal around his throat and he tried desperately to claw it away, but Sinclair only leaned back harder, holding on and choking him until his feet—in the boots that Sinclair had been admiring—stopped scrabbling at the floor and his hands dropped limply to his sides. Even then, Sinclair held on for several seconds more, just for good measure, before easing up on the cuffs and letting Lawson's head loll forward.

The atlas, oddly, had remained open on his lap the whole time.

As the body slumped to the floor, Sinclair pushed the book away, and knelt. He put his ear to the chest and heard the heart still pumping; he had been in this position before, and for a moment the terrible urge to take advantage of the moment rose up in him like a blood tide. But he had neither the time, nor the desire, to kill the man. He put his mouth to Lawson's, and blew into it, just as the seamen had done with the soldiers who had drowned in the botched landing at Calamita Bay. Then he pushed down gently on the abdomen until he saw it rise, then fall, then rise again. Before Lawson could come to again, Sinclair rifled through his pockets and dug out the keys to the shackles. It was tricky work, undoing them all, especially as Sinclair's own heart was already beating faster at the prospect of freedom, new boots... and finding Eleanor.

December 26, 11:30 a.m.

"Are you trying to dissuade me?" Eleanor asked, looking into Michael's eyes.

"No, of course not," he said, inching his chair closer to the bedside where she sat, and clutching her hands more firmly. "It's just that there's a risk involved—a considerable risk—and I'm afraid for you."

She was deeply touched by his concern, but her life, for so long, had been nothing but risk and mortal danger that this was nothing new. She lifted one hand up and placed it against his cheek. "The choice is mine, and I accept it. If I'm going to live on, I don't want it to be in the shadows anymore. I want a life I'm not ashamed of. Can you understand that?"

She could see that he did understand, but he looked, if anything, more apprehensive than she felt herself. After all that she had been through, over such a span of time, even death held no great fear for her. With everything she had ever known—her family, her friends—already gone, how much lonelier could her life become?

And as for Sinclair... even if they were reunited, what would become of them? All that they could really do—she knew this in her very bones—was share their own profound loneliness and isolation from the rest of humanity.

"Should I go and get Darryl and Charlotte then?" Michael asked, and she nodded her agreement.

Michael left, and Eleanor remained, to sort through a tumult of emotions. Despite herself, she recognized that some sense of hope, of redemption, had been rekindled in her. And though she was reluctant to admit it, she knew it had something to do with the way that Michael Wilde looked at her.

And the way she found herself looking back.

A few minutes later, the door to the sick bay opened again, and this time Michael was accompanied by the others. Darryl, with his red hair sticking up like the comb on a rooster, was carrying a clear bag of fluid and Charlotte had a tray with several items on it—cotton balls, needles, alcohol, and a kind of bandage that conveniently adhered to the skin. Eleanor had seen the tray several times and knew the protocols by heart.

Charlotte took the chair that Michael had vacated and put the tray on the bed. Eleanor rolled up the billowing sleeve of her dress and watched as Charlotte applied the rubber tourniquet.

"Michael told you about the dangers of touching ice?" Darryl said, as Charlotte filled the syringe, an unusually large one, from the bag.

"Several times."

"Good. Great," he said, nervously. "And you might feel a certain flushing at first, from the sudden glycoprotein overload—it's a highly concentrated solution—but I think it should pass pretty quickly."

Charlotte shot him a glance and swabbed a spot on Eleanor's forearm.

"I am prepared for anything," Eleanor said. "And I have complete faith in my doctor."

Which was true. After her initial shock, she had come to respect Dr. Barnes for her bold but friendly nature, and her reassuring bedside manner. That was something Eleanor had seen in Florence Nightingale, too—an ability to reach out to any patient and communicate a sense of calm and caring. Of course, in her own day, no one like Charlotte could ever have become a doctor—even if her sex had not barred her, her color most certainly would have done—but in this modern world that Eleanor might be about to join, many unimagined things were clearly possible.

The prick of the needle was barely noticeable, but the immediate effects of the fluid entering her veins was pronounced. Far from feeling flushed, she experienced a strange cooling sensation, like the trickle of a mountain stream running just beneath her skin. She shivered, and Charlotte looked up at her while still holding the syringe and said, "Are you all right?"

"Yes," Eleanor said. "I think so." But was she? What would happen when the chill, which she could feel creeping up her arm, descended upon her heart?

"What are you feeling?" Darryl asked, and Michael, speechless, simply knelt by the edge of the bed, studying her face.

"It's like nothing I've ever felt before," Eleanor replied. "A bit, perhaps, like stepping into a cool bath."

Beads of sweat—a cold sweat—dotted her brow as Charlotte withdrew the needle and hastily swabbed the puncture wound. "Maybe you should lie down," Charlotte said, dropping the syringe on the tray and helping Eleanor to rest her head back on the pillow.

The room was swimming around her, and she tried closing her eyes, but that only made it worse. Opening them again, she saw Michael hovering above her, and she focused her gaze on his face. He had taken her hand, and she could feel the nervous sweat from his palm dampening her own.

Charlotte and Darryl stood behind him, also looking anxious, and Eleanor was moved that she had already been able to find three such friends in this strange and alien place. It bolstered both her hope and her incentive to live. Perhaps the loneliness that she had felt from the moment that she and Sinclair had absconded from the Barrack Hospital in Turkey might not be her permanent lot, after all. Perhaps there *was* an alternative. The internal chill had spread across her shoulders and into her breast, like the petals of a night flower blooming beneath her skin. She shivered again, and Michael quickly fetched a blanket from the closet and tucked it around her. She was inevitably reminded of the voyage aboard the *Coventry*, the ill-fated trip that had ultimately brought her to the Southern Pole, and the night that Sinclair had bundled her in every blanket and coat he could find...before he was attacked by the crew.

Before she, too, was dragged from the bunk and wrapped in a chain on the rolling deck.

A warm compress was placed over her eyes, and as she lay there, she wondered under what circumstances she might emerge— if she emerged at all—from this untried experiment.

Drawing Darryl toward the door, Michael whispered, "What's happening to her? Is there something we should do?"

"I'm not sure there's anything we *can* do at this point," Darryl replied. "The injection should take some time—a half hour, maybe an hour?—before fully circulating in her bloodstream and taking effect. We'll know better then."

Charlotte stepped to the bedside and took her pulse. "It's a bit fast," she reported, "but strong." Then she slipped a blood-pressure cuff around Eleanor's upper arm, inflated it, and watched as the LED numbers flashed. Eventually, they settled at 185 over 120, which even Michael knew was too high.

"We'll have to bring that down, if it doesn't come down on its own," she said, putting the stethoscope to Eleanor's chest and checking her heartbeat. "How are you feeling?" she asked.

"Light-headed," Eleanor said.

Charlotte nodded, pursing her lips. "Just try to relax," she said, removing the blood-pressure cuff. "And rest."

"Yes," she replied, her voice already fading, "Dr. Barnes."

"Call me Charlotte. I think we're on a first-name basis by now, honey." Slipping a call button under her hand, she said, "If you need me, just press this. I'll be right next door."

Charlotte took the tray from the bed and herded them all from the room. Michael took one look back and saw Eleanor, the white compress draped across her eyes, her long brown hair brushing the rim of the ivory brooch.

"Come on," Charlotte murmured. "I'm sure she'll be all right."

But Michael detected a certain lack of conviction.

"Maybe I should keep watch," he suggested.

"You've got packing to do. Get to it."

CHAPTER FIFTY-THREE

December 26, 12:45 p.m.

FOR MICHAEL, packing was easy. All his clothes just went straight from the dresser drawer into the duffel bag, where they were mashed down as compactly as possible. It was the camera gear that took time. He had learned, from bitter experience, that unless every lens and filter and strap went back in its proper case, he might not be able to lay his hand on it when the perfect photo op presented itself. Writing was about deliberation; photography was about serendipity.

All he left out was one tripod and his trusty old Canon S80. He didn't want to leave the base without a few last shots of Ollie, enjoying whatever snack he could bring him from the holiday buffet. And the weather, for a change, was perfectly still—sunny and bright. The calm, Michael knew, before the storm due the next afternoon.

Clearing the top of the dresser, he picked up Danzig's walrus-tooth necklace and slipped it around his own neck. He didn't plan to take it off again until he could hand it to Erik's widow in person.

In Miami.

Where he'd be, with a whole lot of luck, in a couple of days.

He found himself standing stock-still by his bunk, simply contemplating the enormity of everything that lay before him. Everything that had to be done. From inoculating Sinclair, to convincing them both that this was their only way out of Antarctica—sealed in bags, transported on an airplane—a flying machine yet!—over thousands of miles in a matter of hours. And where to? A country where neither of them had ever set foot, in a century they barely knew. There were so many parts of the plan that they would find impossible to believe, he didn't even know where to start. And so many parts that he himself could barely accept—was he truly going to chaperone the two into the modern-day world?—that a kind of mental paralysis threatened to descend. *The journey of a thousand miles begins with one step,* he reminded himself. Confronted by so many variables, all he could do was attend to the small things, one at a time.

When the door opened and Darryl came in, he was tucking a camera case into the bulging duffel.

"Any word about Eleanor?" Darryl asked, plunking himself down in the desk chair.

"Not since we left."

Darryl was eating a mammoth éclair. "You should check out the commons. Lots of leftover Christmas pastry. The hot punch is still going, too."

"Yeah, maybe I will, before we head over to the meat locker."

Darryl nodded, licking the yellow cream off his fingertips. "You told Eleanor yet about the rest of the plan?"

Michael shook his head. "I'm still looking for a better way to say body bag."

"If you think that's going to be hard, try airplane."

"I'm way ahead of you there."

"Charlotte's got a nice supply of tranquilizers in her medicine chest. I'm sure she could arrange for them both to get a heavy dose."

Michael could certainly subscribe to that. His only hope was that Sinclair's belligerence would evaporate once he understood that this was the only way he and Eleanor could be rescued from their immediate plight.

And would he trust Michael enough to go along?

Darryl kicked off his boots, got up, and crawled into his lower bunk. "Eating makes me sleepy," he said, stretching out his legs. "Come wake me whenever you want to go over to see Prince Charming."

"Will do."

Darryl stretched his legs out. "By the way," he added, "you do know that what you're doing is crazy, right?"

Michael nodded, while yanking the zipper halfway up the duffel.

"Glad to hear it. 'Cause if you didn't, I'd have to start worrying about you."

––––––––––

Eleanor awoke with a start, the picture of Miss Nightingale's reproachful face still before her. She had never overcome the sense of guilt at betraying the great lady—and the profession itself—by absconding with Sinclair, and she often dreamt of making amends somehow.

Her limbs felt cold and dead, even under the blanket, and she rubbed her arms vigorously to get the blood circulating. Sitting up, she gave herself a second to get her bearings, then pushed the blanket aside and stood up beside the bed. She was about to stamp her feet on the floor, too, but then thought better of it—the sound might bring Dr. Barnes running from the next room, and she didn't want company, much less medical attention, just yet.

Had she been cured? And if she had, would she feel the way she did—slightly numbed, a trifle chilly—forever? Was that the price?

Wrapping the blanket around her shoulders like a shawl, she stepped to the window and drew back the black curtains. It was preternaturally still outside, and it occurred to her that this might be the calm before the storm. The snow on the ground glinted in the sharp, cold rays of the sun. She had to step back and shield her eyes from the glare.

And then something crossed her field of vision, a flash of red—and she stepped closer again.

It came again, moving swiftly, surreptitiously, down the snowy concourse, looking this way and that. She put her face closer to the window and peered out . . . and the figure stopped, raised a hand to shield its own eyes, and peered back.

It was Sinclair, the red coat with the white cross billowing out over his cavalry uniform.

Before she could even raise a hand to signal him, he had run across the snow, skidding and nearly falling several times, and she could hear the door to the building flying open down the hall. She hurried on tiptoe to the infirmary entry, and when he saw her she put a finger to her lips and waved for him to follow her inside.

Once there, she closed the door to the hall, and had no sooner turned around again than he had clasped her in his arms.

"I knew I would find you!" he whispered. He quickly surveyed the room, taking in the cabinets filled with medical supplies and said, "This is the field hospital?"

"Yes," she said.

"And this is where they've been keeping you? Are you all right?"

"Yes, yes," she said, gently trying to extricate herself from his too-eager grasp. "But how did you get here?"

He brushed the question aside, and said, "We have to go."

"Where, Sinclair? Where would we go?" She grabbed his hands and stared into his bloodshot, half-mad eyes. "These people can help us," she said, imploringly. "They have helped me already, and they can help you, too."

"Helped you? How?"

"They have a medicine," she said, "a medicine that can help us . . . change."

His breath was short and ragged. She knew he was in the grip of the terrible thirst. She cast her eyes wildly around the room, and then settled on the fridge, where she had found the bag of blood. Surely that would be where the other bag, the bag with the medicine in it, was stored.

"Wait," she said, moving to the refrigerator and flinging it open. A bag identical to the one that Charlotte had used to fill the syringe— perhaps the very same one—sat on a wire shelf; a label on it read AFGP-5. She prayed it was the right one.

"Come on," Sinclair urged. "Whatever this is, we haven't time for it."

But Eleanor ignored him. If she could save him, she would, and she had seen the procedure with the needle done enough times that she was confident she could do it herself.

"Take off your coat—quickly!"

"What are you saying? Have you lost your mind?"

"Just do as I say. I'm not moving an inch until you do."

He yanked the coat off in exasperation.

She took out the bag and found a fresh needle in the cabinet.

"Roll up your sleeve!" she said, filling the syringe.

"Eleanor, please, there is no hope, or help, for us. We are what we are."

"Be quiet," Eleanor whispered. "The doctor might hear you."

She swabbed his skin with the alcohol, patted his arm to bring up a vein, then pressed the syringe, as she had seen Charlotte do, to remove any air. "Stay very still," she said, inserting the needle and slowly depressing the plunger. She could guess what he must be feeling—the blossoming chill in his bloodstream, the slight disorientation. When she removed the needle, he seemed at first to be unaffected, and she was seized with fear. Had she used the wrong medicine, or administered it incorrectly?

"I don't know what witchcraft you think you've just performed, but can we go now?" he said, rolling down his sleeve again, and pulling on the coat over his uniform jacket. Loose strings of gold braid dangled like tassels. "Where's your coat?"

He barged into the next room and found her coat and gloves there, then came back and began to bundle her into them. ·

"I have a plan," he said, "to launch a boat, from the whaling station. We'll be picked up at sea . . ."

Then he shivered, from the top of his head to the soles of the boots—different boots, she noted—on his feet. And stumbled backwards onto the edge of the bed.

It *was* the right medicine. Eleanor breathed a sigh of relief. Now he would be incapacitated—at least long enough for her to explain everything to him. She knelt by the side of the bed, the tails of her long coat hanging down to the floor, holding his cold hands in hers. "Sinclair, you have to listen to me. You have to understand."

He looked at her with rolling eyes.

"The medicine will take time for its full effect to be felt. But once it has, you will no longer feel the need you feel now." Even at their worst, sleeping in cellars or spurring their horses through mountain passes in the driving rain, they had always referred to their affliction in only the most oblique terms. "But the doctor tells me—"

He harrumphed at that. "The doctor . . ." But then he could not go on.

"The doctor, and the others too, tell me we must not touch ice. Do you understand that? We must not touch ice! If we do, we will die."

He stared down at her as if she were the one who had truly lost her wits. He chuckled, bitterly. "A fairy tale and you believe it."

"Oh, Sinclair, I do. I do believe it."

"And this in a land of nothing but ice. Is there any better way to make you their willing prisoner?"

Eleanor bowed her head in despair. "We are not their prisoners. They are not our captors. This is not the war."

But when she looked up, she saw that for Sinclair, it was, and would always be, the war. Even if the physical need were relieved, the affliction had struck its roots so deep into his soul that there would be no extracting them, ever. Even then, with sweat beading his brow and his skin clammy to the touch, he staggered up, as obediently as if a bugle had sounded, and pulled on his coat and gloves. She waited, praying for the medicine to further sap his strength, but he seemed to be using all of his willpower to fight its effects.

"Sinclair! Have you heard a word I've been saying? We can't go out there unprotected."

"Then in God's name, button up!" he said, grabbing her by the sleeve of her own coat. She just had time to snatch the brooch from the bedside table before he dragged her from the sick bay. "It's a lovely day outside."

He lumbered down the hall and threw open the door to the outside ramp. Sunlight glinted off the snow and ice, and Eleanor instinctively pulled the goggles from her coat pocket and put them on.

"The dogs are already in harness," he said, with satisfaction. "I made sure of that first."

He had? How long had he been haunting the camp?

He was clambering down the ramp with Eleanor in tow, when he suddenly stopped short and said, "Of all the damn bloody nuisances . . ."

Eleanor had pulled the hood of her coat tightly over her face, but when she peeked out from under it she saw Michael—slack-jawed—standing a few yards away, a black metal contraption with three legs tucked under one arm. He seemed to be trying to make some sense of what he was seeing.

"If I were you," Sinclair said, "I'd turn tail now and run."

Michael's eyes went straight to Eleanor's, searching for some answer.

Sinclair pushed the flap of his overcoat away, revealing the saber that hung at his side, but when he tried to move off, Michael hastily blocked their path.

"Good God, I'm in a hurry!" Sinclair exploded, as if he were scolding a slow-witted stableboy. Letting go of Eleanor's arm, he pulled the sword from its scabbard. "Now get out of the way," he said, brandishing the sword in the gleam of the polar sun, "or I'll drop you where you stand."

"Michael," Eleanor interceded, "do as he says!"

"Eleanor, you can't be out here! You have to get back inside!"

Sinclair's eyes flashed at the exchange, and moved from one of them to the other. But when they returned to Michael, they burned with a cold fury.

"Perhaps I've been blind," he said, advancing on Michael with the tip of the sword extended.

To Eleanor's horror, Michael did not retreat, but raised the metal contraption—it had three legs, like an artist's easel—and held it out like a weapon.

This was madness, she thought, utter madness.

"You can go," Michael said, standing his ground. "I won't try to stop you. But Eleanor stays."

"So that *is* what this is about." Sinclair sneered. "You're a bigger fool than I thought."

"Maybe you're right," Michael said, taking a step closer, "but that's the deal."

Sinclair paused, as if mulling it over, then suddenly lunged at Michael, the sword whistling through the air. The blade struck the legs of the tripod, and blue sparks flew into the air. Michael fell back, struggling to hold on to it.

Sinclair advanced, baiting Michael with the end of the sword, twirling it in small circles. Eleanor saw now that the back of her lieutenant's head had a gash in it, and the blond hair had been cut short, as if someone had tended to the wound.

Michael feinted with the tripod, pushing it back at Sinclair, but Sinclair knocked it to one side and continued to advance on him.

"I'm pressed for time," Sinclair said, "so this will have to be quick."

He slashed once, twice, and on the third blow the tripod was wrenched from Michael's hands and clattered to the hard ground. Michael scrambled after it—he had no other weapon—and as Sinclair swung the gleaming saber back over his left shoulder, ready to deliver the fatal blow, there was a bloodcurdling scream and Charlotte—in a green silk bathrobe, with her braids flying about her head—hurtled down the ramp and shoved Sinclair off-balance. He stumbled forward, barely hanging on to the sword, before whirling around and swinging at his new assailant. The blade caught the doctor's leg, and she fell, blood spraying onto the snow.

It was Eleanor's turn to scream, but before she could go to Charlotte's aid, Sinclair snatched her by the sleeve of her coat again.

"Can you bear to be parted?" he said, seething, and dragged her toward the kennels.

She went willingly, if only to give Michael and Charlotte time to escape.

CHAPTER FIFTY-FOUR

December 26, 3 p.m.

KNEELING IN THE SNOW beside Charlotte, Michael tried to ascertain the damage.

"It's not bad," Charlotte said, sitting up and wincing. "It's a flesh wound."

"I'll help you back to the infirmary."

"I can get there myself," Charlotte said. "Go get Eleanor!"

But when she tried to stand, her knees buckled, and Michael had to sling an arm around her waist to get her back up the ramp and into the infirmary. As he lowered her into a chair, and followed her instructions to bring the antiseptic, antibiotics, and bandages, he heard the jingling of the harness on the dogsled passing by outside. Glancing out the window, he saw Sinclair in his red-and-gold jacket, standing on the runners. He'd pulled a ski mask over his head and goggles covered his eyes; apparently, he'd learned quickly about how to weather the Antarctic. Eleanor was huddled low in the bright orange cargo shell, her head down and her hood drawn tight, as the sled whooshed past.

"Tell me that was Santa Claus heading home," Charlotte said, saturating a cotton pad in antiseptic.

"He'll head for the old whaling station," Michael said. "There's nowhere else he can go, especially with a storm coming on."

"Get rolling," Charlotte urged him again. "But get a gun first from Murphy." She cringed as she applied the pad to her leg. "And take reinforcements."

Michael gave her a comforting pat on the shoulder, and said, "Anybody ever tell you not to take on a man with a sword?"

"You never worked the night shift in an ER."

Michael ran back down the hall, but instead of alerting anyone else, he made straight for the garage shed. Gathering a posse could only take time, and a gun could always wind up injuring the wrong party. Besides, he knew he could catch up to them on a snowmobile—the only question was if he could catch up to them before Eleanor was fatally exposed to the ice.

The snowmobile in front was a yellow-and-black Arctic Cat, and he jumped into the saddle, checked the fuel gauge, and revved the engine. The vehicle burst out of the shed, skidding wildly on the slick snow, and Michael was nearly thrown free. He had to slow it down, at least until he'd made it out of the base, but as he came around the corner of the administration module, he nearly ran over Franklin, who jumped out of the way in the nick of time.

"Go to the meat locker!" Michael shouted at him over the roar of the engine. "Check on Lawson!"

Michael hated to think what might have happened there. But if Sinclair was free, it couldn't be good.

Once past the main quad, Michael took a firm grip on the handlebars and gunned the engine. With one hand he had to tighten the hood around his head to keep it from blowing back. Far ahead, he could see the red of Sinclair's uniform and the blazing orange of the sled, as the dogs raced across the snow and ice. *Please,* he prayed, *let Eleanor's skin be covered.*

Michael could see that Sinclair had harnessed the dogs in pairs instead of fanning them out on wider leads, and he knew that doing so was particularly dangerous under the current conditions. With the dogs bunched together, the weight of the whole sled could cross onto a fragile snow bridge all at once, and if the bridge gave way, the dogs first, then the sled itself, could be dragged straight down into the bottomless crevasse below.

For that matter, Michael could plummet into one, too. That was why he tried to stay on the same path the sled had already taken. But it wasn't easy. The silvery glare off the terrain was harsh and penetrating, and the scrum of snow and ice thrown up by the front runners of the Arctic Cat kept flying back, sticking to the windshield and coating his goggles.

Even as the distance between them closed, Michael began to wonder what he could do when he did catch up. He racked his brain, wondering what was likely to be in the snowmobile's emergency compartment. A first-aid kit? Some nylon ropes? A GPS? A flashlight?

And then he remembered the last essential item sure to be there—a flare gun!

Sinclair would never know the difference between that and a real gun.

The sled was turning slightly, toward the coastline, and Michael could see Sinclair's head turning, aware now that he was being pursued. Though the sun glinted off his goggles and golden epaulettes, and the scarlet flaps of his jacket whipped out behind him like a fox's tail, the black ski mask made him look less like a soldier than a burglar on the run.

The sled was rounding a coal-black nunatak, and the danger there was even greater, especially as Sinclair wouldn't be aware of it. Crevasses often formed around the base of such rocky outcroppings, and increased in number and depth as the glacier field approached the sea. Sinclair was continuing to bear toward the water, no doubt because it made navigating easier. In Antarctica, it was as hard to judge distances as it was direction—there was seldom any landmark to rely on, everything looked the same for hundreds of miles sometimes, and the sun, which on that date was very nearly straight overhead, offered no help either. Your shadow clung as close to your heels as an obedient dog.

Michael was torn between quickly overtaking the sled—and forcing a confrontation on the unstable ice—or waiting until he had reached the solid soil of Stromviken. But that was Sinclair's stomping ground, and who knew what other advantages he might be able to call upon once he got there?

The sled was slowing down a bit, because it had to. Michael could see the chunky blocks of a serac field rising up from the ground, like the tines of a giant fork sticking up from the earth. The dogs were snaking their way through the obstacle course, and Sinclair was bent far forward over the handlebars, urging them on.

Michael wiped the snow and ice from his goggles and lowered his head below the windshield. Wispy white clouds were draped like muslin across the sky, muting the sunlight and dropping the temperature another few degrees; Michael pegged it at about thirty below zero. The snowmobile was rapidly closing in on the sled. He was near enough that he could see Sinclair's sword slapping at his side and Eleanor's head, tightly bound in a hood, poking up from the shell.

Sinclair, hearing the roar of the Arctic Cat, turned again and shouted something Michael could not hear, though he doubted it was an offer of surrender. If there was one thing he knew about Sinclair, it was that the man's will was indomitable.

But then, with no warning, Michael saw the snow beneath the sled begin to crumble. There was a wild, terrified yelping from the pack and, as Michael watched in horror, the snow bridge collapsed, and the lead dogs disappeared. Each of the pairs behind them, barking madly but yoked to the same harness, were dragged into the widening chasm. The sled, too, rocking like a canoe in the rapids, its blades screeching across the ice, was pulled sideways toward the crevasse.

Michael steered to one side of a looming serac and hit the brakes, skidding to a halt. When he leapt off the snowmobile and lifted his goggles, he saw the sled teetering on the edge of the crevasse, with Sinclair pounding his feet on the claw brake, and barely holding on. Michael knew that the fissure could run in any direction there—it could be under his own feet even then—but he had no ski pole to gauge the snow with. All he could do was approach at an oblique angle and hope for the best. He yanked open the snowmobile's storage compartment and grabbed the rope and tackle, but before he could go ten yards, the back end of the sled rose into the air like the stern of a sinking ship, with Sinclair still clinging to the handlebars, and after hesitating there for a second or two, slipped from sight.

"Eleanor!" Michael cried, throwing all caution to the winds, and stumbling across the patchy snow and ice, slipping and sliding most of the way. When he neared the edge of the crevasse, he went down on all fours and crawled to the rim, terrified at what he might find.

The crevasse was a deep blue gash in the ice, but the sled had fallen only ten or twelve feet before becoming wedged between its narrow walls. The dogs dangled below it, like terrible ornaments, the ones that were still alive twisting in their collars and harness, their weight and frantic struggles threatening to dislodge the sled altogether.

"Cut the leads!" Michael shouted. "And the towlines!"

Sinclair looked up uncertainly from his perch on the rear of the sled, then drew his sword and started hacking at the tangled lines that were within his reach.

Eleanor was still huddled in the shell, her face entirely covered by the hood.

First one, then several, of the dogs' bodies dropped away, caroming back and forth against the icy walls and thumping, with hard wet splashes, onto the unseen floor of the crevasse. A few agonized howls echoed up from the bottom of the blue canyon, but then they too died away.

Michael hurriedly wrapped the rope under his own arms, then tied a loop and lowered it into the chasm.

"Eleanor," he said, lying on his belly with only his head and shoulders extended over the edge, "I want you to slip this rope over your shoulders and then tie it around you."

The loop hung down like a noose above her head, but she was able to peer out from under her hood, reach up with gloved hands, and grab it.

"Once you've done that," Michael said, "I want you to climb out of the sled, as carefully as you can."

Sinclair hacked at another lead, and another pair of the hanged dogs plummeted into the purple depths. Even so, the prow of the sled, jammed at a slightly lower angle than the back, slipped another foot or two down.

"I've tied it," Eleanor said, her voice muffled by the hood.

"Good. Now hold on."

He would have given anything for some kind of anchor—a rock, a snowmobile, something to fasten the rope around—but all he had was his own body. He sat back, dug the heels of his boots into the snowpack, then pulled up, his bad shoulder already complaining.

"Use your feet, if you can, to grip the wall, and push off it."

She broke free from the shell and her body instantly swung against the ice. He heard her groan, then saw the toes of her black boots grip the surface. He coiled the rope around his arm again, and pulled harder. He could feel the tendon straining, and the thought—*not now, don't snap now*—endlessly repeated in his head.

She had come up a yard or more, but her feet suddenly slipped away from the ice and dangled in midair.

"Michael!" she cried, hanging above the sled and the chasm that yawned below. Michael dug his heels in deeper, but he could not get enough traction; he was slipping toward the fissure himself, his arms shaking almost uncontrollably. Just as he thought he couldn't hold her up for another second, he saw Sinclair stretch forward over the handlebars, put his hands, still encased in thick gloves, on the bottoms of her boots, and push her up. Although the lieutenant's face was obscured by his black ski mask and goggles, Michael could well imagine his fear and anguish. But Eleanor rose, just enough that Michael could grab the rope encircling her and haul her the rest of the way out of the crevasse.

She crawled onto the snow, gasping for breath, only her green eyes, wide with terror, visible under the tightly drawn hood.

"Stand up!" Michael said. "The ice!" There was snow on her coat, snow on her mittens, snow on her boots. With the back of his hand, he brushed as much of it away as he could, then quickly steadied her on her feet.

"The rope," Michael said. "I need the rope."

But it was cinched so tightly around her, he could not get it free. Michael dropped his head back over the rim—the sled had slipped farther down, and was tilted at an even-more-precarious angle—and stretched his good arm out as far as he could. "Stand on top of the sled," he said, "and try to grab my hand."

Sinclair could barely move without the sled sliding again, its blades grating on the ice. He swept his goggles and ski mask off, then, after carefully unfastening his sword belt, held it out and let it fall.

"Quickly," Michael said, "before it drops any more!"

Sinclair gingerly stepped off the back runner, and onto the hard orange shell. With his arms extended like an acrobat's, he inched closer, his boots squeaking on the slick surface of the shell. He reached up and put his gloved hand into Michael's. Their eyes met.

"Hang on!" Michael said, but Sinclair's weight on the front of the sled was too much, and with a sickening crunch it started to give way.

"Don't let go!" Michael begged, though he himself was being drawn over the rim. The breath in his throat was as raw as a blowtorch, and the ice and snow under his arm started to crumble.

A fine white powder drifted down into the crevasse.

"I've got you!" Michael insisted, but as he stared into Sinclair's face, a few flakes of falling ice wafted down onto the young lieutenant's moustache, then his cheeks, and a look of confusion crept across his features. He started to speak, but a pale frost crackled across his lips, draining them of all color. His tongue became a stick of wood. A glassy sheen rippled across his jaws, then raced down his neck so fast and so hard that his body went rigid, and his fingers loosed their grasp.

The sled made a grinding noise and dropped another foot or two.

"Sinclair!" Michael said, but the only thing that still looked alive in him were his eyes, and then they, too, were marbled over by a tide of ice. His body managed to stay upright for only another moment before the sled suddenly broke free and plunged, prow first, toward the bottom of the blue crevasse. There was a terrible screech and clatter, and finally a shattering crash, as if a crystal chandelier were exploding into a thousand tinkling pieces. Echoes welled up from the jagged walls, but the chasm was too deep for Michael to see any sign of Sinclair, or the wreckage.

When the reverberations died, Michael called his name. Several times. But there was no sound other than the whisper of the wind finding its way into the freezing canyon.

He raised his arm, numb and aching, out of the hole, and rolled over onto his back. His lungs felt as if they would burst. Eleanor was standing where he had left her, her back to the wind and her arms wrapped around herself. Her head was down, the hood of her coat drawn tight around her face—nothing of her skin exposed to the elements.

"Is he gone?" she said, her voice barely audible from under the hood.

"Yes," he said. "He's gone."

The hood nodded solemnly. "And I must not even cry."

Michael clambered to his feet.

"My tears," she said, "might turn to ice."

He went to her, and put an arm around her waist. She was suddenly so weak he felt she might have fallen to the snow herself. Perhaps willingly. As he gently guided her around the edge of the crevasse—now and forever an unmarked grave—she paused, and under her breath said something he could not make out. He did not ask what it was—it wasn't for him to know—nor did he see what she had pressed to her lips, before she let it fall into the blue chasm. But when it twirled down, glinting gold and ivory, he knew.

With the polar sun hanging lifelessly above them, they picked their way back through the ragged field of frozen seracs.

CHAPTER FIFTY-FIVE

December 29, 2:45 a.m.

WHEN THE CABIN LIGHTS FLICKERED on and the pilot announced that they should prepare for landing, Michael downed the last of his Scotch and looked out the window.

Even at that hour, Miami was ablaze with long, sparkling grids of light that only stopped at the black shore of the ocean.

The flight attendant took his plastic cup and empty bottle. The guy who'd been sleeping in the aisle seat roused himself, and stowed away the laptop he hadn't worked on for hours. He'd told Michael he was a "resource specialist," whatever that meant, for some American company building a telecom network in Chile.

Michael hadn't slept a wink—in days. Even now, all he could think of was what lay in the hold of the plane.

The guy on the aisle said, "What are we? Only four hours late?"

Michael nodded. Every extra hour, every delay, had been excruciating.

At least clearing customs in the middle of the night went faster than usual—until Michael mentioned that he had been traveling with human remains and needed to know where to go to claim them.

"I'm sorry for your loss, sir," the customs agent said. "Make a left on your way out and report to the international cargo desk. They'll be able to help you."

At the cargo desk, a kid in a blue uniform, who didn't look like he should be up this late, slowly combed over the NSF forms provided by Murphy and the medical documents drawn up by Charlotte, while Michael struggled not to show his impatience. He knew he had to keep cool and do nothing to draw any attention. The kid called over a more senior employee; the laminated tag hanging around the guy's thick neck identified him as Kurt Curtis. After verifying the paperwork himself, and rechecking Michael's passport and ID, he said, "Sorry for your loss, sir."

Michael wondered how many more times he would have to hear that.

Curtis picked up the phone, punched a button, then muttered a few words with his back to Michael. He grunted "yeah" three times, then turned around and said, "If you'll follow me, I'll escort you to the cargo transfer station." Pointing at Michael's duffel bag, he said, "Don't forget to take that."

Outside, the Miami night hit Michael like a hot, wet towel. *Get used to it,* he told himself. For Eleanor, life in snowy, sleety Tacoma would be an impossibility. Curtis wedged himself into the driver's seat of the cart, while Michael tossed his duffel into the back and sat beside him. It must have rained in the past hour or two—the tarmac was wet, and there were puddles an inch deep here and there. A taxiing jet blew a foul tornado of even hotter air at them, and the roar of its engine was deafening. Curtis took no notice, but steered the cart past a row of terminals and into a vast open hangar where a van marked MIAMI/DADE COUNTY CORONER was parked. A petite woman in black trousers and a white blouse was leaning against the door, smoking a cigarette. She looked up when Michael grabbed his duffel and got out of the cart. Curtis did a wheelie and left.

"You're Michael Wilde?" she said, dropping the cigarette on the concrete floor. "I'm Maria Ramirez. Erik Danzig's wife."

Michael extended his hand, and very nearly said he was sorry for her loss.

She looked at him closely, with dark eyes, and said, "Long trip, huh?"

He suspected he looked like crap, and she had just confirmed it. "Yes. It was." He couldn't keep himself from looking around. Where was the body bag? Had it already been delivered, or was it still in transit somewhere?

"If you're looking for the bag, it's already in the van."

"It is?" His heart nearly leapt out of his chest, and his reaction did not escape Maria's notice.

"So," she said, crushing the still glowing cigarette butt under one shoe, "before we have to drag in the police, the FBI, the INS, or whoever, maybe you want to tell me something?"

He had been rehearsing for this moment for days, wondering how he was going to tell her his story, but now that it was on him, all he wanted to do was throw open the doors of the van and rescue Eleanor.

"First of all," she said, "I don't know who's in that bag—I haven't opened it—but I know it's not Erik. He's about a foot taller, and a hundred pounds heavier, than whoever that is."

"You're right," Michael said. "It's not Erik."

Maria looked surprised at his immediate capitulation. "Then where is he?"

Michael lowered his head and said, "You're going to have to bear with me, because what I'm about to tell you is strictly prohibited by the NSF." And then he launched into his story, reminding Maria that she'd said Danzig—Erik—was never happier than he was at the Pole, and how he would have wanted to be buried there. Michael confessed that he had been. "But we would have caught hell for doing it, so I couldn't let you know about it until I could tell you here myself, privately, in person." Then he reached under his shirt collar and pulled the walrus-tooth necklace over his head. When Maria saw it, her eyes welled with tears. "I know he would have wanted you to have this," Michael concluded. "He always wore it."

Clutching the necklace in her hand, she turned and walked a few yards away, her head down, shoulders heaving.

Michael waited, feeling his shirt sticking to his skin and his long hair plastered to the back of his neck. It was all he could do not

to break into the van, but there were other people not far off—
mechanics and a couple of baggage handlers—and he knew he
needed to hold on just a little bit longer.

Maria composed herself and retrieved a clipboard from the
dashboard of the van. The necklace was hanging around her neck
when she returned.

"Okay, so thank you. Erik got what he would have wanted. I
owe you one." Handing him the clipboard, she said, "Sign at all the
places I've put an X"—there were at least a dozen—and when
Michael had finished, she tore off a couple of countersigned copies
and handed them to him. "Now it's official. Erik came back."

"Thanks."

"But that still doesn't tell me who's in the bag."

Michael knew that this was going to be the really hard part of
the sell. Who would believe it?

"A friend of mine," he said. "Her name's Eleanor."

"You mean, *was* Eleanor."

"No, she's alive."

Maria stopped and looked at him appraisingly, as if trying to
decide if she should reconsider everything else he had just been
telling her. "Not in that bag, she's not. Not all the way from the
South Pole, in cargo holds."

"She is," Michael said, taking Maria by the hand and all but
dragging her toward the rear of the van. "Please let me go in and
get her."

One of the baggage handlers looked over at them curiously.

"Mother of God," Maria said, "are you nuts? What the hell
happens to you people down there?"

But she didn't stop him when he opened the back doors,
climbed inside, and pulled them closed again.

The bag was laid on a metal shelf and held in place by two canvas straps. Michael hastily untied them, whispering, "I'm here, I'm
here," all the while. But there was no sound from inside the bag.

He grabbed the zipper at the top—the one he'd mangled just
enough so it wouldn't completely close—yanked it down and pulled
the flaps to either side.

Eleanor was lying as still as death, her arms at her sides.

"Eleanor," he said, touching her face with the tips of his fingers.
"Eleanor, please, wake up."

He put his head close enough to feel her breath on his cheek. Cool breath, not warm. Her skin was cool, too.

"Eleanor," he said again, and this time he thought he saw her eyelids flutter. "Eleanor, wake up. It's me. Michael."

A troubled look crossed her face, as if she resented being disturbed.

"Please . . ." he said, placing his hand on hers. "Please." Unable to resist any longer, he bent down to kiss her. But then, remembering Darryl's warning, he put his lips to her eyelids—first one, then the other—instead. It wasn't how he would have chosen to awaken his Sleeping Beauty . . . but it was enough.

Her eyes opened, staring straight up at the roof of the van, then shifted toward Michael. For a second, he was afraid she hadn't recognized him.

"I was so afraid," she said. "Afraid that if I opened my eyes, I'd be back in the ice."

"Never again," he said.

She lifted his hand from hers and cradled it against her cheek.

Maria Ramirez made him swear on all that was holy that he would never tell anyone how this strange woman had illegally entered the United States, and Michael made her swear in turn that she would never divulge the true fate of her husband's remains. Then, driving through the muggy night, Maria dropped them off at a little hotel she knew on Collins Avenue, a block from South Beach.

"When we need to bring in a forensics expert from out of town," she said, "it's where we put them. Nobody's ever complained."

Michael took Eleanor up to the room, turned on all the lights, and started filling the tub for her. The moment the bathroom door closed, he thought he heard a low sob from inside. He was torn between knocking and trying to comfort her, or simply letting her emotions run their course. How could anyone have endured all that she had endured—in the past day or two, or in the centuries that preceded them—without breaking down at some point? And what could he say that would be of the slightest help?

Instead, he went back downstairs and convinced the elderly woman at the front desk to open the boutique shop for him so he could buy a sundress—the most demure he could find, a gauzy yel-low cotton with short sleeves—and some sandals. The woman, who'd looked at Eleanor like she was dressed in a Halloween cos-tume, understood, and even threw a couple of other items onto the pile. "Bloomers won't work under that," she said, laconically.

When he got back to the room, he rapped on the bathroom door, then inched it open and dropped the bag of new clothes in-side. A cloud of steam billowed out.

"I thought you might like to dress for the climate here," he said, before pulling the door closed again. "If you're hungry, I can go out and get some food."

"No," she said, her voice sounding almost sepulchral, "not right now."

He went to the window, and pulled back the bright floral cur-tains. A few lights were still on in neighboring buildings. A street-sweeping truck lumbered past. How could he tell her the rest of what she needed to know? That it was not only ice she had to fear . . . but human contact. Intimate human contact.

How could he tell her that even though her craving was gone, her contagion was not? That she posed a threat to anyone she might wish to embrace?

How, for that matter, could he tell himself?

Once the rumbling of the street sweeper had faded away, he went back to the bathroom door and wound up spending the next half hour trying to assuage her shocked sensibilities. Eleanor was so appalled at the shortness—and sheerness—of the dress that she would not come out at all until he had sworn—repeatedly—that these were the latest fashions and that everyone dressed that way. "A lot of the time, they wear even less," he said, wondering what she would make of the first bikini-clad rollerblader they passed. When she finally relented, and stepped, blushing madly, into the room, she took his breath away.

Even that early, Ocean Drive was busy with traffic, and Eleanor shied away from the buses as if they were fire-breathing dragons. The cars, the clamor, the traffic lights, Eleanor clung to his arm as if it were a life preserver. But whatever warmth she had absorbed from the bath was fast receding; her hand, he noted, was cool.

At Point Adélie, she had confessed the thing she most longed for was the hot sun on her face, and he was eager to show her the sunrise over the ocean. They had just stopped at a crosswalk when a vendor pushing a cart of Italian ices pulled up alongside them, almost the only pedestrians out at that hour, and gave them a hopeful glance. He might as well have been selling dynamite, and as Michael instinctively dragged Eleanor away, the vendor looked at him like he was crazy. But Michael knew the rules, and knew, too, that he was never going to be able to let down his guard. He would always have to be vigilant, and until the time came when the rest of the secret had to be divulged to her, he would also have to be secretive. But why burden her—at that rare moment when she might begin to experience happiness again—with something that he could carry alone?

As they crossed the street and then the scrubby dunes, the sky seemed to fade from an inky purple to a rosy glow. Michael led her past the towering palms, swaying in the sea breeze, and down to the surf. As the sun rose on the horizon, they sat down on the white sand and simply watched. Watched as it climbed up into the sky, turning the ocean into a silver mirror, burnishing the clouds with a ruby hue. Eleanor's green eyes glistened in the morning light, and as a gray-and-white osprey swooped low over the water, she followed its path. It was then that he noticed her rueful smile.

"What is it?" he said.

"I was just thinking of something," she said, her long brown hair, still damp from the bath, blowing loose over her shoulders. "A music hall ditty, from another time."

"How did it go?" He felt her fingers slip through his; exposed to the morning sun, they were perceptibly warmer. The osprey darted between the rolling waves.

" 'And oh won't there be, by the side of the sea,' " she liltingly recited, " 'coconut palms as tall as St. Paul's, and sand as white as Dover.' "

Her gaze swept across the bright horizon, the broad white beach, and Michael saw something like joy kindled in her eyes. "And so," she said, still clutching his hand, "there are."

ABOUT THE AUTHOR

ROBERT MASELLO is an award-winning journalist, a television writer, and the author of many other books, most recently the supernatural thrillers *Vigil* (which appeared on the *USA Today* bestseller list) and *Bestiary*. His articles and essays have appeared often in such publications as the *Los Angeles Times*, *New York*, *People*, and *Parade*, and his nonfiction book, *Robert's Rules of Writing*, has become a staple in many college classrooms. His produced television credits include such popular shows as *Charmed*, *Sliders*, and *Early Edition*. A long-standing member of the Writers Guild of America, he lives in Santa Monica, California, and may be reached at www.robertmasello.com.